# THE TEMPERING OF MEN

TOR BOOKS BY SARAH MONETTE
AND ELIZABETH BEAR

*A Companion to Wolves*

# The Tempering of Men

Sarah Monette

AND

Elizabeth Bear

A TOM DOHERTY ASSOCIATES BOOK
NEW YORK

THE TEMPERING OF MEN

A Tor Book
Published by Tom Doherty Associates, LLC
175 Fifth Avenue
New York, NY 10010

www.tor-forge.com

Tor® is a registered trademark of Tom Doherty Associates, LLC.

Library of Congress Cataloging-in-Publication Data

Monette, Sarah.
  The tempering of men / Sarah Monette and Elizabeth Bear.—1st ed.
      p.  cm.
  "A Tom Doherty Associates book."
  Sequel to: A companion to wolves.
  ISBN 978-0-7653-2470-2
  1. Wolves—Fiction.  I. Bear, Elizabeth.  II. Title.
  PS3613.O5246T46 2011
  813'.6—dc22

                                                                2011013459

First Edition: August 2011

Printed in the United States of America

0  9  8  7  6  5  4  3  2  1

# ACKNOWLEDGMENTS

◦❦◦

The authors would like to acknowledge their debts to Snorri Sturluson (1179–1241), the author of the *Prose Edda;* the Viking Answer Lady and her fascinating and tremendously helpful website, www.vikinganswerlady.com; Dr. Robert J. Hasenfratz (for teaching Bear Anglo-Saxon all these years ago); Mitchell and Robinson's *A Guide to Old English;* Jennifer Jackson, agent beyond compare; and Beth Meacham, for being the extraordinary editor that she is.

# THE TEMPERING OF MEN

# ONE

Vethulf and Skjaldwulf did not get along.

They had almost nothing in common. Where Vethulf was red, Skjaldwulf was dark. Where Vethulf was sharp-tongued, Skjaldwulf was taciturn. Where Vethulf's temper ran hot and savage, Skjaldwulf would brood and consider before he spoke or acted.

There was only one thing they could agree on, and that was Isolfr. And agreeing about Isolfr did more to increase the tension between them than relieve it. For they both wanted him, desired him, cared for him, though he was as cold and distant and dutiful as any jarl's daughter given in marriage unwilling. They needed him, not merely as men, but as the pair-yoked wolfjarls of Franangford. His recent two-month absence had made this unhappily manifest, even though he had returned from it with the unlooked-for svartalvish allies who had been the salvation of the entire Wolfmaegthing.

The Franangfordthreat could not manage without its wolfsprechend; it was too new, the ranks too unsettled, and the second bitch, Ingrun, and her brother Randulfr were not mete to fill a konigenwolf's place in the pack.

That konigenwolf, Viradechtis—already a legend in the fifth year of her life, a konigenwolf of the sort who ruled songs and stories that were old when Skjaldwulf's grandfather told them to the boy-child at his knee—had chosen two wolves to mate with, black Mar and odd-eyed Kjaran, and in that binding had bound their brothers Vethulf and Skjaldwulf to her brother, pale Isolfr. Thus they were bound also to Franangford, to lead its men as Viradechtis led its wolves.

Some mornings, still, Skjaldwulf woke disbelieving. He had never expected that Mar, his rangy wolf-brother, would be willing to fight and die to win Viradechtis. That half of his willingness had been Skjaldwulf's own bone-deep longing for Isolfr seemed a greater gift than Skjaldwulf could ever be worthy of. It was not in either of them to wish to lead wolves, or wolfcarls, but if that was the price, they would accept it and call it fair.

Skjaldwulf was lucky and more than lucky that neither he nor Mar had died in the violent night that had founded the Franangfordthreat. For when Skjaldwulf had looked at Vethulf Kjaransbrother, he had seen in his eyes the same willingness to kill or die that he felt in his own heart. It was Viradechtis who had changed the story. She had come between Mar and Kjaran, and chosen them both.

Thus Isolfr was Skjaldwulf's wolfsprechend, and Skjaldwulf thought that he was unlikely to lose that gift unless Mar through some unlikely circumstance offended Viradechtis. Whatever the tension between their brothers, Viradechtis, Mar, and Kjaran frankly doted on each other. Skjaldwulf (dark, ill-favored, spidery, and silent, as he had always thought himself) had that which he most wanted. He had Isolfr, who was like a white shadow drifting through the wolfheall—everywhere at once, listening, understanding, speaking quiet words that calmed men drawn taut by war or rut or personal enmities, or the enmities of wolves.

But he did not have Isolfr's desire.

It could have been worse, Skjaldwulf admitted to himself, grimly snowshoeing over fluffy drifts, grateful enough that his turn at breaking trail afforded him a few hours' isolation from the creaking, swearing mass of men, svartalfar, and wolves bound for Othinnsaesc and the battle that would, one way or another, be the resolution of a war between men and trolls that had cost them more than he cared to reckon. It could have been worse; Isolfr could have preferred Vethulf. Isolfr could have been actively cruel, rather than simply Isolfr: honorable, meticulous, ferocious in battle, reserved in peace. But Isolfr was also inward-looking—Skjaldwulf knew the signs, being afflicted with the disease himself—and as unwilling to be unkind as he was to accept Skjaldwulf as a lover. At least Skjaldwulf had the comfort, or the torment, of knowing that he would likely have Isolfr again, if only when Viradechtis went into season.

The memories were sharp, unhazed by the blur of wolf-rut, and that made them no easier to bear. Because while he wanted Isolfr, he wanted *Isolfr*, not Isolfr driven wild with Viradechtis' heat, not Isolfr half-mad and half-lucid. He wanted an Isolfr who could demand as well as surrender.

And that problem would not admit of a solution.

Skjaldwulf snorted and shook his head, resting for a moment under his pack while the rest of the group caught up to him. His breath steamed; his calves were aching. It was time someone else took his place breaking trail.

So many of the wolves and men and svartalfar were wounded

after the fighting to retake Franangford. So many, too wounded even to march, had been sent back to Bravoll, and Isolfr and Leitholfr's care. So many, unfit for fighting, were at work as quartermasters, managing the rearguard, or sledging supplies along the extended line from Bravoll.

Skjaldwulf was unsurprised when Othwulf and Vikingr came up next to him. They were big and strong, wolf and man, and would have no trouble taking their turn. Othwulf patted Skjaldwulf on the shoulder and Skjaldwulf fell back, ready to return his snowshoes and switch to easier skis now that he was no longer engaged in tamping down the snow for the sledges. Mar would be glad of the opportunity to run free and hunt.

Skjaldwulf sighed heavily as he struggled with his bindings. He should just find a lover who *wanted* him. But that would only put the unfairness on another man, who did not deserve it, whereas this situation, Skjaldwulf thought with a bitter grin, he had brought deliberately and knowingly upon himself.

❦

Skjaldwulf left his pack on one of the sledges, told Grimolfr where he was going, and checked Mar's pads for ice crystals before they headed out. His plan was to strike out perpendicular to the hard-skiing column, to hang a little back from the front and keep an eye out for animals flushed by the advance. It was a strategy that had served them well in the past. They had good hope of bringing down a red deer or something similar in size, enough to feed many wolves and men.

Logistics: they had to march hard to have a chance of reaching Othinnsaesc before the trellwarren had bulwarked against them. But they also had to reach the overrun town hale enough to fight. Which, in the hard winter, meant they needed food and lots of it.

He heard crashing ahead—downwind, inconveniently—and

skied softly toward it, Mar swinging wide to flank. Once Skjald-wulf was in position, he drove his ski poles into the snow and freed his fingers from his mittens. He nocked an arrow and drew his bow, sighting down the shaft—

—and paused when he head human voices, raised in argument over the crunching of snow. Voices he knew: Eyjolfr and Vethulf, and it did not sound like a friendly difference of opinion.

"I've my own tongue to speak my mind," Eyjolfr said, and Skjald-wulf could not hear Vethulf's answer, but he knew his wolfsprech-end's other wolfjarl well enough to know that whatever he said, it would be scathing. Skjaldwulf sent his mind out to Mar, who was still swinging out on his arc. Mar had heard the wolfcarls, too, and knew this was not prey, after all. Skjaldwulf asked for silence and discretion.

Vethulf's Kjaran and Glaedir—who was bound to Eyjolfr—knew they were there, but the wolves were keeping a good distance from their human brothers. The wolves were of different threats, Nithogs-fjoll and the fledgling Franangford, this was not a fight that con-cerned them: it was not an argument over territory or bitches, but rather some obscure point of human dominance, and the wolves would not interfere unless it came to more-than-casual blows.

Skjaldwulf at first had a good mind to follow their lead. It was even odds that Vethulf had started the shouting match. Moreover, Skjaldwulf had had enough experience of Vethulf's sharp-edged pride to have a pretty good idea of how he would react to Skjald-wulf's interference.

But then he heard Eyjolfr's answer to whatever Vethulf had said—"Have you ever considered that he avoids you because he doesn't *like* you, wolfcarl? You'd not be the first to receive Isolfr's grudging endur-ance, leavened by a little cruel flirtation"—and Skjaldwulf cursed un-der his breath, shoved the arrow back into his quiver, and grabbed for his ski poles even as he lifted the bow over his head with the other hand.

He had forgotten that Vethulf was not his only thwarted rival for Isolfr's affections.

Skjaldwulf was skiing fast, the snow hissing under his feet, when he broke through the screening brush and came upon them. Both turned as he planted his poles to skid to a stop, and from the way Vethulf's fists were clenched inside his deerhide mittens, Skjald-wulf had not arrived too soon. Glaedir appeared like a slanting beam of moonlight among the trees on the far side of the clearing. Skjaldwulf reached out to Mar with a thought.

Mar was beside him in a matter of moments, Kjaran running at his hip. And then there were three wolves, and three men, and Skjaldwulf released his ski poles and let his hands fall to his sides. "Eyjolfr," he said, "your wolfjarl will want to speak to you."

Which was truth, as far as it went, and through Mar and Gri-molfr's brother Skald, Skjaldwulf made sure that Grimolfr knew what to expect—a small example of the great conspiracy of wolf-heofodmenn, so like the conspiracy of adults that Skjaldwulf had, when he was a child, already suspected. Meanwhile Eyjolfr still stared at him, arms folded, wide-legged on his snowshoes. "You are no man to order me, Skjaldwulf. I am not of your threat—"

"No," Skjaldwulf said. "But Vethulf is of my threat. And Gri-molfr is your wolfjarl. You will kindly heed my words."

Eyjolfr looked down first. He huffed, glanced over his shoulder to collect Glaedir, and tromped off through the snow, showshoes hissing, arms swinging viciously.

When Eyjolfr was well away, Skjaldwulf regained his poles and skied to within conversational distance with Vethulf.

The next thing he knew, he was on his ass in the snow. Vethulf stood over him, face as red as his braids, shaking his right hand as if it hurt as much as Skjaldwulf's jaw. "Hel take you," Vethulf said venomously. "You have no idea what he was saying about Isolfr. He needs his foul mouth stopped."

"Believe me," Skjaldwulf said, "whatever poison he's spreading, I've heard it."

It would be awkward standing up in the skis. He was lucky he hadn't twisted his ankle in the fall. He held up his hand for assistance, and Vethulf, after a grim pause, reached out and hauled him to his feet. At the edge of the clearing, Mar and Kjaran eyed them curiously, and then Mar turned and unceremoniously began to wash Kjaran's ear.

"How can you stand to listen to it?" Vethulf asked, after an uncomfortable few moments in which Skjaldwulf dusted himself off and cast about for his ski poles.

Skjaldwulf shrugged. "I don't listen. Eyjolfr is hotheaded and hurt in his pride. Anyone with sense knows that Isolfr hasn't a cruel bone in his body. That, if anything, he gives too much to his wolf."

"It's what makes him a good wolfsprechend," Vethulf said, stubbornly loyal. And then he looked down and cleared his throat, turning away.

Skjaldwulf closed his eyes. "Oh, Baldur's tits. You, too?"

"Me, too, what?" Vethulf was defensive, arms crossed, the tails of his snowshoes denting the drifts as he rocked back on his heels, almost far enough to overbalance before he caught himself.

"You love him," Skjaldwulf said, and—unwillingly—Vethulf nodded.

"He doesn't care," Vethulf said, with a shrug that lifted his bearskin coat around his ears. "He'd rather I were anyone else in the Wolfmaegth."

"Vethulf, you idiot, he'd rather you were a *woman*."

The look on Vethulf's face, as if Skjaldwulf had cracked him over the head with one of his ski poles, was very nearly worth it.

"I've been threatbrother to him five years," Skjaldwulf said carefully, "and I have never seen him choose a man when it was not for

his sister's sake. It is never easy for him to lie down for a man—
*never*—and Viradechtis' open mating . . ." Skjaldwulf couldn't say it,
for his own dignity, for Isolfr's. His voice trailed off, and he shrugged.

"Aye," Vethulf muttered. "I have heard a little." And he tilted his
head toward Kjaran and Mar. But Vethulf still wasn't meeting Skjaldwulf's eyes, staring stubbornly at the wolves, who lay in the snow, secure and warm in their fur coats.

It was uncomfortable, stringing so many words together when
he wasn't telling tales. But Skjaldwulf reminded himself that
Vethulf was still a rather young man, sharp emotions not yet worn
smooth by the passage of time. And Vethulf had not known Isolfr
for five years, had not watched him grow from skinny jarl's son into
wolfsprechend of Franangford. "He isn't playing us for jealousy. It's
not his nature. But what you want of him . . . is not his nature, either."

Vethulf swallowed hard; Skjaldwulf saw his throat work under
his scarf and his furs. "I would lie down for him, if he wanted," he
said, and then jerked his chin upward, sideways, as if a violent motion was the only way he could force himself to meet Skjaldwulf's
eyes.

"I know," Skjaldwulf said. "So would I."

⚜

By the time they returned to the army, camp was made, and
they entered it in silence, Vethulf trudging along on his snowshoes as Skjaldwulf skied ahead. They had slung poles over their
shoulders, and between them hung the gutted body of a winter-thin
doe. Their beards and their wolves' faces were red with the blood of
the steaming, raw liver they had shared. Skjaldwulf sank down by a
fire and unlaced his skis, exhausted, while Vethulf found someplace
to pitch their tent. Mar and Kjaran insisted on sharing sleeping
quarters—though Skjaldwulf would have expected them to form a

ferocious rivalry, but perhaps wolves were more sensible than men in this as in so many things—and Skjaldwulf and Vethulf lived by the whim of their wolves.

When Vethulf was done, Skjaldwulf brought him hot wine. They sat side by side to eat their meager suppers.

Things were easier between them, somehow, though Skjaldwulf could read Vethulf's lovesick misery in the set of his shoulders, and hated himself for forcing Vethulf to admit it—to himself as well as to Skjaldwulf. Meanwhile, Vethulf kept shooting him sidelong glances, as if he, too, were wrestling with some private guilt.

When Mar had finished crunching the raw, meaty marrowbone of the doe that he'd been allotted, he scrubbed his face and paws in the snow, leaving behind furrowed claw marks and pink-red blood-stains. He shook ostentatiously, sending snow flying, and nosed the flap of the hide tent. Kjaran, whose insufficient dinner had been slightly more than half of a hare, was right beside him, and Vethulf stood as well. "Good night, Skjaldwulf," he said—the first words other than "thanks" and "hand me that" that had passed his lips since they'd killed the deer.

"I'll be in as soon as I put the fire out," Skjaldwulf answered. He smothered it quickly with handfuls of snow. All around, clustered on the lee side of tree trunks, other fires still burned in the darkness. Isolfr's shieldbrothers—Ulfbjorn, Frithulf, and Kari—had the next camp over. Skjaldwulf wondered for a moment if they had promised Isolfr to keep an eye on his wolfjarls. It would be like Isolfr to worry.

And like him to keep it to himself, if he did.

Skjaldwulf pissed against the runners of the nearest unloaded and upturned sledge, so his urine would freeze into lubricating ice. He tucked himself away before anything more important could freeze, feeling the ache of the cold and the deer-hauling in his once-broken ribs and collarbone. Upon entering the tent, he peeled off his boots. The boots went into a sheltered corner of the tent beside Vethulf's, with Skjaldwulf's snowy trews laid over them. He spread his coat over the pile of bedding, snowy side up, but did not otherwise undress as he crawled over sleeping wolves and man to find his place.

The tent reeked of damp wolf and unwashed wolfcarl, but between the body heat and the insulating snow that Vethulf had heaped over its canvas walls, it was halfway warm. Under the covers, it would even be comfortable; Vethulf and two dog wolves threw off a good amount of heat. And Vethulf had made the sacrifice of crawling into the cold tent first, to warm it with his body. It was a sort of peace offering, like Skjaldwulf's mulled wine.

And so was the way Vethulf—not yet asleep—lifted the blankets and furs, inviting him into the warm, reeking nest. Skjaldwulf went gratefully, drawing his knees up to his chest so his chilled, stockinged feet would be in the warmth.

It was a long way to Othinnsaesc still.

◈

This time of year, the days shortened fast, to solstice and the inevitable endless nights that surrounded it. Hands of hands of days had passed by the time they came within striking range of Othinnsaesc. The assembled might of Wolfmaegth and svartalfar and wolfless men now rose and walked and slept again in darkness and brutal cold, stamping and swearing, breath smoking from straining lungs to rime hoods and beards with hoar.

On this morning, Vethulf, sliding from under the furs, cursed mightily. Skjaldwulf wanted to tell him to wait fifteen years. Skjaldwulf felt the teeth of winter sunk in every bone he'd ever broken, every joint he'd torn or strained. At his age, that sometimes seemed like most of them.

One of the sledge reindeer had died in the night; by the time

Isolfr's shieldbrother Kari found it and brought Skjaldwulf out to see it was already frozen almost too stiff for butchering. Mittened hands pulled into the sleeves of his coat, Skjaldwulf frowned into the fur of his hood and shuddered.

"I hope its heart gave out," he said, unwilling to contemplate an army at the mercy of cold intense enough to drop a reindeer in its tracks. He sent Kari to fetch svartalfar to handle the butchering. Their knives were better, and the smiths and mothers would see the meat equally distributed. Skjaldwulf was developing the beginnings of an appreciation for the svartalfar's sense of fair dealing, uncompromising though it was.

This particular alf was named Iolite, which if Skjaldwulf had the convention right meant it was a male—not that that seemed to matter, to svartalfar, except in that females had two means of attaining the highest ranks of the council, and Skjaldwulf thought the most important were both smiths *and* mothers.

In any case, Iolite was neither a smith nor a mother. He seemed young, his teeth not yet etched with elaborate inlaid decorations, the hands at the ends of his spidery limbs smooth-nailed and quick when he eased off his mittens. The alfar also seemed less susceptible to the cold than men, and Skjaldwulf watched with curiosity as Iolite handled the knife bare-fleshed in chill that would have blackened Skjaldwulf's flesh in minutes.

Skjaldwulf was not so strong as an alf, either, but Iolite seemed happy when Skjaldwulf grasped the reindeer's legs and pulled it onto its back, belly exposed to the sky for butchering. Gelid blood clotted Iolite's knife as he cut from the genitals to the sternum without puncturing the entrails. Pale intestines and blood-dark liver flopped loose, oozing from the wound as Iolite snaked an endless arm up behind them to cut free the diaphragm and esophagus.

Trellwolves were already gathering in a respectful circle, their coats so dense they seemed more like animate clouds of thistledown than enormous gaunt predators. Skjaldwulf recognized Mar, Guthleifr, Kari's Hrafn—almost as black as Mar but smaller—and a half-dozen from alien wolfheallan. At a glance from Iolite, Skjaldwulf rolled the reindeer onto its side, spilling the guts on stained snow. Now Iolite reached inside the pelvis, cutting the anus and genitals free.

Mar whined, elbows hovering above the snow. Under that thick fur, Skjaldwulf knew Mar was painfully skinny—skinnier than he should have been, with so many months of winter still to come. The wolves lingering behind him were in no better condition.

Neither, truth to tell, was the dead reindeer, but there was meat still on it.

Skjaldwulf wiped his mitten across his frosted beard. Frozen and dried blood from the liver of yesterday's deer crumbled and caught in the yarn: he rubbed his palm clean on the reindeer's leg. "Iolite," he said, catching himself before he called the svartalfar "Master." "Divide this meat among the wolves, please? Everything but the intestines. They can have the hide and legs, too."

Iolite glanced up from his bloody work and made a good attempt at a svartalf elder's somber frown. "I'll see it done."

Leaving Mar to his breakfast, Skjaldwulf shuffled off through packed snow, in search of Vethulf, recognizable by his buff-colored hide hood. The other wolfjarl was moving from campfire to campfire, speaking with men as his brother spoke with wolves, making sure of everyone's health and strength—making them laugh, even, which was something neither Isolfr nor Skjaldwulf himself could have managed right now. For a moment, Skjaldwulf stood with his arms folded and watched.

His attention must have drawn Vethulf's notice, because between conversations Vethulf turned to him and caught Skjaldwulf's gaze, raising his chin challengingly. Skjaldwulf bit back hard on a momentary flare of irritation and came down a little slope. He took

Vethulf's sleeve and turned him aside, leaning their hooded heads together. "We need to start butchering the reindeer."

"We'll have to pull the sledges ourselves," Vethulf said, but he didn't argue. Nor did he suggest that perhaps the svartalfar could help out by butchering a few of their shaggy dwarfish ponies, for which Skjaldwulf was grateful.

"Us and the wolfthreat."

"Right." Vethulf leaned back, his mittened hands thrust up his sleeves for a little additional warmth. Snow creaked under his boots: here in camp, it was packed enough that he didn't absolutely need snowshoes or skis. "I'll tell Grimolfr."

⊙⋎⊙

Trellwolves were more sensitive to scent than men, but even Vethulf could smell Othinnsaesc before the Wolfmaegth heard the sea, for all that winter had frozen the stench of unburied corpses. On a night shortly before the solstice, after slaughtering the first three trellish sentries they came upon, the army camped inside the woods, a mile or so from the border of hewn trees their scouts reported.

Vethulf joined the wolfjarl of Nithogsfjoll, grizzled and wiry Grimolfr, in picking his way silently and without lights to the edge of the trell-harrowed lands. Across a rude clearing leading down to the cliffs over the sea, the smoke of trellish fires was almost invisible on a blackened sky. Two wolfjarls stared unhappily at the smudges blurring crystal stars.

The sun-turning was upon them. Vethulf could not shake the sense that if only they could hold on until its return, it would prove an omen of survival.

"They've marked out the boundaries," Grimolfr said. "They're burning our woods." Weariness made his voice crack and sag in the middle.

Vethulf understood. He couldn't muster much outrage himself, or much emotion besides grim resignation. They had come this far, and they would fight now. It was as inevitable as snow. "It saves us time," he said. "We won't have to kindle our own bonfires to burn them out.

"Skjaldwulf will be pleased," Grimolfr said.

Vethulf snorted. If it made a good story, Skjaldwulf would like it.

Grimolfr said, "I hope we got all the sentries."

It wouldn't matter. The trolls had to know they were coming.

"I don't fancy fighting a whole warren of trolls in the dark," Vethulf offered.

Grimolfr's mouth worked behind his scarf. "There won't be a morning," he said. "And the dark is when we fight trolls. Come on. You post sentries and collect the jarls. I'll gather the wolfheofodmenn and the smiths and mothers. We'll go in as soon as we can form up. There's no sense in giving the trolls time to tunnel under and flank us."

⚜

The wolfless men camped on the left flank of the army, and their sentries knew the wolfheofodmenn of the army by sight. Vethulf was ready for the usual mutters and sneak-eyed glances, but this fur-swaddled sentry greeted him with a raised hand. "Wolf-jarl," he said. "Are you looking for the other wolfcarl?"

"I was looking for the night heofodman," Vethulf said. "Which other wolfcarl?"

"Yellow-bearded and about as tall and old as you. The wolf was a tan bitch, gray around the neck. He wanted the heofodman, too."

Vethulf nodded approval of the sentry's sharp eyes and made a point of remembering the man's face. Even now, most wolfless men heeded only the man and did not look at the wolf. And Vethulf recognized the description of the wolf more surely than the description of the man. Blond men there were aplenty, but wolf-bitches were a different matter.

*Randulfr and Ingrun.* A wolfcarl and subordinate bitch of Isolfr's former threat. What would they want with wolfless men? Vethulf found that he did not like mysteries in the approach to a battle. If Kjaran had been with him, his hackles might have spiked at Vethulf's rising irritation. As it was, Vethulf shrugged himself tighter in sweater, tunic, coat, and cloak. He stamped his feet to shake the snow from his calf-wrappings and warm the blood in his feet; he was more successful at one thing than the other. "If it was the heofodman he sought, then I may accomplish two errands in one. Who and where?"

"He's with Fargrimr Fastarrson, the heir of Siglufjordhur," the sentry said. Siglufjordhur was a big southern keep, far down the peninsula in what Vethulf had heard were impossibly temperate climes—four months of winter, no more, and only a week dark at the heart of it. "Head northwest. About a quarter hour's walking."

Vethulf was three steps away when he remembered himself. "Thank you," he said over his shoulder. "Othinn guide your hand."

The sentry nodded in return. "Othinn guide your hand, wolfjarl."

As the sentry had promised, the walk was short—even less than a quarter hour. Vethulf passed several campsites, and at each the wolfless men were unwontedly polite. A close and common enemy made for quiet camps. At the last fire Vethulf walked by, the jarl of Siglufjordhur's graybearded housecarl told him the jarl's fire was the next. "But the jarl's asleep."

"I'm to speak with the son," Vethulf said.

The housecarl snorted. "Well, all right. But I'll wager he's not your type."

Vethulf's arms crossed as his spine drew itself erect. Bilious words scorched his throat, but he bit down on the inside of his cheek and rebuked himself, *What would Isolfr say if he saw you screaming like a fishwife at some wolfless man?*

"I'll wager you're right," Vethulf snarled, and turned as crisply as he could in snowshoes to stalk across trammeled drifts to the next fire.

He could make out Randulfr and Ingrun at their ease on skins beside a shielded fire, and a lean, sword-wearing man dressed in well-sewn seal fur seated beside them. As Vethulf entered the ring of light, both men and the wolf looked up. Vethulf suddenly understood the housecarl's amusement.

The face over the seal fur collar was beardless, framed by hard blond plaits that sharpened its features but could not coarsen their delicacy. Fargrimr Fastarrson was either a very pretty, very young boy—or he wasn't a man born at all.

Vethulf's hesitation and confusion must have been obvious, because Randulfr popped to his feet while Ingrun's tail waved negligently once or twice. "Vethulf," he said, with every indication of delight. "Are you looking for me? This is my brother, Fargrimr. He became my father's heir when I went to the tithe. Grimi, this is Vethulf Kjaransbrother, Franangford's wolfjarl."

"So it was your yard we cleaned the trolls from," Fargrimr said. "I'd wondered whose mean huswifery that was."

Perhaps the words should have offended, but rather than being mocking, Fargrimr's teasing invited camaraderie. The voice was high and sweet, but the intonation was a man's. Vethulf fought the urge to shake his head like a wolf to clear his ears.

"It wasn't mine when the trolls moved in," Vethulf said. "I just inherited the problem."

Randulfr extended a hand to clasp. Vethulf put his own hand in it and let Randulfr transfer the clasp to Fargrimr's, once Fargrimr had dusted the snow from his trews and bindings. He had a good grip, solid and meaningful through his mittens, hard from the sword.

In the southern lands where there were no trolls, it was not entirely unheard of for a man without sons to make one. An unlucky sire could choose one of his daughters as heir and raise her as a sworn-man, a functional son. Such a girl never grew to be a woman; instead, she grew to be a man. She would take a man's name and would not marry, though some took girls as lovers, and thus she could head her father's household when he died. Upon her passing, one of her—his—sister-sons could then inherit. Sworn-men supposedly submitted to a course of herbs and surgeries that would unwoman them, but on the evidence of his eyes Vethulf thought that might be slander. The furs were thick, but Vethulf could see no sign that Fargrimr, at least, had had his breasts burned from his body.

Vethulf had also heard that there were four or five sworn-men with the company of wolfless men—one an archer who had died in Franangford, as it happened—but he hadn't realized any ranked.

"I didn't know you were a southerner," Vethulf said to Randulfr, so he wouldn't stare at Fargrimr's chest. "You don't have an accent."

Randulfr extended his right arm through the gap in his cloak and shoved up the nested sleeves of his coat, sweater, surcoat, and tunic to expose a naked white arm. "No tattoos, either. I went to the heall too young."

Beside his brother, Fargrimr also stripped his sleeve, showing—by contrast—muddy wriggling swirls of blue-green wode and hairless forearms banded with muscle like barrelstaves.

"His fault," Fargrimr said, fondly, and punched his brother. "I would have had washerwoman calluses, instead of learning the axe."

"I was born Fasti Fastarrson," Randulfr said. "Someday I'll tell you how I wound up in the borderlands. It's a long story, involving a trade negotiation and a young wolf-bitch who tagged along with her mother after being told to stay home." He grinned at Ingrun, who had sprawled on her side as if the snow were a featherbed, her feet extended toward the coals. "But you have the look of a man with a message, wolfjarl."

"I've come to speak to your brother, actually," Vethulf said. "Fargrimr, I am sent by Grimolfr to pass the word: the heofodmenn of the wolfless men are summoned immediately to a council of war."

# TWO

As Grimolfr and the season predicted, there was no dawning, but nevertheless the torches of the Wolfmaegth almost sufficed to stain the deep-blue sky in crimson. Vethulf stood with his brothers of the wolfthreat and werthreat, awkward at the back of the human and svartalfar army. The svartalfar had insisted on the honor of the vanguard. When Grimolfr and Gunnarr Sturluson protested, the foremost smiths and mothers of the svartalfar had been polite but adamant. The svartalfar were guests of the men, and they would fight at the front. Furthermore—as Tin, the master-smith who had befriended Vethulf's wolfsprechend, Isolfr, pointed out—her people did not rely upon torches to see in the dark and so should have the lights at their back, where they would blind the trolls but not the svartalfar.

The light of the men's torches still revealed the svartalfar, though—their hunched backs draped in cloaks worked with elaborate quilting; richly, raggedly decorated in subtle rusts and umbers; mail and weapons showing the dull glint of oiled steel. Some of the svartalfar stood no higher than a man's waist and the tallest were only eye to eye with a trellwolf, but their legs bent strangely under the skirts of their hauberks, and when their arms extended, their reach was half again Vethulf's span.

Behind the svartalfar were ranked the wolfless men, Gunnarr the jarl of Nithogsfjoll and his warriors and all the rest of the jarls and their men. Here again the trolls had done them a favor, because the hewn trees, trammeled snow, and scraped-clear hillsides made it easy for the wolfless men to line up shoulder to shoulder, lock shield-edges and advance in a double-rank. Boys and old men not strong enough for service under arms stood behind them, bearing spears and torches.

Down the slope from the crest of the hill to the seacliffs, Vethulf could see the tumbled walls and ruins of what had been Othinnsaesc. Trellfires blazed at the boundaries, glittering on drifts slumped over broken stones.

It griped Vethulf for wolfcarls to fight behind wolfless men when trolls were the enemy, but the wolfcarls were sortie fighters, and a shield wall was only as effective as its cohesion. Somewhere among those wolfless men were Fargrimr and the other two surviving sworn-sons. Vethulf allowed himself a moment of pity for the father of the one who had fallen, who must have burned all his born-male heirs and also now had lost the sworn-male one. Perhaps there were sister-sons to stand the family's obligations.

Perhaps.

Vethulf shook his head. Many fathers had lost sons and sons had lost fathers. Tonight—unless it was today, and who could tell, in the bleakness of midwinter?—there would be more. Beside him, Kjaran whined, reading Vethulf's distress as plainly as the wind, and shifted his paws uneasily. Vethulf leaned his hip on the wolf's shoulder in apology. No warmth penetrated either his woolens and furs or Kjaran's coat, but the contact was comforting. He wanted to strip off a gauntlet and bury his fingers in the wolf's thick ruff, but the cold was too dangerous and the fight was at hand.

He hoped. The worst part of organized action was the waiting.

All around him, men and wolves groaned and fidgeted. The Franangfordthreat surrounded Vethulf and Kjaran, stretching off to the left where Skjaldwulf and Mar made a lynchpin for the southernmost flank of the Wolfmaegth. Only half the Wolfmaegth moved with the svartalfar and the wolfless men. The rest were with Grimolfr, circling wide to the south.

Vethulf felt them and all the rest of his brethren through the pack-sense. Waves of disquiet and eagerness flowed through them, a tumult of conflicting desires. But a driving purpose underlay that, and Vethulf knew that once battle was joined, the Wolfmaegth's passion would be unified.

A cry went up from the back of the press, the howl of wolves and the bellow of men, the horrid ecstatic clatter of axes on bucklers and breastplates. The rearguard was in place. The clamor swept forward, and as the cry reached Vethulf he took it up, head thrown back, Kjaran howling beside him, the press of trellwolf and wolfcarl bodies on each side rocking forward and back in abrupt eagerness. The waiting wore men down, made their bones ache with anxiety, until the splashing terror of open war could come as a relief.

Vethulf shouted his throat scraped and hot, Kjaran rearing up beside him to paw the air like a striking stallion. Far to the front, the dark glitter of torchlight reflected on svartalfar halberds wavered as the forest of weapons dipped forward and the svartalfar tumbled downslope like an avalanche.

Behind them, the torches of the wolfless men dipped and fluttered, following. Then Vethulf was running, too, the axe swinging comfortably in his hand, Kjaran's feet silent and his tongue lolling between dagger teeth as he paced alongside. Trolls poured out of the warren below. Vethulf ran harder, each bounding downhill step jarring his legs to the hip. He had to check himself as he overran the wolfless men's line. As the armies of the humans and alfar poured down the slope, he kept an eye on the woods to the south. Trolls moved underground as easily as fish through water, and there was another logic to placing the wolfcarls in the rearguard.

The svartalfar met the trellish legion with a sound like a thousand falling trees. They plunged among the trolls with a great wailing and the terrible clash of wood and metal. Vethulf reached out to Kjaran with his mind, listening to the evidence of the gray wolf's senses, sharing what he himself observed from atop the moving tower of his height. Together they knew more than each alone. Vethulf could see across the press, down into the ruined town where battle was already joined, as the wolfless men formed their wall again and quickly advanced, shields locked and feet shuffling in unison while swords and spears poked through.

These trolls fought frantically, savagely, blocking the entrances to the warren with their bodies while miners tunneled behind them to close the gaps their warriors defended. The attacking archers loosed upon the miners, but when the trolls fell, their comrades only buried them in the bulwarks so black ichor stained the rough-shaped rock. Vethulf saw a man fall and his comrades close ranks around him, sealing the shield wall before the line could be broken. A second rank of men walked behind the first, some with spears, some merely leaning on their shieldbrothers' backs, reinforcing one man's strength with another against the superior weight and strength of the trolls. One of the second rank shoved the wounded warrior's shield over him to protect him; the fallen man curled in on himself like a beetle.

A moment later, Vethulf heard a roar that drowned even the noise of battle and looked left to see a band of trellwarriors break cover, running for the human army's flank—and the Franang-fordthreat. Skjaldwulf's powerful baritone carried over the creak of leather and the breathless yelps of running men: "To me! To me, Franangford! For Viradechtis!"

Skjaldwulf could not have found a better rallying cry. The throats of the Franangfordthreat were opened, and the battle-howl that rang from them rivaled the ululations of the oncoming horde of trolls. Vethulf shifted his grip upon his axe haft and leaped forward, meeting the enemy midcharge.

What followed was a slaughter. These were not warriors, he realized as he hewed one and another, boots slipping in ichor-black, ichor-slick snow. These were house-trolls, decked in scavenged armor, swinging weapons they barely knew how to hold. A *distraction*, he thought, as Grimolfr's troop broke from the trees behind them and fell upon their flank.

It was not hard to disengage when all around him men and wolves were pulling trolls down like sheep. He drew back, scrambling upslope, finally locating a boulder with the hewn stump of a murdered forest giant still crouched beside it. He clawed up the vantage one-handed, awkward in buckler, leathers, and mail. Blood-clotted boots slipped before he jammed the toes in crevices and heaved himself up. *Where are the warriors?*

Kjaran floated effortlessly up the rock to crouch beside Vethulf, ears pinned as he scented a bloody wind. Down by the ruins, the last of the trellish defenders had fallen. A great cheer went up among the wolfless men as svartalfar smiths and sappers approached the sealed tunnels. Then men and alfar drew back from the tunnels, the last few sappers moving at a scuttling svartalfar run, and Vethulf was only prepared for what came next because he'd witnessed the purging of Franangford.

A rising ice-sharp wind off the ocean brought him an acrid scent of burning, followed some moments later by a dull, heavy sound that struck his ears like a cup-hand blow and lifted and dropped the boulder under his feet. He swayed but kept his balance. Kjaran looked at him and whined.

"I know," Vethulf said. "I hate it, too. Wolf-brother, where are the *trellwarriors?*"

Even Kjaran's nose could not find them. Perhaps the reek of rock tar, as the svartalfar hauled forward barrels of the stuff on sledges and tipped them down into the cracked holes of the trellwarren, drowned out the scent. Or perhaps there were no more warriors to be found.

In any case, for the moment the fighting was over. So Vethulf stood on his lonely promontory, his wolf pressed to his thigh, and watched as the torches were brought up to the tar-soaked trellwarren and the oily black smoke belched forth.

The stink scoured his head and made bile rise up his throat. He couldn't name the thing that left him cold and shivering, but it wasn't the ice of the arctic night.

⟡

All Skjaldwulf could smell was rock tar and blood.

When the fires burned themselves out, the wolfcarls, trell-wolves, and svartalfar had entered the tunnels. This was no job for wolfless men, so Gunnarr Sturluson pulled his troops back to cordon the town and hunt for trellish stragglers.

In the tunnels, they found the trellwarriors whose absence had so concerned Vethulf, and Vethulf had been right to be concerned. The trolls had been too canny to waste their best fighters out in the open, holding them in reserve in the twists and traps of the trell-wrought caverns. The trolls had learned from Franangford as well, and they had built channels and baffles and cisterns to keep the blazing rock tar from their dens. More had survived than not, and it was terrible fighting—so terrible that in the end the wolfless men had to be brought into it.

At least Skjaldwulf found that the trolls' advantage over men was more than balanced by the svartalfar's advantage over both other races. The trolls might twist stone, but if they left it wide enough for a troll to pass, they could never twist it so that alfar could not follow. And follow the alfar did, tenacious and terrible.

Skjaldwulf came to understand, in the days of butchery it took to clear the warren, that the trolls had always relied first on their superior size, and second on their ability to escape. Here, as they had no further bolt-hole to fall back to, but had to stand and fight, they were defeated time and again.

Men and wolves slept and fought in shifts, grabbing a few broken hours of exhausted rest before dragging themselves from their tents and blankets to kill again. Skjaldwulf was sure that svartalfar must sleep, but he never caught them at it.

Skjaldwulf and Mar were in on the kill in the queen's chamber, though neither drew her blood; they had to content themselves with her body-servants. Skjaldwulf was old enough to find that sufficient glory in which to clothe himself. The honor of the queen's death fell to Othwulf Vikingrsbrother and Gunnarr Sturluson, who were brothers in blood though one had gone to the heall and one remained a jarl, and Skjaldwulf was skald enough to find poetry in that, which was more satisfaction than glory would be.

After the trellqueen was disposed of, along with her kittens—and that was a grim piece of butchery, as the kittens screamed and cowered and the adult trolls threw themselves at their enemies' weapons as desperately as drowning men—the remaining trolls fled along tunnels deep in the earth that would have to be painstakingly quartered, explored, and scoured over more days than Skjaldwulf cared to consider. But the svartalfar assured the men that the crucial thing was done. With queen and kittens dead, what was left was merely the tidying away of loose ends. And a blood-boltered tidying it would be.

Skjaldwulf, for his part, sought the comforts of the sauna and his supper. Vethulf was not to be found, and Mar vanished off to sleep while Skjaldwulf was steaming the filth from his skin and the ache from his bones. Vethulf's absence was a sort of blessing. Skjaldwulf had the energy for neither stony silences nor outright warfare, and that was all there had been between them since the battle for Othinn-saesc had started. He continued to be wearily astonished at Mar and Kjaran, who were as inseparable as litter brothers even in the absence of their konigenwolf. The pack-sense was no help to him, as Kjaran's sense of humor was unfortunately all too wolfish. *It would be worse if they fought.*

The first dawn in days was breaking when Skjaldwulf returned to their tent to find it occupied, not just by Mar but by Kjaran and Vethulf. Skjaldwulf ducked inside. The air within was not even cold enough to make his breath steam but still chilly after the bath-house. He quickly stripped off his snowy boots and calf-bindings and coat and without speaking slipped into the furs. He could tell from Vethulf's breathing that he was awake, but neither of them spoke as Skjaldwulf settled himself between Vethulf and Mar.

Mar stirred in his sleep and pressed against Skjaldwulf's chest, and Vethulf, uncharacteristically, draped himself against Skjald-wulf's back, one arm around his waist. *I thought he was awake,* Skjaldwulf thought, and then, *Oh,* as Vethulf flattened his palm on Skjaldwulf's belly, as if to hold him close. Skjaldwulf blinked, abruptly wide awake in the warmth of the brief morning light staining the tent walls golden.

"Vethulf," he murmured, but it wasn't a protest, and when Vethulf nuzzled past Skjaldwulf's plaits and pressed warm, dry lips to the nape of his neck, Skjaldwulf moaned low in his throat. The scrape of teeth, the brush of tongue as Vethulf burrowed through clothing to nip the place where his neck ran into his shoulder was delicately erotic. Skjaldwulf shivered in pleasure.

And it was an answer. A crude sort of answer: a little bit desperate, a little bit sad. But neither one of them was lying to the other or would be expected to pretend. And that alone might make it all right.

And it was so much better than fighting.

Skjaldwulf turned in Vethulf's arms and pressed a kiss to his open mouth. Vethulf kissed him back, tasting of charred meat, sour milky skyr, and the birch twigs he must have chewed to clean his teeth. His hands clenched on Skjaldwulf's braids, dragging their mouths together until Skjaldwulf groaned and met tongue with tongue, force with force, mouths slipping and grating and sliding, hot and wet. Vethulf's hands groped under his tunic, under the linen shirt he wore against his skin. Their clothes were filthy and stank with old sweat and the rancid bear grease with which they coated exposed skin to prevent chapping and frostbite, and it didn't matter in the slightest.

Vethulf wormed out of shirt and tunic and sweater and jerkin with a writhing grace, breaking the kiss only long enough to drag the clothing over his head and shove it aside. Kjaran grunted, waking enough to complain, and Mar put a cold nose in the back of Skjaldwulf's neck. Skjaldwulf pushed him away, laughing, and stripped off his own layers of clothing. It wasn't warm enough in the furs to be naked, but he let Vethulf peel off his loincloth and leggings, too, and rubbed his hands over the bony, muscled architecture of Vethulf's shoulders and back to create heat while Vethulf kicked his own underclothes aside.

They were both too thin, both exhausted and closer to heartbroken than not, and it didn't matter. Heat grew between their bodies where they chafed and slid together, though Vethulf shivered as he pressed against Skjaldwulf. It might have been cold or sexual thrill or both, but Vethulf's sex jutted against the soft inside of

Skjaldwulf's thigh. He groaned like an animal in a trap when Skjaldwulf lowered his head to bite along Vethulf's throat under the short paired plaits of his beard. Skjaldwulf tasted sweat and bear grease and didn't care, because Vethulf's hand slipped between them, cradling Skjaldwulf's stones, kneading gently.

Mar whined, twisting restlessly against Skjaldwulf's back as Skjaldwulf arched against Vethulf, purring deep in his throat, encouraging the touch. Vethulf's hand slid up Skjaldwulf's shaft, moving rhythmically, creating just enough contact to tease. Skjaldwulf curled forward, the burn of cold air on his neck, and pressed his forehead to Vethulf's shoulder.

It was stupid to undress, stupid to do this now, here, when there was always the half-chance that they would have to scramble from the tent at any moment, jamming feet into the wrong boots and struggling with axes. Stupid, and Skjaldwulf suddenly didn't care about that, either, because Vethulf was pressing against him, drawing his legs up around Skjaldwulf's hips, and rolling to pull Skjaldwulf atop him in a wordless, unmistakable invitation. It was quiet in the tent, except for Vethulf's scattered breathing and the irritated moaning of a wolf as Kjaran scratched his ear with a hind foot, aroused and awakened by the wolfcarls' groping.

If Skjaldwulf shut his eyes, the hard, clutching body in his arms could belong to anyone. He kept his eyes open. Solace was one thing; falsehood—no matter how tempting, no matter that he knew beyond need of asking that Vethulf would understand—was something else, and something Skjaldwulf wanted no part of. He had learned from the wolves that a lie was a weakness in the pack.

A coarse beard rasped Skjaldwulf's chest before the mouth it surrounded latched onto his nipple, sucking hard, nipping. Skjaldwulf drew a breath deep enough to make the healed cracks in his ribs ache in protest. He braced himself up on one arm, grinning as Vethulf yelped and burrowed closer against the cold draft, and scrabbled through his coat pockets for the birch bark packet of bear grease. And there it was; he dropped onto his elbows, ignoring Vethulf's *oof* of protest and Kjaran's grumpy whine, and fumbled open the sinew ties, digging his nails into the cold grease until a glob clung to his fingertips. He knelt back while Vethulf gripped his shoulder with one hand, the other still wrapped around Skjald-wulf's sex, moving smoothly but not at all gently now.

Mar lurched to his feet, still half-crouched in the close darkness of the tent, his claws scoring Skjaldwulf's shoulder accidentally. Skjaldwulf hissed at the sting but shook his head as Vethulf opened his mouth to ask. If he was bleeding, it was not enough to matter. Mar dropped back to his elbows, whining, and there was a heave of furry body over Skjaldwulf as Kjaran went to join his threatbrother. Kjaran mounted Mar, though Mar snapped at him halfheartedly. The snow shook off the tent as Kjaran began masturbating against Mar's hip and Mar, with a put-upon sigh, let him.

There were no secrets in the Wolfmaegth. No secrets and no lies.

It wasn't like the wolf-rut—human intercourse was so transitory, so much less obsessive than the pack's response to a bitch's heat— but Kjaran whined as Skjaldwulf pressed his greased fingers against Vethulf, *into* Vethulf, and Vethulf gasped and clutched and almost convulsed with pleasure. He grunted and then keened softly be-tween his teeth as Skjaldwulf slid deeper, seeking, pressing, easing his way. Vethulf was so hot inside, so much hotter than the chill air and even the relative warmth of the furs. Skjaldwulf wanted to crawl into that heat and never come out.

*"Now,"* Vethulf demanded.

Skjaldwulf hissed, "Don't talk," and kissed him silent, and then obeyed.

They came together harshly, Vethulf fisting his hands under his ass to raise himself, his sinewy legs like iron shackles on Skjaldwulf's hips. Skjaldwulf pressed hard, roughly, so that Vethulf swore and

Mar growled under his breath, a vibration in the blankets more than a sound. And then they were together, linked, *locked*. Vethulf's low moan became a stuttered gasp as Skjaldwulf braced himself with one hand, found Vethulf's sex with the weaker one, and began to move against him, hard, matching the rhythm with twisting strokes.

A creased blanket gouged Skjaldwulf's knee; a mouth found his throat in the darkness and sucked hard enough to bruise. Vethulf bit his shoulder, clenching and writhing against him, around him, his nails carving runes in Skjaldwulf's flesh to match Mar's scratches, his sex pulsing in Skjaldwulf's hand, splattering both of them with slippery heat. Kjaran whined and then Mar yipped softly, like a wolf in a running-dream.

Skjaldwulf let himself drop to his elbows, slumped against Vethulf, surrendered to the powerful legs clamped around his hips and the strong hands yanking his plaits, the softness of flesh and the strength of hard muscle as he spent himself deep in Vethulf's receptive warmth.

The hands that stroked his hair grew gentle and the mouth that kissed his was soft, until they disentangled and dried and dressed themselves in silence and fell asleep curled together, warmed by the snoring bodies of their wolves.

# Three

When he was a boy, Brokkolfr was afraid of wolves.

Not that he'd ever seen a wolf, except for the brawling, bellowing sea-wolves who came to the limestone caves along the cliffs to rut and fight, but his grandmother told stories. And then when he was twelve and his village drew lots to decide whose boy had to go to the heall, it seemed like everyone he knew had a story about wolves. Terrible stories about wolves hunting men like rabbits, wolves devouring babies—

*Cubs?* Amma said hopefully, and Brokkolfr smiled. Amma loved cubs of all species: trellwolf, human, the cats who hunted mice in Franangford's new storerooms, the geese on the nearby lake. It left Brokkolfr wondering what she would do if she were a wild wolf and there was nothing to eat but baby geese.

She loved visiting the heall-born babies and made no objections even to having her ear used as a teething rag. And any bitch who littered in Franangford was sure to have Amma hovering carefully out of range until such time as the mother deemed help acceptable. Viradechtis had a particularly long-suffering sigh with which she signaled permission.

Right now, Amma was thinking mostly of Viradechtis' pups, and Brokkolfr said, "Maybe later, sister. Work first."

Amma huffed but flopped down agreeably beside him. The seasons had passed from winter to spring since the liberation of Othinnsaesc, and Brokkolfr was taking advantage of the sunshine to sit in the courtyard—or what passed for a courtyard at Franangford, which was actually just the clear space, roughly rectangular, in the midst of the tents gifted by Bravoll. But it was much better than the close, reeking darkness of the tents, which was all they would have until the construction of the wolfheall and its outbuildings came further along. In the months since the founding of the new Franangford heall, Brokkolfr had taken charge of the saddlery, and leatherwork was best done outdoors in strong light.

Most of the Franangfordthreat were away from the heall this afternoon. Some were hunting, some were felling trees for the outbuildings, and one wolfjarl had gone to negotiate with the master of the Franangford quarry about stone and payment. Skjaldwulf, not Vethulf. No one sent Vethulf when negotiations were at hand. If Brokkolfr listened, he could hear Vethulf now, tearing strips off somebody for wasting the good weather by dawdling about. Brokkolfr winced in sympathy and bent his head to his own work. Amma, resigned, rolled belly-up to the sun and slipped into a dream.

Some time later, Brokkolfr and Amma both became aware of a stranger approaching. Amma went from asleep to standing up with no transition. Brokkolfr stood more slowly. He knew he was staring, but he couldn't help it. The man approaching was not only a stranger but the strangest stranger Brokkolfr had ever seen.

He was tall and broad, balding except for a gray fringe. Brokkolfr had never seen a wolfcarl so old, and it was obvious this was no wolfcarl. Over his tunic and leggings he wore a caftan that came to his boot tops but left his arms bare. Those arms were blue from knuckles to shoulder with tattoos, and a copper medallion stamped with the intricately decorated image of a sow swung on a leather cord about his neck.

He stopped a polite distance from Brokkolfr, shifting from side to side as if to ease sore feet. "Hail," he said. "I am Freyvithr, servant of Freya. Is this the Franangford Wolfheall?"

From the way he was eyeing Amma, he knew it was. A prickle of something uncomfortable shivered along Brokkolfr's spine. He knew about monasteries, although there were none within less than a fortnight's travel of any wolfheall. In the south, there were many strangenessess—isolated farms and crofts, halls where godsmen congregated, places where people did nothing but trade and teach. Not just bondi—tradesmen—and their apprentices, but whole heallan devoted to craft. In the north, one did not group men together except to fight or for self-defense.

Although that, too, might be changing. Brokkolfr was no wolfsprechend, not like Isolfr, but no one in Franangford could have avoided hearing the ongoing, sometimes bitter, discussion between wolfjarls and wolfsprechend, and every visitor the heall had, about what the wolfheallan would do now that all the trolls were gone. Even men who wanted to think no further than their next meal, or their next fight, knew there was something to worry about.

"Aye," Brokkolfr said, "it is. I am Brokkolfr Ammasbrother." And he tilted his head to let the monk know that the great shaggy creature beside him was Amma. "Can we help you?"

"She'll not eat me, then?" Freyvithr said, with a quirk of his eyebrow to let Brokkolfr know it was a joke.

But a joke, Brokkolfr reckoned, with some genuine disquiet behind it. If the wolfheallan did not see monks, it was just as sure that the monasteries did not see trellwolves. And Isolfr was vehement about the need to teach wolfless men the ways of wolves—that trellwolves were no threat to anyone who did not mean harm to them or their brothers. "Amma? No, if she slays you, it will be with kisses. Offer your hand, as you would to a dog."

"Or a pony," Freyvithr muttered, but he extended his hand, and Amma went forward happily to snuffle and then lick it. *Wet wool and old blood*, she told Brokkolfr, and he felt it go into the pack-sense as Freyvithr, accepting that the fell beast before him would not take his hand off at the elbow, began to rub her ears.

"She may knock you down unmeaning," Brokkolfr warned him. "She's young yet and doesn't fully know how big she is. But she means no harm."

"I can see that," Freyvithr said, smiling under his beard.

*Wool and blood?* Curiosity in the pack-sense, and odd-eyed Kjaran appeared between the tents on the other side of the courtyard, quickly followed by Kothran and Hroi, because Viradechtis was away from her den and her mate and shieldbrothers were her eyes in her absence. Freyvithr noticed and glanced at Brokkolfr.

Brokkolfr shrugged. "They want to know what's going on."

"Am I so interesting?"

"You're a stranger, and a wolfless man. We don't see very many such."

"Ah," said Freyvithr, and Amma nudged him to keep rubbing. "I suppose you wouldn't."

Inevitably, the wolves' curiosity had drawn the men as well. Vethulf strode past his brother, his eyebrows going up as he took in the scene. "Hail, traveler," he said. "I am Vethulf Kjaransbrother, wolfjarl of Franangford."

"Freyvithr, servant of Freya. I had been told the wolfjarl was named Skjaldwulf?" Freyvithr said.

Brokkolfr winced, but for once Vethulf did not hackle.

"It is confusing," he agreed. "There are two of us, Skjaldwulf and myself, and our wolfsprechend, Isolfr."

"Ah," said Freyvithr. "Then I *am* in the right place. It is your wolfsprechend I have come to speak to." When Vethulf made a spooling gesture in the air, as if drawing the words off a spindle, the monk continued. "Word has reached Hergilsberg that Isolfr Ice-mad claims he has been spoken to by the lady I serve."

"Isolfr *Viradechtisbrother*," Vethulf said, "has gone with his wolf to practice hunting with her litter."

"She is supposed to have come to him in a dream," Freyvithr said, a little dreamy himself. "In a dream!"

Vethulf looked at Brokkolfr. *You're a bitch's brother. You think of something.*

Brokkolfr looked back. *Yes, because I proved just how much* that *means when Othinnsaesc fell and I saved only the barest scrap of the threat. You're the wolfjarl. You do it.*

But Vethulf was about as suited to politics with wolfless men as he was to flying. Brokkolfr sighed and pushed a few scraggling strands of black hair out of his eyes. He would have to get one of the women to wash and rebraid it; it was too fine ever to stay plaited for long.

"Come with me," he said to Freyvithr. "I'll show you where you can stow your bag and take you to the sauna. When you're clean, we can track down the kitchen-mistress and find out what she has on which to feed you."

"I'm grateful," the godsman said, hefting his pack. From his

expression, Brokkolfr believed it—though whether for being wel-
comed or for not being fed to the wolves was a different question.

⚭

There were not many wolfcarls in the half-built bluestone halls
of Franangford, with their flags not yet worn smooth under
the rushes. Maybe thirty of the threat-that-had-been, plus Isolfr
and his wolfjarls and his shieldbrothers, a few wolves from Nithogsfjoll like Ingrun and Glaedir who had preferred their chances of
advancement under Viradechtis to the established structure of the
old pack. And then the odds and ends, wolves and wolf-brothers
who had chosen to follow Kjaran or Mar from Arakensberg or Nithogsfjoll, a single wolf here and there from other heallan who had
made the same choice for reasons that his brother might or might
not understand. And Brokkolfr, traded from Othinnsaesc like an
extra daughter sent for fostering.

Not that he would not have begged to go, away from the rubble
and ashes and memories of failure. Away from all the empty places
in the pack-sense where his shieldbrothers had been. Away from the
dreams. But it had not been necessary. His wolfsprechend had been
kind, had asked him if he minded, but Brokkolfr had known that it
wouldn't have mattered if he *did* mind. Othinnsaesc wanted one of
Viradechtis' daughters; it did not want a bitch who was remarkable
only for her complete lack of ambition.

That evening, after dinner, he watched Isolfr sit between his
wolfjarls, his gaze on his hands, while Freyvithr recounted all the
news and gossip from the south—as any traveler would, in return
for the heall's hospitality. And Brokkolfr watched from his place
along one of the half-empty trestles and told himself, *Be glad of it.
See what greatness does to Isolfr and be glad you have it not.*

Isolfr looked tired and unhappy, a pinched line between his eyebrows that had nothing to do with the scars from the trellqueen he

had slain. He nodded when the godsman addressed him directly, and he picked at the food on the trencher he shared with Vethulf Viper-tongue and Skjaldwulf Snow-soft, but Brokkolfr could not miss that most of the food that found his hand made its way under the table to Viradechtis. Or that Isolfr cast more than one longing glance down the table to his shieldmates, the bond-pairs who had come with him from Nithogsfjoll—gray solid old Hroi and the Stone Sokkolfr, fleet pale Kothran and Frithulf with his fire-scarred face. Randulfr caught Brokkolfr's eye, and they exchanged the same helpless look they'd been exchanging for months.

No one in Franangford would accuse Isolfr of deliberate malice, Brokkolfr thought. Not after what he had done against the trolls. And those of the old Franangfordthreat, Ulfmundr and his scarred wolf Hlothor, Herrolfr and snake-fast Stigandr their leaders, were so grateful to have a konigenwolf, to *be* a threat still instead of divided among the other heallan, that they would not speak—or hear—a word against their wolfsprechend.

But they could resent the former Nithogsfjollthreat and the favor those men found in Isolfr's eyes.

Isolfr knew it, Brokkolfr thought—although as brother of Franangford's third bitch, Brokkolfr lacked both the status and the nerve to breach his cold-eyed wolfsprechend's silence. But Isolfr was better with wolves than with men; Brokkolfr was awake enough to the pack-sense to feel Isolfr's unease with men who were strangers to him, his even greater unease with men who thought him a hero.

And for most of the new Franangfordthreat, that was all they knew. Isolfr Ice-mad, slayer of trellqueens. And so Isolfr, already carrying a heavy burden as wolfsprechend of a new wolfthreat and a new wolfheall, retreated to the men he knew, to Sokkolfr and Frithulf, who had known him before Viradechtis was more than a squirming pup, to Skjaldwulf and Vethulf, who knew him in the deep multilayered bond that Viradechtis had made between her brother and her consorts and their brothers.

Brokkolfr also knew that he and Randulfr should be doing something, but Randulfr, though friends with every man in the heall, had no taste for leadership, and Brokkolfr himself knew he had no skill for it. He had proved that at Othinnsaesc, when he saved so few from the fire and the trolls. If he had been a true leader, like Isolfr or Skjaldwulf or even sharp-tongued Vethulf, there would not have been so many deaths. With that knowledge heavy about him, Brokkolfr did nothing, fearing that anything he did would only make matters worse.

And so the conversation faltered on for some time, and Freyvithr—something of a spinner of tales—seemed content to talk about everything except how he had come some thousand miles by longship and shank's mare to Franangford, of all the Hel-spawned places.

But travelers did not come to the heall, not without wolves, and finally Isolfr Ice-mad looked up and caught Freyvithr's eye. The godsman fell silent, and the wolfsprechend said, "I do not understand what you want of me."

The godsman rocked back on his heels and folded his ink-marked arms across the breadth of his chest. "I wish to speak with you about your dreams, wolfsprechend," he said. "Because your adventures are the stuff of sagas. And as I am a follower of Freya, and she sent your dreams and spae unto you, it should be in her house that the memories of your exploits are kept."

"My exploits?" Isolfr's mouth quirked bitterly. "You should ask Skjaldwulf, not me. He is our teller of tales."

"But I do not wish the tale," Freyvithr said patiently. "Tales I may hear anywhere. Only from you can I hear the truth."

Isolfr seemed to stiffen, and Viradechtis emerged suddenly from beneath the table. She was the largest wolf in the heall, daughter of Nithogsfjoll's immense Skald, and although Freyvithr did not flinch, he became wary. She gave him a deceptively lazy sideways look and then butted her brother solidly in the shoulder with a deep grumble that made the werthreat laugh; even Isolfr managed a real smile.

"My sister," he started to say to the godsman, but at that moment conversation became impossible, as Viradechtis' adolescent pups realized their mother was awake and leaped on her, barking at the top of their still shrill puppy voices. There were five pups. Amma adored them, and they her. So Brokkolfr could even tell apart the twin dogs black as Mar, Letta and Lofi. There was also the massive brindle, Ottarr; and two bitches, a rarity in any trellwolf litter: tawny Geirve, odd-eyed like Kjaran, and storm-gray Signy, already a konigenwolf and fearlessly ready to prove it against any wolf in the threat.

Freyvithr threw his hands up in mock surrender. "I know when I am bested," he said, pitching his voice to carry over the din. "But I hope you will speak with me later, wolfsprechend. In Freya's honor, if for no other reason."

Isolfr hunched his shoulder in something that could have been either agreement or refusal as his sister and her pups and her consorts herded him out of the great hall. Skjaldwulf and Vethulf looked doubtfully at each other; then Vethulf followed Isolfr, and Skjaldwulf moved to sit next to Freyvithr. Doubtless collecting the tales Freyvithr had spoken of, Brokkolfr thought.

While other men left the great hall, Brokkolfr toyed with the remains of his dinner. No mere longhouse-and-kitchen, when it was complete the new wolfheall at Franangford would boast a courtyard surrounded on the other three sides by dormitories, workshops, and galleries. All were already ringed by a palisade that also enbailed the kitchens, stables, smokehouse, well, and granaries. There would have been a motte and keep, one day, but the earthworks were still under construction. And might now never be finished, given that peace had broken out.

Brokkolfr poked his trencher with the knife one last time before a thrall came to clear his leavings for alms. He stood, realizing that he was almost the last one in the hall. Some wolfcarls undoubtedly took their wolves to hunt in the lengthening evening; others might seek work, play at arms, or women.

As for Brokkolfr, he decided the best thing he could do with himself was sit in the sauna and boil some of this prickly restlessness out of his brain. Amma followed him—which surprised him less when he found Hrafn lying mournfully beside the sauna door.

Gray-masked black Hrafn had been born a wild wolf; he had found his bond-brother Kari mostly by accident in the aftermath of the sack of Jorhus. They had joined the Franangfordthreat before the old konigenwolf had been killed, but they remained here because of Isolfr. Kari had been with Isolfr when Isolfr slew the trellqueen in the Iskryne—the story Freyvithr Godsman had come to collect.

Grateful that he would not have to build the fire and heat the stones himself, Brokkolfr nevertheless wondered if Kari was in hiding. Hrafn lifted his head, ears pricked, his tail thumping the boards twice in greeting as Amma flopped down beside him. Brokkolfr shed his clothes and untied his straggling braids, then pushed aside the first of two hanging blankets to enter the sauna.

"Has the godsman given up, then?" Kari asked as Brokkolfr stepped into bone-deep warmth. Kari was a slight man, wiry and scarred, his yellow-brown beard still ragged as a youth's.

"For tonight. That one, I think, does not give up easily." Brokkolfr hesitated, but Kari waved him over amiably. They were close to the same age—and Amma liked Hrafn. Brokkolfr settled on a sharp-smelling cedar log, his shoulders against warm stone, and cupped a hand across his mouth and nose so he could breathe the cooler air it caught. Water beaded on his face as Kari reached forward and switched soaked spruce branches across the coals. Steam billowed up, and Brokkolfr reached for a scraper. He checked the edge for nicks that could draw blood.

Kari leaned back, body slack in the heat, licking at beads of sweat and condensation. Brokkolfr stood into dizzying heat and dragged the horn edge of the scraper down his chest, watching as a week's soot and grit peeled away with the sweat. He flicked the scraper clean and started under his chin once more.

He almost opened his mouth to say, *You and Frithulf went to the Iskryne with him. Do you understand him?* And was stupidly grateful that Kari spoke first, before he could make a fool of himself by prying into another man's business. "We haven't any shortage of candidates for this litter," the wildling said. "And the next will be spoiled for choice. But that won't last more than a couple of summers."

Brokkolfr hung the scraper carefully. "What do you mean?"

Kari's torso swelled and shrank with deep, slow breaths. He spoke between them. "This year, we're heroes. We saved all the northlands. We'll eat well and have all the women we want. Boys will compete to come be wolfcarls—at least they will once there's food in from the fields, and the memories of the deaths is a little further off, and until then we have wolf-widows to spare. But in two summers' time, or come a lean winter—gratitude is soon forgotten. And the werthreats will die away and the wolves will go wilding. And why should they not? With the trolls gone, what need is there of the Wolfmaegth?"

Brokkolfr sat again heavily. The steam lessened, and he took his turn with the branches. It had the sound of something Kari had been thinking about for a long time. "Of course, you've spoken of this to the wolfsprechend."

Kari shrugged heavily. "To the wolfjarl."

*Which one?* Brokkolfr wondered. "I'm more worried that there *will* be a need for us."

Kari slitted one eye, a pale glimmer behind his lashes. Brokkolfr knew it for encouragement.

"Isolfr Viradechtisbrother *is* the treaty with the svartalfar," Brokkolfr said. "When the ice pushes *them* out of the Iskryne, like it pushed the trolls before them, and when Isolfr is gone—what then?"

There was a long pause. Kari sighed and let his eye fall shut again. "Skjaldwulf has thought of that, I'm sure."

*Yes*, Brokkolfr did not say. *But has he thought of an answer?*

# FOUR

"You were hardly hospitable to him, were you?" Vethulf said as mildly as he knew how. Isolfr's head was bent over one of the pups—who was at last tired enough to lie still and be checked for ticks—and his long blond braids shielded his face very well, but Vethulf was becoming something of an expert on Isolfr's shoulders. Those shoulders said he didn't want to talk about the godsman, or anything else, and in fact wished Vethulf would go away.

*Sorry to disappoint*, Vethulf thought, and settled his own shoulders more comfortably against the door frame. Viradechtis leaning against one leg and Kjaran flopped across his feet told him he was right. Vethulf counted beats of his heart and was at nine when Isolfr's well-studied shoulders slumped and he muttered, "Hospitality surely doesn't mean I have to take my heart out of my chest to show him."

"Is that what he's asking you to do?" Vethulf said. "I only heard him asking about a dream."

That got him a glare. "Would you feel the same if it were your dreams he wanted to hear?"

"I never remember my dreams," Vethulf said cheerfully.

For a moment, he thought Isolfr might smile, but he sighed instead. "I don't want to talk to him. That's all."

*In a pig's eye,* Vethulf thought but bit his tongue before saying. He had grown up the ninth of his father's ten children, with nieces and nephews older than he was, not to mention more cousins than a man could count in a night, all of them brawling in and out of the longhouse his father's elder brother ruled; he had learned early to fight fierce and fight dirty if he wanted to get anything for himself—if he wanted to be heard. The edge that upbringing had given his tongue and his wits had served him well in Arakensberg Wolfheall, which was much enmeshed in the politics both of the Wolfmaegth and of Arakensberg Keep.

But then he had become wolfjarl to Isolfr Viradechtisbrother, and sharp words no longer served him. Vethulf didn't have to scramble to be noticed; it was the men of Franangford who scrambled to be noticed by him. Skjaldwulf, whom he had thought his rival, had turned out to be his best ally—and unimpressed with his flyting. And Isolfr, whose notice he most craved, retreated from the kind of fighting Vethulf knew best like a wolf retreating burn-footed from a hot coal.

He knew—had learned the hard way—that it was not cowardice. Isolfr was one of the bravest men he knew. But fighting with words was not Isolfr's way. And Vethulf, for once in his life wishing *not* to hurt another with his words, found them clumsy and twisting in his mouth.

⟡

After the meal, Skjaldwulf took Freyvithr outside into the
bailey, where they could watch construction of the stables.
Freyvithr leaned forward on the hewn log they shared, thick arms,
roped with images of cats elongated until they almost seemed like
serpents, propped on his knees. He let a horn of mead rest in one
hand. There was no need for fire on a sweet spring evening, and
Freyvithr seemed unconcerned by black Mar sprawled at his feet.
The breeze ruffled the wolf's fur so the lighter undercoat showed in
waves like the silver turning of leaves.

Despite himself—despite his loyalty to Isolfr—Skjaldwulf found
he liked the godsman.

Freyvithr said, "You haven't much use for scholars here in the
north, have you?"

Skjaldwulf snorted dismissively, at first hearing only implied
condescension. A moment's reflection on Freyvithr's tone told him
he might have reacted prematurely. "We have skalds," he said, flip-
ping a braid behind his shoulder. He scratched at his beard. "But
you mean more than that, don't you?"

Freyvithr nodded. "Written records. Men whose duty it is to
maintain and expand them. We have books—" He shook his head.
"We have books from the days of the High Konungur, Njall Waroak.
The actual words and thoughts of men who lived nine hundred years
ago. Not what skalds remembered, or the songs people asked for."

Skjaldwulf rolled his own drinking horn between his hands,
feeling the copper piecework of its badges and bangles press into
both palms. Songs and sagas were not supposed to change—one
was meant to repeat them as one received them. But even the most
trained memory failed, and even the most scrupulous skald could
tune a story to an audience's liking.

And what audiences liked changed over the years.

The wolfheall kept records, written records, but they were records of wolf lineages and troll behavior, not the deeds of men. Still, Skjaldwulf could imagine writing down what men did and thought, as well—

He nodded his apology. "And you wish to add my wolfsprechend's thoughts to this . . ."

"Archive," Freyvithr supplied. "Simply put, yes. So that nine hundred years on, others may read the plain words of Isolfr . . . Isolfr Viradechtisbrother as if in his own voice, rather than what others have written or remembered of him."

"That doesn't seem to leave much place for skalds," Skjaldwulf said. It had been his first apprenticeship, before Mar chose him. He still sometimes wondered what his life would have been had he never come to the wolfheall. He might have starved or died by some wayside, or of drink or some lord's or rival's passions. Or he might be wealthy and respected, with (he supposed dubiously) wife and sons and house in a warm southern town.

Such as the one Freyvithr came from.

"You could come and see," Freyvithr said blandly.

Skjaldwulf sent him a searching look, afraid for a moment that Freyvithr had used some witchcraft to read his thoughts.

The godsman obviously misread the stare. "Isolfr. Or if a wolfsprechend cannot travel alone—I am sorry, wolfheofodman, I do not know your customs—you and Isolfr, or Vethulf Kjaransbrother and Isolfr. As suited you. People do come, you know. To Hergilsberg. There is a tree there said to have been planted by the goddess herself. The archive grew up around it."

Skjaldwulf turned his head one way and then another. He could have swept half-built Franangford up with a gesture of his arm, but that might have been a touch too sarcastic.

Of course, in Skjaldwulf's place, Vethulf probably would have bitten the man's head off.

"We have a half-built wolfheall here, and a half-mended pack. I should send you my wolfsprechend and his konigenwolf, the very core of our success? Would you take the queen from a shattered hive, godsman? There will be no hive in that place come springtime."

If any of them went—and it was madness to think it, even as the thought enticed him—it would have to be Skjaldwulf. Who could read the runes.

He was old for such travel. But then, he was old for a wolfcarl, too.

"What need have you of stout walls if the trolls are truly gone?" Freyvithr seemed to take no offense. He sipped his mead, rolling the spiced-honey wine across his tongue until Skjaldwulf could almost taste it for him. "If the Lady has given you an answer to the very problem that forced your existence, what then?"

"Wolves are Othinn's answer to the trolls," Skjaldwulf said. "He will have an answer to the wolves, if there are truly trolls no longer." *Something will come up.*

"Will you become farmers, then? Wolves like ponies, tamely pulling plows? Will you become brigands, or turn to viking? What will you do when the winters grow colder, and you are driven south like the trolls and the svartalfar?"

Skjaldwulf shrugged. "I have heard that you in Hergilsberg have your own problems. Raiders from the southlands burned the town ten years since, did they not?"

"The town," Freyvithr admitted. "A portion of it. But not the archive."

"And have they vanished like the trolls?" Skjaldwulf knew very well that the seacoast was still harried by raiders. Not so far north as Othinnsaesc. But then, there was little so far north to raid for except pine trees and trellwolves, and neither of those things were particularly transportable.

"Perhaps the Wolfmaegth's future lies with the temple guardians."

Skjaldwulf rocked back on the log bench, his long legs straightening as if to kick the suggestion away. Even if Skjaldwulf could stomach selling himself into the service of someone like Gunnarr Sturluson—or even someone like Freyvithr—how could he bring Mar with him? You could not take the wolf from the pack, nor the wolfcarl from the wolf. And warriors might be hired to hunt men, but that was not the purpose of trellwolves. A wolfheall could not be a weapon of conquest.

How would a konigenwolf and her wolfthreat deal with the demands of a human lord? What human lord who was not a wolfcarl himself would understand the delicacies of working with a wolf pack? And what of the inevitable spoiled sons who wanted a trellwolf of their very own?

Better to let the pups run wild.

Skjaldwulf looked at the men working, at the heaps of felled timber and the mounds of quarried clay that filled the air with their smooth, distinctive scent. Would those half-built fortifications ever be needed? Was it possible—an all but incredible thought—that Skjaldwulf himself would live to see another ten summers? Wolfcarls, beloved of Othinn, did not die in bed.

*Perhaps we will have to learn how.*

"We would make poor mercenaries," Skjaldwulf said mildly, and left it at that.

❧

In the morning the wolfsprechend's daughter—long awaited and much delayed—arrived for fostering. Vethulf wondered if it was the wolfheall's current state of chaos—half-constructed, wolfcarls and stonemasons underfoot, sledges laden with bluestone rumbling along rutted tracks far into the lingering evenings—that served as a beacon to attract still more pandemonium.

Alfgyfa was not the only child in the wolfheall—wolfcarls bred sons and daughters, after all, and something must be done with them. But she was the only one who was Isolfr's daughter, and his wolf was nearly beside herself with the preparations, the clamor of her arrival, and the upheaval and excitement of her presence. Vethulf could feel *cub* all through the pack-sense the whole day long. Things calmed finally, and that night found all three wolfheofodmenn in the room the wolfjarls had claimed for their own use—and sometimes that of the wolfsprechend. Isolfr propped himself on a four-legged stool in a corner with his toddling daughter sleeping on his knee, awaiting a nurse hired from the town who would take charge of her.

Vethulf leaned over to Skjaldwulf and whispered in his ear, "I think Viradechtis would nurse the bantling herself, if she still had milk in."

"Raised on wolf's-milk!" Skjaldwulf whispered back. "What a start to a hero's saga. Pity it's a girl."

Isolfr lifted his head, pale braids draped across the sleeping child's blankets. His rocking must have been the right sort—it looked like what Vethulf's mother and older sisters had done to quiet the youngers—because Alfgyfa made no more protest than might a poppet.

The wolfsprechend gazed benevolently upon the two wolfjarls, an expression that made Vethulf want to bite him for his damned condescension. Instead, Vethulf sat on his hands. *Temper.*

The old wolfcarl beside Vethulf elbowed him, but when he glanced at Skjaldwulf, Skjaldwulf was smiling, and Vethulf had a sudden, vivid memory of the taste of his mouth.

Cursing his complexion, Vethulf looked down quickly.

"Yes?" Isolfr said. "You two are plotting. I can smell it from here."

"The godsman," Skjaldwulf said reluctantly. Isolfr recoiled and might have leaped to his feet except that it could have awakened the baby. That wouldn't have stopped Vethulf, but he read the wolfsprech-end's guilty glance at his child and understood it.

Skjaldwulf, however, pressed on, though Vethulf could sense the tension in him. "He said to me that they have records almost a thousand years old. Written records, books. What if we could get access to those?"

Isolfr shook his head. "I don't understand."

"What if they have books old enough that they talk about the last time the ice came south? What if they remember where it stopped?"

"The svartalfar might remember," Isolfr said. His eyes went to his axe, the axe the svartalfar had given him.

"They might," Skjaldwulf agreed while Vethulf drew his arms close around himself. "But not just anyone can go ask them. And have you thought about what will happen between men and the svartalfar when you are gone, Isolfr? They can push us out as easily as they pushed out the trolls. It is only your deed and their debt to you that stays them. What if there is something in the monks' archive that can help us plan ahead?"

Isolfr spread his unburdened hand. The babe made a thready awakening sound until he jiggled her quiet again. "I can't leave the wolfthreat now. Viradechtis has pups, and the dogs—too many dogs, from too many packs. Amma is too sweet-natured to keep them from killing each other, and Ingrun . . . And then there's *this*." He pointed with his chin to Alfgyfa.

"Talk to the godsman," Skjaldwulf said. "Buy us his goodwill. I will go south with him and see what his books of memories can tell us."

Isolfr looked down. One thing Vethulf could never imagine him doing was shirking anything he saw as his duty. But he frowned deeply before he said, "Vethulf, I want you there when I do the telling."

*Why me?* Vethulf thought. *Why not Skjaldwulf?* Although Isolfr did not play favorites with his wolfjarls the way Vethulf's sisters had with their suitors, it was not a secret that he was more comfortable with Skjaldwulf than with Vethulf. They had known each other—

been part of the same threat—for years, and Skjaldwulf, who (Frithulf said) had been known to go days at a time without saying a word, was far more restful company.

*Perhaps he hopes I will yell at the godsman and save him from this duty he does not want.* The thought was grossly unfair—to Isolfr if not necessarily to Vethulf—and he did his best to push it away. But it would not, quite, go.

⟨⟩

*C*ub, Amma said with great firmness.

They had been busy all the day before, clearing a deadfall and three of the most massive tree stumps Brokkolfr had ever seen—a horrible job, exhausting and filthy, and he'd wished for Amma's pelt to protect him from the tangled briars—and then hunting in the long evening, with Kari and Hrafn and two other bond-pairs who had helped sire the pups Amma was carrying.

Ulfmundr had walked beside Brokkolfr for a while, as Amma and Hlothor ranged ahead, talking about temperament and bone, what they could expect from the pups Amma was carrying, and why Ulfmundr thought Hlothor would sire better wolves on her than he would have on Ingrun. Brokkolfr was very grateful, not only for Ulfmundr's teaching, but for the fact that the senior wolfcarl—as old as Skjaldwulf, nearly fifteen years older than Brokkolfr himself—was bothering to talk to him at all. Brokkolfr asked him if he thought the whelping would be as difficult as Amma's first, but at that Ulfmundr had laughed and disclaimed. "That's wolfsprechend's knowledge. If Isolfr isn't worried, you need not be, either."

*I don't know if Isolfr is worried or not,* Brokkolfr had thought, but he hadn't said it, afraid that it would sound as if he thought the wolfsprechend wasn't attending to his duties. He knew Isolfr was watching Amma carefully; he just didn't know what Isolfr thought about what he observed.

They had come back to the wolfheall late, tired; Brokkolfr found food for himself and his wolf and fell gratefully into his bedding with Amma, as always, an immovable weight across his feet. He had slept deeply, dreamlessly, and now, in the bright morning sunshine, Amma was not to be gainsaid. *Cub,* she said again, and Brokkolfr trailed helplessly after her as she tracked an unerring graceful arc across the courtyard to where the wolfsprechend was sitting with his daughter.

The child was clearly Isolfr's; she had his pale hair and eyes. If she was lucky, Brokkolfr thought—considering his own sisters— under her puppy-fat roundness her father's bones were lurking. She sat beside Isolfr on a rough bench, bright eyes taking in every- thing.

"Wuf!" she said clearly, pointing at Amma, and slid off the bench.

"Good morning, Brokkolfr," Isolfr said with one of his rare, quirked smiles.

"Good morning, wolfsprechend," Brokkolfr said and added sheep- ishly, "Amma insisted."

"Of course she did," Isolfr said, smile widening into a grin as he watched Amma and Alfgyfa meet each other. Amma's tail was waving wildly, and Alfgyfa's delighted giggles turned more than one head among the wolfcarls crossing the courtyard to and from the sauna and kitchen.

"All babies are Amma's babies," Brokkolfr said, and Isolfr laughed.

Amma ignored them. She and Alfgyfa were playing a game that involved the wolf pushing the toddler down on her well-padded bottom with her nose, and then standing patiently while Alfgyfa used her ruff to haul herself back to her feet again.

"She's got enough mothering instinct for ten bitches," Isolfr said. "I know her first whelping wasn't easy?"

It was an invitation to talk about it, exactly the invitation Brokkolfr had been hoping for. But he found himself saying, "She's fine. I'm fine." And then, the truth breaking free like a chick from a shell: "I'm more worried about you."

The confession lay between them for a moment, Isolfr's face contorting around the troll-scars as if he sought to ignore it. But he couldn't quite bring himself to say, *There's nothing to worry about.* Finally he said, although he clearly knew it was a weak effort, "It's my job to worry about you, not the other way around."

"I know I'm not a wolfsprechend," Brokkolfr said doggedly, "but if I were, I would not be here. And I know a little—surely it is not wrong for Randulfr and me to be your seconds?" He hadn't meant to sound quite so plaintive, hadn't meant to reveal his own desire for a place in the Franangfordthreat that was more than simply brother to the third bitch, and he knew from the sudden sharpness in Isolfr's gaze that his self-betrayal had not gone unnoticed.

But before Isolfr could speak—on that head or on any other—Freyvithr the godsman came into the courtyard, closely followed by Vethulf.

"Good morning, wolfsprechend," Freyvithr said, smiling, and then his canny eyes seemed to size up the two of them. "Am I interrupting something?"

"No," Isolfr said, although he didn't sound sure, and Brokkolfr said hastily, "Nothing important, godsman." He had fallen foul of Vethulf once and had sworn he would never do so again.

"Then—do we have business this morning, wolfsprechend?" Freyvithr said.

"My daughter," Isolfr began, but Vethulf interrupted with a snort.

"I think Brokkolfr and Amma can be trusted to mind the child for an hour or two."

"Yes, all right." Isolfr stood, and then turned anxiously to Brokkolfr. "Do you mind? It shouldn't be too long."

"Are you joking, wolfsprechend?" Brokkolfr said, finding a smile somewhere to reassure both Isolfr and himself. "Surely you see that getting Amma *not* to mind the child would be far harder?"

Isolfr smiled back, and Vethulf tugged him away. "Come on, Isolfr. Let's get this done."

Brokkolfr watched them go, uneasy, but his attention was claimed by a sharp tug on one braid; the baby's hand might be tiny and plump, but her grip was relentless.

"Ammy-wuf!" said Alfgyfa, as if that settled everything.

"Amma-wolf, indeed," Brokkolfr agreed, lifting the tiny child onto his hip as he stood. "Come on. Let's go see about some butter and porridge."

# FIVE

Try as he might, Vethulf could do nothing against the awareness of Isolfr's presence that filled him every moment they
were in one another's company. It wasn't a sharp sensation, not
painful, but nagging. Distracting. So that he thought he should wish
Isolfr far away, except that never happened. Instead, he sought out
excuses to spend time in the wolfsprechend's company.

Like now, when he was unwisely grateful to be following Isolfr
and the godsman across the rutted yard, through humming clouds
of biting flies and into the cool of the wood beyond. They left the
wolves behind—Viradechtis instructing her pups on the finer points
of murdering mice among the woodpiles and Kjaran dozing in the
dappled shade of immature fruit trees planted outside the south-
facing fortifications.

If the godsman meant to decoy two of Franangford's three wolf-heofodmenn into ambush and assassination, he was making a good start of it. But once they were following a narrow track among the pines, the godsman dropped back unobtrusively and let Isolfr lead them. And Isolfr brought them toward Franangford proper, not deeper into the taiga, leading Vethulf to wonder if his mind was wearing similar paths of worry. Vethulf had a tendency to think of Isolfr as naïve, but of course he wasn't. Isolfr was only a little younger than Vethulf himself—Skjaldwulf had fifteen winters on Vethulf and a few more than that on Isolfr—and he was a jarl's son and an experienced wolfsprechend, with all that implied.

He was anything but naïve.

What he was, was idealistic. And that was a disease without a cure, save time. Still, watching Isolfr walk on ahead, pale gold braids plaited to stiffness bouncing against his shoulders, Vethulf could not help but wish the inevitable delayed.

The track was well-trodden by boots and pads, though Isolfr rapidly turned them off the sun-baked ruts of the road and into the shade of trees. Here the path rose and dipped over polished roots and the terraced earth trapped between them. Isolfr lengthened his stride so Vethulf broke into a comfortable lope, half-surprised and half-not that the godsman did, too, without apparent struggle to keep up. Well, of course; if he had walked from the southern peninsula, he could hardly avoid being fit. Though no one was as fit as a wolfcarl.

A quarter hour's easy trot brought them far enough from the path to ensure privacy of speech. It was cooler under the trees, the damp air collecting in stagnant pools. At last, they came to a tiny clearing, a space where a spruce—as great through as three trees fit for the roof-beam of a heall—had fallen and sun filtered through the spreading branches. Oxeye daisies grew here, thick white petals spreading flat around yellow cores, and ferns furled from every surface, even growing up the mossy trunks of the trees.

Isolfr leaned back against the trunk of the dead giant, folded his arms, and waited for Ragnarok, as near as Vethulf could tell. Vethulf had assumed that the godsman would ask Isolfr all sorts of leading questions, but Freyvithr seemed content to hop up on the dais made by the intersection of torn-free roots and earth and wait. Eventually, he spoke, but it wasn't to ask questions.

"She's made herself known to me as well, you know."

"She?" Isolfr asked, almost unwillingly.

"Freya," Freyvithr said. "It's how I came into her service, who was Othinn's man when I went viking and fought for a jarl."

"You were a man-at-arms?"

"I killed for my meat and ale," the godsman said. "Not so differently from you."

Vehulf picked at soft moss on the nursery log he'd leaned his butt against, and waited. It was hard.

Isolfr raised his hands in a placating gesture, pressing his back against the trunk. "I meant no insult, godsman. I was a jarl's son, once. I was just . . . surprised, I guess."

"That Freya would speak to a warrior?" Freyvithr's mouth twisted. He kicked one foot, dislodging a shower of moss fragments. "Half the war-dead are hers, when it comes down to it. She has an interest. And you cannot be more surprised than I was, I tell you truth."

"Will you tell us?" Vethulf asked softly.

"There's little point in bringing it up if I won't," Freyvithr said, smiling. "I thought at first—I was far from home, in a land where the trees were wrong and the deer were wrong and the water was wrong, and the women we captured would do nothing but weep and starve themselves to death, and I thought at first it was only that I missed my wife."

"You were married?" Isolfr said, and then blushed scarlet. Vethulf glanced away, pretending distraction as a dull brown bird darted between summer-green boughs.

"I *am* married," Freyvithr corrected. "My wife entered Freya's service with me, and prays in Hergilsberg now for my safe return." When Vethulf glanced back, Freyvithr was still grinning at Isolfr's mortification. "I renounced bloodlust, not the other kind. For indeed, Freya is not a goddess to be pleased by celibacy. But you distract me from my point. I was dreaming of a woman, at whose throat glittered a necklace more beautiful than anything I had ever seen, and who held apples in her hands. I never saw her face clearly, only the necklace and her hands and her breasts. She stood on a green hill beneath a great green tree, and the air was right and the tree was right, and I knew that I was home. And then the captive women began dying, and each night in my dream I would see the woman who had died that day kneeling at the feet of the woman with the necklace. And the dead woman would look at me and say, 'I cannot come to her, because of you.' And then another woman would appear—I could never tell where she came from, though after the third or fourth time I had the dream I watched for her—a woman who I could not see at all, all shadows and flint, and she would take the dead woman away. And the woman with the necklace would weep and drop one of the apples she was holding so that it rolled to me. But when I picked it up, it turned to ashes in my hand."

He took a deep breath, running one hand over the lower part of his face. "And then, one day, we burned a village on our jarl's command. We left no one alive, on our jarl's command. And that night, the woman with the necklace had no apples in her hands. The tree was dead above her, the grass was dead beneath her, and the burned bodies of the villagers were all around her, stacked like firewood. And she wept until I wanted to gouge her eyes from their sockets so that they could not weep, and keened until I wanted to rip her tongue from her mouth. But I could not reach her, no more than I had ever been able to, and finally I said, 'Lady, tell me what I can do for you.' And she said, 'These are not warriors you slaughter. There is no glory for you in these deeds. Go home and kill no more.' And I woke in a cold horrible sweat and I saw—I swear to you I saw—the cold woman, the woman of shadow and flint, standing over me. She was one side white as chalk, and one side black as the blood that settles in a rotting body, and I saw the starlight glitter among her teeth, and I saw the blood running black from her mouth. I knew her then, and I knew the woman in my dreams, and I knew I was being shown a choice."

"Shown," Isolfr said, not quite a question.

"Oh yes," said Freyvithr. "Not offered, for that is not the gods' way. But I was shown, and I chose. Just as you were shown, were you not?"

It was an invitation, and Vethulf watched Isolfr respond to it, chewing his lip and looking aside. Vethulf never would have thought to do what Freyvithr had, to give something of himself in order to encourage another to give something in return. He leaned forward to interject a comment, to deflect Freyvithr's attention from Isolfr, and remembered himself just in time. The Wolfmaegth needed the godsman's help, and it didn't rankle Vethulf to admit it. The Wolf-maegth had always existed on trade, not on charity. Their skills and ferocity, the wisdom of their wolves, the meat they hunted, in return for rye and barley, skyr and butter, cabbages and turnips and apples. All things the Wolfmaegth found too little time to farm.

But perhaps they could learn. And perhaps they could learn to trade other things, because Vethulf did not see the wolfcarls learning to exist meekly on charity now.

Isolfr hunkered down into a squat, leather trews stretching across the knees he laid his elbows on. He pushed his fingers together and let the latticework support his forehead, as if he could not bear either the weight of his head upon his shoulders or the eyes of Vethulf or Freyvithr upon him.

"I prayed for mercy," Isolfr said. "I prayed for something to save us from the trolls. It was a womanish prayer, and a woman answered it."

Vethulf saw his shoulders rise and fall on the breath. If Kjaran were there, he would have whined at the wolfsprechend's distress.

Vethulf felt the wolf notice his awareness, and soothed him. *We're all fine. I was just thinking of you.* Kjaran understood the emotion, not the words, but it was enough. All the way back in the heall, he laid his jaw on his forepaws again.

"I never saw her, unless she came to me as a konigenwolf with rainbow eyes. She sent me a dream of where to go. Some of my friends—wolves and men—would not let me leave them behind. And when I went where Freya sent me, the svartalf Tin—who was a friend, of sorts—had a plan to convince her people to help us. So we did it. I'm pretty sure that part is in the songs."

"You prayed for mercy," Freyvithr said softly. Vethulf couldn't hear condemnation in it, but he imagined Isolfr could provide his own, and even delivered kindly the words themselves were harsh. "And were you merciful in your own turn?"

Vethulf had winced at the first statement. With the second, he wasn't sure what Freyvithr was driving at. Vethulf started forward anyway, because Isolfr flinched as if flystung. But Vethulf's intervention proved unneeded.

Because he was Isolfr Ice-heart, he lifted his head up off his hands and stood, arms at his sides, rocking forward on his toes.

"We were dying," he said. "Call me a nithling if you will, but that prayer bought life for all the northlands. There would have been trolls in Hergilsberg next winter, fighting it out with the raiders, else."

"Oh, aye," Freyvithr said, catching Vethulf's eye like a conspirator. "Because what you did to earn that mercy was so a nithling's deed."

Vethulf burst out laughing, unable to stop himself. Isolfr's head went back, offended as a wet cat, and then, reluctantly, he must have seen the humor, for he smiled.

Freyvithr said, "Do you think me a nithling, wolfsprechend?"

Isolfr went a beautiful scarlet. *Daft creature,* Vethulf thought fondly. *Why* do *you persist in wrong-footing yourself like this?*

"'Tis not what he meant," Vethulf said, hoping that it would be acceptable for him to defend Isolfr on this point. "He judges himself only, no one else."

"And judges himself harshly," Freyvithr said, frowning. "No god asks this punishment from you, wolfsprechend."

Isolfr shook his head. "I know what my choices make me, godsman."

"A nithling?" Freyvithr said. "If that is what you think, you know nothing, either of choices or of yourself."

And Vethulf wondered—although he knew he would not ask—whether it was chance that brought Viradechtis' pups charging into the clearing at just that moment, swarming from Isolfr to Vethulf and back again and making conversation an impossibility. Their mother followed them, coming to rest her massive head on her brother's shoulder. She was watching the godsman, Vethulf saw, not with hostility but with a kind of cool assessment that reminded him of Kjaran in the days leading up to the mating that had made the Franangfordthreat. Each wolf they encountered had been scrutinized with that same dispassionate thoroughness. Kjaran had known all his potential competitors, all the wolves that might stand between him and what he wanted, long before Viradechtis went into heat.

And Viradechtis was far more protective of Isolfr than she was even of her pups. She turned her head for a moment, meeting Vethulf's eyes, and he got a clear, wordless impression: she had had, and would have, many puppies. She had only one Isolfr.

And she was going to keep him.

☙❧

fter dinner, as Brokkolfr was wondering whether he ought to go hunting—whether he *wanted* to go hunting—or whether he should use the last of the light to mend his spare shirt, Kari approached him. He did it carefully, after the manner of a wolf approaching a stranger, stopping where Brokkolfr could see him and waiting until Brokkolfr raised his head to come closer. Hrafn didn't bother; he bounced up to Amma and playbowed as if they were littermates. And Amma, not yet so gravid to disdain tag-and-wrestle, took him up on it. Kari and Brokkolfr both watched them a moment; when Brokkolfr looked back at Kari, the wildling was smiling.

Then he dropped his head, the tips of his ears going pink, and said, "I wondered if you wanted to go for a walk?"

"A walk?" Brokkolfr said. "To hunt, you mean?"

Kari shrugged. "If Hrafn and Amma want to. But no. Just a walk." He looked up, and he was still smiling, although clearly embarrassed. "There's something I think you'd like to see."

Brokkolfr remembered Amma's mating; Kari had been last of the five men who had covered Brokkolfr as their brothers covered Amma. By then, Brokkolfr had climaxed three times, and although he wanted, *needed,* a fourth, he wasn't sure he was physically capable of it. He and the blanket he knelt on were sodden with sweat, every part of his body ached, and the long muscles in his thighs were starting to quiver. Kari had slid into him easily and then stopped, hands on Brokkolfr's hips, body poised and tense. Brokkolfr had been on the verge of cursing at him to move when he said, "Here. Let's—," and wrapping both arms around Brokkolfr, much as Hrafn at that moment had his forelegs around Amma's barrel, he rolled them both down onto their sides.

"Oh," Brokkolfr said in surprise and relief, and then, "Oh!" as Kari's hand slid from his belly to his sex. And he'd gotten that fourth climax after all.

And since then, like the other men whose brothers had covered Amma, Kari had been . . . "kind" was the best word Brokkolfr knew, even though it was a calumny to suggest that anyone in Franangford had been *unkind*. For they had not. But they were all strangers to him, for he and Amma were the only pair who had come to Franangford from Othinnsaesc, and Brokkolfr had been keenly aware from the start of the little packs within the pack, like Isolfr and his shield-brothers; the remnant of the original Franangfordthreat; the men from Nithogsfjoll; the men from Arakensberg. There were closed circles everywhere, and Brokkolfr, his own shieldbrothers' deaths still vivid in his dreams, had not had the strength to try to find his way in.

But maybe a new circle was opening.

"All right," he said, and got up.

Kari took him north and then east of Franangford, following something that might once have been a path, although it was now little more than a thinner patch in the forest. They had to go single file, and there wasn't a lot of breath to spare for talking, but Kari offered bits and pieces over his shoulder. "This isn't a secret," he said. "The wolves know about it . . . but they don't like it. . . . You'll see why." Then, a little later: "I found out about it before the war." *Before Franangford Heall was destroyed and our konigenwolf killed,* he meant. "One of my threatbrothers showed me. Aldulfr. He was a little like Skjaldwulf—didn't like talking. He said sometimes he needed a place the pack wouldn't follow him. And he thought maybe I did, too." He glanced back and made a rueful face. "I do, sometimes. Not for the same reasons. But . . ."

"It's different for you," Brokkolfr said, not wanting to make him finish that sentence.

"Once a wildling, always a wildling," Kari said, and then yelped as he walked into a spiderweb. He ducked and spluttered and, when Brokkolfr came up beside him, grinned. "That'll teach me not to watch where I'm going. We're almost there."

"You think I need a place away from the pack?" Brokkolfr said, direct in the manner of wolves.

"I don't know," Kari said. He straightened. Brokkolfr was taller, but Kari was standing on a slight rise, so that they were eye to eye. "I think you'll *like* it, whether you need it or not. And sometimes . . . sometimes you look hunted, you know."

"I do?"

"I don't know if it's the living or the dead who hunt you," Kari said, "but sometimes I do think you need a place where *this* pack won't follow you."

"Oh," Brokkolfr said, feeling gut-punched.

"Anyway—" Kari clapped him on the shoulder and turned to continue. "I'll wager you've never seen anything like it before, and that's worth something."

As Brokkolfr followed him, Amma appeared out of nowhere, the way trellwolves did, and bumped his left hip gently. "I'm all right, sister," he said. Trellwolves did not grieve as men did, but they understood *absence-in-the-pack* and *loneliness* very well. Amma gave him a very brief memory of *sea salt and new grass*, which was how the wolves had named Brokkolfr's shieldbrother Ulfhethinn, but she followed it emphatically with *winter apples*, her way of saying, *I'm still here.*

"I know," Brokkolfr said. "I do."

She surprised him then with the scent of *wood smoke and pine sap*—Kari—and the slick, acrid scent-taste of spurting wyvern blood, which was . . . Hrafn emerged from the woods, ears pricked inquiringly, and Kari gave Brokkolfr a startled glance over his shoulder.

"Amma's trying to tell me something," Brokkolfr said, feeling his face heat.

"You should always listen to your wolf," Kari said mock sententiously, and Amma bumped Brokkolfr again, harder this time.

"Two against one isn't fair!" Brokkolfr protested, laughing.

"Never mind," Kari said. "We're here."

"Here" didn't seem to be much of anywhere: a massive boulder—no, not a boulder, Brokkolfr realized as he looked more closely, but an upthrust shelf of rock like a petrified wave.

"Around this side," Kari said. Brokkolfr followed him and found that at the tallest side of the rock, it encountered a tree, nearly as massive, and in the place where thick, gnarled roots and mossy rock met, there was a hole big enough for a man, leading down into the darkness.

"You don't mean . . ."

Hrafn whined uneasily.

"I told you the wolves hate it," Kari said, sitting on the root that framed the hole.

"We'll need torches," Brokkolfr said.

"Got 'em," Kari said and pulled a tar-treated stick halfway out of his jerkin. "But there's a bit first where we can't use them." He grinned at Brokkolfr's expression. "Trust me. I've been here a dozen times. And anyway, I'm going first."

"All right," Brokkolfr said.

Hrafn whined again as Kari slid into the hole; then the wolf lay down against the rock and put his head on his paws. Brokkolfr scruffled Amma's ears and said, perhaps foolishly, to Hrafn, "Take care of her." Then he carefully copied Kari's example, sitting on the root and sliding down into the earth.

The drop was farther than he'd expected, although it really was more of a slide than a straight drop. At the bottom, there was only just enough light for him to see Kari's shape, and the warmth of Kari's hand briefly clasping his upper arm was a welcome reassurance.

"This is the only hard part," Kari said. "We have to crawl on our bellies like worms—but it's not more than two body lengths, and after that there's plenty of room. And I'll be able to light the torch."

"This had better be worth it," Brokkolfr said, trying to joke and not sure he was doing a very good job.

"It is," Kari said. "Look, I'll go first and light the torch. Then you'll at least have something to crawl to."

There was a thread of tension in Kari's voice that Brokkolfr had not noticed before. Or perhaps it was his own tension looking for company. The uncertainty made him reluctant to speak, and in another moment it was too late. Brokkolfr half-saw, half-felt as Kari knelt down. He knelt down, too, learning with his hands the size of the opening Kari expected him to crawl through.

"I know it doesn't feel like it, but you'll fit," Kari said. "Aldulfr was bigger than either of us." And with that, he lay on his stomach and slid under the overhanging rock.

Brokkolfr waited, counting his breaths—and forcing himself to keep them slow and steady. He had not reached ten tens when Kari called, "I'm through!"

He *did* sound nervous, but this was a foolish position for a conversation.

As Brokkolfr waited, listening to Kari rummage with flint and steel—each sound amplified, echoing, the sharp crack like the irregular beat of a giant's heart—his eyes adjusted to the dimness. He still could see only shadows, but when somewhere ahead a spark flared in scraped birch bark and Kari raised it to breathe across, even the filtered brilliance was dazzling. The flare died, and Brokkolfr squinched his eyes shut, wincing.

Ten breaths more and the rock of the passage was scraped with the dimmest yellow glow. It grew stronger as he watched, and then steadied, and if he wasn't going to humiliate himself, it was time to move.

He lowered himself carefully, not sure whether he was glad of the light or not, for it showed him just how narrow the crack was. But Kari had done it; Brokkolfr touched the rock, craned back for a glimpse of tree roots and faraway sky—for luck—and slid forward, arms outstretched.

It was moist in the belly of the earth. Cool at first, but though Brokkolfr expected increasing chill as they left the sun's filtered light behind, the air instead seemed to warm. It moved, too, a breeze strong enough to shift the hair at his nape where it curled too short for his braids.

Even though the rock above only brushed his back at intervals, he felt its presence like a Jotun's hand, a fatherly pressure to keep an infant flat in the cradle. The rock under his hands and belly was glossy, polished by the passage of many creeping men before him. He found that reassuring, for as they had crawled in, surely they had also crawled out again. He wriggled forward doggedly, focusing his attention on the light ahead. Although it felt like a slow eternity, he knew it was not very long at all before he was able to heave up onto his knees, and then to his feet, and Kari said, "Well done."

Brokkolfr looked at him; the torchlight showed sweat on his temples and upper lip. "Are you all right?"

"This was easier," Kari admitted. "Before."

"Before what?"

"Before the war. Before the troll warrens. When you've seen men die in them, men and wolves, because the trolls know how to pin them into spaces where they can't swing an axe—" He stopped speaking abruptly, and Brokkolfr was standing close enough that he saw Kari's throat work. Brokkolfr remembered the troll-sapped and undermined floors of Othinnsaesc caving under his feet, and glanced away. "I wasn't going to let the trolls have this, too. And I wanted to . . . share it." He gave Brokkolfr a shy glance; he'd brought himself back from the memories of the war. Then, briskly, before either one of them could be embarrassed: "So, come on. Let me show you."

He stood, or half-stood, his back curving under the domed roof of the cavern. He lit a second torch from the first—he had already tucked away flint, steel, and kindling—and handed it to Brokkolfr. The light revealed oily streaks across the ceiling, the layered soot of many torches. Icicles of guano were evidence of bat habitation, though no bats were currently roosting.

Kari, still half-stooped like a svartalf, struck boldly out down a floor less smoothed by slithering bodies but still marked by the passage of many boots. The walls grew wet as they descended, the air ever warmer and less sweet, until Brokkolfr could detect a distinct, unmistakable reek as of spoiled eggs.

Here the cave melted into a fantasia of flowstone. The walls might have been beeswax, candles dripped for centuries down giant sconces, except they were as dry and chalky as weathered bone, and when Brokkolfr brushed a hand across the surface it was rough rock. Soon, though, it glistened with wet, and then he could see the colors that streaked it like some frozen aurora.

"How does this happen?" he asked Kari, not really expecting an answer—but then again, the wildling knew surprising things.

"There are stories," Kari said. He moved confidently but cautiously, placing each foot as if on ice, testing it before shifting his weight over.

Brokkolfr, not wishing to fall and slide who knew how far down to whatever waited at the bottom of the passage, imitated him. "I take it you don't believe them?"

"There's one that Thor and a Jotun named Frost-cock fought here, and melted the stone. There's another about a svartalf forging the aurora into garments for Sigyn, and staining the stones that were melted by the heat of her forge."

He paused for a moment, and Brokkolfr paused with him, admiring both the stones and the stories. Ahead, a fringe of stone icicles like ragged wyvern teeth decorated the arched ceiling, glittering rose-white and translucent as petals in the torchlight.

"But it doesn't look all that different to me from the stones you get around hot springs. Or all that different from icicles. I think the stone is dissolved in the water, like sugar—you know water can do that, you've seen how rivers make their beds by melting the stone away—and when the water evaporates the stone is left behind."

Brokkolfr had seen candy-making, the beetroot juice evaporated in the sun, cracked into sticky crystals, and the crystals, pressed into brown loaves. He'd seen wax soften, run, and harden again.

He could imagine stone doing the same.

He nodded, then pointed at the hanging icicles.

"The cave has teeth."

"That's not all it has," Kari said, moving forward again. "Duck when you go under. They're brittle."

Brokkolfr had no desire in this life to destroy any more beautiful things. He crouched down, careful of the torch, and sidled through the cluster of stone fangs without touching them. The texture of the floor underneath suggested that Kari was right: each fang was matched by a complementary dimpled protrusion, and in one place upper and lower fangs had merged to form an orange-streaked column.

A scatter of water droplets, perhaps disturbed by the hot draft from the torches, fell upon them as they scuttled under. On the other side, though, the ceiling arched away, and the echoes of their footsteps—and the receding border of the torchlight—told Brokkolfr that they were entering a much wider space.

The sulfur smell was stronger now, the heat almost oppressive. "Here," Kari said, pausing, and thrust his torch up high.

As Brokkolfr imitated the gesture, a draft caught the flames and let them flare. Light spilled across a cavernous space, a vastness wrought of stone jewels and tapestries, grander than any thane's hall. Grand as any dream of Othinn's Valholl, Brokkolfr thought, or Freya's Sessrumnir, where she received her tithe of the worthy dead.

Drapes of white and colored stone swathed the walls, ruched

and gathered like the fabric of a queen's gown. Pillows and clouds and billows of white and gold and orange stone heaped like batts of wool everywhere Brokkolfr's eye traveled, and from the ceiling overhead depended a forest of white stone reeds slender as a young woman's white hands.

The whole was reflected in a pool of still water so broad Brokkolfr could not see the far edge of it, a mirror smoother than any that might have been wrought of rare and precious glass and silvered across the back, to show that white-skinned woman's face. The water, Brokkolfr came to understand with a flash of comprehension heady as wine, was warm.

"A hot cave," he said. "It's a hot cave."

Kari turned to him and grinned. "Very nice to come thaw your toes in the midwinter."

"It's beautiful," Brokkolfr said, doing it no justice at all.

Kari nodded. "You have heard of such places?"

"A svartalf—" Brokkolfr shrugged. "In the troll war. I spoke with one of their smiths one night, on sentry duty. He said it was the hot caves that had allowed them to live in the Iskryne, and kept a valley warm enough to grow crops and see them through the winters. . . ."

Brokkolfr felt his voice trail off. It seemed as if he was sharing too much, bragging on a tenuous relationship—and one he was tempted to hoard, as if in exposing it to the light he could rob it of potency. Halite hadn't been friendly at first, but all sorts of confidences tended to creep out in the darkest hours of the long winter night. They'd wound up talking more than Brokkolfr had expected—or intended— and a good deal of family history had been shared on both sides.

Halite, he'd learned, was young for a smith, and uncertain. As uncertain, in his own way, as Brokkolfr. It was the first time he'd seen one of the svartalfar as a person instead of a story.

But Kari—he stopped himself just in time from shaking his head in awe, thus inviting questions—Kari had traveled with Isolfr to the Iskryne itself, and there killed a trellqueen and returned with the mastersmith Tin, a svaftalf hero as great to her people as Isolfr was to his. Whatever Brokkolfr could say about svartalfar would seem like pretension to Kari.

"It's beautiful," Brokkolfr said. "Thank you for showing me this."

Kari smiled again in clear pleasure, a pleasant flicker that made Brokkolfr wonder where was all the weariness of his wildling life, his village destroyed, his threat scattered.

Hidden? Vanquished. Or simply put aside so that this moment could be, as he had said, shared? They were not close enough that Brokkolfr could ask. But someday they might be.

"You're welcome," Kari said.

⚘

Vethulf looked up from his inspection of a trade-offering from Franangfordtown to see Randulfr standing before him, wolfless and hand-twisting in his nervousness. Vethulf was immediately nervous himself. Randulfr was several years older than he, and moreover, Randulfr was a Nithogsfjoll man, on friendly terms with both Skjaldwulf and Isolfr. If he was seeking out Vethulf, it was for a reason, and his nervousness said it was not a good one.

"Randulfr," Vethulf said as neutrally as he could. One of the things he had learned from Skjaldwulf was not to borrow trouble—not to make a bad situation worse by getting upset before he knew everything.

"Vethulf," Randulfr said with an awkward bob of the head. "You remember my brother Fargrimr, don't you?"

Fargrimr the sworn-son, born Randulfr's *sister*. No, Vethulf wasn't going to forget him in a hurry. "Aye," he said, still wary.

"Today I went to Franangford for . . . well, never mind that part. But I met a man—a thane of Siglufjordhur, I knew him before I was chosen—who was trying to find the way here to give me a message."

*From* Fargrimr or *about* Fargrimr was the next question. Vethulf raised his eyebrows and made a gesture not unlike a man turning a well-capstan.

"Fargrimr sent him," Randulfr said. "To ask for help."

"Help?" Vethulf said. "What sort of help does a jarl's son ask from a wolfcarl?"

"It's the southlanders."

"Fargrimr has gone viking?"

"No!" Randulfr said, half-laughing. "It's not to his taste, and our father would skin him alive besides. No, it's the southlanders. *They've,* um, gone viking."

Vethulf could feel his patience slipping, like a knot in old rope. It showed, too, either on his face or in the pack-sense, for Randulfr said, "Siglufjordhur is all but beseiged. Fargrimr sends to ask me to come home."

"To die in the halls of your ancestors?"

"To help," Randulfr said. "Siglufjordhur suffered greatly at Othinnsaesc, as I'm sure you remember." Vethulf raised a hand in acknowledgment and apology. He'd earned that jab—and he did indeed remember. Almost half the men Siglufjordhur brought to Othinnsaesc did not go home again; cool blond Fargrimr had led them into the thickest and most bloody areas of fighting again and again, and not a man of them had faltered, even as their shield-brothers died at their sides.

Randulfr nodded and continued more mildly, "He asks me to bring Ingrun—apparently the southlanders have stories about the great demon wolves of the north, and Fargrimr thinks that if they see that Siglufjordhur has one, they will become less willing to attack. And he adds that any of my friends who wish to come will be welcome. There are—women widowed, he says."

*Well, of course they will be,* Vethulf thought, but this time he managed to keep a rein on his tongue and even swallowed a couple other sharp comments. Instead, he said, "You don't need permission to leave."

"No," Randulfr said. "But I thought, when Fargrimr asked for just Ingrun and me, that I could do better than that. And if I wish to form a threat to travel south, I would rather do so with the good-will of my wolfjarls."

"Huh," said Vethulf. "Skjaldwulf has this crazy plan about traveling south with the godsman, you know." He put the stack of hides aside and got up, heaving a grumbling Kjaran off his feet. "Come on. Let's go talk to Skjaldwulf."

# SIX

The Franangfordthreat traveled light and they traveled quick. Skjaldwulf had to hide his amusement at the apparent wonder with which the wolfless men—Freyvithr and Adalbrikt, the messenger from Randulfr's brother—greeted the speed at which preparations were completed once the decision was made to move.

Two days after Randulfr's mumbled and awkward conversation with Vethulf (for so Skjaldwulf's co-wolfjarl had recounted it) the gray of morning twilight, moist and loud of birds, rich with smells, found a small collection of wolves and men gathered among the tents and rubble of Franangford's ongoing construction. In one group, burdened chiefly with weapons of the hunt and of self-protection (and a few bundles of food and furs, in case the spring turned bitter), stood Adalbrikt and Freyvithr Godsman. Around them gathered black

Mar and his brother Skjaldwulf; the gray-tawny bitch Ingrun and her brother Randulfr; Viradechtis' fleet, diminutive littermate Kothran and his brother, fire-scarred Frithulf; Afi and Geirulfr, a wolf and his brother who had followed Kjaran from Arakensberg; and Dyrver and Ulfhoss, a silver-brindle yearling from Thorsbaer and his young, wiry brother.

In the other group, representing the less than three dozen remaining wolves-and-men of Franangford's depleted threat, stood slope-shouldered Kjaran and Vethulf, his red braids whipping in a sharp wind; Viradechtis surrounded by her half-grown cubs, shedding her winter coat in streamers and rags; Isolfr ice-pale and ice-calm behind the troll-clawed scars that rendered his face so impassive; young Sokkolfr and old Hroi, the steady housecarls; massive Glaedir, who had been Mar's rival for Viradechtis, and his brother, Randulfr's lover, Eyjolfr; Dagmaer, the heallbred woman who was the yearling wolfcarl's lover and one of Franangford's better herbwives and spinners; and a few others, obviously attached to one wolfcarl or another, of whom Skjaldwulf still knew little other than their faces and their names.

Seven men, five wolves, and three ponies would head south to Siglufjordhur and thence to Hergilsberg and Freyvithr's monastery, a journey that might take two summers to complete, there and back again. So few, and yet really more than could be spared.

Unless they could all be spared. If the world did not need them anymore—if the great deeds of the previous winter would be the last great deeds sung of the wolfcarls and their brothers—then it didn't matter how many went and how many stayed.

But Skjaldwulf would not accept that just yet.

Skjaldwulf stepped forward, clasped Isolfr's upraised fist, and pressed their forearms together. Isolfr thumped Skjaldwulf's back with his free hand. Skjaldwulf could have leaned into it but instead moved aside for his own safety as Mar, Viradechtis, Kjaran, and their pups circled one another, sniffing and nipping. Wolves greeted one another, but they did not leave-take; the little pack within the pack was merely playing. Vethulf came forward next, and when Skjaldwulf would have clasped fists there as well, Vethulf surprised him with a hug and a sharp, fisted tug in his hair. A pale gaze burned into Skjaldwulf's eyes as he stepped back. He nodded. There was nothing here that needed words.

"Bring them back in one piece," Sokkolfr said to Frithulf as they, too, broke an embrace. Hroi whined, and Skjaldwulf could sense his frustration, but Hroi knew as well as any of the men that he was too old to walk a thousand miles in any but the direst necessity. And he was needed here, where there were cubs to educate, just as Sokkolfr was needed where there was a hall to build.

Skjaldwulf sighed. The stiffness in his own limbs told him that he, too, was too old for thousand-mile walks.

Eyjolfr's hug with Randulfr seemed stiff, awkward, but Skjaldwulf was too old and too much a scholar of men to be fooled into thinking it insincere. He didn't pretend to understand that relationship. But whatever their bargain was, it seemed to have survived Eyjolfr's now-abandoned pursuit of Isolfr intact. And Skjaldwulf, stealing a sideways glance at Vethulf, knew by the itch in his own breast that it was not his place to judge.

Skjaldwulf caught Sokkolfr's eye, half-smiled so the tall young man would know it for a vote of confidence, and said, "I'm counting on you to have a finished keep waiting for us on our return."

Sokkolfr snorted. "With sunken tubs to soak your feet in hot water, and thrall-women to beat their willow withies across your back?"

"And honey-cakes and sugared apples," Vethulf said.

Wolves don't linger, and it was Skjaldwulf's opinion that that was a matter in which men benefited from their example. "It's in the hands of the wolf-god now," he said, and turned away.

❧

For a long time, it didn't really feel like leaving. They walked, and some of the wolfthreat walked out with them. Not Viradechtis, but two of the cubs, and Hrafn, the black wildling wolf chasing pale Kothran until Frithulf yelled after them to save some energy for the march. Franangford was visible behind them for a while, and after that they were still on familiar roads.

And would be through Bravoll, and for some of them—including Skjaldwulf—as far south even as Arakensberg. There they would pick up the Hergilsberg road, which would take them within a hundred miles of Siglufjordhur and Randulfr's errand.

And then on to Hergilsberg and its archives and the answers he hoped they might contain. Skjaldwulf hadn't spoken of it, not even to Vethulf and Isolfr. Something superstitious stopped his tongue—the idea that to speak of an ill fate was to summon it, perhaps, or that to speak of a solution to a sticky problem might frighten it away, push it aside like the wind of a hand could bat aside the very mayfly one had meant to catch. But he had had the inkling of an idea. The beginnings of a solution to the dilemma the wolfcarls faced, most of them still unknowing.

Now, suddenly, when it was too late, he doubted the wisdom of keeping his own counsel. He was not a young man. And this would not be an easy journey.

❧

When they made camp on the first night, the Franangford wolves stayed with them, sleeping in a great pile against the seasonable cold of a clear, starry night. When the men rose in the frosted morning and pissed out the embers of the fire, Hrafn and the cubs had already vanished, their paw prints visible in the silvered leaves beside the road—although "road" was a grand term for something that was little more than a track, wide enough for a wolf and a man abreast, or one man riding.

Skjaldwulf gnawed a cold breakfast of hardtack, butter, and jerky, washing it down with water that tasted of the leathern bottle it had traveled in. There was a spring a few miles on at which to refill it, and so for now he drank freely. Hopefully, as they were headed south into gentler and more settled lands, water wouldn't be a concern. But tonight, or the next day at the latest, they would have to hunt if they wanted to keep eating.

On Skjaldwulf's left, the wolfless man of Siglufjordhur rolled up his furs, breath steaming faintly. It wasn't true cold, but he chafed his bare tattooed arms anyway, the skin prickled.

When he straightened, Skjaldwulf tossed him the pouch of hardtack. "Eat."

"I overslept," said Adalbrikt, as humbly as if he thought Skjaldwulf his jarl. A southerner, and raised not around wolfcarls but only among the stories of them. Skjaldwulf rather imagined the awe would wear off in a week or two—especially with Frithulf along. "Aren't we in a hurry?"

Skjaldwulf shrugged. "We are. But not so much of a hurry that we can leave before everybody else's bedroll is packed up. Use all the time you have, young man. And use it for something other than pacing."

Adalbrikt plunked down on the ground beside the log Skjaldwulf sat on, rather than the log itself. More of that respect. "Yes, wolfheofodman."

Skjaldwulf hid a smile.

Across the burned and overburned charcoal circle of the fire— apparently they were not the first to camp here—Frithulf, too, was chewing hardtack as if he found it onerous and using his own found moments to assure himself of the soundness of his wolf. Kothran, for his part, snored quite audibly. Mar, Skjaldwulf reached out into the pack-sense, seeking his wolf—

Mar had gone on ahead and was waiting by the fork in the road, where their route led to Bravoll and an even less-traveled path led seaward, where a dozen nameless fishing villages crouched. Mar, too, was resting, lounging in the shade and concealment of a grove of red pines, aware of his pack behind him and waiting for them to make up some of the distance before moving forward.

Farther than Mar, Skjaldwulf could feel Kjaran and Viradechtis, their awareness like a breath stirring the fine hairs of his skin. Behind them, both nearer and farther at once, the rest of the pack waited—Kothran and Ingrun and Afi and Dyrver, here by the fire; Hrafn and the cubs jogging tirelessly back north, making faster time now that they were unburdened by horses, packs, and wolfless men; Hroi ranging wide on a patrol-cum-hunting-expedition with two of the young wolves that remained of the old Franangfordthreat.

Isolfr had taught Skjaldwulf how to do this. And it was Viradechtis, Skjaldwulf thought, who truly made it possible. Her intelligence and command of her pack—her unmistakable presence—were such that even its human brothers, with their dim sight and hearing and even dimmer second senses, could perceive what every trellwolf knew of its brothers and sisters.

Skjaldwulf crunched the last of his brittle rye hardtack and chewed until it was soft enough to swallow. He stood and chafed the crumbs from his palms against his thighs. "How far do you suppose the pack-sense stretches?"

"As far as wolves have gone," Frithulf said, looking up from checking Kothran's furry paws. Burrs and stones sometimes stuck in the crevices, and the small scrapes they caused could become infected and wear a crippling sore. "To the Iskryne and back, at least. I've been that far. Beyond that, I suppose we'll have to find out."

# SEVEN

Vethulf was irritated by how much he missed Skjaldwulf.

He had fully expected the Franangfordthreat to feel off-balance, men and wolves both. They were missing a wolfjarl, even if one still remained, and although he had no idea of how to put it into words, he understood what Viradechtis has done in choosing both Mar and Kjaran. So it was not surprising that there was a Mar-and-Skjaldwulf-shaped hole in the pack. Vethulf had also expected that he would suffer from Skjaldwulf's absence, in the sense that all Skjaldwulf's work and responsibilities now rested on top of his own.

As the moon waxed and waned, Vethulf became aware: he did not do that work as well as Skjaldwulf did. Vethulf was at his worst with the tithe boys, but there were any number of things he did nearly as badly, and he found himself wondering how ordinary wolfjarls, wolfjarls who had to do all of this themselves *as a matter of course,* could even function.

He had even expected—or at least wasn't surprised by—the effect on Viradechtis and Kjaran, both of whom became even more insistent that they and Vethulf and Isolfr had to sleep together (along with varying numbers of Viradechtis' pups); on one occasion, Vethulf saw Viradechtis actually *herding* Isolfr into the room. Isolfr looked up and caught his eye; after an impossible to read moment, he gave Vethulf a sheepish grin and said, "I've never pretended she wasn't the one in charge." Vethulf grinned back and was saved from having to find something safe to say by Viradechtis coming around to bump him in the back of the legs, too.

So that was all expected and reasonable. But why was he missing Skjaldwulf so much? Why did he keep turning his head and expecting to find the man there, as dark and silent as a shadow? Why did he lie awake at nights feeling as if he had to be in the wrong bed?

There was an answer, but it was ridiculous.

Vethulf threw himself into his work to avoid it, grimly determined to be so exhausted at the end of each day that he wouldn't *notice* what bed he was in, much less care.

Fortunately for him, there was no shortage of work.

⚘

Tithe boys were Sokkolfr's business, and the rest of the threat were glad of it. But as the spring progressed, it became evident to Brokkolfr that this time the situation was peculiar. First of all, Sokkolfr had only four tithe boys for Viradechtis' five pups; tithes would pick up again, the older wolfcarls said, but boys came with the harvest, not in planting season, and too many were dead of trolls.

Although it could have been, it wasn't a problem, and that was another reason the situation was peculiar. There were only four boys, but there were three times that many wolfless wolfcarls. So many wolves had died in the war, even more wolves than men, and this was Franangford's share of what at Othinnsaescheall Brokkolfr had heard called wolf-widows. The Nithogsfjoll men didn't like the term, but one of the wolf-widowed men had said when Sokkolfr objected, "Isn't it true?" And Sokkolfr had had no answer.

The final reason Franangford's situation was unusual this spring was that two of the wolf pups who would be choosing their brothers before the summer solstice were bitches, and one a konigenwolf. Trellwolves threw bitches less often than dog pups, and everyone at Franangford agreed that two bitches in a litter was as great a rarity as a human mother throwing twins. One of the boys or the wolf-widows was about to become a wolfsprechend, and another was about to become a man like Brokkolfr, a bitch's brother.

Brokkolfr was glad enough not to claim the title of wolfsprechend. He couldn't do what Isolfr did, and he didn't think he would have been able to even if Amma were a konigenwolf. But he was, maybe, a wolfsprechend's second, if what the wolfsprechend did was like a holmgang, which it wasn't except on the occasions when it was.

At Othinnsaesc, what that meant had been clear. The wolfsprechend had been Skjaldwulf's age or thereabouts, an old man, for a wolfcarl. He had known his pack and his duties, and Brokkolfr's task was mostly not to get in the way. But Isolfr was only a few seasons older than Brokkolfr, and while his knowledge of his pack was bone-deep, he was uncertain about his duties and uncomfortable about taking some of them up. And even more uncomfortable with the almost worshipful way both boys and men tended to look at him.

And that was one of the reasons Brokkolfr liked him.

When Randulfr had been there, he had taken over that part of the wolfsprechend's duties easily and without fuss, but now that Randulfr was gone, Brokkolfr was the only one left to talk to those Signy and Geirve seemed to favor.

His first instinct when Sokkolfr approached him had been to refuse. If Isolfr felt he was not fit to mentor, then Brokkolfr was surely unimaginably less fit. But Sokkolfr had dropped his gaze and shifted his weight uncomfortably and said, "I'm not sure Isolfr would be the right person in any event."

Almost inaudibly, Hroi whined.

"What do you mean?" Brokkolfr said.

Sokkolfr brought his chin up then, unhappy but resolute. "Viradechtis has had only one open mating, and it was . . . bad."

"Was he hurt?" It did happen, although everybody did their best to prevent it. Men had died; tithe boys and yearling wolfcarls made sick, uneasy jokes about it, and Brokkolfr's wolfsprechend at Othinnsaesc had said, "The ones who die are the ones who fight. So *don't fight.*" It had been good advice, and Brokkolfr had taken it.

"No worse than Randulfr has been a half-dozen times," Sokkolfr said. "No worse than you were, this last time."

"Then I don't understand."

"I don't, either, really," Sokkolfr said. "He doesn't talk about it. But it was worse than war for him. Worse than . . . I don't know what. But I don't think he can teach other men how to accept it when he has so much trouble accepting it himself."

"All right," Brokkolfr said, and so he'd taken care to be around when the tithe boys and wolf-widows were introduced to the pups, taken care to watch, as the pups grew older and bolder, which of their potential brothers Signy and Geirve seemed to favor. Signy was easy; after a few days of licking everyone's hands indiscriminately, she began to focus her candlelight-yellow eyes more and more steadily on a tall fair boy named Eymundr. The wolf-widows backed off and made the other tithe boys back off, too.

Geirve was more difficult. She had Kjaran's odd eyes, one as deep yellow as Signy's, the other the pale blue of moonlight on snow, and she had something of Kjaran's temperament as well; even in her puppy exuberance, she was more watchful than her littermates, and Brokkolfr and Sokkolfr both thought she was early in developing the sardonic sense of humor common among wolves.

"Konigenwolf, no," Sokkolfr said, "but she will be a terror nonetheless."

And Geirve wagged her whole hind end with enthusiasm and tried to lick Sokkolfr's ears off the sides of his head.

She watched all the men and boys who came to be introduced to her and her brothers and sister; she was not unfriendly, but Brokkolfr could almost feel her holding herself back, waiting for something that only she would recognize when it came.

And when it came, it was nothing that anyone but Geirve expected.

One of the wolf-widows was a man from the old Franangford threat named Motholfr; like Isolfr's shieldbrother Frithulf the Half-Burned, Motholfr had been badly injured in fighting the trellish smiths in the Iskryne, the same battle in which his wolf Raskvithr had been killed. But Frithulf's injuries had been to his face and neck; Motholfr had lost two fingers and most of the use of his right hand. Even now, as healed as it would ever be, it was a crippled claw, the skin shiny and gnarled and with only the thumb still moving freely. He had suffered other injuries, but the hand was the worst; the hand was what would keep Motholfr dependent on the wolfheallan for the rest of his life.

He knew it and hated it. Brokkolfr thought that Motholfr was presenting himself to Viradechtis' cubs, which he did more than a fortnight after the others, not so much out of desire—he still mourned Raskvithr, to whom he had been bonded for almost ten years—but out of a bitter determination that he should not be useless.

Neither Brokkolfr nor Sokkolfr thought Motholfr had any chance of attracting one of the pups; he was late, and his presence in the pack-sense was too dark, matching perfectly the wolves' name for him, smoke-blood-burning-fur. He had had a different scent-name before the Iskryne, but it was lost now, along with Raskvithr and Motholfr's right hand.

It was a surprise, therefore, to them as much as to Motholfr when Geirve began to follow him purposefully about. She was not pushy about it—not like Signy, who took over Eymundr's life as shamelessly (Sokkolfr said) as Viradechtis had Isolfr's—simply, wherever Motholfr went, Geirve trotted after him. She did not come close unless invited but watched Motholfr with patient interest; when she *was* invited, she reverted to the puppy she was, wagging her tail wildly and crawling into his lap to lick his face and ears. If he ordered her away—and he was good enough with the pack-sense to tell her to go to her mother—she would go, but she went with ears and tail drooping. And it was never very long before she was back.

Finally, wryly, Motholfr said to Brokkolfr, "I give in. I guess you'd better tell me about being a bitch's brother."

"Right," said Brokkolfr, feeling keenly ridiculous. Motholfr was nearly thirty, almost twelve years his senior. But he had never been bonded to a bitch before, and Brokkolfr had. And this was exactly the conversation Sokkolfr had recruited Brokkolfr in order to have.

He had already had a version of it with Eymundr, and that had been uncomfortable in its own way, since Eymundr was not heallbred and had had to be told what he would be facing in another two years. He'd taken it well; in fact, he'd even been relieved. His older brothers and cousins had told him all the worst stories they knew about the unnatural practices and bestial habits of the wolfheallan. An open mating, scary though it could be, was not nearly as bad as the stories wolfless men told.

Motholfr did not need to be told that part; he'd been part of several open matings in the old Franangford heall. But there was another set of things he had no idea of at all.

"It won't be the same bond," Brokkolfr said. "Bitches are more forceful. They boss the dog wolves around, and they'll boss you around just the same. Geirve's not a konigenwolf, so it won't be *as* bad, but even Amma is—"

Amma grumbled at Brokkolfr, shoving her head against his stomach, and Motholfr was surprised into laughing.

"Well, like that," Brokkolfr said.

"I had noticed already," Motholfr said, glancing aside to where Geirve waited. "She's *there*, in a way Raskvithr wasn't." He said his dead wolf's name steadily, calmly, and looking into his eyes Brokkolfr saw that while the grief was still there, the devouring bitterness was eased.

"Yes," he said. "That will only get stronger."

"Come here, wolfling," Motholfr said, and Geirve threw herself at him instantly. He said around her, "I'm more worried about her mating. I've been on the other side, and, well, it looks a little different now that I'm imagining myself underneath."

"Yes," Brokkolfr said. "There are things you can do to make it easier."

"The salve," Motholfr said.

"Yes. And, um, if you stretch yourself with your fingers first." The blood was rushing into his face, but he continued doggedly, "And some men practice beforehand. With, um. Someone they trust."

"Aye," Motholfr said noncommittally. Brokkolfr wondered if there was anyone left whom Motholfr trusted or if they were all in Franangford's burying ground or lost to the Iskryne's ice.

Brokkolfr tried to think of something else he could say, but most of it Motholfr would know already. He'd probably been a part of more open matings than Brokkolfr had.

"Ah well," said Motholfr, gently removing one of his sandy-red braids from Geirve's mouth. "We've time yet. Come along, wolfling."

He stood up, nodded to Brokkolfr, and strode away. *Oh, well done,* Brokkolfr thought. And since he was already dissatisfied with himself, he got up and went to find Isolfr.

He found Viradechtis first—it was always easy to find Viradechtis in the pack-sense—playing a hunting game with Ottarr, Letta, and Lofi around a woodpile. Three tithe boys and a handful of wolf-widows were nearby, keeping their hands busy with a variety of work; Isolfr was sitting against a half-finished wall in the sun, whittling pegs for the stockade wall. He wasn't watching the wolves' game, but Brokkolfr knew that, had Isolfr been a wolf himself, it would have been easy to watch his ears cock and twitch.

He squinted up at Brokkolfr. "Have a seat if you've a mind to."

"Thank you." Brokkolfr sat down facing Isolfr; Amma immediately shoved her head in his lap, closely followed by her front paws and as much of the rest of her as she could manage. "Sister," he said, "you are not a pup. You won't fit."

Amma huffed and settled her weight.

"You won't be going anywhere in a hurry." Isolfr smiled.

"No," Brokkolfr agreed, and began picking mud out of Amma's coat.

Both men were quiet for a time; Isolfr would not speak first, and Brokkolfr was trying to sort out what he wanted to say from all the things he didn't. Finally, he said, "Signy is going to bond Eymundr."

"Yes," Isolfr said. "He's chosen his name: Hreithulfr."

"Good," Brokkolfr said. And then, before cowardice could get the better of him, "You have to talk to him."

Isolfr said nothing.

"Signy is a konigenwolf," Brokkolfr said. "I talked to him about . . . about open mating and about the ways of trellwolf bitches"—that got a tiny quirk of a smile, and Brokkolfr was glad of even that much encouragement—"but I can't tell him about being bonded to a konigenwolf or about being a wolfsprechend. No one here can tell him that. Except you."

"I know," Isolfr said.

"But you haven't."

"I don't know what to say."

"Neither did I," Brokkolfr said. "And I didn't know what to say to Motholfr just now, either. But saying nothing isn't better than saying something badly."

"No?"

"If I hadn't said anything to Eymundr"—he corrected himself and finished grimly—"to Hreithulfr, he would still be expecting Vethulf to hold him down over the table in the hall while everyone else in the threat took turns with him."

Isolfr stared down at the half-finished peg in his lap; his ears were turning red.

"You're his wolfsprechend," Brokkolfr insisted. "He needs you to talk to him. He needs to know you're not unhappy that Signy chose him."

"Unhappy? Why would I be unhappy?"

At least his head was up and he was listening. "He asked me if I thought you disliked him. I told him of course not, but he's scared of you, Isolfr." *I'm scared of you.* "At the least, he needs to know he has your support."

"Of course he does," Isolfr said, putting down the knife and rubbing his scars as if they ached.

"He doesn't know that." Brokkolfr wondered when he'd turned into a nagging wife. "He's only just beginning to feel the pack-sense. He certainly can't read anything in it. And that's the only place you say anything at all."

"The werthreat is not my responsibility," Isolfr said. "The wolfthreat is."

Brokkolfr raised his eyebrows. He didn't need to say it; in

Skjaldwulf's absence, the werthreat were Vethulf's responsibility and Vethulf had not yet grown into that role. *And might never,* Brokkolfr thought, before he could force himself to charity.

Surely Viradechtis had chosen Vethulf for some reason. Even if it was not immediately obvious. Or was Vethulf simply an unavoidable drawback that came kit and kindle with Kjaran?

Except Kjaran was a sensible wolf. And so he, too, must have chosen his brother for a purpose.

Isolfr bit his lip. How long had it taken him to forget what it was like, being half-deaf to the pack? Or had Viradechtis simply overwhelmed him with her senses as she overwhelmed the pack with her presence?

"Hrolleif—," Isolfr said, which was the name of the dead wolfsprechend of Nithogsfjoll. However he might have ended the sentence, however, was lost.

"Are you complaining about your wolfsprechend, Brokkolfr Ammasbrother?" Vethulf, approaching from behind, startled Brokkolfr so badly that he dislodged Amma—which meant he was able to lurch to his feet.

*Thanks for the warning,* he told the wolf, and heard only her irritation at being awakened in return.

"No," he said, wondering if Vethulf really was a spirit who could be conjured with a thought. Before he could stop himself, Brokkolfr added, "I'm trying to help."

"Help?" said Vethulf, his eyebrows going up in exaggerated disbelief. "That's not what it sounded like to me."

"Vethulf," Isolfr said, irritation plain in his voice and in the packsense.

"You never stand up for yourself," Vethulf said past Brokkolfr.

"And so you're going to stand up for me? I don't recall asking for that favor, wolfjarl." Isolfr very rarely lost his temper—Vethulf was the only one who seemed able to provoke him that far—but when he did, wolves and men alike prudently found business elsewhere. Brokkolfr, face burning and stomach in a knot, backed away as Isolfr stood up, leaving the space between wolfsprechend and wolfjarl clear.

"I won't have you browbeaten," Vethulf said between his teeth.

"Unless you're the one doing it," Isolfr said, face white and set, pale eyes glittering.

Brokkolfr swung about and headed for the woods as fast as he could walk, Amma anxiously at his heels. The pack-sense followed him, wolfsprechend and wolfjarl snapping and snarling for dominance. Brokkolfr was aware in a distracted way of other wolves and men slinking off into the woods or finding urgent work elsewhere in Franangfordheall and town. Amma, gamely following, was heavier on her feet than when she had been lean and virginal, the pups slowly becoming an impediment. It would not be long now, Brokkolfr thought, and contemplation of pups and potentials was enough to distract him for some time.

He was working so hard not to dwell in the conflict or replay that disaster of a conversation in his head that he paid very little attention to where he was going and was surprised to discover he'd found his way back to the cave that Kari had shown him.

*A place where* this *pack won't follow you*, Kari had said; just at the moment, Brokkolfr couldn't think of anything he wanted more.

A cool draught wafted from the mouth of the cavern. Brokkolfr stepped toward it, and Amma made a low, concerned moan. "I know you don't like it," he said. "You don't have to come."

But he wasn't quite confident to go in alone, with nobody except his wolf the wiser. He reached into the pack-sense, relieved that the tension of Isolfr and Vethulf's snapping match had dissipated. What underlay it was still there, the sense of off-balance and awkward, but that wasn't his problem anymore. He'd done his duty and brought it to the wolfsprechend's attention, and the wolfsprechend could take it from here.

It was a relief, he thought, to fold up a responsibility that way and hand it off to the next man. Not for the first time, he pitied Isolfr.

But right now, he did not want Isolfr. He wanted Kari.

He reached out through the pack-sense, through Amma's awareness of the wolfthreat. Not a konigenwolf's understanding of her pack, but still. Nothing to be trifled with. Amma would understand that he wanted Hrafn and Hrafn's brother, and sooner or later, with the relaxed timing of wolves, Hrafn and Kari would appear.

*Wyvern blood, nose-stinging and slick,* Brokkolfr thought, knowing that his attempts at the language Amma shared with other wolves were no more than a toddler's babbling. She looked at him quizzically, head tilted, and he thought Hrafn's name again.

Amma looked away, leaned her head back, and howled. A long eerie descant, a summoning cry. By the end of it, other wolf-voices picked it up, and such was the carrying power of those wolf-voices that he heard it echoed and echoed back again.

"Show-off," he accused the wolf, who laughed at him and flopped down on the leaf litter to wait.

With a sigh, Brokkolfr settled down beside her and pillowed his head on her flank. Puppies wriggled in her belly, one a warm kicking bump against his ear. If she was determined to embarrass him, he might as well nap.

༺༻

Kari and Hrafn must have been in the area, because it wasn't a candlemark later that the patter of footsteps across dry leaves roused Brokkolfr from his doze. Amma craned her neck up, but upon seeing—and scenting—that it was packmates, she let her head thump on the soft earth again.

For his part, Hrafn sniffed Brokkolfr's hand in brief greeting and then dropped down beside Amma, yawning so elaborately that Brokkolfr imagined him turning his teeth to the light so the facets could flash like displayed gems. He laid his head down on his paws and watched the men with slitted eyes.

"So I was thinking," Brokkolfr said by way of greeting, "that we could try to explore deeper. If you were game."

"I was born game," Kari said. "Come on. Let's go."

The darkness seemed less oppressive this time and the tight squeeze more comfortable when Brokkolfr knew what to expect. This time, he managed to follow Kari closely, not waiting for the torch to be kindled, and on the other side of the tunnel they sat for a moment in a darkness as utter and abject as a trellwarren, just listening to one another breathe in the dark.

Brokkolfr could feel Kari beside him, as if a tattered envelope of warm air surrounded the wildling. Now that they were quiet and still, Brokkolfr also felt the moving air lift and stir the fine hairs at his temples and on his nape, where the part between his braids fell. After long silent moments, the scrape and the brilliance of a flint struck on steel were brazen, startling.

The torches kindled easily, flickering just a little. Silently Brokkolfr and Kari descended to the pool room and there stood shoulder to shoulder, staring across the unrippled water.

Kari cleared his throat. It echoed over the pool and back, the bounce of sound around that arched and hollow space covering his voice with overtones like a wolf pack howling in harmony. "So what makes you think there's more to the cave? I mean, the water has to come from somewhere, but we can't exactly follow it underground."

"Can you feel the breeze?" Brokkolfr said.

The stark light of the torches moved terrible shadows across Kari's cheeks and forehead as his head bobbed once. "It's more or less always like that."

Brokkolfr swallowed. "You know how in a longhouse, if you

only open one door, the heat stays inside? But if you open two, the wind blows right through it?"

The way Kari's expression stilled was not an artifact of the firelight. "You think there's another entrance."

Brokkolfr let one shoulder lift and dip, ridiculously aware that here he was, a bearded man with a wolf of his own, coy as a maiden with his opinions, seeking Kari's approval. But Kari, though no more than a year or three older than Brokkolfr, was a tested warrior, shieldbrother to Isolfr Ice-heart. And all Brokkolfr had done in his short life was bond a wolf who liked playing with puppies, and manage to lose four-fifths of a heallthreat to a troll incursion. "Air can go where we cannot."

"Still," Kari said, the impassive expression breaking into a grin, "it doesn't hurt to look."

⚭

If air could go where they could not, Brokkolfr was somewhat startled to discover where they could go. The flicker of the torches led them: the strength of the air currents blowing from any given crevice was their clue.

"Don't get the water in your eyes," Kari said. "It's safe to drink, but the old Franangfordthreat said that if it got into your eyes or ears, it could eat holes in your brain and you'd die in six months with a head full of sea-sponge."

"Well," said Brokkolfr dubiously, "I suppose if it can dissolve stone, it can dissolve brains."

When they crossed the pond, they crossed it one at a time, holding each torch high, wading up to their chests in steaming water, stirring silt from the bottom that might have lain undisturbed since nothing but Jotun, trolls, and svartalfar ruled the world.

Brokkolfr tried to be careful of the brittle laceworks of stone floating atop the still water—stone! floating!—but inevitably his ripples swamped some. It left a feeling of sadness in him, a sense that perhaps one could not see a thing without destroying it. When he waded out of the pool, though, Kari was waiting, grinning, on his belly before a passageway no taller than the span of three hands. "I found something."

Brokkolfr was careful to look back over his shoulder whenever the tunnels were wide enough to crane his head around—he'd spent enough time in the forest to know that the same place could look very different viewed from one direction as opposed to another—and Kari produced a bit of charcoal from a trouser pocket and sketched arrows on the damp yellow-white stone of the walls. It still looked to Brokkolfr like candle wax, but it tasted of salt and was brittle enough that a few needle-fine filaments shattered against Brokkolfr's hair before he learned to avoid them.

As they descended, sweat added itself to the condensation beading Brokkolfr's brow. The warmth he had noticed on his last visit became heat; the water seemed warmer but not yet warm enough to burn.

Some springs could burn you, though. So Kari and Brokkolfr approached each rivulet or puddle with care, especially the ones that could be seen steaming.

The cavern seemed to run forever, down and down and down again, endless crawl spaces and serried galleries and draperies of stone. Brokkolfr could have imagined that they had spent the world's time here, worn out Ragnarok, and passed through the mists of Hel, were it not so hot in the depths—and if he were not grounded in the pack-sense, aware from Amma that the sun was not yet low in the sky.

They burned their first torches and kindled the second. Sometimes they had to push the spares through narrow passages ahead of them or drag them behind, bumping on repurposed boot cords. It was good that there was water, because they had to pause and drink it often, although it was bitter with limestone and smelt of sulfur. They sweated out so much they would be dizzy otherwise. If the stones by the entry had been polished, these were rough, and Brokkolfr had a sense that no one had ever passed this way before.

"It's not like a trellwarren," Kari said when they paused under a great rose-and-white arch to rest and breathe.

"It's as hot as one."

Kari snorted what might have been laughter, and Brokkolfr grinned back. "One more half-torch," he said, "and we have to turn back."

"Next time," Kari said, "we'll carry extra and find someplace to make a cache."

Brokkolfr levered himself up, dusting muddy silt off his rear. He had to walk stooped through most of the passages, scuttling like a crab, and he knew that in daylight his knees would be black-and-blue. "How will you keep them dry enough to kindle?"

"Oiled cloth?" Kari rose and took a hesitant step forward. He passed under the arch, into a crooked squeeze that did not—yet—require crawling, and vanished from sight. "It opens out past this!" he called back, and Brokkolfr followed.

Brokkolfr was still in the crooked passage, his torch held out before him and his arm bent at an awkward angle to keep the flames from his face, when he heard a snap like slate split with a chisel and Kari's sharp, truncated cry.

*Hurry and you die,* Brokkolfr thought, feeling the sudden urgency and fear in the pack-sense. Amma was there within him, and he stepped carefully, meticulously, one of the heall cats stalking a brown rat through the grain stores. One foot, hesitate, shift weight. Bring the other up to the first, careful of the rippled and crooked floor, because the passage was too narrow to step through. And re-peat, crouching, trying to peer past the flames of the torch to see anything beyond.

Four agonized steps brought Brokkolfr to the open space that Kari had found, a floor ahead smoother than good flagstones, flat as that pool in the first large chamber had been, a ceiling above as elaborate, arched, and beautiful.

"Stay there!" Kari called before Brokkolfr could see him. "The floor gave way."

The strain in his voice betrayed him. Kari was hurt, and that was the distress Brokkolfr felt in the pack-sense. Kari was hurt, in pain—but not dead.

Brokkolfr would not allow Kari to be dead. Not when this expe-dition had been his idea. Enough werthreatbrothers had already died because Brokkolfr had not gotten to them in time.

Brokkolfr breathed out softly, and without moving his feet ex-tended the torch and leaned around the corner.

Brokkolfr had seen enough winters to know what it looked like when a man fell through ice. And Kari had fallen through stone in the same manner—stone laid over water, half an inch thick and looking as solid as any tabletop until Kari had gone through it up to the chest. Or farther; from what Brokkolfr could see, water dripped from Kari's hair and eyebrows, and he'd lost his torch. But now he supported himself on the flats of his hands and his forearms laid on the broken stone, the water bearing most of his weight up.

He'd had the sense to go still once he fell, and the sense and luck to find the hole he'd made going in. So he was alive and not vanished under the floor of stone, drowned already. No steam rose around him, and he wasn't screaming, so the water was not boiling him.

Did he get it in his eyes? Othinn, what a way to go—but if he had, there was nothing to be done about it now.

It was better than falling through ice, Brokkolfr told himself. The temperature was not freezing; he had minutes to save Kari, not seconds. And like any wolfcarl, like any northman, he knew how to handle an ice rescue.

"My ankle is broken," Kari said. "Go for help, Brokkolfr."

"And leave you there in the water to drown?" Brokkolfr scoffed, keeping his voice light, as if the situation they were presented with was nothing but an amusing complication. "That would be bad manners."

The flowstone gave him more than one place to wedge a torch, thankfully. Brokkolfr did so, waving it first to make it burn brightly, and hoped the draught through the cave would be enough to feed the flames for a little while. Then he turned back to Kari.

"I'm going to crawl out to you," he said. "I don't suppose you've got some bottom there?"

"Nothing," Kari said. "I picked a bad place to go through. Brokkolfr, you outweigh me."

"And I'll be on my belly, not my feet."

Lying prone on the smooth stone, he scooted forward, inching by rippling his body like a snake. It was only perhaps twice the length of his body to where Kari had fallen through, but it was a long and arduous crawl for a tired, frantic man on bruised knees. Especially when he did not dare press his knees, feet, hands, or elbows to the stone to push himself forward.

With every wriggle, Brokkolfr felt as if the thunder of his heart alone were enough to break through. He imagined he felt the stone creak and settle, heard the crackle where the thin shelf of stone laid over the water might be breaking away from the supporting walls. He reached out slowly and felt the back of Kari's wet hand, the viperlike quickness with which Kari flipped that hand over and grasped Brokkolfr's wrist, the strength with which he clung.

"Brokkolfr!" Kari whispered hoarsely, his voice almost lost in the rasp of his own breathing and Brokkolfr's. He jerked his chin to the side. Pointing with his head, because he could not point with his hands.

Brokkolfr turned slowly left, scanning the dark recesses of the cave. And there, at the farthest reaches of the torchlight, found the glitter of not one but two pairs of eyes in the dark.

# eight

The days went by in hands, and the farther south they traveled, the greener the land became. Skjaldwulf, Ulfhoss, Frithulf, Geirulfr, north-bred all, were as round-eyed as babies, and Randulfr spent half the day with a smile tucked at the corners of his mouth. The wolves were uninterested in trees and bushes, but Mar shared with Skjaldwulf his satisfaction in the rabbits and ground squirrels they caught and devoured. All five wolves became sleek and smug, and Mar, Afi, Kothran, and Dyrver were courting Ingrun assiduously with choice tidbits. They were forming their own tiny pack, and Skjaldwulf wished Isolfr were here to tell the story. He himself could communicate very well with Mar, and he could feel the pack-sense, but he couldn't find the patterns of it the way Isolfr could.

The wolfcarls agreed that Freyvithr would have made a good threatbrother—high praise and well earned. Freyvithr took a fair share of the work when they camped at night and when they broke camp in the morning, neither complaining nor seeming to feel that his status as godsman entitled him to special treatment. He asked questions—endless questions—and listened to the answers, both plaguing Skjaldwulf for his store of eddas and lore and begging Frithulf to talk about the Iskryne campaign. Freyvithr had taken pains to learn the name of each wolf and something of their various personalities, and when he found that otherwise silent and suspicious wolfcarls would happily talk for hours about their wolves, he settled in to learn about konigenwolves and lineages and the web of relationships between the wolves of Franangford and the other heallan of the North.

Adalbrikt did his best, but he was not Freyvithr. Even Frithulf's wicked tongue and Ulfhoss' seemingly endless hoard of filthy jokes could not entirely rid him of his awe for the wolfcarls, and he treated the wolves as if they might eat him at any moment. Skjaldwulf had barely prevented himself from passing on Mar's comment that rabbits tasted better and were more fun to run.

The night they spent in Arakensberg—the most southerly wolf-heall that lay on their line of march—did not help. In truth, Skjaldwulf would have been just as pleased to have avoided Arakensberg; he had never had any fondness for the wolfjarl Ulfsvith, and the few things Vethulf had said had not changed his mind. Geirulfr had not seemed any too pleased to meet his former wolfjarl again, either, although Skjaldwulf did note that other members of the Arakensbergthreat gave the young wolfcarl a warm and happy welcome.

It had been an uncomfortable night all around—the Arakensberg konigenwolf disliked having Ingrun in her territory, and Ulfsvith's brother seemed inclined to take Mar as a threat to his power. And Adalbrikt, who had stayed in the village of Franangford except for a couple of brief forays to the wolfheall, had reeked so strongly of tension and fear that Skjaldwulf could nearly smell it himself. He was positively grateful to bid Arakensberg farewell, and he heard Geirulfr humming under his breath as they set out. Freyvithr was visibly making mental notes, and Skjaldwulf expected there would be a number of questions later. He found he didn't mind.

Freyvithr might have made a wolfcarl, if he'd come to it before the goddess chose him; Adalbrikt never would. But he was anxious to please, and he was very good with the ponies. The farther south they got, the more Skjaldwulf appreciated those ponies—not for their strength, although they were sturdy and patient beasts, but because they served as a marker of respectability. The people the travelers met along the roads and when they passed through villages, like Adalbrikt found the wolfcarls alarming, even if the wolves were nowhere in sight. Skjaldwulf supposed he could see their point. Wolfcarls were warriors, and they looked it, even those who did not have Frithulf's scars. These southern folk were farmers, craftsmen; none of them had ever seen a troll, nor had their parents or their parents' parents. Skjaldwulf wondered how far back he'd have to go to find the last time trolls had come within a hundred miles of the southern sea. Maybe the archives at Hergilsberg could answer that question, too.

But the ponies seemed to reassure villagers and wayfarers, even more than Freyvithr's tattoos and medallion. Skjaldwulf wasn't sure why—bandits and murderers could certainly have ponies just as much as honest people—but he wasn't about to argue with it. Anything that made a fight less likely was a blessing. It was one reason why, even now in a region peaceful and wealthy enough to have inns, they continued to camp beside the road. There were a number of other reasons, but most of them boiled down to the same thing: staying out of any situation that might turn into a fight. Isolfr wasn't the only one who worried about teaching the wolfheallan to interact with wolfless men, and vice versa.

They had camped one night under a tree so vast that Skjaldwulf was tempted to think it must be a child of Yggdrasil, and now in the soft gray before sunrise, he was sitting on one of its massive gnarled roots, his back braced against the trunk, watching the other men sleep and listening in the pack-sense to Mar and Kothran playing a hunting game; it was far more complicated and subtle than the games puppies played but very much a development of the same thing. He hadn't known adult wolves would play like that—except with puppies—but Mar had shown him the explanation, in pictures and scents and things that were not quite words: here where all the rabbits were fat and slow, and with their brothers to cook and keep some of the meat from their kills, they did not need to hunt every day in order to have enough to eat, and they did not want to hunt if they did not need to. The smell-taste of *rotted meat* was clear enough to convince even Skjaldwulf's dull senses. But the wolves needed the feelings of hunting: the chase and the sharpness and the exertion. Skjaldwulf didn't think he understood that part entirely, but well enough to see that the game gave them the feelings they needed without wasting fat rabbits that might—Mar said, almost primly—be needed later.

Skjaldwulf was wondering, half idly, if wild wolves thought like that or if wolves bonded to men changed just as did men bonded to wolves, when something shot through the pack-sense, *bright* and *loud* and completely, utterly unfamiliar.

Frithulf and Geirulfr both went from sound sleep to bewildered defensive crouches. Ulfhoss, whose pack-sense was not as strong, grunted but did not wake. Randulfr, who had been building up the fire from where it had been banked overnight, yelped and swore.

Skjaldwulf, on his feet and trying to figure out what was going on, could feel all five wolves converging on the campsite at a dead run. It was Afi and Ingrun who had raised the alarm; they were south and east of the camp, the direction they'd been intending to travel today. *Strangers,* said Afi and Ingrun through the pack-sense, and Skjaldwulf got a jumble of image-scent-sound: men and horses, metal and leather, and all of it wrong.

*Wrong how?* Skjaldwulf asked, and the wolves gave him another jumble of answers. The leather smelled wrong. The horses were too tall. The men were skin-like-earth, not skin-like-snow. They were carrying blankets on sticks. They had manes like horses.

Most of it didn't make any sense, but one thing was clear. "I think," Skjaldwulf said to his werthreat, "that we've found the raiders."

"Or they've found us," said Frithulf.

⚭

Wolfcarls did not habitually ride to battle, and anyway these shaggy hard-hooved ponies—two bay and one dun—were pack animals from the swish of their tails to the moth-eaten fringe under each throat. Adalbrikt led them deeper into the woods, well out of sight, and there made them fast. He returned at a soft run while Skjaldwulf was picking the ground on which they'd fight. Adalbrikt might be afraid of wolves, but there was nothing wrong with his woodcraft.

The wolves could not tell Skjaldwulf if the invaders had bows, or estimate their numbers beyond a general sense of a group of men more than twice as large as the number of wolfcarls. But at least Ingrun could reach out into the pack-mind and give such information as they had. If they fell, at least Arakensberg would share what little they knew.

The choice of ground was limited. Wolves ran faster than men marched but not so much faster as that, and there would be no hiding the smell of their fire. But the forest giant under whose gray branches they had slept had shaded out a good-sized clear space underneath, and on its east side the wood grew thick with smaller trees and scrub. Across the road, on its sunny side, young oaks had filled up the open space with low branches, heavily leaved now as spring progressed into summer.

They would set their ambush there. Either the enemy would march past, in which case the wolfcarls would have their flank, or they would come into the shaded confines of the clearing and the wolves would fall on them from all sides.

Wolves understood hunting from ambush.

Skjaldwulf found the waiting harder, but he was long inured to patience and made a discipline of it, even when it came with difficulty. He breathed shallowly, straining his ears but straining even more into the pack-sense, for Mar and the other wolves would hear and smell the strangers long before the wolfcarls and wolfless men.

The leafy forest loam lay wet against Skjaldwulf's breast and cheek. The birds boasted loud as vikings in a mead-hall as the slow day brightened, coils of mist fingering down the slope to eddy across the road and deposit another layer of water-jewels on the velvet cushions of the mosses. The treetips sparked golden; soon the sun's rays would filter between their branches and burn off whatever mist was not absorbed by thirsty leaves. Skjaldwulf hoped the strangers would arrive before that happened, for the mist was to the wolves' advantage.

Adalbrikt dropped quietly into the leaves beside Skjaldwulf, his sword already in his hand and reached out crosswise before him. He no longer seemed to regard Mar, stretched out on Skjaldwulf's other side, with fear.

"They're disciplined," Adalbrikt said. "To be on the march this early."

"Very disciplined, for a raiding party," Skjaldwulf answered in low tones.

And now the youngest wolves could make out the march of feet and the jingle of harness. What they told Mar, he shared with Skjaldwulf. And it was strange.

The invaders moved at a trot, like a hunting wolfcarl. But they trotted in unison, their feet hitting the ground at the same instant, like men in a shield wall or rowers in a dragonship moving with a drummer to strike the beat. Mar's ears pricked, too, his hot breaths panting back from the ground to move Skjaldwulf's beard against his face.

That was like an army and not like bandits or vikings.

"Soon," Skjaldwulf said, for the benefit of Adalbrikt. "Soon."

The wolfless man's breath bated, and he flattened himself into the shadow of a laurel branch.

The soldiers—they were soldiers, no mistaking it, and soldiers such as Skjaldwulf had never seen—crested a little rise in the road and came into view.

They were a dozen in number, jogging three abreast and four deep along the road, crowded on each side by boughs and fronds of which they took no notice. They were dressed identically, like a rich man's children, and they were swarthy-skinned, though not black like svartalfar—as if they had been burned dark by some stronger foreign sun.

Their kit, too, spoke to him of climes too warm to imagine— boots made of straps wound round their feet, woven like strainer-baskets with gaps between. Bare legs that rose and fell like the shaft of a treadle, linen shirttails or tunics flapping beneath armor skirts studded with bronze. They wore breastplates—they *ran* in breast-plates—of hammered bronze and helms stiff with crests of horsehair, which gave Skjaldwulf a favorable impression of their fitness.

Each of them carried a large rectangular shield across his back and was armed with daggers, a spear (held high, two or three of them snapped with banners), and a shortsword thrust through his belt. They were a brave sight in red and bronze, bright cloaks furling in the breeze of their own movement.

Skjaldwulf would have liked to get a better look at the blades of those swords, but from his glimpses of the tangs, he imagined steel or iron. Not bronze, anyway.

Of the two, iron would be better.

Behind the soldiers followed what Skjaldwulf took to be a foreign jarl, drawn behind a bay pony in a weird two-wheeled dogcart that he rode standing. Behind *him* came a larger cart, this one laden with the spoils of their foray. No raiding party carried that much baggage, and the cramped wicker cages of chickens and the way the grain sacks bulged suggested to Skjaldwulf that these soldiers came in advance of a larger force and were here to provision. The cart squeezed along the track as if force of will alone made it fit. Had Skjaldwulf been the driver, he would have been tempted to grease it to help it squeak through.

They were alert. As they came abreast of the clearing, they slowed—still in unison, the foreign jarl calling out some phrase in an incomprehensible, barbarian yammering. He reined his horse back as well, dropping from a casual trot to a walk.

Whatever he had said, his soldiers responded to the order without the conversation or quarreling common to a raiding party. Those on the right side fell out of formation, still spaced evenly but spread out, and moved into the clearing. Those on the left turned to face the trees behind which Randulfr, Frithulf, and Freyvithr waited. The soldiers slipped their shields onto their arms, simultaneously locking the edges and lowering their spears. Birds fell silent all around.

*Discipline,* Skjaldwulf mouthed to Adalbrikt. Adalbrikt, pallid, nodded.

Well then. This, and elk, was why wolfcarls carried bows.

As smoothly as old bones would let him, Skjaldwulf stood behind the bole of a tree, leaned his axe against it, and unlimbered his bow. He set an arrow to the string and nocked it, then nudged one foot forward, conscious of twigs and the rustle of dry leaves. Here also the dew was a friend: wet leaves were more silent.

On the ground an armspan away, Adalbrikt gathered himself to lunge. Skjaldwulf drew the bow open around his body and felt the fletching brush his lip.

He was not the best archer in the werthreat, and arrows were next to useless against wyverns and trolls, but he could reliably hit a rabbit at a distance greater than the one stretching between his position and the foreign jarl. The searchers were closer, but they could wait to die.

The breastplate might be proof against arrows, and Skjaldwulf's hunting bow was no mankiller bent to cloth yard shafts. The eye was a slender target and girded in the edges of the helm. But the foreign jarl's horse was nervous—it knew the wolves were there, if the men were innocent—and the foreign jarl must both rein it and gesture to his men.

You could armor over the top of an arm. But there was very little that could armor the softness beneath it and still allow the freedom of movement necessary to swing a sword. And Skjaldwulf, the hunter, knew that in any animal's body the heart lay behind the upper arm in a direct line.

Man was just another animal.

It was strange, Skjaldwulf thought, to put his sights on the life of a man. For all the fighting he had done, for all the wars his long life had encompassed, he'd never murdered before. There was no manprice in war; there was no crime in what he was about to do. But it felt momentous still.

His fingertips tingled from the bowstring as he waited his shot. The light crept down the tree trunks. Mar breathed like a black ghost beside him. The foreign jarl gestured.

Skjaldwulf let the bow pull the arrow from its rest across his fingertips.

It arched softly as it flew, the arrow silent, the twang of the bowstring loud. The thump as the shaft found its target was loud also, and in the silence that followed Skjaldwulf nocked another arrow. He'd have time, he thought, for one more before the soldiers were on him—

The ones searching the clearing turned; the shield wall, however, stood without a ripple. And then the foreign jarl windmilled and toppled, two hands of willow shaft and raven feathers still protruding under his arm as he fell to his knees, slumping over the front balustrade of his peculiar dogcart.

The horse might have bolted—and wouldn't that be fun?—but an alert soldier grabbed the reins below the bit and started pulling the frightened animal forward. Around him, soldiers were falling back, joining shields, linking up to the group. The teamster vaulted from the wagon seat and ran to join them.

Skjaldwulf, who had expected a full frontal attack, was taken aback by the retreat. He loosed another arrow as Adalbrikt ran forward, wailing and waving his sword like a berserk, and then Skjaldwulf, too, was moving.

His axe in his hand, he stepped out from behind the tree. Frithulf and Randulfr were shoulder to shoulder across the clearing; Geirulfr blocked the path ahead, and Ulfhoss quietly moved to block the path behind, Freyvithr with him. Mar was still back in the trees; through him, Skjaldwulf could feel the other wolves. He got a quick, strong flash of a horse herd, the mares circling to protect the foals. That wasn't from Mar; Mar didn't know any more about horses than Skjaldwulf did. Afi, maybe. Arakensberg was proud of their horses. There was a second strong flash, this time of what it felt like when a horse hoof connected solidly with a leaping wolf-body, and at the same time a spear jabbed out of the shield-square the foreign soldiers had made and ran Adalbrikt through.

Skjaldwulf dared not shut his eyes, but he felt the urge all the way down to his guts. He'd seen too many young men die, and although he knew some wolfcarls would tell him Adalbrikt was just one more, he couldn't feel it that way, couldn't feel anything but pain and anger at the loss.

Adalbrikt lurched back and dragged the spear away from the foreign soldier. If there had been fewer of them, and more lightly armed, that might even have been helpful, though not worth the life spattering bright red onto the dead leaves.

A death worthy of a warrior, a death that would assure his place in the afterworld, if songs and sagas could be believed. Everything dies, and maybe it was better to die of a spear in the gut than rot away.

Skjaldwulf was too old—or perhaps old enough—to argue it either way.

Skjaldwulf looked across at Frithulf, who grimaced in answer—an expression made grotesque by his scars, but Skjaldwulf knew what he meant. Even if all six of them charged the foreign soldiers—*herd*, said the pack-sense—at once, the shield wall and spears left the advantage with the defenders. They could all die spitted like pigs. *A four-sided shield wall*, Skjaldwulf thought with reluctant admiration. It would never have worked against trolls, who had the size, and the numbers, to throw themselves against a shield wall until they bore it down beneath them, but it was a clever tactic against men on foot. Bows no use, axes no use unless you got right up close to them, and by then you'd already be dead.

They had to lure or provoke the soldiers into breaking their square, or they'd be stuck here in a standoff until somebody ran out of food. Skjaldwulf was racking his brains for something that might serve against soldiers as disciplined as these when Dyrver came out of the trees to stand next to Ulfhoss.

Dyrver was young—anxious and impatient—and it was a mistake none of the older wolves would have made, but Skjaldwulf was reminded that occasionally making a mistake could be the best thing to do. A soldier in the shield-square caught sight of Dyrver—a dark gray wolf, with light greenish-yellow eyes, not particularly large as trellwolves went, utterly unremarkable to Skjaldwulf's way of thinking—and screamed. Not surprise, not excitement: Skjaldwulf had heard men dying beneath the hooves of the trell-smiths, and he knew a scream of terror when he heard one.

As Skjaldwulf half-crouched, chest heaving, sidling left to cover the gap left by Adalbrikt's fall, he sought out the eyes of the men he knew best. His gaze crossed Frithulf's, and he knew Frithulf was calling Kothran just as he called Mar—as Geirulfr was calling Afi and Randulfr calling Ingrun. And Skjaldwulf was pleased to see that Ulfhoss had the sense to hand off his great-knife to Freyvithr. If the godsman was trained as a soldier, well—now was the time for him to use it.

Now why would a well-trained, well-disciplined soldier scream at the sight of a wolf? Skjaldwolf remembered something Randulfr had said more than once—that the foreign raiders feared trellwolves like nothing else and thought them demons.

A wild babble rose in the foreign soldiers' strange tongue: it could be prayer, or arguments among men suddenly robbed of their commander.

Skjaldwulf and Mar were the oldest, the most experienced, and Mar was Viradechtis' chosen consort; the risk was theirs to take.

Skjaldwulf paced forward, slowly, Mar at his side. The shield-square wavered. Mar, with a sense of the dramatic that Skjaldwulf would never have expected from him, drew his lips back and let a chest-shaking growl out between his teeth. From the other side Ingrun and Kothran howled in hackle-raising harmony.

Perhaps if the foreign jarl had been among them, shouting commands and encouragement, the soldiers' discipline would have prevailed. But Skjaldwulf's first shot had removed that strength. The shield-square buckled and collapsed as the men on the near side fell back, breaking away from the advancing wolf.

The foreign soldiers routed and ran.

Fighting men was not like fighting trolls. It was both easier and uglier: easier because he could predict what a man would do when it was never quite possible to be certain of a troll, uglier because every time his opponent did what he expected, he was reminded he was fighting a man like himself.

The wolves bewildered the foreign soldiers. They fell back against the wagon and regrouped, except the one Kothran hamstrung and the one Ingrun pulled down. But their shield wall was broken, and several of them had thrown their spears away to run. Wolves circled them, seeming to understand as instinctually as they hunted elk or trolls how to hunt men. And the men of the threat had their bows still.

Skjaldwulf and his threat were about a third of the way into their butchers' work when Afi called in the pack-sense, *More strangers! More! More! More!* That explained what this little band of soldiers was doing out here by themselves: they were meeting another band of soldiers. A larger band—Afi's urgency could not be mistaken.

*Fall back!* Skjaldwulf said into the pack-sense. *Fall away!* Luck and cunning had given them the upper hand, but they'd never be able to keep it. Better to disengage, get to Siglufjordhur, regroup. Although, he was thinking as they began cautiously to retreat, if the foreign soldiers *were* as terrified of trellwolves as they seemed, perhaps the five from Franangford would be worth more than a mere show of support to Randulfr's brother.

But for now they must disengage, and disengage quickly. Skjald-wulf fell back, a fighting retreat, Mar circling behind him. He felt his threatbrothers and their wolves withdrawing, too, and wished they had a moment to drag Adalbrikt from the field.

At least Othinn would welcome him. Or possibly Freya, Skjald-wulf thought, realizing that Freyvithr crouched over Adalbrikt's body, fearless in the midst of combat.

Skjaldwulf expected the beleaguered foreign soldiers to accept their reprieve, to regroup and live another day. But the soldier he had been fighting, instead of pulling back with his shieldbrothers, lunged forward. Skjaldwulf blocked the blow on his axe haft, tried to brace himself to throw the man off, and his foot skidded on the wet, dead leaves.

He fell. Falling, he tried to tell Mar to run, and then there was a brilliant flash of blackness behind his eyes and the clearing dissolved into gray, into black, into nothing.

# NINE

Something scraped in the shadows; something rustled. Brokkolfr lifted his head, careful not to push with his elbows, and craned his neck to see better.

There was, predictably, a shape behind each set of eyes, a shape dull and dark in color, like a hunched lump of stone—but they showed up as crooked silhouettes against the pale limestone behind. The torchlight wavered over something with the nap of cloth, something with the shimmer of metal. Kari's torch had gone into the water. Brokkolfr's flickered fitfully against the stone where he had thrust it, and Brokkolfr knew it would soon gutter out.

"Svartalfar," Brokkolfr said, aware of the relief coloring his voice and embarrassed by it. He sounded so damned young sometimes, and Kari was—well, not exactly older. But more worldly. "Maybe they'll help pull you out."

"I wouldn't count on it," Kari said softly. "Come on, Brokkolfr. I can't feel my feet."

Indeed, as Brokkolfr edged slowly backward—and the two svartalfar watched silently, leaning on their staffs, the torchlight catching an occasional glint off their jewelry—the puddle of water that oozed from Kari's clothes and soaked Brokkolfr's frontside was frigid enough to make him shiver and curse under his breath. As for Kari, well, his teeth were rattling, and Brokkolfr didn't think it was with fear.

"How can this water be so cold when the other water is steaming?"

"Different stream?" Kari stammered. Once Brokkolfr had Kari's hips over the edge—tricky work, as it wanted to snag and crumble—he managed to drag his own feet out, and then the two men inchwormed back the way they had come.

"Or maybe it flows in cold, and gets heated up somehow," Brokkolfr offered. It was strange, chatting casually with Kari while the svartalfar watched like statues, but the traverse took a while. When they had regained the edge—and Brokkolfr's torch—Kari tried to stand, yelped, and sank back. He muttered a curse under his breath. "I was hoping I'd been wrong about that."

Brokkolfr looked, a quick, wincing glance, and saw Kari's foot hanging at the wrong angle from his leg. It was bad, then, and he had to focus himself consciously on the immediate problem instead of the babbling chorus of future worries.

"I don't know if I can get you out of here on my own," Brokkolfr said, thinking of the scrambling they'd had to do to get this far.

"I don't think you can," Kari said. He looked across the cavern to the svartalfar. "I guess we'll have to see if they'll help."

"You didn't think they would."

"The svartalfar are funny about things like that. They've got rules, and they want to negotiate everything out ahead of time. I remember Tin's jarls just about swallowed their tongues when they realized we'd gone and killed the trellqueen for them without even *asking*. Help me up."

Brokkolfr wanted to tell him to take his wet clothes off now, before they killed him—but he supposed that even if the water was chill, the air in the cave was warm enough that it would be a few moments before Kari was in dire trouble.

So he helped Kari up, half-hauling, half-bracing, and supported Kari in a lurching, precarious progress toward the svartalfar, Kari cursing vividly under his breath with every hopping step. When they were still about ten feet away, the svartalfar pulled back and Kari said, "All right. Help me down again." Brokkolfr did and then retreated out of the way—beside the torch, kindling a second from it—while Kari, who, sitting, was actually a little shorter than the svartalafar, said, "I am Kari Hrafnsbrother, of the Franangfordthreat. In the names of the smiths and mothers, I greet you." He was panting a little with pain, but Brokkolfr judged it a very respectable speech.

The second torch flared as Brokkolfr waved it, casting better light, and now he saw the svartalfar clearly. The closer and smaller also seemed to be lower-status, judging by the simpler embroidery on its robes. It came a step or two toward Kari, the hems of its layered garments sweeping the rock underfoot, and said something resonant and complex in a language Brokkolfr did not understand.

Kari blinked. And then, haltingly, he answered. Brokkolfr could tell by the pauses and stammering that Kari barely knew what he was saying, and knew even less how to say what he meant. But whatever he got out seemed to satisfy the alf. Brokkolfr brought the torches over and crouched down beside Kari.

The alf turned its head, the long twig-crooked nose showing the direction of its attention. Whatever it said, Brokkolfr could not have missed the tone of query. The larger one made a sound in return that sounded like agreement.

The first cleared its throat. "I . . . am the apprentice Realgar," it said. "The journeyman is Orpiment. We are in service to Mastersmith Antimony."

It hesitated, and Brokkolfr tried to remember if realgar was a metal or a mineral. A mineral, a poisonous one, he thought, one from which red pigment and arsenic could be derived. That would make the svartalf a male, if he understood the way they assigned their names. Or kennings, for maybe their names weren't something they shared with just anyone. That was how it was in the stories, anyway.

The alf cleared its—his—throat again. "What are you creatures doing here? Surface creatures do not come so deep."

Kari and Brokkolfr exchanged a look, and Brokkolfr didn't need the pack-sense to know Kari was as disconcerted as he was. "Exploring?" Kari said. "We didn't know . . . we didn't know any svartalfar had stayed. No one mentioned it."

"Stayed?" Realgar said, his eyebrows drawing together sharply. The other one, Orpiment, said something, and the two alfar began an unmistakable argument. Brokkolfr glanced at Kari, who shook his head. Whatever of the svartalfar language he'd managed to pick up, they'd already exhausted his knowledge.

"What did he ask you?" Brokkolfr whispered.

"I'm not exactly sure," Kari whispered back. "They pronounce things differently than Tin and the other svartalfar I met. But I know he was asking about weapons and whether we intended to fight them. I said no."

"Good," Brokkolfr said, and couldn't help adding, "You need to get out of those wet clothes." Shoulder to shoulder with Kari, he was almost being shaken by the allover tremors wracking the other man's body.

"You want me to strip right now?"

"Not ideally, no, but I don't want you to die. I'm a fisherman's fifth son. I know about cold water."

"It'll certainly persuade them we're not a threat," Kari grumbled, but he dragged his jerkin off over his head. Brokkolfr went to work on his boots, feeling gingerly around Kari's injured ankle. He pulled the laces out completely on that side, stretching the soaked, chilled leather wide.

Kari took a sharp breath but made no other complaint. "Sorry," Brokkolfr muttered. Even through the wool of the sock, he could feel the heat and tautness of the injured flesh. Immersion in icy water had tamed the swelling, and it would also have numbed the pain.

But that would not last.

"Do it," Kari said, and Brokkolfr gritted his teeth—his own teeth, as if what he was about to do could cause him pain—and pulled Kari's boot from his foot as smoothly and easily as he could.

"Ow," Kari said on a long exhale when he was done. Even in the torchlight, Kari's face shone pale through sweat.

"It's over," Brokkolfr said. "Maybe if I strap it up we can limp out of here." Making it worse. Making it more likely that Kari would be permanently crippled—

"Your companion," said Orpiment. "It's injured?"

"He is," Brokkolfr said, wary. He had hoped, he realized now, to pass through this encounter in Kari's shadow. It unsettled him to be required to make an accounting.

"He will heal," said Realgar. "But the cave ice he damaged was the result of centuries of growth. How will you make reparations to the cave for that?"

"Reparations to the . . . the cave?"

*The cave is alive? The cave is a living thing? The cave has . . . property rights?* Brokkolfr shook his head as if he could shake the confusion out of it.

"It can be healed," Orpiment said—to Realgar rather than to the wolfcarls, which made Brokkolfr wonder if the journeyman was taking their side.

Realgar glared at Orpiment. The alf's eyes sparked torchlight like gems secret in the caverns beneath his bushy brows. "A crude attempt could be made," he said. "But such shaping is never as intricate as the natural state of the stone."

"Hsst!" Orpiment said. He lapsed back into the alfish speech, as rapid as a drumbeat now, and after a few halfhearted protests Realgar looked chastened.

Kari nudged Brokkolfr, and Brokkolfr realized that he was staring. He dropped his eyes, glancing at his werthreatbrother instead. The expression on Kari's face wasn't censure, though—it was suppressed excitement, like the face of a man holding the throw of knucklebones. Brokkolfr tilted his head in a question; Kari, having skinned himself down to his breechclout, gave him a subtle little headshake as warning.

"I'll tell you later," he murmured. "I'm not sure—"

If he had been about to say more, it was interrupted. Orpiment's lean tree-limb of an arm reached out, spanning the space between them, and touched Brokkolfr lightly on the shoulder. Brokkolfr froze, feeling the long jeweled fingers like a skeleton hand, aware of how close those filigree-reinforced talons lay to his throat.

"You must come with us to the mastersmith," Orpiment said. "Antimony will know what to do with you."

"Take my shirt and vest," Brokkolfr said to Kari. He slithered out of them quickly and all at once, brushing the svartalf's hand aside, so the shirtsleeves still stuck through the holes in the jerkin. Kari took shirt and vest without a word and struggled into them.

Brokkolfr turned to Orpiment and said, "I need to bind my friend's ankle. And he cannot walk far."

"We shall carry him," Orpiment said. "Have no fear."

❧

Carry him they did, on a stretcher made from their staffs and Realgar's embroidered outer cloak or robe. Brokkolfr had never seen svartalf undergarments before. Under his mantle, Realgar's hunched body was clothed in a mud-colored shift of some fabric more sheer and smooth than lawn. It clung revealingly, leaving Brokkolfr uneasily assessing the power of the svartalf's haunches and thews, the sharp-angled lever arms of his joints. His torso swayed between his limbs with each step, as dwarfed by their strength as a frog's.

Brokkolfr knew that the svartalfar were terrible in war, for all they often looked like bundles of elaborately embroidered rags swaddled up around an awkward collection of sticks. But now, observing ropy muscle and forearms cabled as if with twisted wires of steel, the ease with which this hunched creature carried half the weight of a grown man through cramped tunnels, Brokkolfr found himself with a new appreciation of the svartalf as a dangerous animal.

Brokkolfr could tell when they entered a settled area by the lanterns along the walls and the jeweled and delicate carvings that began to sprout on every side, a garden of stone run riot. In a human house, those carvings would have been on wood and they might have been fantastical beasts or traceries of vine and fruit and flower. Here, though, what work had been done had been done with respect for the stone itself—polishing, opening, showing the layers with delicate incisions.

The floors had been leveled, the spaces opened, and the light the lanterns provided was amplified and reflected through the use of lenses and mirrors to an extent Brokkolfr had never imagined. He thought of the glass prisms in the decks of ships, to bring light below: this was to that as a palace was to a croft.

Bright, clean, warm, and beautiful—the alfden was nothing like a trellwarren, which calmed Brokkolfr's hammering heart a little. In fact, some breaths brought him the scent of familiar flowers and the wet warmth of growing things, leaving him wondering—did the svartalfar grow food underground? And if so, how did they go about it?

As Realgar and Orpiment carried Kari in, Brokkolfr also noticed that the few other svartalfar they encountered seemed to go out of their way to take no notice of the surface-dwellers suddenly in their midst. One or two stared, and the obvious guards at a great door drew aside, nodding—but no words were spoken and no questions raised. Remembering what Kari had said about the Iskryne alfar, the trell-queen, and granting of permission, Brokkolfr thought he understood. The other alfar would assume that either Realgar and Orpiment had permission for their actions or they were on their way to secure it. And so there would be no questions unless it turned out not to be so.

A tidy way to run a town. If everyone could be counted on not to take advantage.

Alfar, he concluded, were even less like men than he had always been told. He caught Kari's eye, wishing that like Amma he could simply reach into Kari's imagination and plant these ideas there. But Kari looked even more white-faced and drawn than before—Brokkolfr grimaced in sympathy as he imagined how the improvised litter and the uneven steps of the svartalfar were jolting Kari's ankle—and Brokkolfr glanced away.

At last, Orpiment turned off the seeming thoroughfare and—still carrying the front of Kari's stretcher—led the little party down a vaulted side-corridor. Brokkolfr wondered if the patterns in the stone were signage. He thought he glimpsed repeating motifs, but that could be artistry as easily as tavern signs. And if this was a *young* svartalf colony, new in the past year, he wondered what glories would populate an old, established one.

Although he was beginning to think that maybe this was not

such a new colony. What had the alfar said when Kari pleaded ignorance that they had remained behind?

Maybe they had been here all along, living under the feet of men, and men had never known it. If they grew food here, need they ever come to the surface? And he'd thought he and Kari had gone deeper into the caves than earlier explorers. Maybe there were svartalf warrens everywhere.

He thought about Isolfr and the fragility of the truce between elves and men, and he caught himself dry-swallowing. *Careful, Brokkolfr. This could end badly indeed.*

At last, they turned aside once more—three more svartalfar passed them in the interim, Brokkolfr burning up under the eyes of each one—and entered a tunnel the walls of which were inlaid with copper and silver between the flowstone. The flowstone itself Brokkolfr took as a sign that this passage was part of the natural caverns and not hewn from the living bedrock as so many of the others had been.

Also, the floor here was waterworn, and though many feet had since polished it, Brokkolfr could make out the eroded shapes of eddies and ripples. They proved a blessing: the descent was steep, and Brokkolfr, though perforce hunched by the low roof, used them to brace his boots against so he did not slide down and send both svartalfar and Kari tumbling. His toes jammed up into the ends of his boots, and he bit his lip to keep from swearing.

Orpiment glanced back over his shoulder. "Fear not, surface-dweller. We are nearly to my master's apartments."

"I'm sorry," Brokkolfr said. Cool air dried the sweat on his chest and back. The alf must have heard his labored breathing and interpreted it correctly. "I did not mean to complain."

The alfar were sure-footed, at least, and even managed to keep Kari's litter somewhat level. Kari himself seemed to have given himself up to pain. He lay back in his borrowed shirt, eyes half-closed, and pulled the slack edges of Realgar's robes over himself as best he could.

Brokkolfr's aching calves and toes—and the hunch of his back—were grateful when the descent ended.

If Orpiment and Realgar's master was a smith, there was here no stench of the forge or clatter of hammers. Instead, a trickle of water flowed down a petal-toned limestone abutment and the floor around it had been leveled with imported slates. The svartalfar paused with their burden, and Brokkolfr paused behind them.

"Mastersmith Antimony!" Orpiment called, after a glance from the apprentice. "It is Realgar and I! We have come to beg your advice."

Brokkolfr had not seen a door since the one that was guarded, and he did not see one now. Perhaps svartalfar simply did not go where they were not invited.

But the scrape of a foot and the swish of fabric came from within, and then around the edge of the flowstone came one of the more elaborately arrayed svartalfar Brokkolfr had ever seen. He had seen mastersmiths before, even Tin in her formal gowns, with her inlaid teeth and her embroidered robes that puddled on the floor all around her. But nothing like this.

Antimony—and now he could not for the life of him remember if antimony was a metal or a mineral, and of course there was no cue to wolfcarl eyes in an alf's face or body what its sex might be—wore ivory woolens that draped in folds like the very flowstone from arms that spanned wider than Brokkolfr's, though the alf scarcely reached his chest. Embroidery in shades of blue and rose and purple trimmed every fold, and around the hem, heavy fringes swung.

Antimony's hair was the same ivory color, looped in braids woven through with a tapestry of wire and jewels. Fingerstalls of some white metal clicked with each gesture, the alf's dark flesh visible through elaborate piercings and filigree.

*This,* Brokkolfr thought, *is what a wealthy old alf looks like. This is an alf-jarl for sure. And I'm standing in the foyer of a grand alf-house.* And Kari's harsh breathing told him it was no dream.

Antimony raised its wizened-apple face and frowned, the edges of a long mouth drawn down sharply between a ragged nose and a precipitous chin. "Well," it said in clear tones and perfectly understandable language. "What have we here?"

Whatever Brokkolfr might have answered was cut off by the patter of running feet—like half-grown kittens, he thought inanely—and the squeal of voices as a tumble of tiny svartalfar emerged from the chambers behind Antimony and sprawled across the foyer floor.

A moment, and he was able to distinguish: there were three of them, each no higher than his knee. Two were dressed in the same deep orangish-red; the third—slightly older?—wore dark blue. But a moment was all he had before Realgar and Orpiment flung themselves across the room, putting themselves bodily between the humans and the svartalf children. They had dropped the litter, and Brokkolfr's attempt to save Kari ended with them both on the floor in a tangle of elbows and knees and bruises.

"Ow," Kari said in a teeth-clenched whisper. He'd gone an ugly color; that "ow" was just barely instead of a scream.

"We have no wish to harm your children," Brokkolfr said with what dignity he could.

"No," said Master Antimony, "and I see that one of you is hurt. Realgar, Orpiment—" He or she—*she,* surely, for those had to be her children now clinging to her robes—dropped into the svartalfar's language, but Brokkolfr didn't need to understand the words to recognize a lecture when he heard it. He stayed where he was, letting Kari grip his hand hard enough to leave bruises, and waited. They couldn't escape, and at least Antimony didn't seem to be angry at *them.*

Then one of the little ones said defiantly and in speech Brokkolfr could understand, "But, Dama, you have guests." Brokkolfr guessed

Antimony's lecture must have widened in scope as it went. Lectures often did.

"Yes," Antimony said, "and this unseemly behavior is preventing me from tending to them as I should. Thallium, please try to keep Cinnabar and Alumine better disciplined."

"Yes, Master Antimony," said the blue-clad svartalf. Not Antimony's child, then—a servant or a fosterling? Watching the assured way Thallium held her hands out to the younger children, Brokkolfr guessed she was a fosterling. The two orange-red svartalfar—twins?—went reluctantly, both of them looking back at Brokkolfr and Kari as Thallium led them away.

"Now," said Antimony, "let us begin again." She held up one long knobbly finger, cutting off whatever Orpiment had been about to say. "I wish the surface creatures to tell me first."

Brokkolfr and Kari goggled at each other. Brokkolfr would have been much happier to let Kari do the talking, but Kari was still too pale and panting and in no shape to play leader. Brokkolfr thought about standing up, but if he did, he would be towering over the svartalfar—which first of all seemed rude, and second of all meant he wouldn't be able to see their faces. Thus he stayed where he was and said, "We were exploring."

Antimony's eyebrows went up, but she nodded for him to continue.

"We didn't know . . . I'm sorry, we had no idea you were here. We didn't mean to trespass."

Realgar said something explosively.

"Realgar says you broke the cave ice in—" A long phrase in the svartalfar language: the harmonics made Brokkolfr want to shake his head like a wolf coming out of the water.

"We didn't mean to do that, either," he said.

"Clearly," Antimony said. "If it had been your intent, you would have been more careful not to harm yourselves."

"Realgar," Kari croaked, stopped, cleared his throat. "Realgar said something about reparations."

"Yes," said Antimony. "Realgar, fetch—what do you surface creatures drink? I do not wish to poison you."

"Ale?" Brokkolfr said, trying frantically to remember what he'd seen the svartalfar drink when they were at Franangford.

Antimony seemed pleased. "We have ale. Realgar, fetch ale, and then I think you should go see if Sceadhugenga Baryta will come."

"But, Master Antimony—"

"It is foolish to discuss reparations until the extent of the debt is known," Antimony said. "I will have to go look at the damage, and in the meantime, the creature is suffering."

"Kari," Kari said. "My name is Kari Hrafnsbrother. And this is Brokkolfr Ammasbrother. We are wolfcarls of Franangford."

"Oh," Brokkolfr said, sharply reminded. "Kari, they're going to be looking for us soon, aren't they?"

"Um," said Kari. "I've lost track of time a little."

"And all Amma and Hrafn can tell them is that we went underground. Vethulf is going to skin me alive."

"No, he won't," Kari said, and his chill fingers closed around Brokkolfr's wrist in what was meant to be comfort.

# TEN

Shortly after first light, Amma burst among the chaos of Franangford's construction like a fox shattering a henhouse door. She jogged heavily, limping on one forepaw, her gravid belly swinging with the jounce of her trot. As she ran toward Viradechtis, Vethulf almost dropped the handles of the barrow he was pushing, remembering just in time that to do so would risk spilling a load of stone over Sokkolfr, who was pulling. Rather than breaking his werthreatbrother's feet, Vethulf set the lever end down carefully and then turned, ready to sprint to whatever assistance was needed.

Amma reached Viradechtis as Viradechtis was standing, still-drowsy, and threw herself at the konigenwolf's feet in supplication like a puppy. Kjaran was there, suddenly, hackles lifted but ears up, and through him Vethulf felt Amma's pleading.

A cool draught seemed to brush over Vethulf's skin, redolent of leaf mold and ancient water. It was Kjaran, relaying for Amma—Brokkolfr and Kari's scent fading, along with the scent of their torches, into that bottomless moistness and then the echoes of their footsteps fading, too. A long time passed. And then, through Hrafn and the pack-sense, Amma felt the echoes of Kari's pain.

"A cave?" Vethulf felt the blood rise through his face. "They went into a cave? Without telling anyone?"

Sokkolfr pushed the loose, sweat-drenched strands of hair off his forehead. "Hrafn waited at the cave."

The pounding of footsteps as Isolfr—lanky, breathing hard—arrived on the scene, the laces of one boot flopping dangerously with each stride. He was running hard enough that he leaned back to slow, arms spread wide like a big bird landing. He rocked to a stop beside Viradechtis and dropped to one knee. One hand in her ruff, he reached the other out to Amma.

Amma, rising to her feet, whined.

"We'll find him," Isolfr said. "Don't worry." He looked up at Vethulf; Vethulf nodded.

"We'll need ropes," he said. "Candles, torches." His mouth dried. They'd need—what would they need? Wolfcarls were not miners.

"Shovels," Sokkolfr said. "Picks. Water. Stretchers."

Vethulf was just turning to begin collecting supplies when something else echoed through the pack-sense—Ingrun in a panic as white as Amma's, reaching out in need across miles of forest to her konigen-wolf. The fear in it doubled Vethulf over, hands on his knees, gasping in referred nausea.

"Skjaldwulf," Vethulf said, the name twisting like a tapeworm in his gut, as Isolfr's ice-pale face went as white as the scar that crossed it.

"Mar," said Isolfr.

◈

Skjaldwulf woke cold and stiff, with Mar's tongue in his ear. That wasn't one of Mar's usual tricks, and when Skjaldwulf tried to push him away, he found his hands were tied behind him. He turned his head and retched, the world spinning. There was nothing in him to vomit except bitter yellow threads of bile, and the effort nearly split his head.

He'd seen men with cracked skulls live and die, and you could never tell which would be the case until a hand of days had passed. It was good news that he had awakened clearheaded, though bad that he had vomited.

*Awake?* Mar said anxiously, and Skjaldwulf could feel that his brother was hurt, pain in his ribs and skull, metal bars on his face, and something twisted choking-tight around his neck. That brought Skjaldwulf to grim alertness. It was full dark, though there was a dim red edge of light from a fire somewhere behind him. *I'm here, brother,* he said to Mar, and the heat of Mar's half-voiced whine washed over his face. *Where are we? What happened?*

Mar was experienced and deep-minded enough to give Skjaldwulf a coherent string of images: *Skjaldwulf slipping and falling hard; the foreign soldiers barking and howling at each other; Mar bounding forward to stand over Skjaldwulf's body, snarling at anyone who approached; the threat hiding in the trees, watching for an opening; the arrival of more foreign soldiers and another jarl, this one riding a long-legged horse rather than driving a cart. The threat doing the right thing and getting out of range,* and Skjaldwulf heaved a sigh of his own, grateful that they had not let themselves be snared with him. *The new jarl barking at the soldiers, a blinding pain in Mar's head, then being dragged by something raw-sharp around his neck, left cold and frightened beside his brother, who would not wake and would not wake.*

That was all Mar knew. Skjaldwulf was still bewildered; they had been taken prisoner, but why? Why capture them when killing them would have been easy and reasonable?

His eyes had adjusted to what little light there was; he could see the chain that bound his brother. It was obviously an improvised restraint, looped around Mar's neck and then around—Skjaldwulf squinted through darkness and blurry vision—a tree. If he'd had his hands free, he could have released Mar easily, but they were firmly tied, and he discovered when he tried to roll over that they were pegged to the ground, so that Mar could no more release him than he could release Mar. The foreign soldiers might not have encountered trellwolves and wolfcarls before, but they learned quickly and they were taking no chances. Skjaldwulf was surprised they'd left him and Mar together—surprised that, even if for some reason they did not want to kill their human prisoner, they'd left Mar alive.

Mar whined again, and a voice said from somewhere beyond Skjaldwulf's head, "Are you awake then, wolf-witch?"

It was a woman's voice. The words were heavily accented but understandable, except . . . "What did you call me?" Skjaldwulf twisted and craned and managed to get the speaker within his field of view, although as not much more than a blot of shadows. And the effort left his head throbbing blackly.

The blot shrugged. "The Rheans say you must be a witch to have command of such a monstrous wolf, and I do not argue with the Rheans."

Skjaldwulf's reflexive response was to protest that he did not *command* Mar; the idea was abhorrent. But it was also not the most important matter facing him. "Rheans?"

"The men wearing skirts. They name themselves for their goddess, Rhea Lupina."

"You aren't a Rhean?"

"Me?" A snort—almost a laugh. *Grief,* said Mar, naming the woman, as wolves did, by scent. *Grief and bitter herbs.* "I'm no Rhean, wolf-witch. I'm a Brython. At least, my mother was. My father was one of six Iskryners who raped her. When I was twelve, the

Iskryners raided again and she killed herself rather than fall into their hands."

Skjaldwulf had seen a few Brythoni and half-Brythoni thralls; they were a comely people, darker than Iskryne-men and finer-featured. He even knew a little of their mountainous homeland, learned when he was a skald's apprentice. Before Mar.

*Your wits are wandering, old man.* "What do these Rheans want with me?"

"They want you to tell them how to defeat your witchcraft. And don't tell them you're not a witch, Iskryner, because if they don't need you, they'll have no reason not to kill you. And they have seven reasons to want you dead, for you killed seven of their soldiers before you were brought down." She got up, a shadow against the firelight, and stood looking down at Skjaldwulf for a moment. "The Rheans burn witches," she said softly, and walked away.

⁊

Skjaldwulf and Mar huddled together as best they could for the rest of the night. Skjaldwulf slept patchily. At dawn, the Brython returned with two Rhean soldiers. They freed Skjaldwulf's hands and hauled him to his feet. One said something, jabbing a finger forcefully at Mar, and the Brython said, "Your wolf companion stays here. If you try to escape, they will kill it."

Skjaldwulf flexed his hands, wincing at the burn of returning feeling. "If I cooperate, will you loosen the chain? It hurts him."

The Brython's eyebrows shot up, but she turned to the soldiers, and Skjaldwulf could only assume she relayed the request. Certainly, it touched off quite an argument, and Skjaldwulf took the opportunity to observe the Brython and the Rheans without being observed in return.

The Rheans were tall, strong men, with muscles corded in their bare forearms and calves. They had dark hair, cut very short, and sallow-toned, sun-weathered skin. Both of them had scars on their hands and arms; one of them had a scar slanting across his face and the other had a nose that had been broken too many times.

The Brython was younger than she sounded—Vethulf's age, or maybe even as young as Isolfr. She was fair-complexioned—not as pale as the men of the North, but she could pass for Freyvithr's kinswoman easily enough—with hair the color of an otter's pelt and hazel-green eyes. She was a full head shorter than either Skjaldwulf or the Rheans and as fine-boned as a bird. She was dressed in obvious Rhean castoffs, a piece of rope serving as a belt, her feet and lower legs wrapped in rags.

She turned, gesturing toward the prisoners, and Skjaldwulf's breath caught. The right side of her face was disfigured with a brand: a two-headed bird, narrow-skulled and broad-winged—the same device the Rheans displayed on their banners. The brand was crisp-edged, carefully placed, not, Skjaldwulf judged, very old.

"It's no different than cropping the hair of a thrall, Iskryner," the Brython said sharply. "They agree to see to your wolf's comfort, but you will stand surety. If he struggles or bites, they will kill you."

Skjaldwulf nodded. "I give my parole."

The Brython nodded—thoughtfully, as if Skjaldwulf's response was a clue to a riddle—and spoke to the Rheans. There was another, briefer round of argument, and then, very obviously, the Rheans gave up. Skjaldwulf wondered if this was how the men of the werthreat appeared to the wolves, at once transparent and completely incomprehensible.

One of the Rheans came around the edge of the clearing and set a sword-edge to Skjaldwulf's throat, reaching up somewhat to do it. *Steady,* he told Mar while the other looped a leather harness around Mar's chest and then ran a second chain before removing the first. Tufts of black fur came with it, and Skjaldwulf could see the wetness in Mar's coat where the links had worn at flesh enough to make it weep.

The wolf needed water as badly as Skjaldwulf did—he could go for days without food—but it'd be in Hel's court that Skjaldwulf would allow Mar to take anything from an enemy's hand.

When they were done, the Rheans flanked Skjaldwulf and the Brython said, "The tribune Iunarius wants to talk to you." Skjaldwulf hesitated, and the Brython said, "I promise, your wolf will not be harmed. Rheans are a methodical and conscientious people. They do what they promise."

And if they didn't, there was precious little Skjaldwulf could do about it. With the best reassurance to Mar he could give, he submitted, following the Brython across the Rhean camp, offering no provocation to the soldiers who stalked beside him.

It was a large camp, laid out in precise, equal squares, every line straight, every surface spotless. Nothing could be farther from the homey, efficient chaos of a wolfheall. Many soldiers paused to watch as Skjaldwulf was escorted past; he saw a mix of curiosity and hostility with more than a little fear, and he remembered the Brython had said the Rheans considered him a witch.

He said to the Brython, "May I know your name?"

"The Rheans call me Lutra. Otter, in your tongue."

Skjaldwulf noted the neatness with which she'd evaded revealing her true name. But Otter suited her—Skjaldwulf had made the comparison himself—and Skjaldwulf could understand her desire to protect what little of herself she still had.

"My name is Skjaldwulf, and my wolf-brother is Mar."

"Wolf-brother?" said Otter.

"Yes," Skjaldwulf said, meeting her quizzical glance steadily. "He is my brother."

Otter said something under her breath in her own language.

Skjaldwulf, remembering the one time he'd tried to visit his family after bonding with Mar, did not ask for a translation.

They came to a tent that Skjaldwulf had no difficulty in identifying as the jarl's. It was twice the size of the others, and there were soldiers standing guard at the entrance.

The soldiers all saluted each other, each pressing a fist to his heart, then extending his arm sharply. One of them poked his head in through the tent flap and said something in which Skjaldwulf thought he picked out the word "Lutra." An answer came too soft for Skjaldwulf to make out any characteristics, and then Skjaldwulf was being pushed into the tent.

There was a table, and seated behind it was a man with black skin. Not dusty-black as a svartalf, but a rich red-black like a dark bay horse. Skjaldwulf knew he was staring, but he had thought the svartalfar were that color because they lived in darkness. He had never imagined a man could be the color of aged leather.

The jarl was staring back. He asked a question in a soft, high-pitched voice, incongruous in a warrior. But Skjaldwulf's first wolf-jarl had had just such a voice, and a young and foolish Skjaldwulf had learned the hard way about making assumptions.

"He asks your name," Otter said. "And—this is difficult—your place? Your styling? Who you are beyond your name."

"Tell him I am Skjaldwulf Marsbrother, wolfjarl of Franangford, and I would have the same knowledge of him."

"Iskryner," Otter muttered warningly.

"Tell him," Skjaldwulf said. "I would know whose prisoner I am."

Otter hunched her shoulders defensively, but she spoke to the jarl and Skjaldwulf could pick out his own name and the word "Franangford." The jarl seemed momentarily startled, and then he smiled widely, revealing two teeth made of gold in his upper jaw. He stood and offered Skjaldwulf the Rheans' salute.

"His name is Caius Iunarius Aureus, commander of the Northern Expeditionary Force of Rhea Lupina, and he wishes to know, what is a wolfheall? Also, he invites you to sit. Call him Tribune Iunarius, Iskryner." Her tone did not change, but he knew that last sentence was advice.

Skjaldwulf took that invitation gratefully and nodded at Otter to show he heard and understood her advice. He was facing Caius Iunarius Aureus across the table. Otter stood beside him and translated for nearly two hours as Skjaldwulf tried to explain the wolf-heallan.

He was, he thought, partially successful. The jarl understood warriors living together, and he understood that trellwolves were formidable fighters. But Skjaldwulf could not make him understand the bond—possibly, he admitted wryly to himself, because he didn't understand it, either.

"But you are the leader of these . . . wolfcarls," Tribune Iunarius said (through the translator) at last. "Do you speak for them? Are you their captain or their konungur?"

"I am their jarl," Skjaldwulf said. "You could say captain. I am not a konungur, just the leader of a war-band." *One of two,* he thought, but that would only lead to more explanations.

"It is not your men who raid in Brython, is it?"

"There are men who raid in Brython," Skjaldwulf said. "They have not come from the wolfheallan. We have little leisure for such pastimes."

Otter stammered over what Iunarius said next, but a raised eyebrow from the man settled her. Through a tensed jaw, she translated, "The Brython lands are under our protection now, Iskryner. It would be easiest for your people if you, too, came under our protection."

Iunarius smiled while Otter spoke. His face, Skjaldwulf was pleased to note, did not blur overmuch, and the nausea was slowly fading. Not too bad a knock on the head, then. With luck, it would not kill him.

"Others have not found the Rhean yoke so onerous. We bring safety, protection. The benefits of trade and travel. My own people have served the empire for less than fifty years, and yet here you find me, a thousand leagues from the place of my father's birth, a tribune"—Otter stammered over the next word and in the end left it untranslated, but the context was clear enough—"in command of two cohorts of Brutus Augustus' legion. Someday I shall be a senator, if I am not made the governor of some province."

The sweep of Iunarius' hand left no doubt what province he might intend.

Skjaldwulf felt his lips thin. But here he was on familiar ground. Iunarius was boasting of his accomplishments like any viking, and Skjaldwulf was, well, skald enough to meet him on those terms.

"Do you fight trolls?" he asked.

Another word Otter had no translation for, and a word that drew a raised eyebrow from the tribune. "Trolls?"

"Earth-hollowers hight horrible," Skjaldwulf said, speaking slowly so Otter could keep up. "Knot-barked and root-clawed, wyvern-friend and foe of farmers. From the north they came, frenzied and frost-fell, tree-tall and broad as boulders, and long we battled."

Slowly, he reached down, and with the arm that still pulled his knotted collarbone when he raised it, he stripped his tunic up, over his head, and let it fall to the floor unimpeded. He stood, aware of all the eyes resting on him—those of the near-forgotten guards by the entrance as well as Iunarius' and Otter's—and spread his arms, turning slowly so there would be no mistake regarding his intentions.

It was a grand dramatic gesture, and Skjaldwulf, schooled in performance before he was ever schooled in war, could not have missed Iunarius' intake of breath. He, Skjaldwulf, did not need to look down to know what Iunarius saw. White scars ran bald and stark among the graying hair of Skjaldwulf's whip-lean chest and

back. The harrowed valley of a troll-axe graze that had gone un-
stitched too long to heal prettily marked him from rib to hip; an
inch more and it would have gutted him. The worst, though, were
the bulging knots of knitted bone that showed lumpy at his collar
and made the muscles of the left arm strange.

"We are not strangers to war," Skjaldwulf said softly. "We wolves
and we men. Do not think that a few shields and banners will daunt
us."

Skjaldwulf looked steadily at the Brython thrall as he spoke
those last words. Otter's cheeks colored and she looked down, but
she translated—as near as Skjaldwulf could tell from the words he
was learning to pick out of the stream of liquid syllables—without
flinching. When she was done, Iunarius nodded and steepled his
fingers, considering.

"You are a young man," Iunarius said, shocking Skjaldwulf to
startled laughter when Otter translated.

"I have thirty-six summers, Tribune."

"You are," Iunarius repeated, "a young man. How many years
would you give me?"

Skjaldwulf studied the other man's face. The cast of the features
was different from any to which he was accustomed—rounder, the
lips and nostrils fleshier, the nose broad and flat. But the only lines
on the tribune's face were at eye- and lip-corner, and if his skin did
not reflect the dewiness of youth, it had also not yet weathered into
leathery folds. There was some gray at the temples of the man's tight-
spiraled, close-cropped hair, but the majority of it was black as Mar.

"Thirty summers," Skjaldwulf hazarded.

Iunarius smiled, and there was that flash of gold again. "I have
twenty years on you, wolfjarl. You use your men up young in this
country." He paused, eyeing Skjaldwulf thoughtfully. "We honor
poets in the empire."

"Poets?" Skjaldwulf said.

"I may not understand your language, but I know poetry when I hear it. The protection of the empire need not mean merely an end to warfare—and do not judge the empire by the unlettered and superstitious men who serve in her armies. We have traditions of scholarship that stretch back thousands of years, to the first breaking of the world. A man could travel, speak to scholars of other lands, teach his poetry to other poets, and learn theirs. There is honor to be found in peace as well as in war."

In its way, it was not so different from the appeal Freyvithr had made, and Iunarius, like Freyvithr, was shrewd enough to see that Skjaldwulf could be tempted that way. Not all men could. But Freyvithr sought merely knowledge; Iunarius sought betrayal. And there was nothing he could offer that could stand against Isolfr and Vethulf—and Mar, waiting patiently and (for Skjaldwulf could feel him when he tried) panting through the ugly muzzle as the sun grew stronger.

Temptation was one thing, and everything Skjaldwulf had ever learned, as a skald's apprentice, as a wolfcarl, and as a wolfjarl, had shown him that all men faced it at one time or another. What Iunarius was trying to do was something else, and Skjaldwulf wanted no part of it.

"A man may find honor in many different ways," he said mildly.

Iunarius frowned, seeing that his arrow had missed its mark, though perhaps not seeing how. Then he smiled again, conceding defeat, and turned the conversation back to trellwolves and the bond.

But at the end, when he gestured to the guards to take Skjaldwulf out again, it was not without the sting of a parting shot.

"Truly, wolfjarl, you should consider my offer. You might live longer."

This time, when they led Skjaldwulf back to Mar, they fixed his hands before him with iron manacles. The sun had risen while Skjaldwulf consulted with Iunarius, and Mar lay in what little shade the tree still provided, his tongue lolling behind the bars of the muzzle, a guard with a spear just out of his reach. Skjaldwulf frowned. He was going to have to make a decision.

He turned to Otter. "Would you ask for water for my wolf?" *And for me.* But Mar came first. Otter had said the Rheans were honorable, and Skjaldwulf thought that if a female slave said so in a language her masters did not speak, it might indeed be true. Beside which, dying of thirst did not make one any less dead than dying of poison, and if the Rheans *were* honorable, then Mar need not die of either.

"You must need water as well," said Otter.

Skjaldwulf was trying not to think of the dryness of his mouth or the foul taste on his tongue. "If I do not ask for him, no one will," he said.

She spoke to the soldier on guard—a man with a square, dished face not unlike a shovel—who scowled and shook his head. Skjaldwulf was surprised when one of his escorts, the broken-nosed fellow, entered into the argument against his threatbrother. Finally, the first soldier snapped something, jabbing a finger at Otter.

Otter bowed her head and said to Skjaldwulf, "I will fetch water for you and your wolf."

The silence after she left was awkward, the Rhean soldiers eyeing Skjaldwulf sidelong. He wondered what they would have asked if they had been able to. He had a list of questions himself, worthy of a skald. But he was also aware that there was fear in the way they watched him. He had grown very tired of the word *veneficium*, witchcraft; it seemed to be the word the Rheans used for anything they didn't understand.

Otter returned, a bucket in one hand and a shallow pan in the other. She stopped in front of Skjaldwulf, looking doubtfully from him to Mar. "Is it safe to approach him?"

"He will not harm you," Skjaldwulf said, at the same time asking Mar to treat Otter as a . . . a werthreatsister? The thrall-women of the heallan had little to do with the wolves, and Skjaldwulf had never chosen a female lover; he'd never had to wonder about how Mar would react to a woman before.

*Cub,* said Mar, an odd echo of Viradechtis and also a promise.

Skjaldwulf had to admire Otter's courage. She did not hesitate any longer, but stepped forward to set the pan down where Mar could reach it, chained as he was. She poured water from the bucket into the pan, the muscles standing out on her thin arms, and then stepped back and offered the bucket to Skjaldwulf. Skjaldwulf raised it to his mouth even as Mar dipped his head toward the pan, drinking through the metal bars that caged his jaws; if they were to be poisoned, at least they would be poisoned together.

The water was cold and tasted fresh. Skjaldwulf drank deeply, aware of Mar's splashy lapping. The relief was almost painful to the parched meat and bone of Skjaldwulf's body, and he had to be careful lowering the bucket so that he did not drop it on his feet. He handed it back to Otter, who gave him a strange, very firm, little nod, as if they had sealed some sort of bargain.

The first guard snapped out another string of syllables, jabbing his finger first at Skjaldwulf, then at the tree Mar was chained to. It was clear he was giving orders and clear he expected them to be obeyed.

"Does he hold high rank among the Rheans?" Skjaldwulf asked Otter.

She almost laughed. "No. But if you don't want to be run through, you'd better sit down. And keep your hands where he can see them."

Skjaldwulf looked at his manacles, then at the leather and chain restraining Mar. "They did a better job than that," he said, sitting down with his back to the tree. Mar leaned over to rest his wet face on Skjaldwulf's thigh, the metal of the muzzle denting flesh. Skjaldwulf cared not.

"It's not that," Otter said. "Witches can work magic by playing the air like the strings of a harp. Iron is supposed to stop them, but I think Sixtus is doubtful."

"I'm not a witch," Skjaldwulf said wearily.

"So you say," Otter said. "But you talk to animals."

"I talk to Mar."

"Who is an animal."

"Who is my brother."

The guard—Sixtus—interrupted again, more angry nonsense.

"I'm not to conspire with you," Otter said with a shrug. "And I have other duties. If you need . . . well, ask for me. Remember, they call me Lutra."

"I remember," Skjaldwulf said. She gave him the Rhean salute and walked away. Judging by the expressions on the faces of all three Rhean soldiers, she wasn't supposed to do that, whether because she was Brython or because she was a woman or because he was a prisoner or perhaps some combination.

The two soldiers who had escorted him saluted the man on guard and departed. Skjaldwulf leaned back against the tree and closed his eyes, pleased that the darkness did not swoop in distressingly and that he knew even without the aid of his eyes where the ground was. Truly, he might survive this head wound, and the greatest honor to Othinn, he had been told once, was to put off your meeting with him so that you might bring the heads of more enemies to lay at his feet.

Skjaldwulf had not been resting long when a confused, excited commotion caused him to open his eyes again. A Rhean, drenched with sweat and breathing like a bellows, was standing in a knot of soldiers. He held something that looked like a very smooth, fat stick in his hand—a roll of parchment, Skjaldwulf realized. A message. And an urgent one. He watched as the man was escorted off in the direction of Tribune Iunarius' tent, and he listened to the ensuing, intensely orderly bustle until he watched a procession of soldiers walk past his tree, four abreast and all marching perfectly in step. Iunarius was with them, on the leggy horse Mar had remembered. Skjaldwulf realized he had no idea of how many men this camp held and therefore no idea what fraction of them this group repre-sented. He noted that they all looked very grim, although that was perhaps an effect of their helmets.

They marched out of sight, but Skjaldwulf did not close his eyes again. The atmosphere of the camp had changed; he wasn't sure whether he sensed it himself or Mar shared it with him, but it was impossible either to miss or to ignore. His guard got up and walked over to the cook fire, speaking to the men on duty there. Skjaldwulf watched with growing uneasiness as one of those men left, only to be replaced by two more. And the crowd kept increasing. The shovel-faced man was soon speaking like a jarl to his armsmen before a battle, and from the way he kept pointing at Skjaldwulf and Mar, Skjaldwulf was very much afraid he knew who the enemy was.

The broken-nosed soldier came and stood on the edge of the crowd for a while and then, frowning, walked across to Skjaldwulf. He said something with a rising inflection at the end—a question, but none of the tiny hoard of Rhean words Skjaldwulf had gathered applied.

"Lutra?" Skjaldwulf said.

The soldier looked doubtful and asked a question again. It might have been the same question, but Skjaldwulf could not be certain.

"Lutra," Skjaldwulf said as firmly as he could. He would have used his hands to show that he did not understand the soldier's words, but he remembered what Otter had said about witches.

The soldier nodded and strode away. Skjaldwulf could only sit and hope that it had been a nod of agreement, not a nod of, *Yes, this man is clearly a witch.*

Time crawled by. Mar's head was up. He was watching the growing crowd of soldiers intently, and every so often Skjaldwulf would feel an inaudible growl where Mar's rib cage was pressing against his leg. Shovel-face was getting louder, more confident. Surely, Skjaldwulf thought, the tribune had left some competent man in charge of the camp—to keep the defenses orderly, if nothing else. So where was he? This could not be the sort of thing the Rheans approved of in their perfectly maintained camp with its perfectly straight lines.

The broken-nosed soldier returned, Otter trotting at his side.

"What's going on?" Skjaldwulf said to her.

She blew out a disgusted breath. "Sixtus is trying to convince them to burn you."

"Because I'm a witch."

"One of the men you killed was his shieldmate. They'd served together since they were boys, and—"

The broken-nosed soldier interrupted her sharply. She listened, nodded, and said to Skjaldwulf, "Lucius says he does not think you are a witch. He thinks you are an honorable warrior. But he's worried that he's wrong." Her glance at Mar, most likely inadvertent, showed why.

"I swear on the life of my wolf I am not a witch," Skjaldwulf said. *"Non veneficium.* Did I say that right?"

"Not even close," Otter said, and she gave him a funny quirk of a grin, as if her face wasn't used to moving that way. But Lucius looked relieved, and he saluted Skjaldwulf with crisp, vigorous movements. He spoke at length to Otter and then left.

Otter sat down beside Skjaldwulf, where—he realized—his body would shield her from the crowd by the fire. "Lucius is going to get the centurion—the leader since the tribune's away."

"Why isn't the centurion here already?" Skjaldwulf would have been if there'd been this kind of clamor in his wolfheall.

"The centurion also served with Sixtus and his dead friend. They're twenty-year men, so the centurion is . . ." She muttered to herself. "I don't know how to say this in your language. The centurion is keeping himself very busy with something else so he won't notice what Sixtus is doing."

" 'Turning a blind eye,' we say."

"Thank you, yes. He is turning a blind eye. And he's trusting Sixtus to get this over with before the tribune comes back."

"Won't the tribune be very angry?"

"Yes, but too many of the men are scared of witches. The centurion can say things got out of hand before he could stop them, and with you dead, Tribune Iunarius won't have any reason to pursue it—and the Rheans are a very long way from home, Iskryner. The tribune knows he can't push frightened men very far."

"What can I do?" Skjaldwulf asked.

Otter touched the brand on her face. She glanced aside. Despite himself, Skjaldwulf found himself wondering if Isolfr would find her attractive. "Vanish, wolf-witch."

She shoved to her feet and walked away. Skjaldwulf almost raised his voice to call after her, but it would have drawn Rhean attention. And he suspected it would have been futile, anyway.

# eLeveN

haste though they would, night was all but falling before the threat assembled to the rescue. Vethulf was not overly concerned: night nor day would matter in a cave, the wolves were at home in the dark, and wolfcarls were accustomed to fighting in darkness. Trolls, after all, did not venture out in daylight.

Still, he did not expect to see the figure of a woman running flat out up the Franangfordtown road.

*Troubles come by tribes,* Vethulf thought as Thorlot the blacksmith's widow, who had come from Bravoll after her lover was killed at Othinnsaesc, hurtled toward them, her skirts kilted too high for decency, a puff of dust rising from the impact of each leather-shod foot. She breathed heavily, sweat soaking the collar of her shift and making half-moons in the underarms of her bodice, but she was still running strongly until the moment she drew up before Isolfr.

Vethulf knew she was acquainted with his wolfsprechend. They had served the Bravoll siege together. Why would the town send a woman to run with an urgent message? Unless it was personal business—

Whatever brought her, Kjaran shied from her scent. Iron-hot, he named her, and he did not think she should stink of sourness and terror. ·

"My lord wolfsprechend!" she cried as Isolfr reached out a hand to steady her. "Franangfordtown begs the assistance of the heall. We are under attack!"

Vethulf stepped close as Isolfr glanced to him.

"Attack?" Isolfr said.

"A great bear," she said. "And in daylight. We have seen it scavenging the middens for some days, but now it has staved in the wall of the bakery and killed the baker's son and a thrall. I ran—" She took a breath, bosom heaving over her bodice. "I ran, because the men are harrying it with torches and mastiff dogs. Hurry, I beg of you, my lord wolfsprechend."

"A great bear," Vethulf said. "White or brown?"

"Brown," she said, and Vethulf made the sign of Mjollnir with his right hand, in silent gratitude. The brown cave bears were larger than the white bears of the sea ice and the far north, but they were also far less vicious. Where the white bears would kill and devour any beast on two legs or four—or swimming—that they met, the brown did not by preference prey upon men, or meat in general. Still, if this one was raiding houses in high summer, something was terribly wrong.

If it had run mad—

Vethulf hooked his thumbs in his belt to still the shaking of his hands as he thought of a mad trellwolf, poisoned by a sick bear's bite. How would Skjaldwulf handle this?

"Isolfr," Vethulf said, "take half the threat."

Isolfr's hand went to the haft of his storied battle-axe.

Vethulf shook his head. "The smallest and most slender."

"Yes," Isolfr said. "Of course." He sighed, and Vethulf swallowed his irritation enough to hear the gratitude in it. Isolfr turned to Viradechtis and ran one hand between her ears and along her ruff.

"Go with Vethulf, sister," he said. "Your fight is there."

He looked up at Vethulf, ice-blue eyes unreadable, and let a smile's phantom shape his face. "The wolves go with you," he said.

"And the god of wolves go with you," Vethulf answered, then turned to call, "Spears! We will need spears!"

🟡

Vethulf jogged through the blue dusk with Thorlot back to Franangfordtown. Kjaran trotted on one side of him and Viradechtis on the other, where she sometimes brushed against Vethulf's thigh and sometimes against Thorlot's. Thorlot did not shy away from her, even resting her hand on Viradechtis' head for a moment, and Vethulf told himself first that it was not his business, and second not to be a jealous fool.

Doggedly he asked Thorlot questions about the bear instead of questions about Isolfr. But she could tell him little beyond what she had already said. There was a bear, a male she thought by the size, and it seemed entirely intent on raiding whatever food it could find.

A hunter's experience told Vethulf that the cave bears were largely eaters of plants, as their white brothers were eaters of flesh. It also told him that they would not scruple to dine on carrion and that they would hunt, in lean times or for the bones they crunched with gusto, which made their droppings white and crumbly. The peak of a big male's shoulders stood as high as Skjaldwulf, who was taller than either Vethulf or Isolfr, could reach with an upraised hand.

That same male's paw would wear finger-long claws, and span as wide as a carthorse's hoof.

Vethulf had observed cave bears many times. He had once seen a female of moderate size—with cubs to feed—break a reindeer's back at one blow. But he had never tried to kill one.

Still, it couldn't be worse than a troll. He devoutly hoped. And a trellspear should work on a bear as well.

Familiar terrain and the scent of smoke from cooking fires told Vethulf they were approaching the township, but he heard the shouts and the barking carried on the wind long before the walls of outlying houses came in sight. The wolfcarls redoubled their pace—running to battle now rather than saving their wind—and the wolves spread out between houses in a hunting fan.

Thorlot fell back as Vethulf sprinted forward, bending to put her hands to her knees, her service done.

The wolves howled. The wolfcarls shouted—perhaps to spook the bear, if they could, and certainly to let the beleaguered towns-men and the jarl's thanes know they were coming. Franangford-town's jarl, Roghvatr, had rallied his thanes and his war and hunting dogs. As Vethulf broke out into the square—Kjaran running on one side, Viradechtis as konigenwolf stretched out and leading the charge on the other, a cross-pieced trellspear jouncing before him—he heard the voices of women and children rise in a ragged cheer. The running thunder of a dozen wolfcarls' feet and those of twice as many wolves rattled the walls. Some of the spearmen turned at the sound, and they cheered, too.

Vethulf's first thought was that Thorlot had undersold the size of the bear.

The mastiffs were great heavy-jowled dogs, their faces droopy with an armor of hide and fur, some near as large as a small trellwolf. The thanes and their jarl were doughty warriors, broad-shouldered in their chain and furs.

The bear dwarfed all.

It was a great sloped boulder of a thing, and it was as shaggy as a boulder, too. It was bloody here and there from the boarspears of the jarl's thanes and the jaws of his mastiffs, standing at bay in the ruins of the bakery, protected on three sides by the standing walls, the roof half-collapsed across it. The high, humped back was draped with thatch and timbers; the head that swung below and before its awesome shoulders snarled to reveal bone-crushing teeth in a mouth that could have consumed Vethulf's head entire.

A mastiff—a dog of fifteen stone if it was an ounce—lay crushed under the bear's right paw, limp as a stomped rat. Behind the bear, Vethulf could see tumbled racks of loaves and the torn body of the baker's son, unless those rent white limbs belonged to the dead thrall. Before it, the dogs and thanes darted in and back, harrying the beast—as Thorlot had said—with fire and spears.

As Vethulf closed, the head of the trellspear bobbing with each stride, he saw the bear pin one of the boarspears to the ground and swipe at the thane who had held it. The thane danced back, swift and sure-footed, and for a moment Vethulf hoped the bear would be lured out of its shelter to follow. If they could get its flanks—

But no. It lunged once and then retreated again, shifting from paw to paw and groaning. From this closer vantage, Vethulf could see the crumbs in its fur and the angry glare of its eyes. He checked his stride as the Franangford jarl, Roghvatr, pulled back from the fight and turned toward him.

One benefit of the long campaign against the trolls was that wolf-less men now showed less fear of the trellwolves and more respect. Roghvatr, a grizzled, black-bearded man at least as old as Skjaldwulf, did not flinch in the slightest as Viradechtis and Kjaran drew up beside him. They faced the bear, and the jarl faced Vethulf.

"Well met, wolfjarl," Roghvatr said. He gestured over his shoulder. "I don't suppose you have any ideas?"

"Fire the roof," Vethulf said, realizing the flaw in his plan even as he uttered it. "But then we'd be fighting the bear and the fire." He hefted the spear in his hand. "I suppose you have tried arrows?"

"We haven't a bow that will do more than sting the beast," the jarl said. "I fear it's spears or nothing."

Vethulf humphed. "Spears it is, then. We'll drive it out to you."

To be honest, he was relieved to find something in which direct action might work. He was tired to the teeth of subtlety and nuance and politics.

*Brother,* he called in the pack-sense.

Kjaran's attention was clear and bright in him. Vethulf showed the wolf what he planned, and the wolf agreed.

*It will be dangerous,* Vethulf said.

*Battle is dangerous,* the wolf replied, or images to that effect. Vethulf turned over his shoulder. "I need a set of volunteers, wolf and man. The rest of you go with Viradechtis and join the thanes. We will drive the bear out to you."

Viradechtis gave him a look, her eyes cunning and bright. "You are the konigenwolf," Vethulf said, "the pack's life is in you." He only realized when Roghvatr hid a smile that anyone might find it strange for a man to converse with a wolf. Vethulf swallowed a flare of irritation at being made sport of. *At least I can be a distraction in troubled times.*

Viradechtis sighed and turned away, every line of her body saying, *You never let me have any fun at all.* When Vethulf looked away from her, Sokkolfr was there. "I'll do it," he said.

"Hroi is old," Vethulf cautioned. In truth, he wanted Kothran for this. Frithulf's ghost-colored brother was quick and small and sly; he would be at least risk in close quarters with the bear. But Frithulf and Kothran were off with Skjaldwulf and Mar—and Skjaldwulf and Mar, the pack-sense told him, were in terrible trouble.

He could not think about that now. And in truth, why did it

worry him so? If something happened to Skjaldwulf, that was one less rival in the threat.

Was it not?

Sokkolfr shook his head. "Herrolf went with the cave rescue team. I can work with Stigandr—"

Stigandr was fast, perhaps even faster than Kothran, if not as small and sly. From where Vethulf stood, he could see the leggy tawny wolf behind Sokkolfr, regarding him with eyes the same color as his coat. Vethulf opened his mouth to agree when Eyjolfr said, from the other side, "We'll do it."

Vethulf had to lift his chin to stare the bigger man in the eyes. Speaking of rivals, Eyjolfr and his big wolf Glaedir were first among them. It had been a surprise to everyone when Glaedir had chosen to follow Viradechtis, after all the bad blood caused by Eyjolfr's pursuit of Isolfr. But since the reformation of the Franangfordthreat, Eyjolfr had been better-behaved than Vethulf had imagined possible.

Perhaps he was a changed man. Perhaps he only needed to be valued to blossom into an ornament to the threat. Or perhaps he had merely been biding his time, awaiting just such a perfect opportunity for treachery. If something happened in the close confines of that tumbled bakery, who would ever know?

Vethulf did not like Eyjolfr Eagle-faced. But he still had to lead him. And to lead him, he must not be afraid.

"Better a wolf and man that know each other well," Vethulf said. "I'm sorry, Sokkolfr. Eyjolfr, check the lashings on your spear."

Another man might have stormed off—Vethulf himself most certainly would have. Sokkolfr, whom they called Stone, simply nodded. He was no older than Vethulf. Who was he to be so calm?

A jarl was meant to be foremost in battle, last in retreat—and doubly so a wolfjarl. Vethulf firmed his suddenly sweaty grip on the bindings of his trellspear and straightened his spine.

"No worse than fighting in a trellwarren," he said.

Eyjolfr surprised him with a smile. "Better," he said. "No trolls coming up behind you through solid stone. Come, soonest begun is first ended."

Eyjolfr and Vethulf separated and—each accompanied by his brother—went the long way around the other houses, out of sight of the bear. Each pair chose a place on one side of the gap, and Vethulf knew through the pack-sense when Eyjolfr and Glaedir had found theirs.

Viradechtis joined the thanes before the bakery, her wolves and wolfcarls around her, and the thanes broadened their formation to allow the wolves access. A dog or two snarled at a wolf, but the wolves replied only with cold indifference. The plan was all through the pack-sense, passed from wolf to wolf and wolf to man. Only the wolfless man had to be told in words.

When everyone was in position, Vethulf glanced down and let his left hand brush Kjaran's ruff. He felt Viradechtis' readiness, and Glaedir's.

*Go.*

Viradechtis and her threat lunged forward, men and wolves snarling, harrying, thrusting with spear-tips, and gliding out of reach again. Vethulf smelled sharp blood as wily old Hroi got his teeth in a bear-paw, just a slash and release. The bear roared, enraged, and surged forward. *Now!*

Vethulf dove around the corner, past the bear's flank, behind it. Into the destruction of the bakery, the blood-soaked bread, the rags that had been a man. Beside him, Kjaran, and then—though the wind of the bear's paw swept by his ear and shoulder—they were behind the beast, and Eyjolfr and Glaedir were there as well.

The big wolf laughed and lunged, but narrow-backed Kjaran was a hair faster. And Eyjolfr got his spear down—twisted around in the tight confines to level it—even as Vethulf pressed forward. All four at once, they struck the bear's unprotected haunches.

The bear sprang away, astonishingly fast for something so large, bellowing louder than the thunder of the mastiffs' voices. The men and wolves ran after, stumbling amid torn lath and wattle, tripping on crumbled mud plaster. Vethulf felt the shock up his hands and forearms as he struck the bear again. He realized they were in daylight, the bear surrounded by wolves, and men, and wolfless men, and dogs as fearless as the others. Sokkolfr was on Vethulf's flank, of a sudden, in the midst of a wave of snarling wolves. Then the bear was facing them, trying to rush back into the shelter of the bakery, and Vethulf set the base of his trellspear against earth and leaned into it with all the strength of his arms.

The impact of the bear's weight would have torn the spear from his grip, but other hands were beside his, broad shoulders, Sokkolfr and Eyjolfr supporting the spear against the charge. The bear came up the spear snarling, the point entering its chest and emerging behind its left leg, and Vethulf knew it could not survive this.

But it could survive it long enough to shred the puny humans who had killed it.

The spear's crosspiece cracked under the bear's charge, shattered and pushed back before it, doing nothing to hold its weight. The bear lunged again, teeth snapping just shy of the men who tormented it. One more push, Vethulf knew, and it would be on them. He felt Kjaran tense, ready to dive past him and into the range of the bear's teeth and claws. "No!" Vethulf yelled, in the pack-sense and aloud, knowing that Kjaran would not listen with Vethulf's own life at stake.

Viradechtis hit it from the side, twenty-plus stone of killing fury, her teeth a mouthful of daggers as she ripped through dense matted fur and into flesh. The bear, off-balance and impaled, toppled onto its opposite side and thrashed weakly, ripping the spear from the hands of the shouting men.

Vethulf hardly felt the sting. He staggered back, trying to find his feet, failing, and was only saved from dropping to his ass in the dust when he bumped into the remains of a leaning wall. He put his left arm out to support himself and only then realized that he was bleeding from his upper arm and shoulder.

"Ouch," Sokkolfr said, touching the slickness. The bear was still quivering. "Come on, I'll stitch that for you."

Vethulf turned to Eyjolfr. He extended his right hand. "Well fought."

Eyjolfr returned the clasp. "Bear for dinner tonight," he said with a grin.

Vethulf felt a returning pang of worry—for Brokkolfr and Kari, for Skjaldwulf and Mar—and could not force himself to return the smile. Coming up alongside the bear, Roghvatr shook his head and swore by the god of smiths. "What a mess," he said. "There's the widow and children to house and feed, the bakery to rebuild . . . And did you look at this thing? It's half-starved. In the height of summer. What's going on?"

⚬✿⚬

The sceadhugenga was much younger than Brokkolfr had expected, even granted that he had no idea how to judge the svartalfar's age. But Baryta was obviously younger than Antimony, possibly even younger than Orpiment, and Brokkolfr might have worried, except she had the most commanding presence of anyone he'd met, including Grimolfr Skaldsbrother, the wolfjarl of Nithogsfjoll. Every time she looked at him, he felt her glittering glance cut through him. He would not have dared to argue with her even if it had not become speedily apparent that she knew her work and knew it well.

She set Kari's ankle and gave him something that he said was like drinking flowers. It certainly returned the color to his face and stopped his shivering. Brokkolfr suspected it made him more than a little drunk, for he became remarkably tractable. Brokkolfr was glad of it, as he and Baryta manhandled Kari into a cupboard-bed, and Baryta said firmly, "Sleep, surface creature."

At that point, Kari would have been hard-pressed to do anything else.

Baryta led Brokkolfr away from Kari's bed—a real bed, not merely a pallet. Brokkolfr could not fault svartalfar hospitality, though he feared again there would be a price. They passed more fluted stone, carved with such delicacy that Brokkolfr imagined the tools must be as fine as wires. How did the svartalfar smiths make them so fine and yet strong enough to carve stone?

He tried to remember if Kari had mentioned any such carvings in the svartalfar cities of the North and could not. The only work Brokkolfr had ever seen of such intricacy was in the trellwarrens that undermined all Othinnsaesc.

He swallowed against the chill in his gut. This was not a trellwarren, and where that stone had flowed as this did, the designs had no comparison. A trellwarren was disturbing, nauseating, full of head-splitting asymmetries. *This* was as restful as any herb garden.

Baryta led him to an antechamber whose floor, sloped like a shallow bowl, was padded with elaborate carpets and tassled cushions. They were rich and soft enough for a jarl, but years and use had dulled the colors and worn the embroidery smooth. *Not a new settlement,* Brokkolfr noted, and wondered.

The svartalf settled among the cushions. At her gesture Brokkolfr, too, sank down gratefully. He had not realized it until now, but his limbs ached with weariness and the aftermath of struggle and fear. He sighed and let his back curve into the cushions.

"Your friend will do well," Baryta said, "though he will be lame for some months. The break was a clean one and did not involve any of the *difficult* bones."

Of course, what the sceadhugenga considered relatively simple might have been beyond the skills of the wolfheall's best bone-setters. Brokkolfr had seen men—fishermen and wolfcarls both—permanently lamed by broken ankles, even if the flesh rot did not set in and kill them. Kari was blessedly lucky that the svartalfar had decided to help him, and Brokkolfr, as his friend, felt that blessing deep in his own chest. "Thank you," he said, and was not surprised that his voice wavered.

Baryta turned a bright inquiring eye on Brokkolfr. "And you? Are you hurt?"

"No," Brokkolfr said. "Thank you."

She shook her head. "I am in Antimony's debt. Thank him for choosing this way to," and she used a svartalf word, with the harmonics that made Brokkolfr's teeth ache.

But his attention had been caught by something else. "Him? I thought . . . I beg your pardon."

Baryta raised her eyebrows. "Antimony is a male. Why does this surprise you?"

"I thought . . . Antimony is a metal, isn't it? And the svartalfar I have seen—women are high-ranking, are they not?"

Baryta exhaled a long breath, almost like the snort of a horse. "It is a complicated question that you ask, surface creature."

"You don't have to answer," Brokkolfr said.

She cocked her head, the crystals in her long braided sideburns catching the light. "But curiosity is the mark of," another svartalf word, which she translated, "those who are awake. And if you are awake, then I may make a bargain with you."

"There are stories about svartalf bargains," Brokkolfr said uneasily, and Baryta crowed with laughter.

"So there are, surface-creature-who-wakes. But I have in mind only information. For I, too, wake, and I am curious. So we will trade questions. I will ask first, so that if you do not wish to answer, you will not be left owing me."

"Should I not be speaking to Mastersmith Antimony?"

"Antimony has gone to view the destruction you have wrought, and will not be back for some time. He does not move as swiftly as once he did. But fear not. I will not cause your debt with Antimony to mount."

Brokkolfr hesitated, a hundred stories telling him he was being a fool. But Baryta seemed scrupulous, and one thing he knew from having seen the svartalfar and men speaking to each other during and after the trellwar: along with information, one could also trade goodwill.

"All right," he said. "What question would you ask?"

"You have met svartalfar before." She smiled, showing inlaid teeth almost as elaborate as those of Isolfr's friend Tin. "How is this so? We are a secretive people."

Brokkkolfr paused, marshaling his thoughts. "We would never have entered the caves if we had understood they were the home of a clan of svartalfar. We had no idea you were here."

He remembered Realgar's reaction when Kari had let slip the comment about svartalfar staying, and frowned, wondering again: was it possible that this alf-clan had been here all along, secreted in the deep caverns, burrowed in away from the surface and the sun— and no one had ever known? If so, just how greivous an offense was this trespass? He also remembered what he knew of svartalfar from watching Tin and her allies during the war. He knew that they had held a special honor for Viradechtis.

"My wolfsprechend—one of the leaders of my threat, a man bonded to a konigenwolf—"

"A Queen Wolf!"

Brokkolfr nodded. So that was not different. Did this count as Baryta's second question, or would that seem ungenerous? "He is her brother, as I am Amma's brother."

Baryta's face furrowed, and Brokkolfr imagined his own expression often looked the same, as he attempted to ferret out the hidden complexities of her words. She said, "Your wolf is a she."

"My sister is a she," Brokkolfr said. "But not a konigenwolf."

Baryta nodded. "Continue, please."

"Isolfr, my wolfsprechend, is a hero of the svartalfar of the Iskryne. He and his sister, and their allies, including my friend"—had he any right to call Kari friend?—"and a smith named Tin slew a trellqueen in a warren the Iskryne clans wished to appropriate. In return for this service, the Iskryne clans agreed to come to our defense against the trolls who were migrating south and attacking our towns."

Baryta opened her eyes wide over the crooked twig of her nose. "The Iskryne clans have come south!"

"Well, it was the svartalfar driving the trolls out," he said. "They needed the room. It was only fair they help deal with the problem." She grimaced at something in what he said but gestured for him to continue.

"We thought when we first encountered Orpiment and Realgar that they must have stayed behind when Tin and her people returned north."

"Hmm." She nodded. "That is a good and fair answer. And you have given more than promised."

From what Isolfr and Frithulf had taught the werthreat about svartalfar, Brokkolfr remembered that the race of smiths cherished generosity as highly as any thane or wolfcarl cherished valor.

"Ask your question, Ammasbrother," Baryta said.

"Antimony," he began, and then hesitated. "But it's not just about Antimony. I know your councils are made up of smiths and mothers; I have heard Tin say so. As our councils are made of warriors."

"It is so," Baryta said. "But that is not much of a question, if you know the answer. You would leave me in your debt."

"I guess my question is, then, what is Antimony?"

That sparkle of her inlaid teeth again. "Antimony is a smith. A mastersmith, in point of fact, and one of our eldest. But he is also by-honor a mother, as he has adopted children in need and is raising them as his own. He is one of our most honored elders."

Baryta had felt free to ask ancillary questions, so Brokkolfr did not stop himself. "By-honor?"

The sceadhugenga used one of those windy, harmonic svartalfar words. "*Andetnessa*. By-honor," she said. "*Andetnessa ne-sooth.* By-honor-if-not-in-fact. A matter of perceived reality in contrast to objective, in a positive context. He performs the service and offers the sacrifice of a mother, so he has the honor of one."

"Can one be anything by-honor?"

She did something that might have been a shrug but—under the drape of her layers of robes—more resembled a bullfrog inflating and deflating itself. "One can only become a smith by skill," she said. "Of course, skill is earned, like honor. But it sounds as if your wolfsprechend has become a svartalf by-honor, through his service to . . . to the Iskryne clans."

There was something funny in how she said "Iskryne," and Brokkolfr didn't think he was imagining it. Discomfort, veiled anger. These emotions looked and sounded different on a svartalf, but they weren't unreadable. Just different.

"Your question," he said.

"You are male."

That wasn't a question. "Yes."

"And your companion is male."

"Yes."

"Does your kind have females?"

Brokkolfr gaped at her for a moment. "Yes, of course."

"There is no *of course* about it," she said. "Trolls have no males, save those who breed their queens. I thought perhaps you creatures were the same way, but in reverse."

She had thought no such thing; he saw it in the creases around her eyes as they deepened.

He wasn't quite sure how to accuse a svartalf of teasing him; it seemed better simply to answer her question. "Our women are not as powerful as yours," Brokkolfr said, "but we certainly have them. In fact, there is a woman in the town near my heall who is a smith. She is a widow, and widows sometimes stand in their husbands' stead."

"Huh," said Baryta. "But not a mastersmith."

"We do not have mastersmiths as you do, even as we do not have sceadhugengas." He stumbled slightly over her title, but she seemed pleased that he had made the effort.

She said, "Your question."

A sensible man would have asked through trickery or kept his own counsel and learned by observing. But Brokkolfr was very tired of being sensible. "Are your people the enemy of the Iskryne clans?"

It drew her up short. The silver-shod butt of her staff scratched on the stone between cushions and carpets.

"Rather," she said, "the Iskryne clans hold us in enmity. These caverns are our exile, for practices the old ones found to be anathema. It is why we call ourselves aettrynalfar—poison elves—in commemoration and defiance." A pause, in which the sceadhugenga made a sound like *humph*. "And now you come from the surface, with news that the Iskryne-folk have begun inhabiting and reworking the very trellwarrens that we were once persecuted for seeking to understand? They will spurn our smithcraft, and yet inhabit the dungheaps of trolls?"

Brokkolfr had heard svartalfar raise their voices to cry across a battlefield or be heard in open council. He had never heard the words of one shake with rage before. He drew a breath and thought about how Skjaldwulf would handle this.

Fortified with the semblance of calm, he said, "I have a feeling there's something here I do not understand."

She spoke with the same sort of brittle pride he had heard from wolfcarls whose families disapproved of their lives. "We practice forbidden arts here. Did you not observe?"

"No," Brokkolfr said. "I am ignorant in this as well."

That hushed her. Momentarily at least. She cocked her head left-and-right and said, "The stone shaping, wolfcarl. The beauties of our lair. You have noticed?"

How could he not? He nodded, thinking of airy stone, filigree, chrysoprase roses that shone with a light of their own.

"It is a trellish art, and some would say unclean."

It . . . staggered him. Not that svartalfar had politics—he knew that—but that they had *these* politics. These divisions. These excuses for conflict.

"Who does it harm?" he asked.

This time, the sound her gnarled stone staff made was an intentional sharp rap, and the tiny bells along its length jingled sweetly.

"The soul of the stone? So say our northern cousins. Our ancestors believed that the art of shaping stone with the hands was worth learning." She shrugged. "Of course, they also forswore warfare and murder."

He wasn't sure he understood her. "Your people are sworn not to . . . ?"

"To kill," Baryta said. "The mother of our mothers, the master-smith Hepatizon, who named herself Vaidurya when her sisters cast her out, taught that each death remained in an alf's song, making her darker and weaker. She taught that it was killing that was poison, not the working of trolls, that if we believe the world is the song of the First Mother, then how can we say we have the right to silence so much as a note of it? We follow her teachings. We hide; we do not kill. And now you and your threatbrother have found our hiding place. . . ."

Her openness bothered Brokkolfr. If she had never met an outsider—which was seeming more and more likely—she might be frighteningly naïve. "Should you tell a potential enemy that?"

"I would not." Her voice ran cool and deep with certainty. She spoke as sceadhugenga now, he realized, and not as Baryta. The shift in roles was as astounding as when Vethulf put aside his snappish, temperamental exterior and became a man in command of a war-band. "But you are no enemy of mine, Ammasbrother. Nor, I think, shall you ever be."

⚭

The first Brokkolfr knew of the rescue party was somewhat past suppertime—he assumed it was suppertime—when Isolfr appeared. Or rather, was waiting for Brokkolfr in the company of Mastersmith Antimony, when Realgar guided him and Kari—awake again, and hobbling on stone crutches as light as if they were withywoven—into a room arrayed for dining.

The wolfsprechend seemed hale and hearty, if a little smirched about the knees and elbows, and he rose from a stone bench by the wall—one that might serve as a sideboard for a svartalf—to greet the prodigals.

"Amma is beside herself," he said.

Brokkolfr did not wince only because he had expected nothing less. "We did not plan to be gone more than a few handspans of sun."

Isolfr smiled in sympathy. "Next time you're falling into a hole in the ground, send a message home. Mastersmith Antimony informs me there has been some damage."

Brokkolfr's face chilled as the blood fell out of it. "I will make it good."

Kari made a noise of protest. "I was the one who fell through the cave ice."

"The heall will make it good," Isolfr said firmly. He glanced from Brokkolfr to Antimony and Realgar. "It may yet serve us to owe them a debt."

Antimony laughed. "Isolfr Alf-friend," he said. "It may also cause you untold trouble. Here comes Orpiment with the children now. Come, dine with us. We have much to discuss."

Brokkolfr wondered how Antimony had known Isolfr's status. Did these exiles, these aettrynalfar, still have contact with their brethren? He would have to tell Isolfr what Baryta had revealed regarding this clan's outcast status. But perhaps in front of the mastersmith and his family was not the correct time.

Brokkolfr kept his counsel close and sat where instructed. There were no benches, although the young alfar had blocks to crouch on. The table was no more than knee-height on a man, and the aettrynalfar ate squatting in their typical resting huddle. Brokkolfr and Isolfr had to help Kari sit on the floor, but once that was accomplished the arrangement was quite comfortable.

"Did no other wolfcarls come with you?" Brokkolfr whispered.

"I have more sense than to go haring off alone," Isolfr said.

"Barely," Kari muttered, and Brokkolfr was surprised and delighted when Isolfr laughed.

"True enough. But, yes, there are half a handful of other wolfcarls—they are dining with the . . ." He looked at Antimony, who supplied, "The quarrymaster."

"Yes," said Isolfr, "thank you. The quarrymaster and her masons. We could not spare more men, as there was a cave bear attacking Franangfordtown."

Kari and Brokkolfr both stared at him. "I assure you," Isolfr said, "I haven't the imagination to make up such a thing, even to make you feel guilty."

"We have guilt enough," Brokkolfr said.

"We will speak of that later," Antimony said. "Not during dinner. Now, please, allow me to make known to you my children."

There were five of them, the three Brokkolfr and Kari had seen earlier—Thallium, Cinnabar, and Alumine—and two more: Osmium, who was even smaller than Cinnabar and Alumine; and Pitchblende, who was almost old enough to be apprenticed. Pitchblende called Antimony "Mastersmith," as Thallium, Realgar, and Orpiment did, while Osmium, Cinnabar, and Alumine called him "Dama." Perhaps the form of address was a matter of age rather than kinship? The children were confident and well-mannered; all of them seemed to speak the language of men, and Brokkolfr finally succumbed to his curiosity and asked why.

Antimony's winging eyebrows shot up. "I see Baryta was correct."

"Correct about what?" Isolfr asked.

"She told me that your people were awake, even if you could not sing, and I see that it is true." Antimony took a sip of wine from a stone goblet so delicately made that it was translucent. "We are taught that in the days when the world was young and the World-Tree but a sapling, there was only one language, and alfar, men, trolls, Jotun—all spoke it. My grandmother's mother said that it was the language spoken by the gods and it was they who taught it to the creatures of Midgard, but I have never heard anyone else say that, and I do not know from whom she learned it. We believe that our language is close to that language, but even the svartalfar could not keep everything, as first the Jotun, then the trolls, then the men turned against us. Some of our oldest writing, we think, may be close.

"But as each race turned to war, their language changed and was lessened. The trolls lost language altogether, as in the dreaming of the mother-mind they did not need speech. And the Jotun, it is said, now speak so slowly that it might take a svartalf her entire life to learn one name. But men are the youngest race, and the last to taste the fire, and their language is still close-kin to ours. We learn it because it is our nature and our task to hold knowledge, lest it be lost as the language of trolls has been lost."

Beside Brokkolfr, Isolfr shifted uneasily but did not speak.

"At least," said Antimony, "that is the story as I was taught it."

Orpiment said, "I was taught that it was the svartalfar who taught language to men, and when they could not teach them to sing, they banished them to the skin of the world."

There was no hostility in his voice—he didn't sound as if it was something he believed, and Brokkolfr listened as all the alfar at the table became embroiled in a discussion of myths and children's tales and variants. He understood why Antimony had said it was their nature to hold knowledge.

Kari said, just loud enough for Brokkolfr and Isolfr to hear, "Skjaldwulf would love this," and Brokkolfr was reminded that it wasn't alf nature alone. Men could hold knowledge, too.

The aettrynalf food was strange; there was something that tasted like beef but did not have the texture of meat, small crunchy things that Brokkolfr could not identify, and a profusion of root vegetables, some of which he recognized and some of which he did not. All of it was good, and since Isolfr ate without any noticeable concern, Brokkolfr decided he probably didn't have to worry about being poisoned by accident. Antimony calmly and patiently refused to discuss the cave ice until the last dish had been cleared off the table by Realgar and Pitchblende—the oldest of Antimony's children and the youngest of his students—and then the mastersmith rolled his knobbled shoulders and said, "And now we must speak of the business between us."

Everyone sat up straighter and tried to look attentive.

"If it will not distress you," Antimony said, "I would wish for my children to stay—so long as they are quiet and respectful," and he offered a glare at the twins, who nodded solemnly. "We would not have sought out contact between our peoples, but since it has occurred, it seems to me foolish and useless to try to retreat. Better that my children should learn to speak with you now."

"I concur," said Isolfr, "and I do not think we will be distressed." He glanced at Brokkolfr and Kari, who both shook their heads.

"Then, Orpiment, if you will please ask the sceadhugenga and the mastersmiths to come."

Orpiment left, and Antimony said, "Although we do not have a council as our cousins of the North do, we have agreed that any important decisions about the"—a buzzing, echoing svartalf word, which Antimony translated, "the life of the cave"—"must be deliberated by a quorum of three mastersmiths, with the sceadhugenga to speak for the lives of the creatures, alf and otherwise. Baryta undertook to host the mastersmiths and to explain what has occurred."

Brokkolfr swallowed hard, and Isolfr patted his thigh, exactly the same tactile reassurance either of them would have offered to his sister. "They understand what an accident is, Brokkolfr."

"All too well," Antimony said wryly, and began to tell a complicated story about something that had happened when he was an apprentice. Brokkolfr couldn't follow most of it, but from Realgar's and Pitchblende's expressions, whatever Antimony had done had been truly spectacular. Brokkolfr knotted his fingers together and told himself not to worry.

Antimony's story was almost finished when Orpiment reappeared and bowed in Baryta and the mastersmiths. Brokkolfr was deeply grateful he'd met Baryta already and was able to recognize the smile around her eyes when she looked at him. The mastersmiths were indistinguishable from Antimony to Brokkolfr's eyes; he never did get their names and was reduced to thinking of them as Bark and Bubble for the way each of them spoke.

They asked Kari and Brokkolfr to tell their story again and asked a number of searching questions, most of which were uncomfortable but at least one of which Brokkolfr was grateful for: Bark asked if either of them had ever seen cave ice before.

"No," Brokkolfr said, and Kari added, "We'd no idea stone could do that."

"It is a marvelous thing," Bubble agreed.

"Now destroyed," Bark said dourly.

"But—Antimony, I have the most fabulous idea! Since the cave ice is broken *anyway*, why should we not—," and she dropped into svartalf, with a long word that was all warble and buzz to Brokkolfr's ears but made Antimony's eyebrows shoot up. The three mastersmiths huddled into a conversation that made no sense to Brokkolfr at all, despite the fact that he could understand or guess at more than half the words. But it didn't look like Orpiment and Realgar were having any better luck. Bark seemed to disapprove of Bubble's idea—unless that look was just habitual—but Antimony was visibly intrigued.

After a fair span of time, when the discussion had neither ended nor even slowed, Baryta cleared her throat and said, "Mastersmiths?"

"Right," said Bubble. "The judgment." Her little twinkling eyes surveyed Brokkolfr and Kari. "You are to be commended for not allowing your corpses to poison the water."

"We may not know about cave ice," Kari said stoutly, "but we do know about water ice."

"That's true," said Bubble, suddenly intent.

There was another, much quicker round of discussion between the mastersmiths while Kari and Brokkolfr exchanged bewildered glances behind Isolfr, and then Bark said, "Very well. It does answer the question of reparations. Wolfsprechend, we ask from your heall that as you have broken the cave ice in"—that svartalf word that Brokkolfr couldn't make sense of—"so will you aid us in a new shaping there. For while we cannot restore what has been destroyed, we can recognize the opportunity of making something entirely new."

"And marvelous," said Bubble, and was not at all subdued by Bark's withering glare.

◦❖◦

In the morning, they returned to the surface of the world, Kari supported by his crutches or—frequently—Brokkolfr. It was not easy going: the tunnels were meant for svartalfar, not for men; they were low, and they twisted with the natural patterns of the rock. But Kari did not complain and only once suggested that they would have been smarter to leave him with Antimony.

"I would have had to explain to Hrafn," Brokkolfr said, and that was all the reassurance Kari needed.

Isolfr had bargained cautiously and hard with the aettrynalfar, but Brokkolfr thought he was pleased to have the heall involved in this shaping. They had shared a bed that night, and Brokkolfr had told him what Baryta had said. "We will be careful," Isolfr said. "But for all that Tin is my friend, this is an opportunity to share, to learn, that her people would never have offered us. And in truth, if we have neighbors who are both delvers *and* shapers, I had rather be on good terms with them than otherwise."

Brokkolfr remembered the way troll ambushes came from beneath one's feet and agreed fervently.

The aettrynalfar took them out a different way—which was a mercy, as neither Kari nor Brokkolfr thought Kari would be able to wriggle out the way they had come in. Brokkolfr knew they were getting close to the surface when Amma suddenly burst into his head, a wild wash of anxiety, love, and loneliness.

*I am sorry, sister,* Brokkolfr said to her. *I never meant to be apart from you for so long.*

Her forgiveness was immediate and as wholehearted as her worry had been. Beside him, Kari exhaled a soft laugh. "Hrafn says I am to leave holes in the ground to rabbits."

"Hrafn may have a point," Brokkolfr said.

"It's not the holes that are the problem," Kari said. "It's breaking my ankle once I'm down there."

"Yes," Isolfr said in his soft voice. "The entire heall begs you will not make a habit of that."

"No fear," said Kari. "If I never fall through solid rock again, it will be too soon."

"Is that what it was like?" Isolfr asked.

"It was *rock*," Brokkolfr said. "Until it wasn't."

The aettrynalf leading them—one of the masons who had hosted the rest of the rescue party while Isolfr dickered with the mastersmiths—said, "Truly, it is a mistake anyone can make. It is why it is the duty of the smiths' journeymen to explore the caves beyond our settlement, and why they must teach the caves to the apprentices before they may attempt their masterwork. So that there will always be someone among us who knows where the cave ice is. Along with other hazards."

"Are there many?" Kari said. "Other hazards, I mean?"

The inlay on her teeth flashed in the torchlight when she grinned. "Oh yes. There are holes we do not know the bottoms of, rooms with unstable ceilings, passages that look safe until you are too far along them to back out again, hot pools that will scald you to death if you fall in. Plus bear dens, bat roosts . . . and the grendle, of course."

"The grendle?" Brokkolfr said. He was beginning to get a feel for when an alf was teasing.

"The monster who eats aettrynalf kits who go exploring where they are not supposed to," she said straight-faced. "It is a wonder she did not eat you."

"Perhaps she thought we'd taste bad," Kari said, just as straight-faced, and was rewarded by a chuffing laugh.

The exit the aettrynalfar led them to was every bit as well-concealed as the one Kari had shown Brokkolfr, a slit between two boulders so narrow that you could not see it unless you stood directly in front of it. There was barely enough room for the men to squeeze out sideways, and Brokkolfr was glad Isolfr hadn't brought any of the more hulking members of the werthreat. Of course, he remembered, they would have been needed for the cave bear.

There was a delegation of wolves waiting: Amma, Hrafn, Viradechtis, and the other wolves whose brothers had made up the rescue party, plus Kjaran, sitting by Viradechtis and looking politely interested as the men emerged from the earth.

Brokkolfr knelt to hug Amma, knowing that she would try to stand up to reach his face if he did not, and she was much too pregnant for that maneuver. He missed the other reunions, his face buried in Amma's ruff while she licked his ear and neck, but finally Isolfr cleared his throat and said, "Vethulf is back at the heall. He was hurt in the fight with the bear, although Kjaran says not badly."

Brokkolfr stood, brushing flecks of dead leaves off his knees. "Yes. We should go."

There was no sign of the aettrynalfar, but Isolfr said clearly, "We will come to treat with you again in a sevenday. And . . . thank you."

Except for Kari's pain, which it was getting harder for him to hide, the walk was pleasant. The wolves ranged widely; about halfway back, the rest of the rescue party split off as a hunting party, leaving Brokkolfr and Isolfr to get Kari back to the heall.

"Sorry . . . about this," Kari said. "Funny thing is . . . not my ankle . . . It's my *arms*."

"I remember how much Sokkolfr hated his crutches," Isolfr said. "We won't make you stir from the hearth once you get there, I promise."

"I'll hold you to that," Kari said, then gritted his teeth and started forward again.

# TWELVE

While the sun set, the Rheans built a pyre. There was no sign of Lucius or the centurion he had gone to fetch; Skjaldwulf guessed unhappily that the centurion had decided to take a more aggressive approach to his blindness rather than make any effort to disrupt Sixtus' plans.

Skjaldwulf could not count on anyone putting a stop to this madness, then. There was no telling when Tribune Iunarius might return, and Skjaldwulf did not want to be a greasy pile of ashes and bones when he did. Otter might help him—and then again, she might not.

*Pack,* said Mar.

*We don't know where they are,* Skjaldwulf said.

*Pack,* Mar said patiently, and showed Skjaldwulf: Ingrun,

Kothran, Afi, and Dyrver, with their brothers warm shadows beyond them. They were not far away, and they were quick to answer Mar. Skjaldwulf could not follow much of the conversation that followed, if conversation it could be called. Wolves did not use words, and the flickering mix of images and scents was confusing to anyone who did. But he understood that their small threat was moving toward them. If he could free Mar, at least they would have a target to flee toward.

And it was not that he *could* not free Mar, merely that he could not do so unobserved. *Perhaps as it grows darker,* he thought, knowing that a misjudgment would mean both their deaths.

He waited, watching the competence and precision with which the Rheans toiled. They'd done this before, and he wondered if they often burned witches, wondered if many Brythoni had been burned for not being what the Rheans expected. *A thousand leagues,* Iunarius had said. Skjaldwulf couldn't imagine a distance that great, much less the different peoples who might live within its span. He wanted to tell the Rheans that burning was the wrong answer, but he thought of Iunarius and Lucius and knew that many of them knew that already. A jarl should not be ruled by villagers, and Skjaldwulf thought it would be a terrible pity to die just to prove that hoary truth one time more.

As he was starting to wonder if the shadows might not be deep enough to hide his movements, a Rhean bearing a torch came to stand just outside the limit of Mar's chain. His face was stony, his eyes hard; even if Skjaldwulf had spoken the Rheans' tongue, he would not have been able to reach this one. Mar whined.

*Easy, brother. We aren't defeated yet.*

Skjaldwulf could feel Kothran most easily, of the other wolves, for reasons he doubted would ever make sense but had something to do with Viradechtis. Kothran's thoughts were bright, clear, and fast-moving; the wolves' name for him was the smell of a wet spring morning, the rich green liveliness of the world waking up. Through Mar, Kothran showed Skjaldwulf the wolves and their brothers approaching the Rhean camp from the south; they had made a wide, cautious circle during the day, while Skjaldwulf and Mar sat chained at the base of this tree.

*Be careful!* Skjaldwulf thought as forcefully as he could, and he felt Kothran laughing at him. *They* were not the ones who'd gotten themselves caught, were they?

Mar grumbled in his throat, and Skjaldwulf hid a smile, even as he cautioned Mar against making that sort of noise again. Their Rhean guard had edged away a step, his eyes showing white like a nervous horse.

*He really does believe that I'm a witch and Mar is my creature.* It was not that Skjaldwulf had not believed what Otter (and through her, Iunarius and Lucius) had told him, but the idea made so little sense to him that he had trouble understanding it. *Familiaris,* the tribune had said, and Otter had struggled to translate: a servant enslaved by magic, something that wore the shape of a giant wolf but was really a spirit. *A ghost?* Skjaldwulf had said, and the tribune had seemed almost insulted by the idea.

Mar was no magical spirit; he was a trellwolf, whelped by the konigenwolf Hafthora of Thorsbaer Wolfheall. He had his mother's black fur and her unswerving focus. He was the truest brother of Skjaldwulf's heart, closer than his blood-kin, closer even than his werthreatbrothers, some of whom were dear and close indeed. But Mar was more than any of them.

Mar pushed against Skjaldwulf's thigh, and Skjaldwulf felt Mar's love for him. It steadied him, and he looked thoughtfully at the Rhean, wondering if they could turn the man's fear to their advantage.

But he did not have to find out, for the spider-thin shape skirting the growing pyre and coming toward them was Otter. As she stepped into the circle of torchlight, she gave Skjaldwulf a flick of a glance that he had no difficulty interpreting, and then she stepped close to the Rhean, murmuring words in that liquid, rippling language. Skjaldwulf watched gratefully as she used her body to make the Rhean move, so subtly he probably wasn't aware of it at all: pushing in to make him fall back ever so slightly, then shifting sideways, the tiniest part of a circle, so that he turned. It was clear by his expression what her words meant—or what he wanted them to mean. The instant Otter had maneuvered the Rhean so that his own body cast a shadow on Skjaldwulf and Mar, Skjaldwulf leaned over, finding the hook where the chain connected to the harness. He'd had all afternoon to stare at it; he felt as if he could draw it in his sleep.

It was a cunning thing, and it took a moment's teeth-clenched effort to release it with his manacled hands. As he did, Skjaldwulf pressed down on Mar's shoulder. This was not the moment to run, not until they knew where their pack was and what they were doing.

Otter drifted back half a step, and the Rhean followed her. Skjaldwulf wondered if her job as translator made her forbidden to the soldiers or if she was the concubine of one soldier in particular, a high-ranking one perhaps, and thus an unexpected opportunity for this man. He was certainly eager enough; she'd gotten him talking now, and from the tone of voice, he was boasting. Perhaps of his bravery in standing guard over the witch?

*Now,* Skjaldwulf thought. *Run.* But trellwolves were not commanded. Mar snarled through the muzzle and leaped.

The muzzle saved the Rhean's life; as it was, Mar's weight bore him to the ground, and there were long gashes where his leather armor did not protect him. Skjaldwulf lurched to his feet and did the only thing he could. He grabbed Otter, iron cutting his wrists, and shoved her toward the edge of the camp. Over the Rhean's scream, he shouted: *"RUN!"*

Otter ran, as fast and agile as if her namesake animal were a deer. Skjaldwulf ran after her, hands held awkwardly before him, throwing his mind open to the pack.

On the other side of the camp, Ingrun howled, a magnificent ululation that made the hairs on Skjaldwulf's neck stand up, never mind that he'd known her since she was a gangly half-grown pup. He could feel Mar's savage frustration with the metal bars that kept him from his enemies, but that frustration was enough that when Skjaldwulf said in the pack-sense, *Run, brother*, this time Mar conceded and ran—on a different trajectory from Skjaldwulf and Otter.

Afi and Kothran answered Ingrun's howl, and without the pack-sense Skjaldwulf wouldn't have been able to tell where they were. He twisted his head for a moment, just as he reached the edge of the trees, and saw that the Rheans were hopelessly disorganized; not one man had managed to start in pursuit, and most of them seemed to be on the verge of flight themselves. Satisfaction flared. If a man spent an afternoon inciting his threatbrothers with fear of witches and wolves, then he was well served when the presence of wolves sowed panic among those threatbrothers.

And then he was crashing through the trees—*blessed trees, lovely trees*, he thought, even as the branches lashed the face he could not protect with his chained hands—and Dyrver's brother Ulfhoss was saying, "Skjaldwulf, what do you want done with this girl?"

"Keep moving," Skjaldwulf said. He'd seen how quickly the Rheans could regroup if a strong enough leader willed it, and he did not want to be anywhere nearby when that happened. "And treat her kindly. She helped me when she did not have to."

"Ma'am," Ulfhoss said respectfully, and Skjaldwulf forced his aching legs and aching head to carry him forward to Otter's side.

"You don't have to stay with us," he said. "Though I cannot advise returning to the Rheans."

"No," Otter agreed; he couldn't tell in the dark, but he thought she might almost have been smiling. "I have no love for Iskryners, but I have not learned to love the Rheans, either."

"The protection Iunarius spoke of?" For in truth, Skjaldwulf had been wondering.

He sensed her shrug, like a woman impatient with a heavy burden. "If you are a landholder, I am sure it is a good bargain, for I do not think your vikings will come raiding again anytime soon."

"No," Skjaldwulf agreed. "But they wouldn't have anyway. Not after the trellwar."

"No," she said softly. "But my people could not know of that, and the Rheans are civilized. They do not burn, and when they pillage, they pay for what they take. And they only rape the women who have no one to protect them. The same women everyone else rapes."

He heard her bitterness and knew he had no answer for it.

They ran south and east, as best Skjaldwulf could tell, picking up men and wolves as they went. When they were all together again, they veered more directly south. Skjaldwulf had no idea of where they were going, but there was some relief in reminding himself that he *couldn't* know; he did not know this land, and having been unconscious, he had no way to determine where the Rhean camp was in relation to the place where they had first met the Rhean soldiers. He had to trust Randulfr and Frithulf to know what they were doing and where they were going.

He stumbled down a hill, and a strong hand caught his arm just above the elbow. "Mar says you're hurt," said Frithulf.

"I took a bad blow to the head," Skjaldwulf said, "but it's not so bad I fear dying from it."

"I'm pleased to hear it. But that means Mar's right. You're hurt."

"We can't stop, whether I'm hurt or not."

"No, but I can stay near you and keep you from pitching top over tail. At least until we can strike off your chains. I did promise Isolfr I'd return you in one piece."

"Because he doesn't want to be left with Vethulf as his only wolf-jarl."

"It's a good reason," Frithulf said. "Come on. It's not too much farther to where we stashed Freyvithr and the ponies." And his hand stayed, uncompromising and yet comforting, across a shallow creek and then into a narrow ravine.

There was the heat and scent of horses and Freyvithr's voice saying, "Did as many come back as set out?"

"I think so," Frithulf said. "Skjaldwulf did most of his own rescuing."

"It was Mar," Skjaldwulf said. "And I must see to him—get that damn muzzle off him."

Mar was there, as he had been there the entire way, near without ever being close enough that Skjaldwulf might trip over him. It had taken several months of the first year they were bonded for Mar fully to understand that Skjaldwulf could not see in the dark and that his nose was not sensitive enough to tell him exactly where his brother was. But once Mar had grasped Skjaldwulf's deficiencies, he had never once forgotten.

"Come, brother, come," Skjaldwulf said, dropping wearily onto his knees. "Let us remove this hateful thing."

"That will be easier with your hands free," Frithulf observed dryly, but Skjaldwulf shook his head and kept working.

Mar held still, whining softly, as Skjaldwulf wrestled with the stiff leather buckle. The muzzle did not fit well; Skjaldwulf felt a dull fury at the raw-rubbed lines across Mar's nose and under his ears. "Frithulf, I packed a salve. . . ."

"I'll find it," Frithulf said promptly, and Skjaldwulf was able to devote his attention to removing the harness.

Finally, the last of the Rheans' cursed bonds was off Mar, and Frithulf had returned with the salve. He spread it carefully on Mar's face and around his neck and across his shoulders, while

Randulfr pulled Skjaldwulf aside and set a chisel against the manacle lock. Mar, for his part, was more interested in trying to lick Skjaldwulf's hands, too glad at being free to have much care for his injuries. Frithulf had to restrain the wolf so that Randulfr could safely strike off the manacles.

Shaking stinging wrists, Skjaldwulf looked up and found his threat surrounding him: Randulfr, Frithulf, Geirulfr, Ulfhoss, with Freyvithr and Otter standing uncertainly behind them. And the wolves: Kothran pressed between Frithulf and Geirulfr, and Ingrun lying before Randulfr's legs with her head on her paws. And Afi and Dyrver at the head of the ravine, watching for trouble.

"Tell me how things stand," Skjaldwulf said, because he was wolfjarl and it was his duty.

"Adalbrikt is dead," said Frithulf. "You probably knew that."

"Yes," Skjaldwulf said.

"Other than that, you and Mar are our only casualties. We didn't even lose the ponies, mostly because none of those foreign soldiers wanted to get more than arm's length away from his shield-brothers."

"They have some . . . unusual ideas," Skjaldwulf said. "Where are we?"

"A day, day and a half, from Siglufjordhur," said Randulfr. "No more than that. We thought perhaps one man should ride ahead and see how things stand there, but we felt we should rescue you first."

"And I thank you for that. They were preparing to burn us."

"To *burn* you?" Freyvithr said.

Skjaldwulf sighed and said, "They thought I was a witch."

⚬❦⚬

There was no sign of pursuit from the Rhean camp, even when Ingrun and Afi made a wider sweep, and Randulfr assured Skjaldwulf they would not find a better-concealed place to rest anywhere short of Siglufjordhur, so the party remained there the next day and night. Skjaldwulf slept a great deal of the time. "Head wounds are like that," Frithulf said cheerfully one time Skjaldwulf was awake. "And if we're going to cart you around the countryside, I'd rather you looked a little less like a corpse first."

Skjaldwulf would have said something rude, but he was already three-quarters asleep again.

He had been careful, in his explanations, to identify Otter as both someone who had helped him and someone who was not to be bothered. In his bouts of waking, he found that she was generally somewhere near his bedroll, sitting quiet and watchful. When Frithulf insisted on waking him for dinner, he found that Mar was lying with most of his body pressed against Skjaldwulf's leg but with his head in Otter's lap.

"Is it all right?" she said anxiously. "I didn't mean to—"

"No, it's fine," Skjaldwulf said. "I didn't expect it, but you've done nothing wrong."

*Brother?* he said.

*Grief-and-bitter-herbs smells like fear and sadness,* said Mar. *And my ears itched.*

Skjaldwulf was caught between a laugh and a cough; he managed a smile for Otter. "Usually, trellwolves pay little heed to anyone beside their brothers. But Mar says you scratch his ears the way he likes."

"Does he really talk to you?" She sounded both curious and slightly wistful.

"Not in words," Skjaldwulf said. "They don't think in words, although most of them know a few. Like 'dinner.'" Mar thumped his tail without looking around. "They think in scents mostly, and images. Feelings. If you've been bonded long enough, you learn to put words to what they say."

"Oh." When she looked down, her face in repose, he could see how young she was. Skjaldwulf remembered the tribune calling *him* a young man.

Comprehension rattled him. He blurted, "You have nowhere to go."

"I know that." She brought her head up to meet his gaze. But she couldn't quite mask the distaste with which she said, "Is it your intent to take me as your leman, then?"

The word she used was unfamiliar—Brythoni, he thought—but the sense of it was plain enough. And it startled him into laughter.

She jerked back. "I know I am branded. And a slave. I did not presume—"

"No," he said. "No." He cast about for an explanation, something that would make sense to a woman who was not just not heallbred but alien in every way. "Women—women don't—"

The furrow between her brows, the puckers around her brand, were only getting deeper. He wondered if her head hurt as much as his did.

He sighed and tried again. "I am a wolfcarl. But I am also a lover of men."

For a moment, the squint grew deeper. And then she jerked as if beestung, her hands flying to her mouth. Mar, his head still in her lap, muttered a complaint.

"But you—" She looked from side to side. "You are a *warrior*."

He spread his hands. "As wolfcarls must be."

And then she laughed, and shook her head, and put her hands in Mar's ruff again. "Where I am from," she said, "no man would admit to such a thing, except if he were a minion."

"Minion?"

"A perfumed lapdog living off the . . . largesse of his patron." Her mouth worked as if she were sucking on something bitter. "I should not speak so harshly. I suppose that's what there is for me, as well, if you will not have me."

She did not sound, in particular, as if she wished him to have her. But rather as if it were the best of a range of bad options. Skjaldwulf stared at her, understanding. When she met his eyes, he remembered himself and glanced down.

"You speak Brythoni," he said. "And Rhean. And Iskrynder. Have you other skills?"

She rubbed Mar's ears until he moaned—Skjaldwulf thought to busy her hands. "Before the Rheans took me, I did what any woman without family would do. I can drudge and cook and earn a living on my back. I know which end of a horse to put the bucket before, and at which end to wield the shovel. I am not useless."

She was little more than a child. Some tithe boys came to the heall older. Skjaldwulf had: barely a tithe *boy* at all.

"You saved my life," he said. "And the life of my wolf. On my honor as a wolfcarl, as I am jarl of Franangford, you will not want for a livelihood. The heall will house and feed you as our own. You are of the Wolfmaegth, the brotherhood of the wolfheall. As far as the pack is concerned, from this day you are my daughter."

Her hands tightened in Mar's fur, knuckles whitening. But Skjaldwulf could see that she clenched only, and did not yank. Her mouth opened. She closed it again.

More gently, tempering the passion with which he had spoken, he said, "Do you understand me?"

"You mean it."

"I swear it. An we all live through this, you will have a home."

Whatever she tried to say next choked her, but Skjaldwulf did not need to hear it. He could read enough truths in the way the tears tracked her cheeks, diverted by the weals and valleys of her brand.

❦

Vethulf felt snappish and tense, as if he might bite anything that drew his attention. For him, it was an unusual reaction to the aftermath of battle, and he did not entirely know what to make of it.

So he bit his tongue instead and allowed Roghvatr to divvy up the remains of the bear in any manner that suited him. Mostly, Vethulf realized, he was eager to get away from the jarl's house and see what could be done to help Isolfr, even though through the pack-sense he knew that Isolfr was fine.

When Sokkolfr came for him and led him into a bed-closet in which he could tend Vethulf's wounds, Viradechtis and Kjaran followed. Upset, they lay pressed close to Vethulf's knees on either side as might any man's dogs. Vethulf could read their fear on behalf of Mar and Skjaldwulf. Surely it was the pack's distress setting him on edge.

The smell of roasting meat already spread through Roghvatr's hall, and a bustle outside the alcove where Sokkolfr worked on Vethulf told Vethulf that preparations were under way to celebrate the combined victory of keep and heall. Sokkolfr dressed and tended Vethulf's wound without fuss, for which Vethulf was grateful.

"I can't afford this," Vethulf muttered.

Sokkolfr looked up from tying off the end of the bandage. "It's summer," he said. "And Viradechtis won't mate this year. You'll have time to heal."

"Roghvatr," Vethulf said, by way of explanation, "I need to be helping Isolfr, not appeasing the local jarl with a victory feast."

"Oh," Sokkolfr said. "Politics."

"Politics," Vethulf agreed, putting a snarl in it.

"If Isolfr gets in trouble," Sokkolfr said, "Viradechtis will let us know, won't she?"

"Hand me my tunic, please?"

Sokkolfr did so, and Vethulf used the time required to struggle into the bloodied garment without tearing open his mauled shoulder to think what to say next. The truth was, he itched to set off southward at a dead run, and not stop running until he had found Skjaldwulf's traveling band and seen for himself that Mar and his brother were safe. Failing that, Vethulf wanted to go haul Kari and Brokkolfr by the ears out of whatever pit they had fallen down and deliver an extensive and scathing tongue-lashing in the process.

Anything—anything—but dinner with the jarl. With Vethulf's rival Eyjolfr on Roghvatr's left hand, as a special gift.

"All right," Vethulf said. "Let's get this over with."

Roghvatr's keep, like all the rest of Franangford, was in the process of being resurrected from the rubble. Houses and workshops, stables and barns could be raised with fair speed—they were but lath and thatch and turf and daub and plaster, after all, and there was no great art in their quick construction beyond the labor of many hands—but a keep, like a wolfheall, had to be defensible, and had to house both men and stores in quantity.

Roghvatr, having been the youngest half brother of the Franangford jarl killed by trolls, was as new to his role as jarl as was Vethulf. But Roghvatr was a man of mature years and experience, a warrior and an adventurer who had done his time a-viking. He knew how to command, and Vethulf could only hope Roghvatr was learning how to govern.

If nothing else, he set a good feast.

As promised, Vethulf and Eyjolfr sat on the jarl's right hand and left, and all three shared a trencher. It was meant to be a mark of signal honor, but Vethulf was so busy avoiding eye contact with Eyjolfr that much of it was lost on him. Still, the food was good, the meat of the great bear lean and tough but flavorful, the plates piled high with summer's bounty. The wolves, under the table, did not go hungry, either, as there were trenchers of rare steaming meat for them to dine upon.

Vethulf ate to keep his mouth full, so that his traitor tongue would not say anything scathing and provoke a break in this fragile accord. Eyjolfr seemed more than content to hold up the conversation on behalf of the wolfheall, judging by his boasting.

There was a line, Vethulf thought, between any warrior's healthy blazon of his victories and attributes, and being a blowhard and a bore. At that moment, he was rather glad his mouth was full of trout and lingonberries.

At last, the feast ended with sweetmeats and savories, and with a winding of horns the skin and skull of the bear were paraded through the hall, tented on sticks borne not by thralls but by several of Roghvatr's thanes. Those doughty men laid the pelt across the cleared table between Vethulf and Eyjolfr.

Roghvatr stood, and those in the hall who owed him allegiance stood also. The wolfcarls did not; they did not answer to the jarls of men.

Roghvatr said, "The pelt of the bear must be yours, wolfjarl, for it was your plan and courage that drove him from his shelter unto death. And the skull must be yours, wolfcarl, for your spirited courage in this same venture. All present, charge your cups!"

He held out a hand; a thrall placed a horn in it. Someone was there, too, with a horn for Vethulf and one for Eyjolfr. Vethulf managed to get his hands around it without fumbling.

Roghvatr held up his horn and cried, "To the rebirth of Franangford, town and keep and croft and heall!"

"Hear!" cried the thanes and wolfcarls, and Vethulf with the rest stood and drained his horn.

⊕ϒ⊘

In the quiet aftermath of the feast, Roghvatr came himself to find Vethulf as Vethulf was assuming his axe and spear, in order to return as swiftly as possible to the heall. Viradechtis and Kjaran paced impatiently beyond the keep's great door; they had told

Vethulf that Isolfr was returning in the morning, both of the missing wolfcarls safely recovered, and Vethulf was in a hurry to be there to greet them.

So his patience and interest when Roghvatr stopped before him were feigned. But he was trying.

Roghvatr extended his right hand. Vethulf, abandoning the ties of his axe for a moment, returned the clasp. The jarl cleared his throat.

"I have a proposition for you, wolfjarl."

*Oh, here we go.* But Vethulf forced himself to nod.

"It is said," Roghvatr began awkwardly, "that the trolls are gone forever."

Vethulf shrugged. *Save us from the dissembling of wolfless men.* "I would say it is too soon to make such a pronouncement."

"Still. The heall . . . If it is true, the heall lacks purpose. What will wolves do, when there are no trolls for the hunting?"

*We've been wondering the same damned thing.* Vethulf did not say it, but his silence was an effort.

"You could come in service to me," Roghvatr said. "We have seen today that trolls are not the only peril from which a wolfcarl and his brother may defend us."

Vethulf finished with the axe bindings. "No," he said.

Roghvatr stepped back. He had not been a jarl long, but perhaps it did not take long for a jarl to forget what it was like to be gainsaid. "No?"

"No," Vethulf said. "Wolves do not fight in men's wars." He paused, uncertain how to explain himself. "They do not fight for men's reasons."

Roghvatr stroked his forked beard. "Not to win wealth and fame? Not at their brother's behest?"

They might, that latter at least. Men fought for wealth and fame, it was certain. But wolves—

He imagined taking Kjaran a-viking. His jaw firmed. "No," he said. "Not wolves."

⊙ᚤ⊙

When Brokkolfr and his companions returned to the heall at midmorning on the day after Kari had broken his ankle, Hroi lay waiting before the gate. When the old wolf saw them, he stood with a welcoming wag of his tail, and moments later Sokkolfr was there, calmly taking charge. Brokkolfr was almost immediately banished to the sauna, and he was glad to go. Amma followed him, and he took care to choose the bench nearest the door, so that although she could not see him, she would know he was there.

Being properly clean was a tremendous relief. He came out to the discovery that it was dinnertime. He found himself not particularly hungry, and although it was still light, he retreated to his bedding along the wall as soon as he could. He slept restlessly but long, waking and rolling over, only to wake again what felt like mere minutes later. Eventually, he woke in darkness with more men beside him—and finally, at the ragged edge of dawn, he woke and realized Amma wasn't there.

He sat up with a jerk, reaching for her in the pack-sense. He found her immediately and was able to breathe again, but she was not in the finished part of the heall. She was— He got up, shoving his feet into his boots, and followed the feel of her out and to the left and down into the newly dug root cellar, where she had made a nest, half bed, half rampart, out of burlap sacks.

"You couldn't have picked a less comfortable spot?" Brokkolfr said, knowing that the affection in his voice would keep her from thinking it was a real rebuke.

Amma thumped her tail, but she was panting, a whine threading in and out. *Hurts,* she said.

"It's your cubs coming," Brokkolfr said, settling in beside her. "You remember what it's like."

*He* remembered. The first pup had been breech, and Amma had nearly died, along with her litter, before Othinnsaesc's wolfjarl had reached up into her body and turned the pup with his fingers. The wolfjarl, of course, because even the most amiable of bitches, which Amma surely was, did not want another she-wolf's brother near her newborn pups.

As if the thought had summoned him, Vethulf said from behind Brokkolfr, "Kjaran says Amma is birthing her pups."

"Yes," Brokkolfr said, not turning around. "Her water's broken—I think that must be what woke me."

He heard Vethulf's boots coming closer. "Hmmph. Sokkolfr will not be pleased with you."

"As her pups are all born healthy, and she does not die in the birthing, I will pay Sokkolfr any penalty he wants," Brokkolfr said, hearing the tightness in his own voice but unable to ameliorate it. He was scared for Amma, and he was remembering too keenly his last encounter with Vethulf.

There was a silence; then Vethulf knelt beside him. "I meant no rebuke," he said, his voice gentler. "Sokkolfr knows as well as I do not to argue with a whelping wolf."

"Sorry," Brokkolfr said.

*Hurts,* Amma said again, and he saw the contraction tighten all the muscles of her belly.

"Comfort your sister, wolfcarl," Vethulf said, "and I will see what the word is from the front."

Brokkolfr couldn't bite back a lunatic giggle. "You mean the back." And he looked up to see Vethulf grinning at him.

"That's better," Vethulf said. Moving stiffly—Brokkolfr remembered that Vethulf's arm was hurt and felt guilty about the confines of the cellar all over again—he shifted to kneel by Amma's back legs while Brokkolfr moved to her head, stroking her ears, and, when she indicated she wanted to, letting her put her head in his lap.

Vethulf said, "No sign of pups yet."

"That was what went wrong, the . . . the first time," Brokkolfr said.

"Breech-birth." At Brokkolfr's startled look, Vethulf said, "I asked every wolfjarl I could for wisdom about birthing wolf pups, and your wolfjarl told me what he had to do."

Brokkolfr blinked, hit with a sudden suspicion. "Is this the first time you've assisted at a birth, wolfjarl?"

"Well," Vethulf said, and with a tight, teeth-baring grin added, "yes. I wasn't expecting Skjaldwulf to go haring off south."

Brokkolfr knew he could have become angry—was even tempted, because it would be easier than the fear cramping his guts. But instead, he said, "It's my second one. And I was only watching the first time."

Vethulf's snarl of a grin eased into something more like a smile. "So of the three of us, Amma's the only one who knows what she's doing."

Brokkolfr was surprised by his own laughter. "I find that's usually the way of it," he said, and surprised Vethulf into laughing, too.

⁂

They got lucky, and Brokkolfr was going to make an offering to Freya as soon as he could find something that would please her. This time, none of Amma's pups had turned the wrong way in her womb; although her labor was long and painful—longer and more painful than Isolfr described Viradechtis', Vethulf said, and Brokkolfr knew the other she-wolves of Othinnsaesc had never had as much trouble as Amma did—she bore four healthy dog pups over the course of that long day. Vethulf only left once, and that was to fetch water for Amma, and food and small beer for Brokkolfr and himself. Brokkolfr hadn't thought he could eat, but when Vethulf set down the platter of rye bread and cheese he discovered he was ravenous. Amma lapped the water thankfully, then laid her head back in Brokkolfr's lap. He fed her bits of cheese when she would take them, but mostly he rubbed her ears and talked to her in the bond while she labored to bring her sons into the world. Vethulf did the bloody part of the work, catching the pups to help Amma push them out, clearing their noses and mouths with his one good hand, then giving them to their mother. Brokkolfr offered once to trade, but Vethulf said, "No. All that's required at this end are steady hands and a strong stomach, and that any warrior can provide. But Amma needs her brother."

And Brokkolfr felt the *winter apples* of Amma's agreement.

❧

Once the four pups were born, and the afterbirths counted and given to Amma to eat, and once it was clear there was not a fifth, Vethulf dragged Brokkolfr back to the heall for a proper meal and another visit to the sauna. "I know you'll stay out there with her until you can persuade her to bring them in," Vethulf said, "but in the meantime, eat and be clean, and I'll have a thrall gather up some extra bedding for you."

"Thank you," Brokkolfr said, then stopped, tongue-tied and uncertain of what he was trying to say. Finally, he said, "Thank you," again, although it was inadequate.

Vethulf seemed to understand. "I've a vile temper and a viler tongue. Does not mean I am not your wolfjarl, Brokkolfr Ammasbrother."

"Yes," Brokkolfr said, meeting Vethulf's eyes. "You are my wolfjarl."

Then Vethulf clouted him on the shoulder and said, "Don't fall asleep in there, or I'll have to send someone in to drag you out," and strode off.

Brokkolfr felt as if the ugly lead-sealed knots in his gut had all been broken at once. He reached for Amma in the pack-sense, giving her his love for her and her pups, and got *winter apples* sleepily in return.

# THIRTEEN

Skjaldwulf and his companions staggered into Siglufjordhur on the evening of the third day, in better order than Skjaldwulf thought they had any right to expect. There was no sign of Rhean pursuit. Determining that was what had caused the delay—the last thing Skjaldwulf wanted to do was lead an army down on a friendly settlement.

An army by his standards, anyway. Because when he had said to Otter, "But it's not that big, the Rhean army. Surely we can—" she had replied, infinitely tired, "Oh, wolfjarl. That is not the Rhean army. That is not even a legion of the Rhean army. That is a mere expeditionary force."

"You mean . . ."

"I saw the Ninth Legion," Otter said, "when they came to

Brython, marching across our wheatfields with the sun dazzling off their helmets. Counting them would have been like trying to count the waves of the sea. Or"—her mouth twisted—"the ants of a hill. You can't imagine the Rhean *army*. Nor can I. I only know that I never want to see it."

It was an idea at once dizzying and horrible, and Skjaldwulf tried neither to dwell on it nor to forget it. *Put out the fire burning your boots first,* he said to himself, and thus took care to be sure they came unencumbered to Siglufjordhur.

The lack of pursuit did not, in particular, reassure him. He understood it to mean that the tribune and his men had some more pressing business elsewhere, and whatever that business was, it boded not well for the Northmen.

But at least they had come to a place of defense.

Fargrimr came striding from the keep to meet them, his dirty-blond braids streaming behind him. The keep of Siglufjordhur was built on a rocky promontory, jutting out of the low hills like a tooth, and the wind scythed across its forecourt as if it had a personal grudge against the stones. Randulfr and Fargrimr met, embraced, and Randulfr made the introductions. Skjaldwulf remembered Fargrimr from the war, remembered seeing him at his father's shoulder on the battlefield, stone-faced and slim and wearing gauntlets of troll blood past his elbows. He nodded respectfully, wolfjarl to jarl's heir, and Fargrimr nodded back. The other wolfcarls at least knew what a functional son was, and Freyvithr greeted Fargrimr as a respected acquaintance, if not quite ally or friend. Otter's eyes were huge, but she held her tongue while Fargrimr led them in, handed the ponies over to a stableboy, and showed them the training arena where they would be housed.

"It rains in Siglufjordhur nine months of the year," Randulfr said, grinning, "and while there are important lessons to be learned about mud, there are equally important lessons to be learned without it. My grandfather had this built when he expanded the stables."

"But there is no need for practice when the real thing is encamped a league from our gates," said Fargrimr, "and I thought the trellwolves might prefer this to the other options."

"And you don't have to worry about your armsmen screaming that they're being eaten in the middle of the night," Randulfr said.

Fargrimr punched him in the arm without even looking in his direction. "If you would prefer other arrangements, wolfjarl . . . ?"

"No, thank you. This is excellent. But two of our party are not wolfcarls."

"No," Fargrimr said. "The godsman knows he will be welcome wherever he chooses to sleep."

"Thank you," Freyvithr said, bowing.

"And this is Otter," Skjaldwulf said. Fargrimr's eyebrows went up as he got a good look at her brand. "She was the Rheans' translator."

"It is no small feat to have taken her from them, then," said Fargrimr.

"Boot's on the other leg," Skjaldwulf said. "They captured me, and she helped me escape."

"Ah," said Fargrimr, and bowed to Otter. "Since my mother's death, we have few women about the keep, but I imagine we can—"

"I would rather stay here," Otter said, and then looked anxiously at Skjaldwulf. "Is that all right?"

"Surely you'd be more comfortable—" Skjaldwulf started, but Otter laughed.

"This is more comfort than I've seen in a while, wolfjarl," she said. "It isn't a tent."

Skjaldwulf nodded in understanding. "She is my oath-daughter," he said to Fargrimr, meeting his eyes steadily.

"Then her choice does honor to you both," said Fargrimr. "You will find that the men of Siglufjordhur do not slander women, and if one of them does, I ask you to bring the matter to me. For he will not do so twice." He nodded to the company, said more softly to Randulfr, "Father would speak with you, when you are settled, and yes, you may bring your sister." Then Fargrimr turned and strode away, back to the entrance to the arena, where an armsman was waiting for him.

"Your people's ways are very strange, Iskryner," Otter said to Skjaldwulf, and Skjaldwulf raised an eyebrow. Compared to the Rheans, what was so strange about any of this?

⊙Υ☉

As if troubles indeed traveled in the flocks that proverb predicted, the next morning brought word to Franangford of a wyvern nest near the village of Othstathr. The boy who had spotted the molted skin at a cave entrance—also the boy sent with the message, and Vethulf appreciated the village headman's economy—had been smart enough not to go any closer, and he said he could lead the wolfcarls to it.

Vethulf wanted, rather badly, to tell somebody else to go. His shoulder had stiffened, swollen and hard, and he knew he was fevered—though Sokkolfr had cleaned the wound with stale urine and stitched it, so Vethulf did not think it would take poison. He was tired with the fight and tired with diplomacy—or what he passed off as diplomacy, in Skjaldwulf's absence—and furthermore, the village was far enough away that it would mean spending at least three nights away from the wolfheall. But he was aware of the thing Roghvatr had not quite said: *If there are no trolls, why should we support the wolfheallan?*

From watching Skjaldwulf and Isolfr deal with the wolfless men of Franangfordtown, Vethulf had learned that while it was important that the problem be solved, it was also important that the wolf-heall be clearly seen to care. That meant sending a wolfheofodman. With Skjaldwulf gone, Vethulf was also aware that, as far as the day-to-day concerns of the heall went, he was the one who could best be spared. You did not send your wolfsprechend to deal with a wyvern, and he did not like to think what would happen to the wolfheall without Sokkolfr paying careful, quiet attention to all the details everyone else missed.

The wolfjarl was a vital part of the heall, but that was because he was the leader when action was necessary, not because the heall's peaceful productivity relied on him.

Also, as wolfjarl, he was the one whose authority the wolfless men most readily recognized.

Vethulf chose three wolfcarls to go with him, being careful to select men whom he had not chosen for the bear-fight in Franangfordtown. He understood favoritism very keenly—more so perhaps than Isolfr, who had been a jarl's heir before he came to the heall and thus would never have seen what it was like *not* to be his father's most important child. Vethulf chose Ulfmundr and Hlothor from the old Franangfordthreat; Throttolfr and red Djurgeirr, threat-brothers of Vethulf's from Arakensberg; and Ulfvaldr and Reykr, the only pair who had come to Franangford from Bravoll.

Saying good-bye to Isolfr was awkward, but Vethulf did it anyway, determined to behave like a wolfjarl, not a child or a fool. Isolfr helped by making a face and saying, "My first night at Nithogsfjoll, I helped kill a wyvern. You may have this honor with my good wishes."

"Thanks," Vethulf said, grinning but also meaning it, and he left Franangford feeling—not lighthearted exactly, but as if he could handle whatever the world was about to throw at him. It helped that the distant pack-sense was no longer jangled and jagged with fear for

Skjaldwulf. Even Isolfr couldn't tell exactly what had happened, but whatever it was, Skjaldwulf and Mar had come through safely.

They made good time to Othstathr. The boy, Haukr, led them confidently and at a pace swift enough to keep even Vethulf from fretting. Haukr was of an age for the tithe, and Vethulf, trying to think ahead as Skjaldwulf would want him to, made sure Haukr saw the wolves properly: not as monsters and not as dogs. When they camped the first night, Haukr asked Ulfmundr, diffidently, how Hlothor had been so badly injured; Vethulf was both pleased and startled to discover he had been successful.

"Ah," said Ulfmundr, and although he was a formidable man with a thundercloud scowl, it was easy to see he was pleased to be asked. "That's the work of trolls, boy. The trolls of the Iskryne." He nudged Hlothor, and the wolf flopped over obligingly, so that Ulfmundr could show Haukr (and the other wolfcarls, who were all watching) the track of the scars, from Hlothor's ragged ear, down neck and shoulder, across his ribs, and over the point of his hip.

"One swipe," said Ulfmundr. "And how he escaped being gutted I still do not know. I slew the troll, and would have slain it twice in my rage, and when Hlothor came crawling to me out of the blood and muck, I carried him back to the surface and the wolfsprechends who stitched him together. I remember one of them told me it was all right to rip my shirts like that, but not my wolf."

Everyone laughed, as Ulfmundr had intended, and Hlothor got up, indulged in a full-body shake, and ambled away to piss on a tree. But Vethulf had seen the look in Haukr's eyes, and he went to sleep satisfied that when they asked for a tithe from Othstathr, there was at least one boy who might volunteer.

❧

The village was one Vethulf was not yet familiar with, for his duties as wolfjarl had so far kept him tied as if by apron strings to the heall. Really, he should be grateful to the wyvern for getting him out in the air, rather than sitting home playing nurse-maid and construction boss. With the trolls gone, he thought, it might not be very long before the northern settlements grew more scattered, families moving out among their fields in isolated crofts. People lived farther apart in the South, he knew, an extended family in a longhouse wherever the soil would sustain them. In the North, folks had until now huddled in stockaded villages for survival.

Even before *this* village came in sight, Vethulf knew they were herders and woodcutters by trade. Its location up the rocky sweep of a fell precluded farming, and the wolves had been stopping to sniff piles of goat droppings for as long as it took the sun to move a palm's-width on the sky—ever since they broke out of the wood, in fact. In addition, Haukr had inquired—without undue anxiety—if he should run ahead and warn his father to lock the herds away before the trellwolves' arrival.

"Don't worry," Vethulf had said. "They won't eat anything we ask them not to."

*And you ask us not to eat so many things,* Kjaran had said—or rather, he'd imagined a brief list of all the many things Vethulf had asked him not to eat over the years, with a somewhat aggrieved sense about them.

But a few moments later, Kjaran and Hlothor had chased and killed a foolish young squirrel between them, and divided it neatly in two. It made about one snap of the jaws apiece, without a speck of blood wasted.

Haukr looked even more impressed.

They reached Othstathr at midmorning, and the whole croft turned out to greet them, from a tottering grandfather who would die abed to a babe so new she was still swaddled up into a package that seemed too small for a child to fit in.

Othstathr was tiny; Vethulf was hard-pressed even to call it a village. It had a baker but no smith, and there were only four houses all together, clustered around a center green. Stockade stretched from cottage-wall to cottage-wall, a man-high wall of lath and withy washed white with lime. It would not stop a troll, or a bandit, or a bear—but it might turn back a wild wolf or boar, and it no doubt gave the villagers some small feeling of security to herd their flocks through the gates at night and draw the latchstrings in.

He strode forward, following Haukr while seeming to lead him, toward the headman. Vethulf introduced himself and heard the man's name in return. Guthbrandr—God's Brand—which Vethulf chose to regard as a good omen.

Guthbrandr was a spare, sparse-bearded man with gnarled hands and nails that ridged and curved like clubs over the tips of his fingers. He clasped Vethulf's forearm strongly, however. "Thank Othinn you've come."

"We are pleased to serve," Vethulf said, stepping back.

Guthbrandr gestured broadly. "Will you be wanting to leave immediately?"

Vethulf glanced at the sky. There was not enough light left even to consider seeking out a wyvern in unfamiliar country. He had fought enough trolls in the dark to understand the necessity for it— but the wyvern would be out of its den for the night, hunting, and though wolves could track it, it would be better to lie in wait for the thing when it returned. And wyverns were stupid in daylight— stupid and ever so fractionally slower.

"We'll go before first light," he said, trying not to think too much about the pull across his shoulder and the heat and throb of swollen flesh he felt with every breath. "It would be kind if your women would have a breakfast for us upon our return."

"They can have it before," Guthbrandr said. "They're used to waking early."

"We won't eat before battle," Vethulf said. He didn't want to shatter the naïveté of this man—a man grown but no warrior. "It's best for a wounded man if he hasn't eaten."

"Oh." Vethulf could see Guthbrandr absorbing the implications. The man might be naïve, but not stupid. "I see. Perhaps I should show you your beds, then."

"We thank you," Vethulf said, and looked neither at Haukr, bouncing with excitement, nor the three wolfcarls and their wolves arrayed behind him.

⟋⥁⟍

They turned someone out of a bed—several someones, Vethulf knew, for these cottages were too cramped to offer guest quarters, and the wolfcarls (divided into pairs) were given the best beds, at ground level, near the hearth. Which meant fathers and mothers had been displaced to the lofts and the children and grandchildren most likely to the stables.

He hoped that old man had a bed by the fire.

The season was past the white nights of high summer but only just—the sun seemed to dip below the horizon and roll along beneath it for an hour or two before lunging again to the sky like a fish to a lure. Still, even a brief rest would serve them, and Vethulf would rather fight beside men and wolves who had caught a catnap between adventures than those who had had no rest at all.

He knew the temperature must be dropping outside, because the doors and window were sealed against the depredations of the mosquitoes and biting flies of summertime, but the cottage did not grow too hot and close. He slept beside his old acquaintance Throttolfr on a straw-tick mattress—luxury to a wolfcarl, though Franangford was a modern heall and offered more in the way of comforts and amenities than a longhouse—across the few short hours of sunset and night until the silence of the cold hours and the pain in his shoulder woke him.

He rose and padded across the cottage's one great ground-floor room, beneath the head-high lofts, to the door that led to the square court between houses.

He pulled the latchstring and opened it a hair's-breadth before the knock. Across the threshold, a young woman faced him. She had a pinched face and a smock of plain homespun. Her ash-colored hair hung straight from a fillet across her brow, the color blurring into her dress in the gloaming.

"Lord Wolfjarl," she said, in soft hesitation. "I was sent to rouse you."

"Thank you," Vethulf said, quelling the grumpiness of pain, hunger, and short sleep. "Where is Haukr, to guide us?"

She gave Vethulf a look that betrayed unsuspected wit. "He," she said, "is eating breakfast. I am sent to inquire as well if you and your wolfcarls will accept at the very least a breakfast draught?"

The thought of rich ale tempted him, but he shook his head. Better to be hungry and sober. "But if you will have breakfast laid in against our return, I shall be most grateful."

She nodded, and he thought maybe that upward glance through lashes was an attempt at flirtation. What must it be like to come to womanhood in such a place as this, with at most two or three young men to choose between?

For a moment, he pitied her. But it was her life, and her wyrd, and she would make of it the best she could, like anyone. Like Vethulf himself.

"I'll get my weapons," he said.

⚬⚭⚬

They gathered in Haukr's father's house. The old man, it turned out, was the lad's great-grandfather, and though his hand shook, he saw them off with a father's blessing. Vethulf bore it in silence and tried not to fidget noticeably.

Afterwards, in a gray dark unbroken by torches, the wolves and Haukr led them through morning's mist and up the high fell. Haukr walked forward, the four wolves around him. Vethulf was sure the boy did not know that they flanked him as they would a cub on its first hunt.

Behind the boy and the wolves, the men walked single file, picking their way along a rough, tussocked path strewn with treacherous stones. It would be easy to turn an ankle here or slip and tumble down the precipitous slope.

They had not been climbing long when they broke above the fog. Coiling tendrils grasped at Vethulf's ankles and tattered when he pulled free. Djurgeirr ranged ahead, Kjaran beside him, and between them the wolfcarls had a sense of how the path twisted and what lay beyond each ridge. The morning grew brighter as they gained altitude, and it was only a little before sunrise when they began again to descend.

Reykr was the youngest wolf, his senses keenest. He was a smoke-brown with a pale fawn chest and points. Each hair of his coat was banded along its length so that pale shadows rippled through the dark fur-tips when he planted his feet and arched his neck up to sniff deeply, the first to scent the wyvern. His recognition rippled through the pack-sense. Serpent-musk, leaf mold, old blood and bone.

A thrill ran through every wolf and man of the threat. Teeth showed behind curled lips; hands fell to the hafts of axes and warhammers. Scarred old Hlothor huffed two or three times, drawing the air in deep, and then sneezed. Ulfvaldr shifted from foot to foot, boot leather creaking. Like his wolf, Ulfvaldr was young—but seasoned by the trellwars he had none of Guthbrandr's naïveté.

"Haukr," Vethulf said, "wait here."

The boy nodded and stepped off the path to let the men go by. "It's two rises on."

"We can find it from here." The wolves, in fact, were straining forward, hackles high and tails curled aggressively, ready for war.

And war it was. They did not move like wolves on the hunt—slinking, stiff-legged, like stormclouds drifting. Rather, they went in as the teeth of an angry pack, ready to drive the interloper from their territory or kill it if they must. Their excitement was a contagion, filling the wolfcarls as well and giving Vethulf's hand the trembles as he unlimbered his axe and made a few experimental swishes.

Nevertheless, when they crested that second rise—moving now in a scuttling crouch—and finally laid eyes upon the crevice in the rocks, Vethulf breathed out in relief. The ghost-white shed skin twined through the shrubs on every side, bunched up in places and torn in others, and the rocks of the cave mouth were papered with scraped-off scales.

But the cave was not large, not by the standards of wyverns.

Ulfmundr, who had the most experience with wyverns, thought so, too, because he whispered harshly, "God of wolves, it's not a big one."

"Big enough," Vethulf answered, gesturing to the skin. The skins stretched when shed, though, so the wyvern itself might be as little as two-thirds the length. Still and all, adequate. More than adequate.

"Is it in the lair?" Throttolfr asked. He wasn't a big man, but Vethulf knew him as an implacable fighter. His hair was sandy and his beard sandy-red. The scars of a troll's claws tracked through it on the left side of his face, three thready bald patches running parallel.

"I don't think so," Vethulf said. Kjaran told him the scent was rank but cold, and no fresher in the lair than in the little vale that fronted it.

This cave would not be a cavern, Vethulf thought. This high, it would be a crevice comprised of jumbled stones, not river-worn deep and muddy. Which was good news, because they would have neither to pursue the wyvern through measureless tunnels, nor to worry that it might enter or exit its lair through another opening and ambush them.

There was no chance of the wolves and men ambushing it. Wyverns had dim eyesight when dazzled by day, but their sense of smell did not suffer when exposed to sunlight. It would know the threat awaited it long before it came in sight. The consolation—if you could call it that—was that wyverns were territorial and if it felt its lair threatened, it would not quietly move on. Nor would it wait for the interlopers to do the same.

The fact that it could smell them, however, did not mean it was smart for anyone to stand up and present a silhouette along the ridge-line. So the wolfcarls waited crouched behind gorse and alongside boulders, and the wolves lay flat, heads on paws, in a relaxed crouch from which they could rise in an instant, fighting.

Vethulf measured the sky. A molten thread of gold spilled across the eastern horizon. The first rays of the sun glowed on the topmost stones of the summit behind him.

It would not now be long.

Their warning was the crackle of grass pressed flat, the rasp of something rough against stone. The wyvern traveled belly-flat, gliding along a tunnel of grass long since adapted to its passage. Its hind legs were hinged up alongside the cylinder of its body, the stubby vestigial wings folded tight.

Vethulf was relieved to see that he'd been right: it was not a large one. The wyvern's triangular head was neither longer nor thicker than his torso. Its dappled scales of lichen-green and stone-gray would vanish among the rocks when it lay still, the scattered colors breaking up its outline and fooling all but the most observant eye. In motion, though, it was unmistakable.

Vethulf felt the tension of the pack around him. His booted toes dug into the earth; he balanced lightly in his crouch, his shield dragging on his stiff, hot shoulder even when he rested one edge on the ground. Then, without any signal but the sense of his threat-brothers that they, too, were ready, he sprang down the slope.

His strides stretched long on the downhill, the heavy axe as light and quick in his hand as if it had a will of its own and merely pulled his hand behind it. Beside him ran Kjaran; strung out in a line abreast were Ulfmundr and Hlothor, Throttolfr and Djurgeirr, Ulfvaldr and Reykr.

They made, between them, a terrible noise.

From the first thumping of feet, the wyvern set its taloned feet and rose from the grass with a thunder and display of thrashing wings. If the hide of the thing was indistinguishable from the rocks and mosses among which it lived, the wings made up for it. They could not carry the wyvern in flight, but between the finger-bones the leather blazed cobalt-blue, eyed with white and purple so bright it was nearly pink. With each beat the sun flashed through them, and Vethulf was hard-pressed to remember that it was only a display and keep running.

The head was far more dangerous, and so Vethulf ran straight for it. This was his threat, and Kjaran had made him the leader of it. The greatest risk was his.

Wolves and men encircled the wyvern as Vethulf lunged toward its head, dancing in and out again. He feinted with his shield—a punch at its throat—and felt the injured shoulder protest. On every side, wolves snarled, men shouted, axes whipped through air with a whistle almost like the clangor of bells.

The wyvern fought in near-silence, after the manner of its kind. Its head hammered down at him, rows upon rows of fangs ripping the sod where he had stood a moment before.

Even through the shield, that blow would have broken his arm if it had landed. But it had missed and in missing left the wyvern's neck for a moment extended. Vethulf stepped in and, with the weight of his body behind it, swung the axe.

The wyvern hissed as its head snapped back. Vethulf would have missed and that was all, except by ill luck the inexperienced Reykr struck the wyvern at just that moment on the opposite shoulder. The lashing beast staggered; Vethulf heard the grunted cry as its tail struck either Throttolfr or his shield, and though Vethulf threw himself backward and raised his own shield, one of the wings slammed him against the ground, the talons—tiny things compared to its teeth but sharp nevertheless—raking across his chest.

He hit hard, the fire in his wounded shoulder fresh and raw, the breath whistling out of him until his lungs ached and then whistling some more. Sparks hung in his blackened vision; the edges of the world fell away until only a bright spot remained at the center.

Through that bright spot he saw a gray blur. Kjaran lunged over his prone body, snarling, and took the wyvern by the throat.

Vethulf forced his elbows against the ground, his whole chest hollow for want of breath, and managed to push down only with the right one. It levered him up but crookedly, and from where he lay he saw Kjaran, head down, hunched and snarling, with the soft underside of the wyvern's throatlatch between his crushing jaws.

The thing wheezed and heaved, tongue flickering, tail and hind parts writhing in coils, its legs scrabbling convulsively through the tattered grass. There was something high on the wyvern's throat—a thick leather band, a collar grown into the hide that bulged on either side of it—and it was that that Kjaran had a hold of, preventing him from tearing the beast's throat out.

Kjaran growled low and continuous, and Vethulf knew he was nevertheless grinding his jaws together, slowly choking out the wyvern's life.

One-handed, Vethulf forced himself onto his knees. His raking hand found his axe; the other arm hung numb. He dragged the shield behind him as he stood.

One step forward. He raised the axe.

Ulfvaldr appeared beside Kjaran, stepping out of the black margins of Vethulf's vision, and split the wyvern's skull between the eyes.

⚬❦⚬

They did not carry Vethulf down the hill on a litter, but that was only because he insisted he could walk.

"All that's wrong with me is my arm, gods rot you," he snarled.

But the arm was seriously wrong. In the absence of a wolfsprechend, Ulfmundr had struggled the clothes off Vethulf's body—more pain, Vethulf thought distantly, even than the blow—and peeled back the jerkin. The scabs had broken, competing with the new gashes to make a gory mess, and the lumps and twists under the skin told their own tale. Ulfmundr thought the muscle was torn, or possibly the tendon.

Still, Vethulf made it down the hill by his own strength. And, having done so, was more than glad to collapse in a chair before the door of Haukr's father's cabin while Guthbrandr's wife, the mother of the girl who had wakened him that morning, examined his shoulder, clucked over it, and bound it up as best she could.

"The muscle's torn, all right," she said. "You see you rest it, or it will never heal. As it is, it's likely to be trouble to you for a long time."

Vethulf sighed. But nodded. And finally accepted that draught of ale while his wolfcarls saw to their wolves and the villagers went out to butcher the wyvern (and admire its size) and drag as much of it home to smoke or salt as possible. One did not eat troll—but there was nothing unwholesome about the meat of a wyvern, and for a village like this, the great snake was an unusual windfall.

As for Vethulf, the pain made him tired, so after he made sure Kjaran's injuries were insignificant, he thumped back to that chair and drowsed in it until Haukr roused him to come out in the square and accept a share of the wyvern-meat that had been roasted by segments over the village's shallow cooking pit. It was more like frog than fowl but unobjectionable either way, and the wolves seemed to enjoy it.

Vethulf sat on the ground, eating one-handed while Kjaran gnawed fibers of meat from a segment of the dead wyrm's spine. Despite Vethulf's aches, he basked in the moment of peace.

Someone sat down laboriously beside him. It was the old ruin, Haukr's great-grandfather, levering himself into place with the aid of a staff polished black from age and use. "Greetings, wolfjarl," he wheezed.

"Greetings, grandfather," Vethulf said. "Did you get enough to eat?"

The old man smiled toothlessly. "I have no means to chew it, or appetite to drive me. It's just as well. Let it go to those as still have need. No, I came to offer a word of advice to a young man, if he will hear it."

The old man smelled rank and Vethulf almost spoke sharply, but pity moved him. What was it like to be such a man, doomed to die in bed? To endure the pity and scorn of other men?

"I will hear it," Vethulf said, surprised at himself.

The old man reached inside his jerkin and drew forth a leather string, knotted here and there, strung with beads of amber the quality of which Vethulf had never seen.

"I had these from the neck of a prince of the Brythoni," he said. "When I was your age. I have kept them since. They will go to my grandson."

"You went viking."

It was hard to credit—that those gnarled hands could have held a sword, that those stooped shoulders could have filled a shirt of chain.

"I was a jarl of the sea!" the old man boasted. His back struggled to straighten against its perpetual bow. His rheumy eyes flashed. "I took a princess from a keep, and gold from a monastery. There were songs of me. Perhaps they sing them still, in other lands. And then with my riches I returned to this place, and built a house for the woman I had raided. And in time she gave me seven sons. Two went raiding in their own right. One went to the monks. Three live here still."

"And the seventh?"

"The seventh," the old man said, "went for a wolfcarl. He is dead now."

"I am sorry."

The old man shrugged. "It was a brave death. He drains a horn at Othinn's right hand now, I have no doubt. Whereas I will dine with Hel. But that is not my advice, wolfjarl."

Vethulf smiled. He wondered what it would be like, to walk away from war. To live as long as this man had, with the memory of one's great deeds dimming behind one. To watch one's sons live so long that they, too, must call on other men for help against a fell beast of the North.

"What is your advice, grandfather?"

"Your arm," the old man said. "I will show you some practices that will help it come back to strength, if you perform them every night and morn without fail. It would be a shame if such a doughty warrior could not lift his shield."

The words went straight to the knot in the pit of Vethulf's stomach, the one he hadn't even really let himself feel. And the knowledge—if the practices did indeed work—would be something he could take back to the wolfheall and share with his brothers. And that was worth the sting to his pride.

"Thank you, grandfather," he said, and in the old man's smile

Vethulf saw, for a moment, the sea-jarl, the warrior and leader of men, he claimed he had been.

⁖

I n the dark before dawn, Vethulf awoke to the awareness that someone crouched beside his pallet. Even knowing that Kjaran would never have allowed an enemy to approach so closely, Vethulf came to alertness instantly, catching a stick-thin wrist before the hand could touch his shoulder.

"Lord Wolfjarl!" A gasp, the unbroken treble of a boy-child.

Vethulf sat up, squinting in the gloom. One of Haukr's brothers, he thought, or one of the other children who tumbled among the crofts like wolf pups. "What's toward?" he said.

"Haukr said to fetch you, Lord Wolfjarl, or Guthbrandr and Leikfrothr will be at feud in truth."

Guthbrandr was the headman, but Vethulf had no idea who the other was, why the two might be at feud, or what Haukr thought he might do about it. But the wolfheall had to be seen to care. He got to his feet, gritting his teeth against the grinding pain in his shoulder. Kjaran was there, butting anxiously against his hand, and Vethulf let himself ruffle his brother's ears for comfort before he said to the boy, "Tell them I will come forth presently and not to do anything rash betweentimes."

The boy darted out, and Vethulf let himself groan. Throttolfr sat up, not even pretending he had not been listening. The courtesy of wolves. "Do you need a hand, wolfjarl?"

"I doubt it," Vethulf said, regarding his jerkin with dislike. "Not against crofters."

"I meant in dressing," Throttolfr said, and maintained a straight face when Vethulf glared at him.

"All right, yes, damn your eyes. You can help me be presentable as Franangford's wolfjarl this cursed morning."

Vethulf had to give Throttolfr credit: he did not tease anymore, and he was not at all rough, even when Vethulf's impatience made him snap. And Vethulf went out into the first weak light of dawn with at least the assurance that he did not look like a madman.

Most of the village seemed to be waiting for him, women and men in a circle around three persons: Guthbrandr, another man who must be Leikfrothr, and the girl who had been sent to fetch Vethulf yesterday for the wyvern-hunt. Guthbrandr's daughter, whose name Vethulf had forgotten. He saw Haukr in the anxious circle of witnesses, with his little brother clinging to his hand, and when Vethulf said, "What is the problem?" it was at least as much toward Haukr as it was addressed to the croft in general.

There was a babble of answers, including outbursts from both Guthbrandr and Leikfrothr, though not from the girl, whose expression Vethulf could not read, and Vethulf had to raise his good hand to quiet them. "One voice, if you please. Haukr?"

Haukr gulped but took a half step forward. "Leikfrothr says Jorhildr is promised to him, and Guthbrandr says she is not."

Vethulf looked around to see if anyone dissented from Haukr's version, and no one did. "Thank you, Haukr," he said, and Haukr bobbed a nod and stepped back.

*God of wolves,* Vethulf thought, neither, quite, a prayer nor a curse. *What would Skjaldwulf say here? What question would he ask?* He knew that disputes like this were always a morass of claims and counterclaims, and these people had neither skald nor godsman to speak oaths before and thus have them remembered. Kjaran leaned gently against his thigh, and Vethulf knew abruptly, if not what Skjaldwulf would ask, then certainly what Isolfr would ask.

"And what," he said, "does Jorhildr say?"

Everyone looked startled, Jorhildr as much or more than anyone else. Vethulf's shoulder hurt from his hip to the top of his head, and he had neither strength nor patience to ask another question. He stood and waited, and finally Jorhildr said, "I do not wish to marry Leikfro-thr, Lord Wolfjarl. And if he should marry me, I will divorce him."

There was another round of shouting, most of it at Jorhildr; Vethulf gathered that she had not been nearly so forthright before and had possibly even been encouraging.

And when the voices died away, Leikfrothr said, "She is prom-ised."

"She is not promised," Guthbrandr retorted. "I said I would be pleased to have you as a son, and that is true, but it is not the same as a promise."

"Then what were the negotiations for?" Leikfrothr demanded. "Why were we discussing her bride-price if she was not promised to me?"

Vethulf resisted the urge either to behead the lot of them or just to go back to bed. Or possibly to behead them and *then* go back to bed. Skjaldwulf and Isolfr would both be very disappointed in him.

"If Jorhildr does not wish to marry you," he said to Leikfrothr, "you would be well advised to look elsewhere for a wife."

"She is promised," Leikfrothr said, his jaw jutting, and Vethulf thought sourly that he could see Jorhildr's point of view.

"Lord Wolfjarl," Guthbrandr said, trying to pull himself to-gether and behave as a headman instead of an angry father. "This is no concern of yours, and we should not trouble you with it."

*No, you shouldn't,* Vethulf thought. But he saw why Haukr had wanted him. If the headman was supposed to settle disputes in the village, what were they to do when the headman was himself in-volved?

*They ask the nearest wolfjarl.* He pinched the bridge of his nose, trying to convince his eyeballs that they did not need to throb out of their sockets. "Has the bride-price been given?"

"No," Guthbrandr said, and after a long grudging pause Leik-frothr agreed.

"Then the matter is not one of actual gain or loss, but merely whether a promise was or was not given?"

"More than a promise passed between us," Leikfrothr said with a spiteful glance at Jorhildr, and Vethulf decided he definitely agreed with the girl. He wouldn't want to marry this one, either.

"Do you carry his child?" Vethulf said to Jorhildr.

"No," she said, and her chin was up. "That can be proved, Lord Wolfjarl," and Kjaran, sitting beside Vethulf and attending with great interest, agreed that she smelled of blood as human females did when they did not breed. Vethulf wasn't sure whether Kjaran was attending to the words spoken or to the images he could read in Vethulf's head, but he was grateful for the support.

"Then you have lost no goods," Vethulf said to Leikfrothr, "and there is no child to claim for your house. What is the injury you claim you have suffered?"

"It is an injury to my honor!"

The girl's eyes caught light as her chin lifted. For a moment, Vethulf thought it likely that she would pick up a stick of firewood and come after the man. Her hands clenched to fists, and the tendons in her forearms showed plain. *A strong wench*, Vethulf thought admiringly.

But she controlled herself and only marched three steps forward to confront the man. "And what of my honor?" she spat. "What of these things you say of me before the entire village, and my family? When you claim me oathbroken, what then?"

It was a good question, Vethulf thought. But the man would not hear that any more gladly from a wolfcarl than from the wench.

Vethulf strode into the center of the circle, putting on an appearance—he hoped—of decisiveness. The girl didn't recoil; she wasn't afraid of him. The young man jumped a little when Vethulf took his elbow.

He was taller than Vethulf and broader across the shoulders, but

Vethulf knew from living among wolves that confidence and authority were more important than size. He never let the boy realize that he had a physical advantage, or that Vethulf was injured. And the boy didn't have the experience to see through him.

*Let's try this again.*

"Look," Vethulf said, lowering his voice so that the boy had to lean toward him to hear. "Do you really want to marry somebody who hates you? It's not a receipt for domestic peace, my lad. Better you find a girl who wants you. She'll be less likely to wash your shirts in nettles, don't you think?"

As he said it, he tried to imagine how Skjaldwulf would deliver the advice. Softly, he thought, but with certainty, and he tried to make his voice go that way.

It surprised him when he found the boy nodding. "You have some wisdom, wolfjarl," he said. "I did not think of it that way."

Vethulf caught himself just short of rolling his eyes at the girl. "And it does you no harm," he added, "to be seen an openhanded and forgiving man. No one likes a man who polishes his grudges."

*Heed your own advice,* he thought wryly, but the boy looked astonished. "Would they say that of me?"

"Yes," Jorhildr said, with relish, and for a moment Vethulf thought he'd lost control of the thing again, but Leikfrothr made a great show of ignoring her and said, "Thank you, Lord Wolfjarl. Your counsel is sage." He bowed and turned away, shouldering a path through the gathered villagers. It clearly didn't occur to him that he might owe his erstwhile betrothed, or her father, an apology.

"He is young yet," Guthbrandr said, and Vethulf was glad to see he was making an effort to recover his temper. "He will gain wisdom with the years."

Vethulf snorted. "Unless he first gets eaten by a bear."

# FOURTEEN

Skjaldwulf didn't mind being excluded from Randulfr's first conference with his brother and father. He knew as well as if he had been instructed that there would be another council after supper and his chance to speak would come then. He used the time seeing that his men and wolves were fed and watered and bedded down warmly. He would have seen to the same for himself, but by the time he came back to Mar, the big wolf was sprawled snoring on Skjaldwulf's open bedroll, a scoured-clean plate and a half-empty water bucket beside him.

Otter had apparently made herself useful in Skjaldwulf's absence.

Skjaldwulf suspected she had gone to get clean, and in that assumption he made his own way to the bathhouse before dinner. It was not as luxurious as the one they were building at Franangford, but some thrall or member of the household had kept the coals stoked, and there was water and fresh green branches.

The heat of the steam was harder to bear in summer than in winter, when it was one of the few things that could take the chill out of a man's bones after a long night patrol. But Skjaldwulf still scrubbed thoroughly, letting the heat soothe knotted muscles.

There were worse things, and if he was light-headed when he came out, it would clear. The headaches were passing, and with them the sleepiness—he hoped with no long-term harm done. His clothes—fouled with blood and the dirt of the trail—were too filthy to put on again, so he bundled them up, intending to walk back to his things and find the clean shirt he had put aside for returning to civilization.

He was not, however, expecting to all but trip over Otter as he emerged from the sauna.

"Oh, dear," she said. "I was looking for you."

She seemed unfazed by his nudity, which he supposed was only natural for a woman accustomed to army camps. She held up a cloth bundle of her own. "Fargrimr was kind enough to give me some of her—of his mother's things. I was looking for a place to wash."

"The sauna is right through there," Skjaldwulf said. "Scrapers and branches inside."

"Sauna?"

"Steam bath?"

She looked blank. He wondered if Rheans and Brythoni just scrubbed themselves in streams with handfuls of sand. Obviously, they scrubbed themselves somehow, because neither Otter nor the tribune had been particularly filthy even by Skjaldwulf's heall-refined standards. He said, "I'm sure you'll figure it out. Flick water on the stones to make steam; use the scrapers to get the dirt off. If you feel sick, drink water or step outside."

"Oh."

He smiled. "Leave your old clothes outside, and I'll take them to the laundress with my own."

She blinked, then nodded. "All right then. I'll see you at dinner."

"You, too."

⊙⥌⊙

Fargrimr and his father fed them well that night, though not elaborately. There was game, baked slowly over coals until it fell off the bone, and rounds of harsh rye cracker to soak up the juices with. Skjaldwulf shared a trencher with Otter. It being summer, there were also fruits and onions and handfuls of wild greens. Better than the food of the trail, anyway, and Skjaldwulf—with his first appetite in days—stuffed himself.

The old jarl sat at the head of the table and made conversation, and though the jarl wore blue tattoos down both arms and up his throat to the jawline, it was the same comforting conversation one found in any hall. Boasts of prowess, complaints about the harvest, discussion of the merits of women and of hounds.

Afterwards, the tables were cleared. When Fargrimr and Randulfr came to fetch him for that anticipated council, Skjaldwulf brought Otter along. "After all," he pointed out, "she knows the Rheans better than any of us."

And what she knew, she did not hesitate to share.

She told them of the vastness of the Rhean empire. Of its resources, its ambition, and how the Brythoni had fought it for their independence for a decade or more before coming under its wing, driven in part by the depredations of the Iskryners. She spoke eloquently and with passion, and her words left no doubt in Skjaldwulf's mind that the Rheans had every intent of setting a governor over his scattered people and making of them vassals and tributaries.

He thought of the Rhean tribune's gold teeth and his confessions of age and wisdom, and frowned.

"The man I met—," he said. "Caius Iunarius—"

"The southerner," Otter said.

"He said his land was a thousand leagues away, and still under the control of the Rhean emperor."

Otter nodded. "They have—they have a senate," she said. "A council of learned and powerful men who advise their emperor, who come from all over his empire. They say that in the farthest reaches of the Rhean domains the sun is setting while it rises here. I don't imagine—"

"If there is to be a war," Randulfr said, his hand automatically reaching toward his absent wolf for comfort, "there will have to be a Thing. And a konungur. We will need unity."

Freyvithr Godsman said, "The monks will fight."

Randulfr bit his lip and did not hide his smile. "That would be a godsend."

Otter threw her hands up and sighed. "You do not understand. How can you fight the Rheans?"

Fargrimr clasped his left wrist in his right hand and laid both fists on the table before him. "How can we fail to?" He looked at his father; his father was looking steadily back at him.

The old man nodded. "You will set out for Hergilsberg, then. On the morrow."

⚯

But on the morrow they could not go. Ingrun was coming into heat.

Skjaldwulf was woken in the coldest, darkest hours of the night by a combination of things: distress in the pack-sense, a burst of arousal from Mar and a throbbing in his own groin, and the mutter of Randulfr cursing under his breath.

Skjaldwulf came up on his elbows in his bedroll. "Randulfr?" No need to ask what was happening; no need, either, to ask what was wrong: of all the dreadful times for Ingrun to choose—not that it was her choice, either—this was . . . Well, it wasn't the worst, because Skjaldwulf could think of worse times, but it certainly wasn't the best. But that still didn't explain.

But by the same token, he didn't have to ask. "My father lies sleeping not fifty yards from here," Randulfr said. "My *father*, Skjaldwulf. He has mellowed these last years, and he is appeased, I know, because Fargrimr is a better son and heir to him than I could ever have been, but he still has not forgiven me for finding my wyrd elsewhere than Siglufjordhur. And he . . ."

Ingrun whined, and Randulfr murmured, "No, my heart, it is no blame of yours. I am not angered with you."

"I could send you and Ingrun from the keep—," Skjaldwulf began, and Randulfr finished: "But the woods may be crawling with Rheans."

On Skjaldwulf's other side, Frithulf said, "What can we do? Randulfr could find us a place to go, no doubt, but we cannot leave the keep safely as a group for this purpose any more than we can send Randulfr out alone."

*You wanted to be wolfjarl,* Skjaldwulf said to himself, and while that wasn't strictly true, it was close enough. He pressed the heels of his palms to his eyes, and oddly, it seemed to help. He said, "There are no other wolves here, nor bonded men to feel our mating. This arena is clean and warm and we have everything we would need."

"But—," Ulfhoss said.

"Otter," Skjaldwulf said before Ulfhoss could voice his objection.

"Yes?" said Otter. She did not pretend she had not been awake and listening, and Skjaldwulf was grateful.

"I need you—*we* need you—to go to the keep and tell Fargrimr that everyone must be kept out of here until one of us emerges and says that it is safe."

"Sh—he will want a reason," Otter said.

"Randulfr?" Skjaldwulf said. He might be wolfjarl, but the old man in that keep was not his father.

"Tell Fargrimr that Ingrun's season has come upon her. Tell him he may decide what to tell our father, so long as he ensures that no man, woman, or child trespasses on us."

"How long will it be?" Otter said; she sounded frightened, for which Skjaldwulf couldn't blame her.

"Not long," Randulfr said. "Ingrun has never stretched matters out. It should be over by sundown. But if it is not—Otter, please be sure Fargrimr understands—*no one must come near*. We will be fine. There is no danger."

"And tell him we'll all be ravenous," Frithulf said, sounding reassuringly cheerful. "Cold food is fine, as long as there's lots of it."

"All right," Otter said. "I will tell him." Skjaldwulf heard her getting up, the rustle of cloth as she dragged on her kirtle over her shift, and then the pad of her feet across the arena floor. She was silhouetted for a moment, a black shape against the scarcely lighter oblong of the doorway, and then she was gone.

"Frithulf, Geirulfr, make sure all the doors are barred and the windows shuttered. Ulfhoss, kindle lights. Randulfr, what do you need?"

A shaky laugh from Randulfr. "Oh, wolfjarl, I could recite you a list. But truly, all I need is the salve and a little time."

As Ulfhoss lit the torches, the wolves became visible: Mar, Dyrvyr, Afi, Kothran, couched in a neat semicircle around Randulfr's bedroll, where Ingrun was standing, her head swinging as she tried to keep them all in view.

"I would judge that you have a little time," Skjaldwulf said. As the best bonesetter of their traveling threat, Skjaldwulf carried their few medical supplies. He dug quickly through his pack and found the small clay pot of salve. It was soothing for skin chapped or rubbed raw, but its slickness also made it a great boon to any she-wolf's brother when her time was on him. He tossed it to Randulfr.

"A little," Randulfr said, "but probably not much." He stood up, stripping his shirt and trews off, making no effort to hide the fact that his sex was engorged. He looked at the circle of dog wolves, looked at Ingrun's half-raised lip and tightly tucked tail. He reached a torch down from the wall and said, "Sister, come." They disappeared together into one of the small storage rooms around the arena. The dog wolves whined, but did not move.

Skjaldwulf looked at his small pack. Frithulf, Geirulfr, Ulfhoss. Geirulfr was a veteran and could be relied on to keep his head. Though Kothran was too small and submissive ever to win the bitch in an open mating, Frithulf was Isolfr's shieldbrother, and Skjaldwulf knew he would be mindful for Isolfr's sake, despite his inexperience. Ulfhoss, though, he had witnessed Amma's open mating, which was all to the good, but he was young and Dyrver was young. Dyrver, Skjaldwulf rather thought, might one day make his brother a wolfjarl—which was all the more reason to be sure they went carefully now.

Skjaldwulf said, ostensibly to all of them, though he knew Geirulfr and Frithulf would know it was for Ulfhoss' sake, "Remember that the man you couple with is your werthreatbrother. Remember that though he is strong, he has not his sister's body, just as you have not your brother's. Follow your wolf, as always, but follow him as a man, not as a wolf."

Frithulf said, "Do you think there will be fighting?" He was watching Kothran, and Skjaldwulf remembered that Frithulf had witnessed the mating in which a wolf of Nithogsfjoll had lost his life. And it was, moreover, a good question. They were in an unusual situation, more like Viradechtis' mating with her two consorts than a proper open mating, and it was hard to say how matters might proceed.

Skjaldwulf opened himself to Mar and the pack-sense and found the turmoil he expected. Mar was clearly head-wolf, and no one seemed inclined to argue about that, but Afi, Dyrver, and Kothran were eyeing each other sidelong. Kothran usually had no chance at mating and was eager to make the most of this opportunity, and Dyrver had been shouldered ignominiously aside as a mere youngster when Amma bred and was equally eager to prove himself now. Afi, perceiving challenge on both sides, was all too clearly willing to fight anyone who offered.

"I hope not," Skjaldwulf said to Frithulf, and had not time for anything more, as Ingrun emerged from the storage room before her brother, and Mar and Skjaldwulf stood up together.

༒

Skjaldwulf had thought more than once that Franangford had been blessedly lucky in its bitches: Viradechtis was a marvel and had been from birth, and Ingrun and Amma were sensible and kind as she-wolves went. Ingrun did not have Amma's indiscriminate love for the young of all creatures, being far more a warrior at heart, but she was a good mother to her cubs, and unlike some bitches, she never went out of her way to encourage fighting when she was in season.

Skjaldwulf knew that among the wild wolves the fighting was no more a matter of choice than was the mating, but bonded trellwolves took some flavor of their brothers, just as wolfcarls tended to the wolfish in their humor and their politics. Conflict was inevitable, but the bitch did have some control over her followers; Skjaldwulf had seen what happened when she used that to incite them to frenzy, and that morning in Siglufjordhur's training arena, he saw the opposite. Ingrun did not want fighting, too aware that they were a small pack, far from home, surrounded by enemies. Deep in the pack-sense, he saw her image of *enemies:* great hulking shadows, mingled of troll and cave bear, that smelled not of death but of disease—of the foaming sickness that could destroy an entire pack in a matter of days.

*Brothers,* Ingrun insisted, a word she'd learned from her brother and from all the men of the werthreat, and Skjaldwulf wondered, when he could ponder the matter clearheaded again, if she had learned to use men's words from Viradechtis. Isolfr had told him that Viradechtis could do that, and Skjaldwulf knew the wolves of a pack learned from each other—and packs learned from packs when they met at a Wolfmaegthing. And Ingrun, though by no means as intelligent as Viradechtis—or Viradechtis' mother, the Nithogsfjoll konigenwolf Vigdis—was *not* stupid. And all wolves were curious and eager to learn, as wolfcarls found out to their dismay with the regularity of the waxing and waning of the moon.

*Brothers,* said Ingrun, and the dog wolves listened to her. There was some posturing and snarling, but Afi followed Mar, Dyrver followed Afi, and Kothran followed Dyrver without any blood being drawn. And they mated with no less vigor, Skjaldwulf noted; some wolfcarls claimed that the fighting heated the blood and made the dog wolves more potent, though Skjaldwulf had thought privately that if that were true, then every raped woman would bear twins.

In the aftermath, they slept, men and wolves in a happily indiscriminate pile, and when they woke, ravenous, and Ulfhoss and Geirulfr threw the doors open, they found the courtyard glowing gold and purple in the sunset.

A thrall or fosterling must have been set to watch for them, for Fargrimr was there with gratifying promptness, Otter close behind him. "We are well," Skjaldwulf said to both of them.

"And hungry," Frithulf said.

"Very hungry," Ulfhoss added.

Fargrimr actually grinned and said, "That, we are prepared for. Come." He led them into the hall, where a thrall was scurrying to and fro, setting out platters and trenchers and tankards. Fargrimr sat down with them, although he did not eat, and said, "I told Father that you were celebrating a mystery of the wolfheallan, in preparation for the work of driving the Rheans from our shore. I do not know how truthful I was, but he is not displeased."

"Truthful enough," Skjaldwulf said. It seemed better for all of them, wolfcarls and wolfless men alike, if the details were not discussed. What was not spoken could not be repeated.

Fargrimr nodded, as much in acceptance as in agreement, and gracefully turned the conversation to tactics likely to be successful in Rhean-hunting, a discussion that the wolfcarls entered into with enthusiasm, and sometimes with their mouths full. Randulfr was tentative at first, but it was soon apparent that whatever Fargrimr knew or guessed about the wolfheallan's mysteries, they did not change his feelings toward his brother, and Randulfr was soon arguing amiably with Frithulf about the best way to break the Rheans' four-square shield wall.

Skjaldwulf asked Otter, "Are you well?"

"Yes," she said. "Fargrimr was very kind. I do not know what to make of you Iskryners."

Skjaldwulf shrugged. "I like wolves better. They are simpler."

Otter gave him half a smile, but he had reminded himself of a question he had been meaning to ask: "What do you know of the Rheans' beliefs about wolves? For surely we can use their fear of trellwolves to our advantage."

"I know a little," Otter said. "Their greatest city, for which they name themselves and their empire, is Rhea Lupina. That's the name of their principal goddess, too, and she's something to do with wolves, although I couldn't ever make sense of it, whether she was eaten by a wolf, or turned into a wolf—or maybe she was a wolf turned into a woman. I don't know. The god they follow is a war god—like your Othinn, I think, but I'm not sure about that, either—and they say their city was founded by the child born when the god raped Rhea Lupina."

Skjaldwulf's mouth opened, surprise like a stone on his heart. "They have gods. Gods of their own, I mean? A war god who is neither Othinn nor Thor?"

"They call him Mars."

Unwitting, Skjaldwulf looked at his wolf. Mar blinked like a cat, immune to the nuances of the conversation but evidently finding *something* the inexplicable men were doing funny. Skjaldwulf frowned, trying to remember if he had told anyone the wolf's name while he was in captivity.

Of course men of other lands would have other gods, he supposed. Men from a warm land would not need to worship winter, nor to appease him with sacrifice. Or perhaps they were the same gods, with different names. Othinn walked in disguise in the stories.

*God of wolves, god of war.* "That's . . ."

Otter grimaced in agreement. "They hold wolves sacred, but I think there aren't very many of them—wolves, I mean—around Rhea Lupina itself. And I'm sure there aren't any as big as your wolves."

"Is that why they decided Mar had to be some kind of ghost?"

"Not a ghost," Otter said. "But yes. I know some of them were saying that maybe the enormous wolves were a sign of Rhea Lupina's displeasure. Now that I think of it, that may be why the centurion was willing to let Sixtus yelp on about you being a witch."

"Yes," Skjaldwulf said. "If I'm a witch, I can be burned. But if the goddess is displeased . . ."

"Probably they burn you anyway," Otter said.

❧

O ne thing," Vethulf said, against the exhaustion that dragged at every limb.

"You need to sleep," said Isolfr, who had been white-faced and peremptory since Throttolfr and Ulfvaldr had half-carried Vethulf into Franangfordheall.

"'S important," Vethulf insisted, because he knew it was, even if he couldn't quite remember why. He pushed himself up on his good elbow and would have reached for Isolfr except that the first hint of movement reminded him not to.

Isolfr looked at him and apparently decided that it *was* important. "All right. Tell me. But then you *rest*."

"Yes," Vethulf agreed. There was nothing he wanted more at that moment. But . . . "The wyvern. It had a collar."

"A collar?"

Vethulf couldn't tell if the frown was perplexity or concern, so he explained, "Too small. Grown since. Trolls."

"You think it was one of the wyverns the trolls kept," Isolfr said cautiously.

"Yeah," said Vethulf, slumping back against his pillows. "Run wild. Like pigs, when the farmer dies."

"And those are the most dangerous," Isolfr said softly. He understood.

"Yeah," Vethulf said again, and fell hard asleep.

෧෨

S kjaldwulf spent the next two days eating the fish and dulse that Siglufjordhur harvested from the sea, and going over Siglufjordhur's defenses with Randulfr, Fargrimr, and their sister's husband, Bjorr. The old jarl, though keen-eyed and keen-minded, was no longer able to walk farther than the length of the longhouse. The trellwar had been the last rally of a long life spent in warring.

*A long life?* Skjaldwulf thought. Fastarr was older than Iunarius, but by how much? Five summers? Ten? How much longer could he have expected to live, had he been born Rhean?

Unprofitable thought, and Skjaldwulf shook it off.

Siglufjordhur, being less than half a mile inland, was built for defense as much as for monitoring the sea. "The jarl of Siglufjordhur is still known as the Watchman," Randulfr told Skjaldwulf, and Siglufjordhur's rocky prominence made sense in another way. There had been less need for watch and defense in Fastarr's time, as the Northmen quit raiding each other and turned their attention to Brython and the southern lands, and although he was too good a steward to let anything fall into disrepair, it was clear that Siglufjordhur's wealth had been put to other uses.

In principle, Skjaldwulf approved. The crofts and cottages about the keep were in good repair, sheep and children alike were healthy, and there was a windmill, its wood still yellow with newness, that every man in Siglufjordhur—to Skjaldwulf's observation—looked on with pride.

Unless he had gone north to the trellwar, no one alive in Siglufjordhur today had ever seen a troll, and only the oldest of the grandfathers might remember their grandfathers telling stories of the troll attacks *their* grandfathers had survived.

*Franangford and Nithogsfjoll could look like this,* Skjaldwulf thought, and it was an almost incomprehensibly strange idea.

But for now the question was how to make Siglufjordhur more like the northern keeps rather than the other way around. Fargrimr had begun the process, but he was hampered by the reluctance of the farmers to believe there was any real danger. The Rheans thus far had been behaving like bandits, attacking travelers and outlying crofts but leaving alone anything within sight of a keep. "It cannot last," Fargrimr said, and Skjaldwulf, having seen the Rhean camp and the monumental self-confidence of the tribune, agreed.

"They are merely waiting until they are dug in," Skjaldwulf said, "and until they have a satisfactory sense of what they are fighting. An invasion force is what I saw, not a raiding party."

Bjorr looked doubtful still. He was his father-in-law's housecarl; from things said and unsaid, Skjaldwulf had gathered that he was also the son of the most stubborn of the farmers. Bjorr was not a warrior. He said, "But perhaps they will see that we are not easy prey like the Brythoni, and they will go away."

Skjaldwulf reminded himself that this was not a wolfheall and he was not leader here. He had no authority save what Fastarr and Fargrimr chose to give him.

And Fargrimr answered in any event. "It is not a chance I like to take. If we prepare our defenses and it turns out that we guessed wrong, we are none the worse off. But if we do *not* prepare our defenses and are wrong, then we are dead or enslaved."

"You will be singing a different tune come winter," said Bjorr, "when we have not enough food laid in."

"Enough," Fastarr said sharply. "I agree with Fargrimr. We must defend ourselves, or our food stores will only serve to feed our enemies. But I know it is also true that if we abandon the farms now, we do not have enough food in the keep to feed all our liegemen and their families. We will have to try to balance one concern against the other."

Fargrimr made a face, and Fastarr laughed. "I know, but we cannot solve one problem by pretending the other is not there. Which brings me to another sty which must be cleaned."

"The bandits," Fargrimr said disgustedly.

"Bandits?" Randulfr said, sitting up straighter. "Since when are there bandits in Siglufjordhur?"

"Since two winters ago," Fargrimr said, choosing to take the question literally. "We played hide-and-go-seek with them for months—and then the call to the trellwar came and had to be answered. And now we have crippled warriors and half-trained boys, and a new danger to contend with."

"And the bandits," Fastarr added, "have the luck of the gods." He and Fargrimr exchanged a dark look, and Skjaldwulf understood what was not being said: *luck—or help.*

Banditry was a problem Skjaldwulf was more familiar with from tales than from experience; the far north was too hard a land, and men too dependent on each other's goodwill for survival. But it took only a very little imagination to see how matters would be different here along the coast. And very little more to see how a pack of bandits could go to a village heofodman with a bargain he would be hard-pressed to refuse. Or, Skjaldwulf supposed with a shiver, it would be easy enough for a whole village to turn bandit.

He said, "Though we do not usually do so, we can hunt men as well as trolls."

Fargrimr gave him a look bright with interest. "That," he said, "would be very useful indeed."

❦

They set out at moonrise, wolves and men, with Fargrimr along both to provide guidance and to mete out justice as might be necessary. Fargrimr knew roughly where the bandits were laired: a gnarled and knotty stretch of forest that was—Skjaldwulf saw at a glance—ideal for emerging to ambush travelers and equally ideal for eluding pursuit.

Unless your pursuers were trellwolves.

The wolves dispersed into the woods as silently as a scatter of raindrops into a pond; their brothers followed them. Skjaldwulf tended to lose track of time in the hunt, so he could not say whether it was quickly or slowly that the wolves picked up the scent of their prey. *Men,* said Kothran, who had the keenest nose. *Dirty, wolfless men. There.*

The wolves turned, Afi swinging wide, Ingrun closing the circle. Mar and Dyrver followed Kothran. *Hunters,* Skjaldwulf thought, and though it was by no means a new thought, it chilled him. *Hunters of men.*

The bandits had rigged a series of dugouts and lean-to shelters, well-camouflaged with tree branches and dead leaves, and all but impossible to see in the soft, cold moonlight. Although it was a rough camp, it had every appearance of permanence—this was no spur-of-the-moment enterprise, existing solely from one opportunity to the next. These men were bandits as other men were farmers or wolfcarls, and Skjaldwulf did not mind nearly so much being a hunter of men if his prey was men like these.

The rout was quick. The bandits, startled and sluggish with sleep, were not warriors, and even those who seemed to have some rudimentary skills were utterly unnerved by the trellwolves. The wolves herded their catch into the middle of the clearing: six men, ranging from a boy barely old enough to start a beard to a paunchy fellow older than Skjaldwulf—this last clearly being the leader and inclined to bluster until Fargrimr stepped out of the trees.

"I know you," he said coolly, and named all six, ending with the leader, who was also the brother of the heofodman of Botarsmyrr. "And thus," Fargrimer concluded, "many things are supplied with an explanation."

He tucked his hands behind his belt and stood in a warrior's wide-legged stance. "Justice demands your execution, but if I execute you here and now—"

The bandits broke out in a clamor, and Fargrimr silenced them with an upraised hand. "Do not think justice will not be done. But if I run you through as you deserve, then I will never have truth from Botarsmyrr, only muttering and discontent and whispered lies. So we will go to Botarsmyrr now, and this will be finished before the sun reaches its height." His eyes were cold, his voice level and uninterested, and the bandits were silenced.

Fargrimr turned to Skjaldwulf. "I must ask you, Lord Wolfjarl, do not let them escape. And convince those that need convincing that death in a trellwolf's jaws is not preferable to a clean killing stroke."

Looking at the bandits' ashen faces, Skjaldwulf did not think they would need much convincing.

⟨⟩

It was not a pleasant morning. The heofodman of Botarsmyrr died beside his brother. But Fargrimr walked with a lighter stride as they returned to the keep, and Fastarr showed his gratitude with gifts. And that night, Skjaldwulf lay beside Mar's warm bulk and knew that if they did not leave for Hergilsberg soon, they would not leave at all.

⟨⟩

May I join you?"

Brokkolfr looked up, needing his eyes' confirmation. It was Isolfr, standing awkwardly in the doorway of the sauna. Without his daughter, for once: Brokkolfr was used to seeing her chasing her father from place to place on plump toddling legs as a wolf pup chases its mother. But she must be with her nurse now or in the care of the women of the heall.

"Of course," he said. "I mean, please do."

Isolfr gave him a flash of a smile and let the hides swing down behind him.

He was not a large man, Isolfr Ice-mad, sighthound lean instead of mastiff broad. Brokkolfr could probably have bested him in a wrestling match, if he'd been daft enough to try. Isolfr sprinkled another dipper of water over the stones and sat down on the bench beside Brokkolfr.

"I've been thinking about what you said," Isolfr said after a few moments of silent and contented sweating.

"What I said?" Brokkolfr could think of any number of things he'd said, none of which he wanted Isolfr to be thinking about.

"About Hreithulfr."

"Oh. Isolfr, you don't—"

"No, you were right," Isolfr said tranquilly. "It *is* my duty as wolfsprechend. I was . . ." There was a long pause, in which Isolfr reached for a scraper and began cleaning his arms. "When you were taught about mating, how did they go about it? At Othinnsaesc?"

"Um," said Brokkolfr, uncertain where this was going. But if Isolfr finally wanted to talk, Brokkolff was willing to try almost any topic. "My wolfsprechend told me the way of things among wolfcarls, and he . . . Oh."

"Yes," Isolfr agreed, with a shy, wry smile. "Hrolleif was much older than I am, and he . . . he was Grimolfr's lover. He understood love between men, and I—I honor it, but I don't . . . only when Viradechtis . . ."

He was becoming hopelessly mired, and Brokkolfr said, "I understand." Because he did. He gathered his courage and asked, "Were you a virgin?"

"No. I had had a lover in my father's keep."

Of course. A jarl's son would be expected to. "I was a virgin."

"Oh," said Isolfr.

"It wasn't bad," Brokkolfr said hastily. "He taught me a lot of things I'd *never* have learned otherwise. And his lover was the heallbred woman who does all Othinnsaesc's dyeing. I just meant, I understand what it was like. And why you're . . ."

"Uncomfortable," Isolfr supplied.

"Yes. Here. If I scrape your back, will you do mine?"

They traded, turn and turnabout, as friends did, or shieldbrothers, and Isolfr said, "It *is* my duty, though."

"Yes," Brokkolfr said. "I'm sorry."

"No, why should you be? I wanted to thank you for making me

see that before it was too late. You said you wanted to be my second, and I thought I should tell you I would be honored."

He was smiling, and Brokkolfr, his heart lighter than it had been in months, perhaps even since the fall of Othinnsaesc, felt himself starting to smile back.

◦Ŷ◦

When they went—five wolfcarls, five wolves, a Brython girl, two ponies, and a godsman—Fargrimr went with them. "To assure the monks of our good faith," he said, and Skjald-wulf wasn't sure whether Fargrimr intended the pun or not. Judging by the spark in his eyes, probably. But the sworn-son was a dry wit, and it was hard to be sure.

Skjaldwulf thought he also wanted a chance to spend some time with his elder brother. It was a pleasure to see them together, their manners so unlike the stiffly polite meetings that were the best Skjald-wulf had managed with his own kin once he bonded Mar. Fargrimr also treated the wolves with respect, not blinking at the wolfcarl habit of including them in conversation. He was a good traveling companion, fast and tireless and with a knowledge of the land as deep as blood.

Once he was comfortable with them, he proved an excellent storyteller—not trained as Skjaldwulf was but with a knack for mimicry and an instinct for timing. And he was not too proud to tell stories with himself as the butt, which Skjaldwulf appreciated in any man, and especially one destined to be a jarl.

Freyvithr and Fargrimr agreed it would take three to five days to reach the coastal town of Hergilsbay, where they would hire a boat for the voyage to Hergilsberg itself. They proved right: the journey was four days, and in that time the small group of wolves and men dealt summarily with one group of bandits and dodged a large Rhean patrol. They also dispatched a smaller group of Rheans, and

Skjaldwulf made sure to claim a sword and a helm to bring along as evidence.

The ponies would be left at the stable the monks maintained on the mainland. There was no point in shipping them to the island city of Hergilsberg, which had as many horses as it needed, and of the monastery itself Freyvithr said: "Our chapel is on a smaller island, and that island is rocky. The settlement is quite small. We got a trio of goats out there some years ago, and that was enough to convince us that larger animals belonged on the mainland."

"What of the wolves?" Skjaldwulf asked. "Are you asking us to leave them behind?"

"I'm not such a fool as that." Freyvithr looked at the wolves and wolfcarls assessingly. "We may have to hire more than one boat."

Skjaldwulf was relieved by Freyvithr's immediate understanding that men and wolves were not to be separated. It occurred to him that by traveling with Freyvithr, he had secured the wolfheallan a sympathetic ear among the godsmen, which seemed unpleasantly likely to be necessary.

*Would have been a marvelously clever notion. Had I thought of it.*

⚶

Skjaldwulf wasn't seacoast bred, but he'd been in a good-sized town and on a boat before. As they wended through the bustle of Hergilsbay, Skjaldwulf was acutely aware of the eyes of the townsfolk on him, his men, and his wolves. And he was just as acutely aware that some of those men and wolves were made crowningly uncomfortable by the attention. Dyrver and Ulfhoss, in particular, were young and needed seasoning, and Skjaldwulf noticed that they kept to the center of the group.

Frithulf, predictably, enjoyed the bustle—and chattered about it ceaselessly. And Randulfr and Fargrimr were entirely at home— they had both obviously spent a good deal of time here.

Not so much time as Freyvithr, though, to whom Skjaldwulf had just cause to be grateful. Because Freyvithr strode through the crowds, his kilted coat swinging against his heavy calves, his staff swinging, too, in time to his stride. And the godsman greeted a face on every street with a wave and a name, which soon made the tired little group's passage seem more like a stroll and less like a procession.

At the third street-crossing, Skjaldwulf leaned across to Randulfr and ducked to speak in the other wolfcarl's ear. "How big is this town?"

"Some thousands," Randulfr said, grinning at Skjaldwulf's bogglement. "Wait until you see Hergilsberg."

They found no trouble in boarding the horses, though the press of people all around made Skjaldwulf feel, more and more, that he was at the heart of a great army. That was the only time he'd seen so many people in one place before, and this group was men and women, racing children and tottering grandmothers. Otter, though, did not seem distressed in the least by it and looked about herself with great delight.

From the stable they made their way to the ferry docks, and there Skjaldwulf was glad to let Freyvithr and Fargrimr handle the haggling once more. The party was in fact divided into two boats, and though Freyvithr assured them all it was perfectly safe, it took all of Skjaldwulf's coaxing to lure Mar aboard.

The black wolf huddled in the bilges, miserable, and he was not the only one distrustful of this seemingly rickety device in the face of the great sea that stretched before them. Skjaldwulf thought Ulfhoss was going to have to actually pick Dyrver up by main strength and set him in the other boat where it floated, gently bobbing beside the dock. But Kothran leaped lightly over the gunnels and then poked his head back over, giving a short, sharp yip as if to say, *Shake your tail, there,* and so Dyrver was shamed into courage.

*And so it is with all of us*, Skjaldwulf thought. Freyvithr piled into that boat as well, and Afi and Geirulfr—leaving Skjaldwulf with Randulfr, Ingrun, Fargrimr, and Otter. As Skjaldwulf turned back to mind his own half of the threat, he caught Otter smiling.

Randulfr assured him that this was calm seas and no chop worthy of the name. But as the blue-armed ferryman and his two strong tattooed sons pulled away from the dock with oars until they were well in the wind, Skjaldwulf still found himself white-knuckled on the edge of his bench. He comforted himself that the ferryman was probably as scared of the wolves as the wolfcarls were of the sea.

"Look, wolfjarl!" Fargrimr gestured as they rounded a long point of land that defined the bay. "There is Hergilsberg the island. The city is farther along; we will pass right under it."

As the big island came into sight, Skjaldwulf understood what Fargrimr had been trying to describe. Hergilsberg stood athwart the mouth of Hergilsbay like a stalwart defender (and hadn't there been a song about Hergil? Skjaldwulf half-remembered it, from the days before his old songs had been buried under nigh on twenty years of wolfcarl lore). The stark cliffs rose up like escarpments, and a walled city with a great keep surmounted the highest point, commanding the strait in both directions.

They did, indeed, pass directly under it. Skjaldwulf felt the hairs on his nape lift as he considered how easy it would be for some defender to simply drop rocks down and hole the boat between his feet. Would the water geyser up or simply roll in—quickly, softly?

He shuddered and looked away.

The tide was running out, sucking them along at a great pace. Good fortune, that—or perhaps Freyvithr had timed it so. As they passed the strait, Skjaldwulf realized that what he had taken as a breakwater or jetty at the base of the cliffs was actually the tail of another island, protruding around the curve of the first. This one was lower but just as rocky, and he could see the white shapes of goats hopping from stone to stone above the sea. They were eating dulse, dancing as sure-footedly on the sea-slick stones as if they moved along a broad promenade. There were too many of them, and much too active, to count.

Above the hissing surf, shining whitely, stood the ragged lime-washed walls of the monastery.

"Three goats?" he said dryly, wishing Freyvithr weren't a hundred yards behind and so out of range of his sarcasm.

Fargrimr shrugged. "Maybe one was a billy."

⚘

There were more godsmen and godswomen than Skjaldwulf had expected. So many people, here, and all of them so intent on what they were doing. The bustle alone, men and woman clustering at the piers as the ferries docked, was daunting.

The wolfless men disembarked first; as the wolfcarl's and wolves began to follow, someone in a shift of onion-dyed homespun, barefoot and her hair caught up in an untidy knot as if she'd just run from her washing, hurled herself into Freyvithr's arms with shameless delight. The godsman picked her up and whirled her before putting her down once more.

"My wife, Brunnhilde, the chatelaine of our little outpost," was what Freyvithr said to Skjaldwulf, when Skjaldwulf, having seen Mar safely onto dry land, made his way to them and she doubled over laughing. "This is Skjaldwulf, wolfjarl of Franangford, who has come to answer our questions about his wolfsprechend."

Skjaldwulf extended his hand as she recovered. "I had gathered the relationship."

She gave him her wrist, and he bowed over it as prettily as he remembered how. He might seem out of fashion, but he was determined not to be taken for a country fool.

If he'd failed in his courtesies, she seemed forgiving. "Lunch will be ready in a span or so," she said. "I imagine you all want more than anything to pull your boots off."

"That's true," Skjaldwulf said. "But we come bearing grave news, as well, and we rely on you to bring it before the jarl of Hergilsberg."

He knew as well as anyone that the jarl of a great keep might hesitate to listen to a clutch of raggle-taggle travelers from far away, even be they ever-so-romantic a band as wolfcarls. But Randulfr and Fargrimr's father had made them a gift of some vellum and ink—rare and expensive items—and Skjaldwulf and Otter had spent their nights on the trail drawing up maps of all she knew about the Rhean strength and movements.

More and more, Skjaldwulf was finding himself grateful that they had come together out of captivity. He'd said as much to Freyvithr, and Freyvithr had smiled slyly and said, "Then thank those who placed her in your path."

*Godsmen,* Skjaldwulf cursed to himself, but it was a mild and amused frustration.

"The jarl," Brunnhilde said. She glanced at her husband. "Is this something the godheofodman needs to know of?"

Freyvithr nodded, frowning. "The Brythoni have made alliance with the Rhean empire, from the far south. And the Rheans have come to take Brython's justice upon us for all the years of viking."

Brunnhilde was fair enough to show it clearly when she flushed. "And this lass?"

Otter was not so clear-skinned. But she ducked her chin none-theless, and Skjaldwulf wondered if it was from the notice, or simply that she was unaccustomed to being called "lass."

"A Brython enslaved by the Rheans," he said. "She has been of great help."

"Hmm," Brunnhilde said. But whether she was thinking of inquiring why it was that Skjaldwulf did not fear Otter as a Brythoni spy or whether she was about to pry Otter loose from the men and take her somewhere to cosset her, he never found out. Because Freyvithr was gesturing them up the pier to the road it fronted on, past an assemblage of shacks strung with fishing nets drying in the sun.

Skjaldwulf's feet hurt, and his calves ached with walking. The maps were safe in his pack, and they would speak with the jarl as soon as the godheofodman secured an audience for them.

They were safe. For a time.

# FIFTEEN

The wolves and men—and Otter—were still settling into their austere quarters, Skjaldwulf with his hand on the door to the cell he'd been allotted, when a young girl came up to him at a run. Her bare feet scattered the rushes softening the monastery's ancient stone floors. Skjaldwulf assumed she was an acolyte, because she wore plain homespun but was not collared or crop-haired like a thrall.

*Sunshine,* Mar said, of her scent. He leaned his shoulder against Skjaldwulf's hip and thigh, and Skjaldwulf leaned a little back.

The girl neither curtseyed nor effaced herself in any manner, but met his eyes as boldly as befitted a priestess. The sunlight through the monastery's narrow windows haloed her. Her bearing contradicted the freshness of her face. He wondered whom she served, and amused himself briefly thinking that it must be Ithunn, of the golden apples of immortality.

After all that, what she said turned out to be reassuringly mundane. She spoke in a light self-confident voice, telling Skjaldwulf that he, Fargrimr, and Otter were summoned to the Hall of Othinn in as much time as it should take the sun to move two fingers' width across the sky, and that she would be pleased to guide him once he had made ready.

"My wolf comes with me," Skjaldwulf said.

That, at last, provoked a smile. And a pair of pretty dimples as she glanced down at Mar. Maybe she was Ithunn herself and no mere servant.

Stranger things happened in epics, and that was where Skjaldwulf, all unwitting, seemed to have landed himself.

She said, "In the hall of the god of wolves, how can a wolf be unwelcome?"

Skjaldwulf let himself and his wolf into the cell and shut the door between them, begging her pardon. He tidied himself as best he could in such haste, which meant that the tangled braids he'd half-undone had to be loosed completely and combed in rough haste, as there was no time to find a threatbrother to rebraid them. At least they'd been spending so little time in beds that he was comfortably louse-free.

Then he stomped into his boots and opened the door to the hall again, to find the Ithunn-girl waiting as if she had scarcely breathed in his absence. "Follow!" she said, and again she ran.

Skjaldwulf ran behind her, his steps in his worn boots significantly heavier than hers. He kept up easily enough, though he had a sense she was intentionally pressing him. But Mar responded to the challenge—a healthy wolf would no more refuse an invitation to run than he would refuse raw meat—and even Skjaldwulf drew up with her before the doors of the Hall of Othinn only slightly out of breath, despite the summer heat.

Fargrimr arrived a moment later, also running behind a young man dressed as alike to the Ithunn-girl as if the cloth had been cut from the same bolt. The sworn-son ran as well as he did everything else save grow a beard. Skjaldwulf wondered for a moment what it was like to take to being a man as a profession, rather than an accident of birth. You'd study it, he imagined. You'd learn it as well as Isolfr had learned swordplay when he had been Njall Gunnarrson and the future jarl of Nithogsfjoll.

Skjaldwulf nodded a greeting. "One more?" he asked.

The Ithunn-girl shook her head. "The Brython is already within."

*Separate and conquer,* Skjaldwulf thought. But in the godheofodman's sandals he would have done the same: gotten an uninfluenced interview with the primary source—and potential spy—before bringing in the leaders of the party.

The Ithunn-girl and Fargrimr's lad stepped to either side of the doors and moved latches. The doors themselves were carved of some wood aged almost black, showing the hack marks of more than one set of ancient axes over carving that had once been an intricate and subtle study of innumerable wolves and ravens.

"God of winter, god of war," Skjaldwulf muttered as they passed over the foot-dished stone and the cool of the chapel's interior enfolded them. It was dim within, and the space was smaller than he had anticipated. He'd imagined something like the great hall of a wolfheall, but this was a more intimate setting—a large empty room with a reliquary on one end, the interior pierced by close-set columns in military rows, no two left alike by the stonecutter's whims.

A low dais supported the reliquary, and on the edge of that dais, Otter perched beside a great shaggy bulk of a man. She turned when the doors opened, gathering about her the skirts of yet another dress

Randulfr's family had given her, and stood. The man beside her rose to his feet like one of the stone columns that surrounded them, and came forward, trailing a visibly anxious Otter.

Erik, godheofodman of Hergilsberg, could not have been more exactly what Skjaldwulf would have imagined, had Skjaldwulf been required for the purpose of some tale-telling to imagine him. He was a man in the last vigorous years of his life, as tall as, broader than, and perhaps fifteen years older than Skjaldwulf.

Unlike the boy-faced tribune, he looked his age. A scar creased his cheek and brow, disappearing under an eyepatch on the right side, leaving Skjaldwulf to wonder if that had been an intentional sacrifice to his god or the manner in which the god had claimed him off some battlefield. His hair, unbraided and caught at his nape in a clasp, had once been black, but years had weathered it to the color of granite. His beard was still black at the center, but the sides and the moustache glittered like hammered steel. He, too, wore homespun, a rough robe with no sleeves, open at the side-seams to accommodate arms as broad as some men's thighs. He had the belly of a man who liked his ale, and the shoulders of a man who carried the kegs up from the cellars two at a time.

And over his priest's robe he wore a cloak of bearskin, thrown back off his shoulders now, the silver-tipped seal-brown hairs ruffling gently in the wind of his movement.

His voice, though, was soft and rough as he extended his right arm to clasp and said, "In Othinn's name, wolfjarl, I thank you your journey. And you, Siglufjordhur's heir, be welcome in Othinn's house."

"Thank you for your graciousness," Skjaldwulf answered, returning the clasp before standing aside so that Fargrimr could have his turn. The godheofodman had a forearm like bandy steel, enough to make Skjaldwulf wonder if he spent his evenings at the smithy. "Unfortunately, as you have no doubt heard, we do not come merely to meet Freyvithr's thirst for histories."

"Alas," Erik said. "I know. And your charming companion has been most enlightening."

Was that actually a flush warming Otter's checks? It was hard to tell, with her complexion and the dimness. But the duck of her head suggested so.

"It seems you are well in advance of all our intelligence," Skjaldwulf said. "And, I would guess, also all our requests. There must be an AllThing; we must prepare for war."

"You wish me to speak to the jarl of Hergilsberg, and plead this case before him."

Skjaldwulf looked at Fargrimr.

Fargrimr nodded.

Erik sighed. "I tell you this because I know the jarl and I know what he will say. He will say, *it seems that the wolfheallan come crying for assistance a great deal of late.* He will say, *did we not send men from Holm and Siglufjordhur to fight their last war for them—*"

"The men from Siglufjordhur," Fargrimr said stiffly, "went of their own accord."

The godheofodman showed broken teeth when he smiled.

Skjaldwulf shook his head. "A jarl would say this?"

"He is old. He had played politics too long, and forgotten what it is to be a warrior. To be a wolf. He will say, *what, the northerners cannot handle a few raiding parties of Brythoni allies? Are they wolves or are they women?*"

"I see," Skjaldwulf said. Over Erik's shoulder, Otter threw him a bitter grimace.

Fargrimr drew himself up. "And when the Rheans sail up to Hergilsberg and say, *we have taken all the farms and all the forest, will you open the gates or will you starve?*"

"He'll open the gates," Erik said. He waited, looking from man to man, and Skjaldwulf nodded.

"You see another option."

Erik spread wide hands, each like the paw of a bear. "Where is it sung that the Wolfmaegth cannot call an AllThing?"

Skjaldwulf felt himself take a step back. "A wolfcarl could not be konungur over wolfless men—"

"Calling an AllThing is not the same as proclaiming one's self konungur," Erik said. "It is proclaiming the need for a konungur. I am sure a suitable selection of candidates for argument could be arranged."

Skjaldwulf folded his arms, too aware that this aged berserk—and who had ever heard of such a thing, a bear-cloak living to retire?—was outmaneuvering him on the field of politics to such a degree that Skjaldwulf was not even certain what Erik's final goal might be.

"Would the wolfless men come to the Wolfmaegth's summoning?"

There was a pause. A hesitation. Then Fargrimr said, "Siglufjordhur would."

And Erik hitched his bear-cloak back with a thumb and said, "The jarl of Hergilsberg might not. But the godheofodman would. And if I came, so would a number of the thanes."

"And if it did not work," Fargrimr said, "if not enough jarls and thanes decided to come?"

"Either they would accept the konungur the rest chose, or they would go to war against him," said the godheofodman. "And the Rheans would inherit a shattered Iskryne for no more effort than the lifting of a hand."

"The harvest is upon us. By the time messengers go out and travelers gather—" Skjaldwulf stroked his beard, wishing the gesture imparted wisdom in life as it did in tales. "There is only just time before winter locks down to do this."

Wolfcarls could travel in winter. Most townsmen could not. It was a bold decision. It was a dangerous decision. It was the sort of decision, Skjaldwulf thought, that would be either honored or mocked in a hundred years of songs.

*Songs.* He breathed in deep. "If we must, so we must," he said. "Listen, I have an idea."

Erik Godsman stared him up and down. "Speak it. Or are wolf-carls known for their coyness?"

"You must have some priests that can sing, aye?"

The godsman's smile took awhile to reach his eyes. "Some," he allowed. "Aye."

◦┆◦

As much as Skjaldwulf fretted to be away from Hergilsberg at once, common sense and experience reminded him that he had come all this way—*through untold perils*—for a task and it would be best if that task was completed. Moreover, there was the song to compose and priest-skalds to send out to sing it.

A song that, having said he would compose, Skjaldwulf hadn't the faintest idea how to begin.

It was easier to extemporize, to unlock a word-hoard and make something up on the spot, knowing that people would quote the best bits and forget the rest. But this had to be memorable, and chantable, and it had to be the sort of thing people would pick up in a hearing or three and repeat to their friends.

And here he was just beyond the walls of a city such as he had never imagined, a city vast as a trellwarren, teeming with people, with markets, with foreigners—

Skjaldwulf suppressed his restlessness for two days. With Frith-ulf, who had been Isolfr's shieldbrother through many of his adventures, he went to the archives each morning after porridge and stayed there, spinning tales and investigating the history of human relations with the svartalfar until the bell for supper rang. The priests ate well, if plainly, and Skjaldwulf soon felt the flesh that travel had stripped from his always-bony frame returning.

Scribes needed good light, and so the archives had broad windows. These were shaded by the tree Skjaldwulf had heard of, the one supposedly planted by Freya's own hand, and the space was very pleasant, if dusty. The priests were skilled questioners and in giving them his history, he found himself learning things he had never suspected. He knew how to piece together a tale as a skald would, how to ferret out the truth behind a warrior's recital of renown— and retell it so the truth seemed more exciting than the lies. But this thing the godsmen historians did—they built a mosaic of tiny details, things that seemed insignificant to Skaldwulf, like the rations needed for a band of men and wolves on the move to war, into a sort of comprehensive whole that he'd never imagined.

They did seem surprised to discover that he was literate, which made him laugh. Who did they think kept the records of breedings for a wolfheall, and who kept the accounts? Admittedly, not every wolfcarl could read or cipher, but in any heall it was good if one wolfheofodman or two could manage his runes and figures.

At Franangford, that meant Isolfr and Skjaldwulf, though Sokkolfr was learning—housecarls often lasting longer in that role than wolfjarls did in theirs.

Strangely, the godsmen seemed interested in those details, too. It made Skjaldwulf understand, a little, how foreign wolfcarls and their ways were to these southerners. (He almost thought, *Soft southerners*, but that was unfair: they might spend all their days hunched over books, but he found it pressed him to the limit of his endurance to keep up with their questioning all the hours between sunrise and sunset. Historians, he concluded, did not sleep.)

By the third day, he had had enough, and the need to complete the song he'd promised the godheofodman was pressing at him. He made his excuses to the priests, took his leave of Mar, pulled on his tattered boots, retrieved some coin from the packs left piled where the wolves slept, and made his way down to the docks. A few inquiries led him to the Hergilsberg ferry, where he bought passage and buns for his breakfast. Some of the more heavily accented individuals seemed to have a hard time with Skjaldwulf's speech, but he used the painstakingly learned skald's dialect of his apprenticeship and managed to get through to them. And honestly, it wasn't like it was such a large marina that he could get lost in it.

Unlike the one he could see across the water, on the big island.

The crossing was no worse than the first, and briefer. As the ferryman and his 'prentice rowed with ropy arms, Skjaldwulf sat, arms crossed, already missing his wolf. But the problem of bringing Mar into a city not accustomed to wolfcarls and wolves was not a wyvern he was prepared to battle. Not this morning, anyway.

Today he meant to write a song. And buy a pair of boots.

The Hergilsberg market square was hard by the docks, a sensible coincidence for which Skjaldwulf thanked his gods. The houses here were of stone or plastered timber and some were three stories tall— like little keeps. It seemed the tradesmen's stalls were in the ground floors of those houses, behind wide, low shuttered windows that opened over a bench or counter directly onto the street. In half an hour's time, Skjaldwulf had located no fewer than three cobblers.

Wary of the sort of tricks a dishonest tradesman might play on a foreigner, he spent some time politely accosting comfortable-looking passersby and asking after the source of their footwear. A few were taken aback, but in general the denizens of Hergilsberg seemed unfazed by weary and tattered-looking travelers, and eager to discuss the merits of various local shops and craftsmen.

In many cases, once they realized who and what he was they were eager to ask him questions of their own, and Skjaldwulf had to prevent two men from all but bodily standing him a drink.

Just walking the street in Hergilsberg was exhausting. Every street was paved in cobbles, and while the civic wealth it indicated was impressive (and the foot and horse traffic heavy enough that he did not wonder at the need), they wore hard on the bones of his feet through his thin soles. And there were so many people! He'd left his axe and buckler behind—somehow, they did not seem like the sort of thing one carried through a town on a shopping expedition— and wore only the dagger at his belt. Nevertheless, it was an effort of will to keep his hand from the hilt each time someone jostled him, or just because of the press of people on every side, as if the whole *world* had gone to market.

None too soon, Skjaldwulf found the shop recommended by four local men as the best available for a moderate price, and set about haggling with the proprietor. He wound up paying twice what he would have in Franangford, but by the deftness with which his feet were measured, and with the boots promised for the next day, he felt like he'd gotten a fairly good deal.

As he turned away from the cobbler's window-bench, he became aware that the general sense of *too many people* had resolved into a specific awareness of being watched. And indeed, there was a thane— obviously a thane, though he wore no more weapons than Skjaldwulf did and no armor—with a heavy gold ring on his thumb, and his blue-worked arms bare to the shoulder. He was a great barrel-chested man, brown-bearded, his cheeks above the hair also banded with runewards needled into the skin so long ago the lines had softened and blurred.

"Are you the wolfcarl?" he asked.

"I am," Skjaldwulf said, and gave his name and styling.

"I am Ethvarthr, thane in the service of Dromundr Dros."

*Dromundr the Fat.* The jarl of Hergilsberg.

"I am at your service," Skjaldwulf said. "Except insomuch as it may contradict my prior allegiances."

"I did not know," Ethvarthr said, uncrossing his arms, "that wolf-carls were so politically spoken."

He said it pleasantly, gesturing Skjaldwulf to fall in beside him as he turned. Skjaldwulf chose to interpret the comment in the most agreeable fashion possible and therefore walked with him, limping a little on sore feet.

"I see you were buying boots."

"It was a long journey," Skjaldwulf said, as if it were a confession.

The thane laughed. His arms were thick, but more of that thickness was muscle than flesh. "The jarl would know what causes a man to come so far, so fast, that he walks his shoes off."

Skjaldwulf glanced from side to side. Though they were surrounded by people, there was a sense that they walked alone. Perhaps in an eternal crowd such as this, each person must create his own bubble of private space. Abruptly, sharply, Skjaldwulf longed for the deep, piney woods of home. "How can I be sure you are the jarl's man? Forgive my suspicion, but as you noted, I am a stranger here."

Ethvarthr extended his hand. That gold signet pinched his thumb, shoved on a hand too large. But there was a callus beside it, such as a man might get from ill-fitting jewelry worn too long. "This mark of his service," Ethvarthr said. "It is the image of the signet he wears on his right hand."

Skjaldwulf studied the ring and the thane's meaty, bearded face. "I think you have lied to me."

The man stopped in his tracks. When Skjaldwulf stopped, too, and turned, Ethvarthr frowned at the wolfjarl's face. "If every man serves himself, in the end, is it a lie to claim so?"

"And the name?"

Ethvarthr shrugged. "Mine by birth, though I have not been known by it for many years."

"My lord jarl," Skjaldwulf said, but softly, so the people on the street with them would not hear. He imagined there were guardsmen nearby. What city was so large that the townsfolk did not know their own jarl by sight?

Dromundr smiled. It folded up creases at the corners of his eyes until they almost disappeared. "My lord wolfjarl," he replied. "I admit, some rumors of your presence here have reached me. Why would a warrior speak first to priests, I wonder, and then come to my city so quietly, without thought of seeking an audience with me? Your renown comes before you; we have heard of the fall of Othinnsaesc, even here, and also of its reclamation. But it's almost as if you sought to avoid me."

"The godsmen have kept me busy," Skjaldwulf said. "So answer me this: if I told you that foreign warriors were striking at villages in the very heart of the North, what would you say?"

"I would say," Dromundr mused, "that those who would raid may in turn be raided and I have a city to defend."

"And if I said these were no raiders but an army? Not the actions of warlords seeking plunder but of an empire seeking conquest?"

"I would say that was a serious allegation, deserving of study."

"And not one deserving to be put before a Thing?"

"In time," Dromundr said slowly. "In time."

Skjaldwulf nodded. "We are not enemies," he said. "And I mean no threat to your power or your steading, Jarl of Hergilsberg. But I do not believe that there is time now to study."

Dromundr stepped back, opening a space between them. A townsman or two walked through it, as oblivious to their presence as a deer slipping between trees. *Townsmen*, Skjaldwulf thought, with wonder.

"May your actions bear out your words, wolfjarl," Dromundr said. "I would not care to be any man's enemy."

He stepped back and turned away, broader than most but no taller than many, until the crowd swallowed up even the width of his massive shoulders. Skjaldwulf watched a moment longer, then turned and limped away.

When he came back the next day to pick up his boots, the cobbler said someone had paid the bill. And left him a pair of woolen socks as well. In the ferry on the way back to the monastery, he finally composed his song.

It was simple and repetitive and had a naggingly insistent rhythm that should worm its way into the memory of anyone who heard it.

As the ferry docked, Skjaldwulf tipped the ferryman handsomely and stomped ashore in his soft new boots. He turned to look back at the big island and smiled. Finally, he had a good feeling about this.

Freyvithr Godsman, waiting for him at the monastery gates, seemed less sanguine.

"Problems?" Skjaldwulf asked, and the sunburnt godsman nodded.

"The godheofodman spoke with the jarl."

"The jarl said no?" Skjaldwulf hazarded.

The priest nodded.

So did Skjaldwulf. "It's no matter," he said. "Wolfcarls are accustomed to defending people who would rather ignore the fact that there is even a fight."

⊙⥋⊙

It took the first moon of her pups' new lives to convince Amma to leave the root cellar. She was as stubborn about it as Brokkolfr had ever seen her about anything; though it made no sense to him, he slept out there with her until the afternoon when all four puppies' eyes were at last open. Then she stood, shook herself, and picked up the smallest pup with her mouth.

*New den,* she said to Brokkolfr, with a very clear image of the room the wolfcarls had built especially for their bitches to whelp in. She indicated that he would be permitted to help carry the puppies, and so Brokkolfr walked back into the main hall with his arms full of squirming wolflings, Amma trotting ahead of him carrying the fourth pup like a viking's treasure.

"Welcome back," said Ulfmundr, with the warmest smile Brokkolfr had yet seen on his face, and Brokkolfr smiled in return.

The whelping room was the most carefully finished room in the heall, and would be, most likely, for years to come. The plaster was smooth and clean, the floor was generously strewn with rushes, and every fur or blanket that was too worn for sleeping—and some that were still soft and bright with newness—had found its way here. Amma put the pup down in the pen built against one corner with carefully smoothed wood and began transporting furs to build a new and better nest with.

The pup squeaked, and Brokkolfr knelt to let his brothers join him. Then Brokkolfr sat back out of the way and watched Amma work.

A shadow in the doorway made him look up. It was Vethulf, looking very white and drawn. "Should you be out of bed?" said Brokkolfr.

"Probably not," said Vethulf, "but I can rest here as well as there, if Amma will have me."

"It's her choice," Brokkolfr said. "Sister?"

Amma tidied a stray pup into the corner, then came across to sniff, and then lick, Vethulf's hands.

"I guess I'll do," Vethulf said with a crooked smile.

Brokkolfr said, "Share some floor with me. There's plenty to go around."

They did not talk much, beyond a few mild reminiscences of Kjaran's and Amma's respective puppyhoods. Brokkolfr was not surprised when, after a long peaceful silence, he looked over and found that Vethulf had fallen asleep where he sat. It did not look comfortable, but—on the other hand—he was resting, and Brokkolfr knew, from the pack-sense and from the talk of the werthreat at mealtimes, that getting Vethulf to rest had been a task nearly beyond even Isolfr's abilities. Brokkolfr did not disturb his wolfjarl, but sat beside him for the rest of the honey-warm afternoon. When Amma had the nest arranged to her satisfaction, she and her family napped, and Brokkolfr watched her sleeping with profound satisfaction.

At sundown, Amma woke, and her pups with her, squeaking their hunger. She arranged herself to let them nurse, but her attention was on the doorway. *Konigenwolf,* she said—a warning, a greeting, too many things tangled in that one scent-image-feeling for Brokkolfr to sort them. He got up and stepped into the hallway, hearing Vethulf wake as he did so.

Viradechtis was sitting a polite three bodylengths back, her eyes averted in a show of submission. *Mother,* she said respectfully. She glanced at Brokkolfr, acknowledging him as Amma's brother, and then turned her head as her own brother came into the hall.

"Wolfsprechend," Brokkolfr said, much as Amma had said, *Konigenwolf.* "Your wolfjarl is within, but he has been sleeping all afternoon."

"Then I won't flay him before dinner," Isolfr said with his shy quirk of a smile. "But it was you I came to find."

"Me?"

"You are a wolfheofodman of this heall," Isolfr said, "as I think you have asked me to remember before this. And with Skjaldwulf and Randulfr gone, and Vethulf ill—"

"I'm fine," Vethulf said irritably, appearing in the doorway.

"Are you still feverish?"

Vethulf gave his wolfsprechend a sour look. "Yes."

"Then you are ill, and Sokkolfr will agree with me if you try to argue. Which means," Isolfr said, returning firmly to his point, "that Brokkolfr, Sokkolfr, and I are the wolfheofodmenn making decisions right now, and there is a decision that needs to be made."

"There is?" Vethulf said.

Isolfr coughed, looking a little sheepish. "It seems that our absent wolfjarl has called an AllThing."

ঔৼৎ

It was impossible to keep Vethulf out of the council, and Brokkolfr was sure Isolfr had known it would be. But it was also impossible for Vethulf to keep himself awake, especially with Kjaran all but draped over him, and so by the time the news was told and the messenger from Arakensberg—a former threatbrother of Vethulf's—had been closely questioned to wring out every last detail, Vethulf was asleep, as quietly and neatly as a cat, and Kjaran was looking smug.

"Is he all right, truly?" the messenger asked.

"He will be," Sokkolfr said. "He kept pushing himself, even when he knew the wound was inflamed. If he will but rest, he will be well again by the time we can travel."

"And if that doesn't make him rest, nothing will," Isolfr said.

The messenger bowed and left, and the three wolfheofodmenn looked at each other.

"Franangford must go," Sokkolfr said.

"Oh, undoubtedly," Isolfr said at once. "We would go even if it were not our wolfjarl who had called the Thing. But it worries me, how we seem to be bleeding wolfheofodmenn. First Skjaldwulf and Randulfr, and now I do not see any way around the fact that Vethulf and I must go to Arakensberg."

"Which leaves Brokkolfr and me," Sokkolfr said. "Do you doubt our ability, wolfsprechend?"

Isolfr smiled at his friend, and at the almost indignant snort from Hroi. "Not a bit. I'm leaving you in charge of Alfgyfa, am I not?"

Brokkolfr felt the warmth of Isolfr's appreciation, unexpectedly, and bit back a smile.

Isolfr continued, "But I do not like placing such a large burden on your shoulders, when it is properly mine."

Sokkolfr rolled his eyes, and Brokkolfr guessed that this was a discussion they had had before. "*Your* burden is representing Franangford at the AllThing. I assure you, I would not swap if you begged me."

"Why do you think Skjaldwulf has called an AllThing?" Brokkolfr asked.

"I would guess that the danger facing Siglufjordhur is much greater than the messenger knew to tell us," Sokkolfr said.

"And jarls are . . ." Isolfr's mouth twisted. "It is much easier to get many jarls to do what you want than it is to get one jarl even to agree that something ought to be done."

Brokkolfr suspected he knew who that *one jarl* was, but it would be both unkind and unprudent to say so. Rather, he said, "Sokkolfr is right. I wouldn't swap if you begged me, either."

He won a crack of laughter from Isolfr loud enough to wake Vethulf—who was most indignant to discover he'd slept through the whole decision.

# SIXTEEN

Skjaldwulf was beginning to feel as if his life were an endless round of rushing from place to place, scarcely in advance of bad news. His new boots galled his feet for a day or two before they settled in. By the second week out, though, he was glad of them, because brief summer was coming to its close already, and as they walked northward they went to meet the fall.

It was more than a month's travel to Arakensberg, although the wolves and wolfcarls traveling alone could have done it faster. But they had Otter with them, and the contingent from the monastery— though Erik and Skjaldwulf had decided between them to travel in advance of whatever party the jarl would—or would not—field. If Skjaldwulf was calling the AllThing, it behooved him to be one of the earliest in attendance.

Still, the Arakensberg road was a good one—the town the heall defended was a hub of trade and textile production, its swift, smooth river lined with mills—and if monks couldn't travel like wolves, they kept up well enough. And Otter either had been hardened by life on the march with the Rheans or simply possessed a good deal of native toughness. Skjaldwulf and his party arrived in Arakensberg only three days behind the messengers bearing word of the AllThing.

The town, keep, and heall were in uproar already. The messenger would have given the wolfsprechend of Arakensberg, Aesulf Aeg-ileifsbrother—a green-eyed blond with a pitted, ruddy face as broad across as a barn door—some advance warning of what was about to descend upon them. Also, if Aegileif were deep enough in the pack-sense, she might have told her brother when and where to expect the arrival of the Franangford pack and their companions.

It was possible. Skjaldwulf had heard a bit of Aegileif from Vethulf, and Vethulf thought her a konigenwolf the match of any—including Nithogsfjoll's Vigdis, their own Viradechtis' legendary dam. Aesulf was her third brother, and neither of the other two had died particularly young.

*Not particularly young as wolfcarls go, anyway,* Skjaldwulf thought, ironically, and did his best to keep the thought from Mar and the rest of the wolves. The Rheans had done him no favors holding up the specter of an easier life.

As the old konigenwolf came out to greet the travelers, Skjald-wulf could see in her the source of Vethulf's awe. Where Viradechtis was still a young bitch, as playful and irreverent in peace as she was terrible in war, Aegileif was the very countenance of a queen.

Big as a boar, she dwarfed even Mar. Her coat was the gray of smoke, the black-tipped gray that showed in ripples when she moved. Skjaldwulf knew from experience that it would make her even more invisible than a black wolf in the darkness, because she'd show no solid outline against bare earth or snow. She was silver to the ears, her muzzle laced with the pink and white lines of many battles, and as she lifted her head and raised her tail to show her dominance over the small pack arriving, both Mar and Ingrun unhesitatingly showed her their throats.

It was a triumph of intelligence over instinct. In the wild, a wolf pack would not suffer mature wolves of another lineage in its territory, and a konigenwolf's pack would consist of her mates, her daughters, and her male pups, until those pups grew old enough to seek out their own packs. Theirs was a society of great queens, and Skjaldwulf had no doubt that the konigenwolf who now regarded him with old green eyes was a very great queen indeed.

Her brother, younger and more brash, nevertheless seemed perfectly at home arranging food, baths, and housing for wolves and men. Otter was found a place with the heallbred women, though not a private chamber—Arakensberg was one of the older healls, and like Nithoggsfjoll, its compound was a log longhouse and outbuildings, not a stone keep as they were building in Franangford. Freyvithr and Erik and their party were housed here and there about the town. Arakensberg, it turned out, even boasted a pair of small inns and one larger one.

In addition to being more southerly, more cosmopolitan, and less isolated than Nithoggsfjoll or Franangford, Arakensbergheall seemed to have a good relationship with the keep and town. The local jarl joined them for dinner at the heall, greeting Skjaldwulf with barely concealed excitement and apprehension. The jarl, too, was young, and embarrassingly overawed by the march of history around him—"An AllThing! Can you credit it?"—and Skjaldwulf was glad enough to change the topic to telling Vethulf's former threatbrothers whatever old news Skjaldwulf could muster about Vethulf's deeds.

Somewhere in the process, he was slightly confounded to realize that he missed Vethulf and that he was speaking fondly of him to men who also seemed to regard him fondly, although it was obvious that all the Arakensberg werthreat (and some of the wolves) retained a sympathetic sense of humor about Vethulf's temper.

Well, maybe Skjaldwulf did not miss Vethulf's scathing tongue—but his forthrightness and indomitable spirit were a different matter. And the Arakensbergthreat were hungry enough for news that they kept Skjaldwulf—and Freyvithr, and Fargrimr, and Erik, and Otter, and the other godsmen and wolfcarls—talking long into the night.

❧

Vethulf had been unshakably determined that Isolfr should not leave him behind, and he paid for it, mile after grueling mile from Franangford to Arakensberg. He started out walking, glaring down anyone who tried to argue, but by the end of the first day he was nearly reeling, his pulse throbbing in every half-healed inch of his shoulder.

Isolfr, mustering a fearful glare of his own, sat Vethulf down on his bedroll and made him strip off his shirt. He then cursed Vethulf roundly, using several phrases Vethulf hadn't thought Isolfr knew. "This can still kill you, you know," he said. "A wound gone bad is not something to take lightly."

"I don't," Vethulf said through gritted teeth as Isolfr began cleaning the inflamed gashes. "Take it lightly, that is."

"No, you just thought you'd walk to Arakensberg."

"Couldn't let you go alone," Vethulf said, and immediately wished himself dead. No way to explain that he hadn't meant it the way it sounded, that it wasn't because he didn't think Isolfr could take care of himself. It was just because he *couldn't*, and there was no way to explain that at all.

But after a moment, Isolfr said, "And you call me a daft creature," and he didn't even sound annoyed.

❧

In the morning, and each morning after, Skjaldwulf found, there was work to do. Pavilions to raise, latrines to dig, plans to contribute to. And already wolfcarls and wolves and wolfless men were filtering in. Some—many, blessedly—brought their own tents and provisions, which were after all necessary for travel for those who did not care to sleep rough and live off the land. The wolfcarls and wolfless men and some of the thanes arranged hunting parties and shared the meat out among the slowly swelling body of the AllThing. . . .

It would be a year or more before the local wildlife recovered.

Despite the serious business they had come here to do, a festival atmosphere prevailed. Kinsmen and friends long-parted reacquainted themselves; feasts and footraces and fights broke out across the landscape. Everywhere he went, Skjaldwulf heard snatches of his tune hummed or sung, and—ridiculously, for the war was not yet won—he felt the burdens that had weighed his shoulders lessening.

Perhaps, he thought, it was not so much that they were lightened as that there were more hands to bear them now. In any case, he spent a good deal of his time moving from fire to fire, listening to wolfcarls and wolfless men, taking a tenor of the times. There was skepticism, and there was a good deal of rancor—some, summoned from the harvest or sent as proxy for others who remained behind to do the work the world set before their hand, were skeptical. Some disbelieved in any Rhean threat at all and saw in the calling of the AllThing only wolfcarls greedy for political power. Some were young men, eager for war and the making of their names. Some were hardened vikings, who wished to take the war to the Rheans over a sea of Brythoni corpses.

Skjaldwulf thought that last a mistake near as bad as ignoring the threat of the Rheans, but he also saw that here, gathered around the keep of Arakensberg, was the nucleus of an army, if he could sway them. Some of the men present had fought in the trellwar, and so he knew them or knew of them. Some were men whose legend preceded them, borne by songs and tales.

Some were men who had come not to his summoning, but to that of Erik Godsman, and Skjaldwulf thought they, too, might be of use.

The question that remained before him—if he could bring them together now, here, in advance of the danger—was, if a konungur they must have, who best should it be?

Although it was early days and the AllThing not even convened yet to decide if a konungur *should* be chosen, some obvious contenders were being put forth. One was the jarl of Hergilsberg, despite his absence from the scene. One, to Skjaldwulf's amusement, was one-eyed Erik Godheofodman. ("Can you be a godsman and a king?" Skjaldwulf had murmured to Erik behind his hand. "Not and be worth a damn as either," Erik had replied.) One was Grettir Gang-arm, a southern jarl Skjaldwulf knew only by reputation until he made a point of cultivating the man's acquaintance, which led him to believe that there couldn't be a better choice for leading a party going viking or a worse one for konungur.

Because of the way the news of the AllThing had traveled—north, from Hergilsberg, a few days in front of Skjaldwulf and his party—the southern jarls began arriving first, even before the wolf-carls of the closest heallan to Arakensberg. It wasn't until the very first heall—Bravoll—arrived that Skjaldwulf realized that some of his agitation was from the tension of holding his breath over whom the Franangfordthreat would send. And then Nithoggsfjoll arrived—both wolfjarl and wolfsprechend—and even his busyness could not stop Skjaldwulf from meeting Grimolfr and Ulfbjorn and the three wolves-and-men who had come with them, along with Gunnarr Sturluson and his wife, Halfrid, and their selected retainers and their mounts and pack animals, and two stout mastertradesmen—bondi—of the village, to make up the Nithoggsfjollthreat's delegation to the AllThing. They dismounted as Skjaldwulf came up on them, and cries of greeting sounded all around.

"Well met," Skjaldwulf said to Grimolfr, full of emotion as Grimolfr clasped his arm with a hard squeeze.

"Well met," Grimolfr said in return while Mar and Skald and Vigdis and the other wolves sniffed about one another in a companionable sort of way.

The first thing from Ulfbjorn's mouth, before even a greeting, was, "Have Isolfr and Sokkolfr come?"

Skjaldwulf hugged the big man warmly and clapped his back. To his credit, Gunnarr did not flinch from the question but only put a hand comfortingly on Halfrid's back as she leaned forward, alight with all eagerness.

"Franangford is not yet arrived," Skjaldwulf said, hastening to explain as Grimolfr's brows began to rise. "I came from the south, with the godsmen from Hergilsberg. It's a long story. But Frithulf is here, and I'm sure he won't wish to wait to see you. And Randulfr is with me also."

He would have said more, but Vigdis, Nithoggsfjoll's great konigenwolf, yawned widely and sat down with a thump. She looked back along the trail, and deliberately forward, and sighed.

Skjaldwulf didn't need an interpretation. "Come on," he said. "Vigdis wants her dinner."

⚶

Skjaldwulf brought his former threatmates back to camp and turned the jarl, his wife, their householders, and the rank-and-file wolves and wolfcarls over to the local housecarl for disposition to such housing as could be made to accommodate them. When he left, Halfrid was insisting that she could sleep on any hard ground under any tent leaf her husband could withstand, and Gunnarr was objecting that for his wife only the best could do.

That accomplished, Skjaldwulf himself led Ulfbjorn and Grimolfr farther into camp. It took only a few questions of bystanders to locate Randulfr and Fargrimr.

They stood in a sunny corner, deep in conference, Fargrimr's inkworked arm draped across his brother's shoulders. Ingrun, visibly pregnant now but not yet too far gone to travel, lolled at their feet, sunning her distended belly. Trellwolves were broad-backed enough to sleep stretched out like a man when it pleased them, though when they did so their forelegs lay against their chests like crossed sticks and their back legs extended ridiculously.

Ingrun didn't seem to care that she looked a clown. When Vigdis and Skald came within sight, though, she rolled herself to her feet quickly for one so gravid, and came to them head held low and tail wagging like a pup greeting its parents. She bowed low, her belly brushing the ground and her haunches elevated, and stayed there while Vigdis sniffed her over. The sniffing must have yielded successful results, because Vigdis threw one massive foreleg over Ingrun's shoulders and then danced back, inviting play.

Three wolves bolted toward the forest, Ingrun running heavily but running, Vigdis and Skald pacing themselves to go easy on her.

When they had gone, Fargrimr sighed, and Skjaldwulf realized that he and all the wolfcarls had turned to watch them run. Skjaldwulf took a breath in but glanced at Randulfr before he spoke; Randulfr nodded and interceded.

"Fargrimr," Randulfr said, "you remember the wolfheofodmenn of my old threat."

There were claspings all around, and then Fargrimr returned to whatever had so troubled him. "Our father, Fastarr," he said, glancing again at Randulfr—the elder, Skjaldwulf recalled. "Has there been any word?"

Skjaldwulf shook his head. The housecarl would have mentioned if the jarl of Siglufjordhur had arrived.

"He should be here by now," Fargrimr said. "He would not fail to come, or send word if he could not get away. And he should have been here in advance of us, or at the very least not more than a day or two behind."

"You want to go find out?"

Fargrimr shook his head. "I thought of going home. But then I realized that if I gave my proxy to my brother, he would be counted by the jarls and thanes as belonging to the Wolfmaegth. And they will be hard enough to convince that a wolfcarl's plan has any merit. You need me here, and it's a boy's fear that would send me home."

Skjaldwulf was still considering whether he would rise to Fargrimr's gentle bait when Grimolfr said, "And?"

"Two days ago, I dispatched a rider on a fast horse with gold for remounts," Fargrimr said. "If the Rheans or the bandits do not get him, he could be at the coast in ten days more."

"By the time he makes it back, the AllThing will be under way."

"We need him," Randulfr said. "We need his voice and his renown to speak against Dromundr. The Hergilsberg jarl will make trouble."

"My word is one thing," said Fargrimr, "for I have seen these Rheans firsthand. But I am only my father's heir. There are those who will not hear me, for my beard is not white and to my belt-latch." His smile invited them to share the irony.

"Thank you," Skjaldwulf said, aware that Grimolfr and Ulfbjorn would need more explanations later.

Fargrimr shrugged. "It seems the least I can do. After all, the Franangfordthreat came to our defense when we sent for you, though you are not the closest wolfheall and we have never sent you a tithe of support."

Randulfr choked lightly. Ulfbjorn thumped him—not hard, but a love tap from Ulfbjorn was enough to make any lesser man stagger.

"Only your brother," Randulfr said.

Fargrimr shrugged, smiling tightly. "That seems to have worked out to the good for both of us."

But it was Grimolfr who said, "Siglufjordhur came to the aid of the heallan when the trolls threatened. Though you were at great remove and might have stood by idly, denying that what threatened the North threatened you, you came with men and arms. Can we do less for you?"

It was a warm smile, warmly returned. "Actually," Fargrimr said, "I've been thinking about that. You must be weary with travel—come sit and drink some wine, and I will tell you."

๑๖๑

It was very strange, Brokkolfr decided, to be even an acting wolf-sprechend. It was not a role he had ever sought out; he wished to be useful in the world, but he had never wished to lead, and it was comforting to find both that leadership was not so bad—at least in this small way with nothing disastrous at stake—and that he would happily hand it back to Isolfr when wolfsprechend and wolfjarls returned.

"Most of a wolfsprechend's job," Isolfr had said, "is listening. And I know already that you do that very well."

The praise was unexpected, almost as unsettling as reassuring, but he realized that Isolfr was trying to tell him that he would not be asked to learn arcane new skills, merely to do what he already did. It was harder for Sokkolfr, who had already had a heavy load of responsibilities as the housecarl of Franangford, and much of what Brokkolfr did was simply to try to take over as much of Sokkolfr's work as he could. He was taken aback when Hreithulfr, Signy's brother, and Motholfr, Geirve tagging patiently along behind, came to ask what they could do to help, but it was an easy question to answer. Hreithulfr, town-bred, was the natural person to speak to wolfless men—and while Signy was every inch a konigenwolf, she was also still puppy enough that even the most nervous weaver or dyer could smile at her.

And Motholfr turned out to be a blessing. Before the trellwar, he had been one of those wolfcarls who could turn his hand to anything; now, it slowly began to show that anything he had once been able to do, he could teach. And in place of the bitterness and grief that had shrouded him, he had found a surprising store of patience.

Much of it, Brokkolfr thought, was Geirve, who was solemnly interested in everything—much more so even than the ordinary run of trellwolves, who were all as curious as cats. Geirve watched and listened, and she remembered what she learned. The second time Motholfr dropped the awl he was attempting to demonstrate, left-handed and awkward, to the boy who had bonded Geirve's brother Ottarr, Geirve picked it up for him. And from there she quickly became Motholfr's extra hand, turning frustration into pride. And Motholfr became in an odd way like the other half of Sokkolfr, the one doing the work that needed doing, the other making sure that it was possible for that work to be done.

Most of Brokkolfr's job, then, was to listen when wolfcarls approached him, as—to his bemusement—they did. None of their concerns was particularly earthshaking, but the werthreat was serious in entrusting them to his judgment, and Brokkolfr took them seriously in return.

Minding Alfgyfa turned out to be the least onerous of duties. Though she had her father's solemnity, she was rarely fussy; the heall-women doted on her, and Amma was inclined to regard her as a fifth pup. Alfgyfa, for her part, seemed happy to be adopted. The wolfheall grew used to her imperious cry of, "Ammy-wuf!" and if ever the little girl went missing, she was sure to be found cuddled against Amma's flank or playing some inscrutable baby-game with the wolf's massive paws. Some of the werthreat began to drag out the old legends of Sigfrothr, the hero raised by wolves, and Brokkolfr, not knowing if Isolfr would be amused or irritated, decided not to say anything. If nothing else, they were good stories, and some of them he'd never heard before.

The other duty that Isolfr, apologetically, placed on Brokkolfr was that of going with the men who volunteered to be the svart-alfar's laborers. Brokkolfr said, "You need not sound so guilty. It was a harder penance staying away." And he succeeded in making Isolfr laugh.

During Amma's sojourn in the root cellar, the aettrynalfar had asked for men whose brothers could come with them and add their strength. Four wolfcarls had volunteered; the only one of them Brokkolfr knew well was Ulfmundr, and he walked beside him, Hlo-thor circling them both, as they went out to the cave entrance. This was a different entrance from the two that Brokkolfr had known, and he wondered how many there were. Remembering what Baryta had said, he wondered if that was even a reasonable question or if the aettrynalfar made and closed entrances as they needed. This one, Ulf-mundr told him, was not difficult for trellwolves, although the men had to walk nearly doubled over, and it was only a short distance to the cave where they were working.

They were met at the cave mouth by two alfar; one Brokkolfr recognized as Orpiment. The alfar bowed and led the way silently; the men and wolves followed single file, the men bracing them-selves with their hands as they entered the tunnel. Brokkolfr, bring-ing up the rear, observed that the wolves showed no reluctance. Whatever the aettrynalfar were doing, clearly it didn't make them smell like trolls.

It was a comforting thought. He didn't know anything about shaping magic, either the kind that the svartalfar used or the kind the trolls used. He'd always assumed, without really thinking about it, that trellish magic was just that: part of what made trolls trolls. But if that assumption was true, it meant some very unpleasant things about the aettrynalfar—and Brokkolfr couldn't reconcile that idea with Antimony's care for his children or Baryta's teasing or Bubble's overflowing enthusiasm.

He'd mentioned the worry to Kari, who, bored and frustrated as his ankle slowly mended, had been happy to talk about it. He'd seen more of trollwork than Brokkolfr had, and he said, "It's not the same. Perhaps the techniques are the same, but—well, it's like Isolfr's axe that Tin gave him. That's svartalf work and you can't mistake it. If one of our smiths made an axe, it'd be just as clearly an axe, but you wouldn't think a svartalf had had anything to do with it. So the svartalf here—they may make their passages with the same technique the trolls did, but there's no comparison."

"So magic is like an axe," Brokkolfr said thoughtfully. "In itself, it's a tool. It depends on who you are when you pick it up whether you use it to chop wood or slay trolls or murder your kinsmen."

"Maybe. What do I know from magic? But I don't think these svartalfar are the murdering type. Tin's people, I could see where the stories came from about svartalfar being dreadful and dangerous, but these svartalfar are craftsmen and scholars."

"And mothers."

"Yes. Although all svartalfar are a little single-minded about that."

It wasn't quite what Brokkolfr had meant, but he had stayed silent, not sure how to explain himself. He kept thinking of Antimony with his five children and two students, all of whom he loved and valued and encouraged. Perhaps, Brokkolfr thought, it was the encouragement that was so compelling—encouragement was something he had received very little of until he came first to Othinnsaesc and then to Franangford. There had been neither time nor strength for such things in the village of his childhood, nor anything great to need encouragement to accomplish. There had only been the endless round of the boats going out and returning, fish to clean, nets to mend, and for his mother, food to prepare, clothes to make, children to bear. Brokkolfr had been afraid when he was chosen for the tithe, but now he could hardly remember what he had feared that could possibly have been worse than being trapped in that village like his father and grandfather and great-grandfather before him. If it had not been for the tithe, he would never have seen a trellwolf, or an alf, or anyone who had not been born within five leagues of his own birthplace. Amma was the greatest of the gifts his wyrd had offered him, but she was not the only gift.

He came then into the cavern of the cave ice, and his breath caught in his throat. Without the tithe, he would never have seen this.

The svartalfar had set the men and wolves to hauling the broken cave ice out, so that where once there had been solid-seeming rock there was now a lake. A mastersmith pointed them onto the path of rock around the rim of the lake—the rock was smoothly finished, and if Brokkolfr had not known better from vivid firsthand experience, he would have said it had been there for decades easily, if not centuries. From several points on this path bridge spans were starting to arch over the lake, each with an alf standing at the end spinning rock like a spider spun her web. The men and wolves' job was to bring the rock for the spinning, and Brokkolfr could see that this was a truly useful job, even if backbreaking and strictly manual labor.

He didn't know how long he had been standing, staring in rapt amazement at the working aettrynalfar, before he realized an alf had come up next to him. He recognized Orpiment by the golden crystals woven through his braids.

Orpiment said, "I must apologize to you."

"To me? Whatever for?"

"To you and your friend," Orpiment said staunchly. "When the cave ice broke, Realgar and I should have helped you. Not doing so was," and he used a svartalf word Brokkolfr did not recognize.

"I'm sorry, I don't—"

"Miserly?" Orpiment said. "Cautious? Closed, perhaps. The ways of our foremothers which we have rejected. We should have helped you, but we were afraid."

"Of the cave ice?"

"Of you."

Brokkolfr remembered Realgar and Orpiment throwing them-selves between the men and the svartalfar children, even though Kari had a broken ankle and neither svartalf knew anything about fighting. "Are the stories told of men so terrible?"

"You are warriors," Orpiment said. "The smallest aettrynalf knows that, just as she knows our cousins in the North are warriors. But men are not our kin and have no reason to spare us. We have hidden ourselves away for centuries out of fear of you."

"We aren't *trolls*," Brokkolfr said.

Orpiment shrugged, one of those complicated alfar shrugs that seemed to involve more joints than it should. "You have proved that you are not so terrible," he said. "But we did not know then, and we held ourselves closed."

"You've changed your minds," Brokkolfr said.

"Yes," said Orpiment. "You are helping repair what you de-stroyed, and you do it even though you cannot share in the making. You are not closed, even though you cannot sing." He bowed over his folded hands, a gesture that Brokkolfr was not familiar with, but which clearly showed respect.

Clumsily, Brokkolfr copied him, and Orpiment gave him a small, shy smile.

"All right," said Brokkolfr. "Show me what to do."

❧

When they—Skjaldwulf, Fargrimr, Randulfr, Grimolfr, Erik Godsman, and Ulfbjorn—were distributed around the ashes of a derelict fire, each man cupping a flagon of wine, Fargrimr leaned forward, elbows on his knees, and said, "I've been thinking about the future of the wolfheallan."

Skjaldwulf snorted. "You are not alone, my friend—"

But here Fargrimr held up one hand, and Skjaldwulf paused. Of a sudden, the sworn-son had a commanding presence, and Skjaldwulf found himself imagining how he would capture it in verse.

Fargrimr had more to say. "I saw a lot of you and your brothers on the trail of war. And I know this—if the trolls really are all gone, you and your wolves must find other meat to hunt. Or there will be no tithes, no tithe boys, and eventually no wolfheallan."

"We are," Ulfbjorn said grimly, "aware." Which led Skjaldwulf to wonder if the same conversation had been repeated over and over in every heall and keep the breadth of the northlands.

"You cannot become mercenaries," Fargrimr continued. "But we have seen that there is nothing like your men and wolves for putting down the bandit trade, for keeping peace on the roads and in the townships. So I say, what must happen is that we, the jarls, must employ you."

"You just said we could not become mercenaries." Grimolfr shifted, dangling his free hand casually between his knees. "A viewpoint, by the way, with which I agree."

There was a flash of the old grit and gray speech that had long made Grimolfr so terrifying, even though he and Skjaldwulf were not too different in age. Hrolleif, Vigdis' previous brother, had been a little older—

Skjaldwulf bit his lip rather than think too long on Hrolleif. He'd died a warrior, and he stood now at Othinn's right hand. And if Skjaldwulf's grief was bad, how much more so that of Grimolfr, who had been a friend, shieldbrother, and lover to Hrolleif since boyhood.

Unbidden, Skjaldwulf found himself thinking of Vethulf, and pushed it aside as an irritation. Much like Vethulf himself.

"You cannot become mercenaries, no. Not and fight for one jarl against another. But what if you fought for all jarls?"

There was fire in Fargrimr's voice, and from the nodding of Randulfr's head the two of them had worked out what Fargrimr would say in advance—or at least, Fargrimr had run it past his brother.

"How do you fight for all jarls?" Skjaldwulf asked.

"All jarls," Fargrimr repeated. "All jarls, all women, all thanes, all bondi—even all thralls."

Erik raked a hand through his hair, so it stuck up disarrayed around the thong that bound his eyepatch on. "What if you fought for Othinn, and for the Law?"

Skjaldwulf blinked. He glanced at Grimolfr and found the other wolfjarl sitting openmouthed, lost in contemplation. "Peacekeepers," Skjaldwulf said.

"Lawgivers," Ulfbjorn answered.

Silently Randulfr rubbed his wolf's stomach. There were cubs in there, cubs that would need bondmates, heallan, a future. Or they might as well be let run wild: they would be safer and happier. Trellwolves were not meant to be merely ornaments.

"Softly," Skjaldwulf said.

"You hate it," said Randulfr.

Skjaldwulf shook his head. "It just takes some getting used to. Herding bandits like cattle for their meat and milk—"

"'Herding' implies some intentional cultivation," Fargrimr said, eyes laughing. "This might be more like 'gleaning' bandits."

"Assuming we survive the war with these Rheans of yours, we'll put it to the Wolfmaegth," Grimolfr said. And as simply as that, it was settled.

⚛

Two days later, Franangford and Othinnsaesc arrived together, having met up on the road. Isolfr was with the Franangford contingent, Skjaldwulf was pleased to see, walking with Viradechtis beside a rust-orange pony not much bigger than the trellwolf. But that gray wolf with her was Kjaran, and—where then was Vethulf?

Skjaldwulf started forward as the combined threat arrived, his heart hammering until he was almost dizzy with it. Three steps more, though, and he could see the litter the pony hauled and the red braids bundled up within it.

"Vethulf?" Skjaldwulf said as he came up to his wolfsprechend.

"Stupid fool is in the pony drag," Isolfr said. "He was injured fighting bears and wyverns, and didn't have the sense to stay home in bed. He will live; it's just wounds and travel that exhaust him. You?"

There was strain in Isolfr's voice, so Skjaldwulf knew that the journey had not been easy. "We have lost none from the heall." He'd mention Adalbrikt later.

"We, too, have come through unscathed," Isolfr said. "Amma whelped four. Kari and Brokkolfr seem to have found a lost colony of alfar, but more on that later."

*Tease,* Skjaldwulf thought. "Ingrun is in whelp."

"To Mar?" Isolfr said, without a hint of jealousy.

"To all four dogs," Skjaldwulf said. "It took us on the road."

Isolfr's eyebrows went up. "That must have been interesting."

A tall man nearly as pale as Isolfr but far more year-weathered came up to them. "Skjaldwulf," Isolfr said. "You remember my uncle Othwulf, of Othinnsaesc, and his brother Vikingr?"

"Of course," Skjaldwulf said. Othwulf's arm clasp was strong and his smile broad. It was he who claimed half the glory of the Othinnsaesc trellqueen's death, the other half belonging to his brother Gunnarr. Skjaldwulf wondered if the two men had spoken since. He knew Isolfr was only barely on speaking terms with his father; Skjaldwulf hoped, although he was not about to say so, that the fact that Gunnarr had brought Halfrid with him might lead to some better understanding. His wolfsprechend had enough worries without being at feud with his kin.

Better to warn them both: "Nithogsfjoll, heall and keep, arrived two days ago."

"Together?" Isolfr said.

"Grimolfr said it was Gunnarr's idea."

"Truly, we live in an age of marvels," Othwulf said with a sardonic and decidedly wolfish smile. "Well—" He clapped Isolfr on the shoulder. "Vikingr says my wolfjarl wants me. I am glad to hear Brokkolfr is doing well." He strode off, his wolf a vast shadow at his side.

Skjaldwulf raised his eyebrows at Isolfr.

"Apparently, Brokkolfr's cohort bore the worst of Othinnsaesc's losses—his shieldbrothers, the men bonded to Amma's siblings. It was one reason they were willing to trade him to us: wolfsprechend and wolfjarl agreed that it might be better for him to go to a new heall, where he would not be reminded of the dead every time he turned around. I think it is working."

Skjaldwulf was not deceived by that innocent tone. "You said something about a lost colony of svartalfar."

Isolfr abandoned the struggle to keep a straight face. "Yes, and I will tell you about it once we are settled, I promise."

"See that you do," Skjaldwulf said, and let himself grin back, and not think too hard about where the Rheans were and what they were doing.

❧

The trouble with having this many jarls (and wolfjarls) heaped up together in Arakensberg like a handful of pebbles was that one had to find ways to keep them from banging and rattling and knocking chips off each other long enough for an AllThing to be convened.

But the Franangfordthreat was the last group definitely expected—saving Siglufjordhur—and with their arrival a certain momentum began to infect the gathering. The knots of conversation and argument grew bigger, the handwaving more intense. Skjaldwulf began to notice the distinctive ribbon-topped staves of skalds wandering the town and the sprawling encampment that surrounded it. Seeing them still evoked a peculiar feeling in his chest, so that Mar whined and bumped him, but Skjaldwulf put his hand on the black wolf's solid shoulder and moved on.

After half a day or so, it dawned on him. *He* had begun this argument. It was his to bring to completion.

It was after midday, and he had been walking along the high street of Arakensberg, idly looking for old friends and acquaintances whom he had so far missed greeting and meanwhile marveling at how the town had been transformed to a metropolis that might rival Hergilsberg in population, if not in architecture. Now he turned and scanned the bustling street for one of those staves— there. Skjaldwulf raised a hand and his voice, pleased that he could still bring up a shout that would carry through the noise of a crowd. "Ho! Skald!"

The skald spun on one foot and came at a brisk walk in the midst of a flutter of ribbons, abandoning the duckling-trail of children who had no doubt been importuning him for sweets or stories. "My lord wolfjarl."

*My lord wolfjarl.*

He looked prosperous, but it was in a skald's interest to look so. He also looked nervous, more so of man than wolf, which left Skjaldwulf wondering where, exactly, he had become the sort of person who made skalds hardened to the antics of drunken jarls and thanes—and their drunken daughters—nervous.

Skjaldwulf extended a coin and said, "Poet—"

"Throstr, my lord." The coin vanished. Up his sleeve, Skjaldwulf suspected, having once practiced the same trick himself.

"Throstr. Pass the word for me: the AllThing commences at sunset, in the longhouse at Arakensbergheall." Perhaps it was a mistake, perhaps it would be seen as still more evidence of partisanship, but Skjaldwulf found he did not much care. Either keep and heall would stand together, now, or they would surely fall apart.

*If the trellwar taught us nothing else, let it have taught us that.*

"As you wish, my lord," the skald said, and stood awkwardly until Skjaldwulf realized he was waiting to be excused, lest he give offense.

⚬ɣ⚬

B efore sunset, the longhouse swarmed.

The majority of the Arakensberg wolves and wolfcarls decided that this would be a fine time to see to some hunting, leaving the heall in the possession of the AllThing—jarls, ladies, bondi, housecarls, horsecarls, thanes, heofodmenn, warriors of renown, skalds, smiths, wolfjarls, and wolfsprechends from all over the North were here, all packed in until when one breathed in, three must breathe out.

Or so it seemed to Vethulf as—trying to walk tall despite Isolfr on his left elbow and Skjaldwulf on his right, each of them holding up far more of his weight than they made apparent—he was led in. *Led in*, like an old man tottering between his sons.

"Gods rot it," he snarled under his breath as Isolfr dragged a stool around for him. But he sat, because there was no renown to be won in measuring one's length on the floor. No renown such as a man would wish to carry, anyway.

Isolfr patted his shoulder mockingly. "Even a poisoned wound can't keep you down long."

"The wyvern might die of biting you," Skjaldwulf teased, and Vethulf shot him a glance that probably proved his point. But there was time for little else, because outside the wolves of twelve heallan raised their voices to sing the sun down—and inside the konigenwolves and their consorts answered the call.

The sound, as always, shivered along Vethulf's nerves like spirits of wine. He'd known trellwolves all his life, but they never quite sounded like living animals when they howled. Their chorus had the voices of ghosts, the harmonics of some otherworldly musical instrument. He felt the hairs across his arms and nape prickle erect.

The reaction of the wolfless men was rather more dramatic. Some of them paled; some huddled close to one another. Vethulf saw at least one lady snatch her skirts up, as if preparing to run. When she dropped them again a moment later and smoothed them overenthusiastically, everyone around her pretended not to notice.

Skjaldwulf gave his shoulder a squeeze, almost startling him off his stool, and as the singing subsided moved to the center of the heall, leaving Mar behind with Kjaran and Viradechtis. Kjaran sighed and rolled over on his side.

"Damn him and his skald's eye," Isolfr muttered.

Vethulf nodded agreement. *That* would be in the songs, how Skjaldwulf had stepped into view amid the dying fall of wolf-howls. Vethulf wondered if Skjaldwulf even knew that he had planned it that way.

But the tall man was clearing his throat, turning in place, spreading his arms wide—wider on one side than the other, because of the old stiffness of his broken collarbone—and the unsettled throng were focusing on him. He had a staff in his hand—a blackwood bough, cut long and gnarled and fluttering with strips of scarlet cloth like a mockery of a skald's staff.

He raised it up. His voice boomed, became great, rang among the smoke-black rafters like a winded horn. "Jarls, thanes, bondi, wolf-carls, warriors, women! Attend, for we have a bright business before us. Attend, for I am Skjaldwulf brother of Mar, called Snow-soft, wolfjarl of Franangford, and I have fought fell trolls in fearsome winter that you might sleep unfettered and unfearing in your warm feather nests. Attend, for it was I who asked you here, and you have done me the honor to come! Attend, for I have gone down into the belly of the earth, and I have come out again, and some of you were there!"

A moment of silence as he paused for breath, and then a voice rang out, "I was there!"

It was Othwulf—no jarl, but Vethulf supposed the slayer of a trellqueen had a place in any war council. And most of the crowd would not know who had shouted. But Gunnarr Sturluson surely did, and he, too, threw back his head and cried, "I was there!"

Vethulf felt Isolfr jump in shock, and Kjaran sat up, looking this way and that. A roar followed as every wolfcarl and thane who had fought—and probably a few who hadn't—raised voice to claim his share of the glory that briefly washed them all. Vethulf was not immune. "I was there!" he cried, and felt Isolfr move behind him but he did not hear his wolfsprechend's voice. When Vethulf turned to catch Isolfr's eye, though, the scarred warrior merely frowned and shook his head. *Later.*

Skjaldwulf waited, arms still wide, until the furor subsided. Then he spoke in a softer voice—still carrying, but it gave the illusion of intimacy, and Vethulf saw men lean forward to hear better.

"You know why we have come here," Skjaldwulf said. "We have come here because our homes are threatened, because an army of the enemy walks the world, putting our land under his feet as he wills. Because this army—this army of *Rheans*—is only the vanguard of more to come."

Someone shouted from the back, "How do you know this?"

"I have seen it with my own eyes," Skjaldwulf replied. "And I have spoken with a Rhean conscript who escaped them."

"A spy!"

Beside Vethulf, Mar growled wetly.

"An escaped prisoner," Skjaldwulf said, and then raised his voice to the attack: "The wolves will fight for us. The winter will fight for us. But we must also fight for ourselves. We must make ourselves ready for war, warriors, because war has surely come. Who among us would lead us against this enemy? He who would be konungur, who would see his name ring with renown from now so long as songs are sung, let him stand forward and speak that name aloud!"

He paused. Around him, the quiet hung as heavy as the silence between strokes of a tolling bell.

Someone stepped forward then, and Vethulf was surprised to see that it was Roghvatr, the jarl of Franangfordtown. He extended his hand for the staff, and Skjaldwulf gave it over. The red rags at the head shivered like fountaining blood in the torchlight as Roghvatr shook it, introducing himself and giving a summary of his deeds.

"You know," he said finally, "that I am as great a friend of the wolfcarls as any man. That without their help, *your* help"—he pointed with the staff to Vethulf—"I would have lost dogs and perhaps thanes this summer, when a bear raided my town. But I must say, who other than a wolfcarl or an outlander has seen these Rheans? We know, do we not, that if the heallan wish to continue to avoid swearing allegiance to their rightful lords, they need to produce a threat against which we can be united!"

There was a mutter from the crowd, followed by a rumble of outrage, rising as jarls and wolfcarls who happened to be standing near one another began to argue.

Skjaldwulf held out his hand for the staff. Reluctantly, Roghvatr gave it back. He walked off stiffly, and Vethulf was surprised to find his distaste for the man leavened by a spike of pity. He was, Vethulf thought, reading the world through his own lens.

In Roghvatr's wake, a tense silence rippled.

Then Fargrimr stepped forward, hand extended for the staff, and the silence became a hush.

*The sworn-son*, Vethulf thought. *Really?*

Skjaldwulf gave him the staff and stepped aside—not retiring to the circle but waiting at Fargrimr's back.

Fargrimr cleared his throat and, in a clear tenor that skied from nervousness, began. His speech was not so polished nor so dense with rhetoric as Skjaldwulf's, and he could not make his voice boom like the sea, but he spoke plainly and sharply of what he had seen in Siglufjordhur, of the rumors of Rhean ships making port in small villages along the coast and leaving them razed and smoking, of Adalbrikt, a young Siglufjordhur thane buried in the woods by his traveling companions after a fight with Rheans. He did not say that that thane's companions had been wolfcarls—just that he had been very, very young.

What Fargrimr lacked in rhetoric he made up for in sincerity, and the room listened.

When he gave the staff back to Skjaldwulf, that same respectful silence followed Fargrimr from the ring.

"Feargar of Hergilsberg!" someone shouted from the back, and after a moment Vethulf realized it was a nomination for konungur.

"Grettir Gang-arm!" someone else yelled.

A third voice yelled "Skjaldwulf Snow-soft!" and was met with a general roar.

"Oh, Othinn, no," Vethulf said.

But Skjaldwulf raised the staff. "Nay, not I. My loyalty is to my wolf and the heall, and a konungur's loyalty must be to all men who fight in his name. Let those who would be made konungur, or those who have an argument for or against the making of one tonight— for now let those men speak!"

And then he passed the staff to the first man who came forward, and beat a retreat back to Vethulf and Isolfr as if the floor scalded him. Frithulf came over a moment later, bearing four horns of mead, and Vethulf accepted one gratefully. Not as gratefully as Skjaldwulf, though, who knocked his back like cold tisane.

"You should have been a skald in truth as well as name," Fargrimr said, under his breath.

Skjaldwulf laughed.

"He nearly was," Isolfr explained.

Who were they to sound so familiar? Vethulf killed a worm of jealousy.

"He's never really given it up," Vethulf added. "He likes the attention too much."

❦

The arguments that followed went on for hours. Men came and went before the staff, some in favor, some against, some nominating themselves or others—despite Skjaldwulf's request—as konungur. It blurred into endless chanting after a while, and Vethulf was glad the dim torchlight let him rest his eyes without being obvious about it.

He didn't care who the konungur was, so long as there was one and he was competent. But that was an issue of some complexity, because others did care. A wolfcarl was not acceptable for the reasons Skjaldwulf mentioned, but a wolfcarl might have been the best compromise candidate. Because the northern jarls did not trust soft southerners and the southern jarls did not trust the barbaric north.

Vethulf was still dozing when the heall doors were flung wide, and on a wash of hubbub from outside someone staggered into the room. He would have fallen, in fact, were he not supported between two wolfless men with the colors of the jarl of Skarth sewn to their sleeves. Wolves, wolfcarls, and wolfless men packed in behind them.

One of them was Frithulf. He shouldered through the crowd, Kothran breaking trail for him, until he was within shouting distance of Skjaldwulf.

And then, being Frithulf, he shouted. "Wolfjarl! There is news from Siglufjordhur!"

"Sweet Freya," Fargrimr said, pushing forward. "That's Bjorr."

Vethulf heaved himself to his feet, wobbling. If Isolfr hadn't been there, he would have fallen, and he cursed Isolfr for it even as he leaned on him. Three wolves clustered around them, a protective wall, and if there were any chance it wouldn't have resulted in him falling and being trampled, Vethulf would have pushed them all away and said he could walk by himself.

And maybe he could have walked by himself, but this wasn't walking so much as forcing through a milling crowd as a wedge found a split in a log.

When they got to the man, he had been lowered to a bench and Fargrimr was kneeling beside him, holding him upright. "What happened?"

Bjorr shook his head. Vethulf could see that his clothes were torn and filthy, his face drawn with long hunger. His boots were so worn on his feet that they flapped open, and raw toes with black toenails showed through the gaps. He had run himself bloody, and beyond.

"Foreign soldiers," he said, between heaving breaths. Someone brought water; Fargrimr held it for him while he drank. When it was gone, Bjorr seemed to realize whose hands his own scratched ones were covering on the cup, because he shuddered, and grimaced.

Fargrimr lowered the cup. His voice shook. He steadied it. "Speak . . . Speak on."

"My lord," Bjorr said, his eyes on the floor until they crept, unwillingly, to Fargrimr's face. "You are jarl of Siglufjordhur now."

Fargrimr closed his eyes and nodded. Someone moved toward him; without opening his eyes he gestured them away. Isolfr leaned down to Vethulf's ear and said, "Are you all right without me?"

"Go," Vethulf said, steadying himself against Kjaran and Mar. At least his shoulder only ached now, rather than screaming protest of every move. He would manage; others needed his wolfsprechend more.

Isolfr slipped from his side. Not toward Fargrimr and his brother, but back, toward Skjaldwulf. Vethulf turned in surprise and wobbled but stayed upright. He saw Isolfr, quick and stern, pull the staff that

Skjaldwulf must have retrieved in the confusion from Skjaldwulf's hand, and Skjaldwulf open his hand as if the staff had scorched it.

Isolfr strode to the center of the room and turned.

He was not a tall man, nor a broad one. His hair hung in ice-pale braids on either side of his face, and the scars that crossed his cheek left sparse lines through his beard. The axe he wore at his belt caught light all along the filigree of its hilt. His wolf, her red and black brindles shifting like a tabby cat's stripes in the firelight, sat by his side like any dog, except her head came to his chest when she stretched it back to yawn.

"I know, sister," Isolfr said softly.

And then he struck the board floor with the butt of the staff, and half the room jumped and turned at the noise. Skjaldwulf spotted Vethulf standing alone and made haste to his side, offering an arm in support.

Swearing under his breath, Vethulf took it.

"I am Isolfr," he said, speaking too softly. "Isolfr brother of Vira-dechtis, wolfsprechend of Franangford. Called . . ." He gathered himself, and Vethulf saw his distaste for the byname twist his mouth. "Called Ice-heart, called Alf-friend. You know who I am."

With a flip of his hand, he let the ritual of boasting his renown pass by like water through the piles of a bridge. A stir passed through the room.

Yes, they knew him.

"I have come to praise a man," he said.

Another stir, followed by a waiting silence. He had them. They all waited to see upon whom Isolfr Ice-mad would call.

Isolfr straightened his shoulders and said, "I come to praise a man who is a great and doughty warrior, who taught me what I know of sword and shield, of valor and of honor. I come to praise a man who has fought trolls and brigands—and raised a daughter and two sons!"

A laugh followed, nervous at first but then rolling all around them.

Isolfr smiled, a rare shy flash. Vethulf wondered how many others saw him swallow. "I come to praise a man who, in the dark trellwarrens under Othinnsaesc, fought a trellqueen and destroyed her. A man who can lead us into great renown as we defend our much-loved land from these Rheans. I come to praise Gunnarr Sturluson, jarl of Nithoggsfjoll. Gunnarr Trollsbane, my father, should be our konungur."

He lowered the staff.

Something swept through the crowd. Vethulf couldn't name it, but he could see it. A silence, and then a muttering. And then someone shouted, "Gunnarr!" From the voice Vethulf thought it was Othwulf. Across the room, he saw that godsman—Erik—catch Skjaldwulf's eye, and Skjaldwulf nodded. "Gunnarr!!" the godsman shouted, and he had a voice like iron hammers ringing on a forge.

At that point, it was inevitable. Roghvatr, who had apparently thought better of his earlier advice—or who saw which way the wind was blowing and would vote for a northern lord while he had the chance—shouted the name. Then Grimolfr bellowed it in his battlefield command voice, and the wolfcarls took up the chant until the whole room was stomping and shouting, arms upraised in the torchlight. "Gunnarr! Gunnarr! Gunnarr Konungur!"

Silently Isolfr slipped from the center of the room and handed Skjaldwulf the staff once more. "Well," Isolfr said, sweat soaking his collar, "that was easy."

A woman Skjaldwulf's age or older came from the crowd to tug Isolfr's sleeve. He turned, and she threw her arms around him before Vethulf could move to intervene. But Isolfr hugged her hard and then set her back at arm's length. "I am sorry, mother."

She grimaced. "He'll hate it."

Isolfr smiled. "He'll be good at it."

She dipped her head, then reached up and squeezed her son's arm. "I know."

⊙↓⊙

In the next few days, it seemed as if Skjaldwulf was needed everywhere at once. He found time—by brute force—to introduce Otter properly to Isolfr and Vethulf, and he began to learn the art of handing tasks on to other men. He did not want to be indispensable to all of the northland, only to Franangfordheall.

He was not surprised that Gunnarr showed every indication of being an excellent konungur; he *was* surprised, although he made every effort to conceal his bemusement, that Gunnarr and Erik Godsman took to each other immediately and enthusiastically. The jarl of Hergilsberg would be outmaneuvered on every flank, and Skjaldwulf was unworthily pleased.

When he was not avoiding the responsibilites other men wished to heap on him, Skjaldwulf was endeavoring to live up to the responsibilities he already had. He managed, with no small difficulty, to convene an actual Wolfmaegthing, and after listening to several wolfjarls echo his own fears—and after Vethulf had told them about his conversation with Roghvatr—Skjaldwulf put forward Fargrimr's suggestion.

There was silence when Skjaldwulf had finished, out of which Vethulf said, sounding puzzled, "But we're already *doing* that."

"Yes," said the wolfsprechend of Thorsbaer. "Which is all the more reason that the jarls should honor us for it."

"And tithe," put in the wolfjarl of Kerlaugstrond.

"And if they *all* tithe," said the wolfsprechend of Arakensberg, "then no jarl can complain that another jarl buys our service away from him." Wolfsprechend and wolfjarl exchanged a dour look; Skjaldwulf wondered which of Arakensberg's neighbors they had run afoul of.

"And it gives us a reason to continue the patrols," said the wolf-jarl of Othinnsaesc, a light in his eye that suggested he had been having trouble with wolfcarls underfoot.

"*And,*" Isolfr said, "it means that wolfless men will become accustomed to wolves, and will continue to be so. Which raises another point: if we are to do this, we must make at least one wolfheall in the south, where I understand"—with a dry look at Skjaldwulf—"the bandits are particularly troublesome. Franangford has a konigenwolf pup, and we would gladly stand her to a new heall."

A mutter ran round the room; Grimolfr and Ulfbjorn both looked as proud as if they'd birthed Signy themselves. Isolfr coughed, looking a little embarrassed, and said, "I would ask only that we name the heall not for the keep it will stand near, but for Freya, as she seems still to protect us."

Another murmur, this one even more approving. Skjaldwulf said, "I will put the question to the new jarl of Siglufjordhur, for I think he may be willing to grant us land."

◦҉◦

Later that night, Skjaldwulf came into the section of the wide-flung camp around Arakensberg that was Franangford's. He passed two small campfires, one surrounded by sleeping wolfcarls and wolves, the other providing warmth and light for a lazy half-drunken dice game between Frithulf and Otter. Otter was winning. They saluted him with their cups as he went by, and he waved back. At the main tent, pitched for wolfsprechend and wolfjarls, he found Isolfr and Ulfbjorn talking while Vigdis and Viradechtis, united in a temporary truce, angled for bits of the smoked ham and cheese laid out on the table, boards over trestles, the men had set up beside the stone-ringed campfire.

"It is not finished," Skjaldwulf said, "but it is begun. As I expected, Fargrimr was not at all averse to the idea."

Ulfbjorn saluted him with his mead-horn.

"So," Isolfr said, "what happens next?"

Skjaldwulf sighed and stretched his spine, listening to the series of small pops as it settled back into alignment. "Everybody dies, and the people who don't get married."

Isolfr smiled crookedly. "Like any other story, then."

Skjaldwulf smiled back. "We all think we are greater than the story, but we aren't, really, and that is no bad thing."

"No," said Isolfr. He looked across the table. "Ulfbjorn and I are talking about konigenwolves, but I think you will find that Vethulf is still awake in our tent. His stamina is improving."

Skjaldwulf stood a moment, arrested by the thought that his wolfsprechend was matchmaking for him—and the delicate pink rising along Isolfr's ears suggested that he was not wrong. But Isolfr met his gaze and said, "You don't want to listen to us, Skjaldwulf. Truly."

Viradechtis snorted in unkind agreement, and Isolfr said to her, "Who keeps the ham, madam?"

"Good night, then," Skjaldwulf said and ducked into the tent, where Vethulf was indeed awake, lying propped among the furs like a viking prince, with Kjaran and Mar, one to each side.

Skjaldwulf sat down and began to undo his boots. "Isolfr says you are improving."

Vethulf made a grumbling noise uncannily like a wolf's.

"Was it a lie, then?"

"No, damn you. I am better. But I do not like being nursemaided."

"I know that," Skjaldwulf said, grinning at him over one shoulder before bending again to his boots.

"So if you were thinking of starting—"

"I wasn't, I assure you."

"Good," said Vethulf.

Freed of his boots, Skjaldwulf lay back across the bedding. Kjaran got up and came to sniff his face and throat. He heard Vethulf sit up, grumbling at Mar to shift his furry black ass, and grinned at the tent pole.

"Oh, this is ridiculous," Vethulf said.

Skjaldwulf rolled up and saw that Mar had indeed shifted his furry black ass and was now draped across Vethulf's lap.

*Brother,* Skjaldwulf said.

Mar rolled his eyes at him, then, with a very pointed thought about the smoked ham, got off Vethulf. Kjaran joined him at the tent flap, and Skjaldwulf got up and tied it closed behind them. He heard Ulfbjorn and Isolfr laugh, but he didn't mind. He stripped his clothes off as he came back to the bedding, and Vethulf said, "I thought southerners were all fat and lazy. Haven't they been feeding you?"

"I could have stayed out there and eaten smoked ham and listened to Isolfr and Ulfbjorn talk about konigenwolves," Skjaldwulf pointed out.

"You could have," Vethulf agreed, and then Skjaldwulf rolled into the bedding and straddled him.

Vethulf was wearing nothing but his shirt—two trellwolves were more than enough to keep a man warm at this time of year—and Skjaldwulf was pleased to feel evidence that the grumbling was just for show. He leaned down, got a careful grip on Vethulf's braids, and kissed him, hard and slow and with all the pent-up loneliness and fear of his long trip south.

Vethulf made a tiny bitten-off noise and kissed him back, just as hard, and Skjaldwulf gratefully lost himself in the pressure of mouth on mouth, in Vethulf's strong hands gripping his biceps. Skjaldwulf shifted himself to lie closer along Vethulf's body, and Vethulf seized the chance to roll them over.

"Easy," Skjaldwulf said. "Your shoulder—"

"Is fine," Vethulf said. "Need I prove it to you?"

Skjaldwulf could not help laughing. "Yes," he said. "I think you should."

And Vethulf did. Vigorously and for some time. And Skjaldwulf happily, happily let him do it, let Vethulf be the one in charge. It could not always be so—and Vethulf would not want it to be so; they were wolfjarls together. But for now, Skjaldwulf could let go and simply feel Vethulf's strength and fierceness and the sweetness that he hid behind his porcupine armor.

Afterwards, they lay together quietly for some time until a soft scrape at the tent flap and a nudge in the pack-sense told them that Mar and Kjaran wanted to come back in. Vethulf got up and loosed the flap; the two wolves sauntered in and annexed the bedding, Kjaran flopping down where Vethulf had been and Mar moving Skjaldwulf around to suit himself.

Vethulf came back and stood glaring down at Skjaldwulf and the wolves. Skjaldwulf was aware of a tremendous spreading feeling of rightness, as if he had finally come back to the place he was meant to be—even if at the moment he was too many leagues from his own heall. Here, with these wolves and Vethulf, and Isolfr just outside with Viradechtis. This was the right place.

Vethulf, still glowering, sat down and kissed him. Skjaldwulf kissed him back.

"I missed you," Vethulf said. He sounded aggrieved.